I0824531

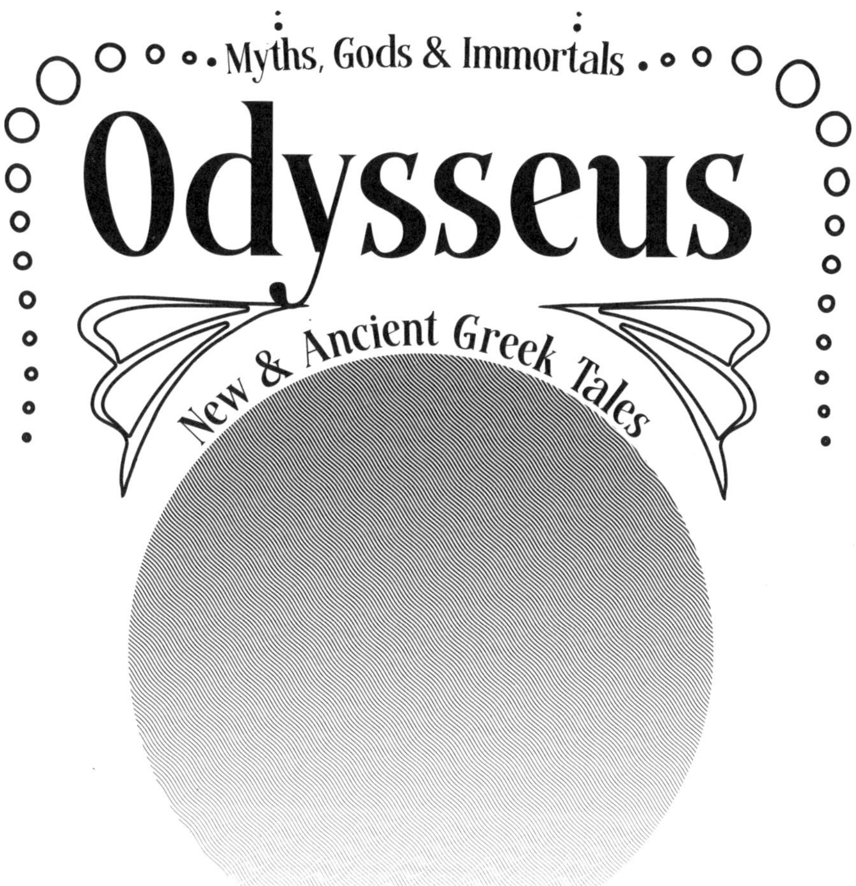
Myths, Gods & Immortals
Odysseus
New & Ancient Greek Tales

This is a FLAME TREE Book

Publisher & Creative Director: Nick Wells
Editorial Director: Catherine Taylor

Special thanks to Catherine Bradley and Tim Leng

FLAME TREE PUBLISHING
6 Melbray Mews, Fulham,
London SW6 3NS, United Kingdom
www.flametreepublishing.com

First published 2026

Note: all translations in the section 'Introducing Odysseus' are by the author
unless otherwise stated.

26 28 30 31 29 27
1 3 5 7 9 10 8 6 4 2

ISBN: 978-1-83562-791-4

Content Note: The stories in this book may contain descriptions of, or references to, difficult subjects such as violence, death and rape, but always contextualized within the setting of mythic narrative, archetype and metaphor. Similarly, language can sometimes be strong but is at the artistic discretion of the authors.

Cover art by Flame Tree Studio based on elements from
Shutterstock.com/Matyuschenko.

A copy of the CIP data for this book is available from the British Library.

Printed and bound in China

Represented in the EU for product safety and compliance by
Authorised Rep Compliance Ltd, Ground Floor, 71 Lower Baggot Street,
Dublin, D02 P593, Ireland. Contact at www.arccompliance.com

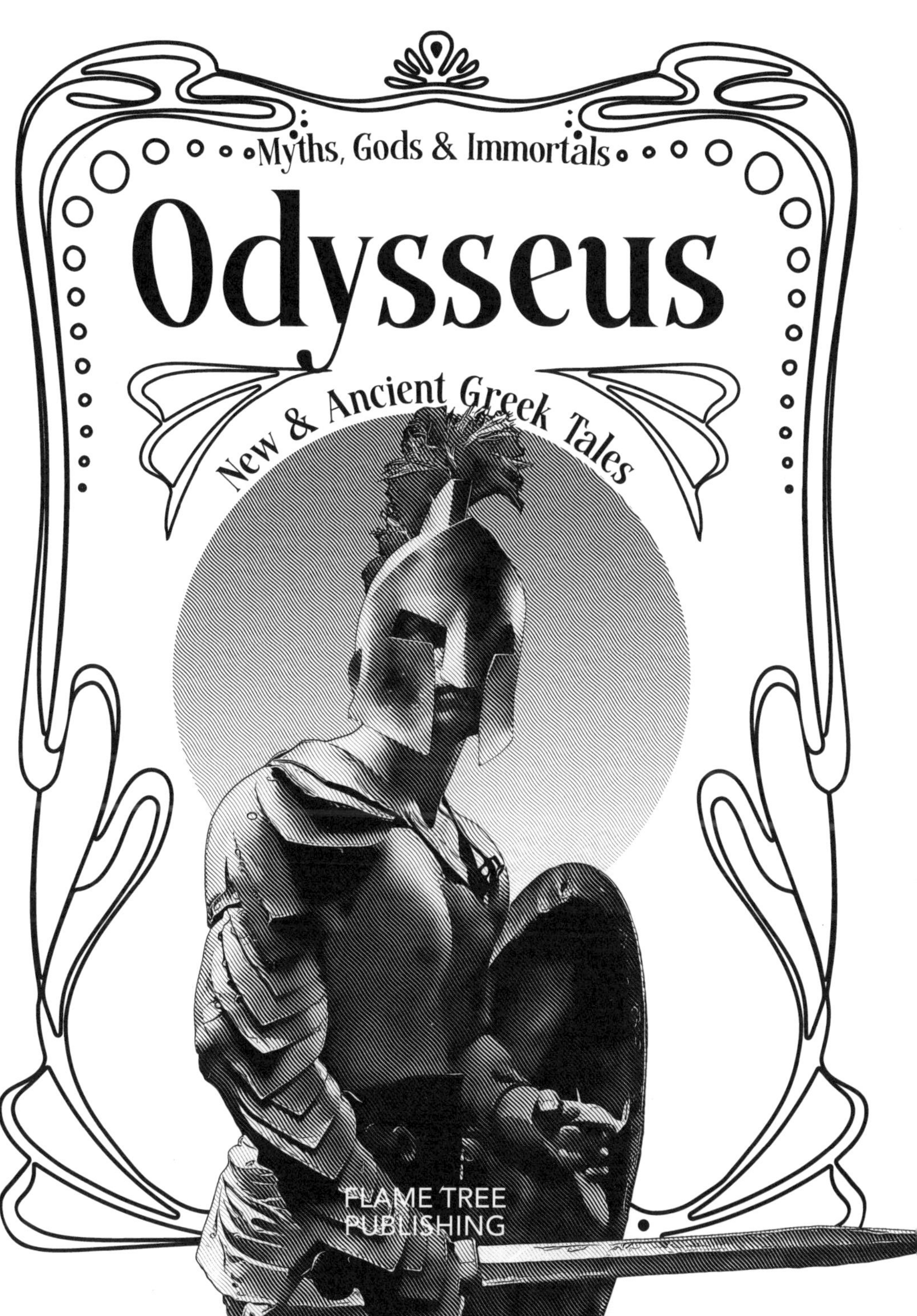
Myths, Gods & Immortals
Odysseus
New & Ancient Greek Tales
FLAME TREE
PUBLISHING

Contents

Foreword

Professor Edith Hall

OF WHOM MANY TALES ARE TOLD

Of all ancient Greek mythical warriors, Odysseus has the most fully formed personality. He is the many-sided hero of a variegated story, but also an incomparable storyteller. This emerges consistently from the ancient sources, whether in the Homeric epics – the *Iliad* and the *Odyssey* – or the Greek tragedies dealing with the Trojan War and its aftermath. Homer uses far more adjectives and titles – epithets – to describe Odysseus than any other hero, a sure sign of his complexity.

He possesses all the necessary skills to win glory on the battlefield, and is an incomparable archer. He is an eminent warrior in the traditional sense, a 'sacker of cities', 'that kingly man', 'great glory of the Achaeans', 'the great tactician', 'cunning' and 'mastermind of war'. He thought up the stratagem of the wooden horse, allowing the Greeks to take Troy. But he transcends social class, since he was also the most relatable of heroes to the ancient peasant farmers who formed the bulk of Homer's audience.

Odysseus is less wealthy than most legendary warrior-kings; his realm is the tiny island of Ithaca, too craggy even to pasture horses. He leads only 12 ships to Troy, compared with Achilles' 50. Odysseus's own orchard contains a mere 13 pear trees, 10 apple trees and 40 figs. He is comfortable sleeping in the humble cottage of his loyal swineherd, Eumaeus. This 'resourceful' hero possesses a far wider range of skills of the type needed by peasant smallholders in the ancient Mediterranean than the other heroes of the Trojan War: beloved by Athena, goddess of crafts, he is an expert carpenter; he is described in action felling trees, boatbuilding, and carving his marriage bed from a living tree. He is a powerful swimmer, as all ancient fishermen and sailors needed to be, and of course he is a 'master mariner', the only Greek hero who fought at Troy whose exploits at sea receive sustained attention.

The varied emotions Odysseus displays invite intense audience identification. We first meet this 'much-suffering' hero seated on the shore of the nymph Calypso's island. He sleeps with her at night, but spends his days on the beach, racked with grief and shedding tears, longing for his homeland. His deep humanity makes him turn down the opportunity of immortality as Calypso's consort, because he loves his wife Penelope, whom he regards as his equal in intellect and leadership qualities. As he says himself to Nausicaa, there is nothing better than when a married couple are of like minds.

At other times, we see Odysseus feeling diverse emotions that enticingly draw us in to relate to him. During his earlier escapades he is 'hotheaded'; he is unwise to give Polyphemus his name, which enables the blinded Cyclops to curse him, but we sympathize with Odysseus's desire to gloat after he has outwitted the hapless giant. We are impressed that he learns from this, and in Ithaca his self-control keeps his true identity under wraps for as long as it takes to ensure that he can entrap his enemies. We admire his curiosity and ingenuity when he wants to hear the song of the sirens and become omniscient. We feel his outrage when he is insulted, dismissed as a mere trader by an aristocratic Phaeacian or belittled by Penelope's maid Melantho. It is impossible not to share his triumph when he shoots his arrow through the axes and throws off his rags to avenge himself and his household. We revel in his poignant reunions with his loyal slaves, his son Telemachus, his dog Argos, his nurse Eurycleia and especially his wife Penelope. Unlike most ancient Greek heroes, Odysseus is also doggedly heterosexual, another quality probably related to his appeal to non-elite ancient audiences.

Odysseus is the type of hero who always wins; part of the pleasure in the diverse episodes comes from knowing that this 'man of action' and 'man of exploits' will always prevail over his foes, usually by subterfuge, and live to tell the tale. And indeed he does tell tales, quite brilliantly: one epithet is 'superb at storytelling'.

The *Iliad* offers us a description of Odysseus the orator. He is not particularly tall, as are the other Greek heroes, but is powerful and broad-chested, like a sturdy ram. When silent, he does not seem particularly distinguished. But when he speaks, his great voice issues from his chest in words that fall like snowflakes on a winter's day. He seems godlike. In the *Odyssey* we hear this eloquent hero narrate the most exciting parts of his own life story; he is the first autobiographer in world literature.

At the Phaeacian court, Odysseus recalls the voyage from Troy – the Cyclops, Aeolus, Circe and the trek to the edges of the ocean and entrance to the Underworld. We listen, enraptured, as Odysseus narrates his spooky invocations of the dead and his heartbreaking meeting with the ghost of his mother. But he suddenly breaks off, before describing his dialogues with the other Trojan War heroes. We yearn for Odysseus to continue, like Alcinous, who would be happy 'to stay up in this hall until the divine dawn' to hear his guest (11.375–6). Eumaeus later tells Penelope that the stranger is a Cretan gifted at telling the story of his adventures (17.513–21). Eumaeus is lying. He knows Odysseus' true identity, and that the tales of the 'Cretan' are thus untrue. But by this point in the *Odyssey*, it is apparent that truth is not a good criterion by which to judge the success of a story.

Odysseus thus becomes an archetypal narrator of both fact and fiction within his own epic. One translation of his epithet *polutropos* – 'of many turns' – is 'of whom so many types of tale are told'. The *Odyssey* is the mother of all stories – Odysseus is a hero of a travelogue, a romance, a revenge plot, a biography, an autobiography and of wanderings in supernatural lands, a sort of proto-science fiction. It is little wonder that his seminal tale has been translated into more world languages than any other ancient text except the *Fables* of Aesop.

Professor Edith Hall

Ancient & Modern: Introducing Odysseus

by Professor Silvia Montiglio

1.
Odysseus in Homer

Tell me, Muse, about the man of many ways,
Who wandered much, after sacking the sacred citadel of Troy.
Of many men he saw the cities and learned the minds,
And many troubles he suffered in his heart on the deep sea,
While striving to secure his life and the return of his companions.
– Homer, *Odyssey*, Book 1

(Note: all translations are by the author unless otherwise stated)

dysseus, for most of us, is the protagonist of Homer's Odyssey, which is generally dated to the eighth century BCE and is divided into 24 books. The invocation to the Muse that begins the epic describes its hero's character in a nutshell: the man of many ways, versatile, multifaceted, multiform (the Greek word is *polytropos*, 'of many turns' or 'much turned'); the sacker of Troy, the wanderer, who came to know places and people and weathered much at sea, fighting to survive and to bring his crew home. The countless and manifold avatars of

Odysseus that will mushroom over the next 2,800 years stem, directly or remotely, from this portrait.

ODYSSEUS IN THE ILIAD

Mediator and Effective Speaker

Some of the features mentioned in the introductory lines of the *Odyssey* already characterize the hero in the *Iliad*, where he makes his first appearance. The *Iliad* begins in the last year of the Trojan War. As the poem opens, a plague is decimating the soldiers. From the prophet Calchas, the Greeks find out that the cause is Apollo's ire, because Agamemnon, the Greek commander-in-chief, has taken as his concubine Chryseis, the daughter of Apollo's priest. Agamemnon is forced to give her back. Who then leads the mission? Odysseus the mediator, the man gifted with many ways of speech, is the one who hands over the girl to her father Chryses, accompanying the gesture with soothing words:

"Chryses, king Agamemnon sent me
to return your daughter and offer a hundred
oxen to Phoebus,
as a sacred sacrifice on behalf of the Greeks,
so as to appease his Lordship,
who has now flung grievous afflictions upon them."

Odysseus displays his diplomacy and political skills more dramatically – and to greater effect – in the epic's second book.

Agamemnon has spoken dispiritedly, exhorting the warriors to abandon Troy. Tired as these men are of fighting, they seize on the call and rush en masse to the shore, shouting and roaring like a huge wave, whereupon Odysseus intervenes to restore order. Applying double standards, with gentle words for the chieftains, but beatings and rough language for the common soldiers, he masters the army – apart from one man, Thersites, 'the ugliest soldier', who insults Agamemnon and urges everyone to pack up and go home. Enter once again Odysseus the peacemaker: he silences the rebellious voice, beats him on his back and tactfully appeals to Agamemnon's image, eventually persuading the entire army to stay on. Instead of blaming the uprising on Agamemnon's speech, he tickles his sense of honour, declaring that "The Greeks want to make you the most disgraced man on earth". Odysseus also shows sympathy for the discouraged warriors: I understand you, he says, for it is hard to stay away from one's wife to fight even for a month, and we have been here nine years. To cheer the host up, he relates a prophecy according to which Troy will be sacked in the tenth year. "So you all stay here, you Greeks who wear well-fitted greaves, until we take the great city of Priam!" Odysseus's speech is greeted with deafening applause by the same warriors who shortly before were rushing to the shore, eager to leave:

So he spoke, and the Greeks shouted so loudly
that the ship around tremendously boomed
under their shouts,
as they approved the speech of the divine Odysseus.

Ambassador

In the following book Antenor, one of the Trojan elders, remembers Odysseus in the role of ambassador, prior to the war. He had come to the city with Menelaus, supposedly to negotiate the restitution of Helen to him. Antenor, who got to know both men, describes their physical appearance (Menelaus was more impressive standing, Odysseus seated) and, at greater length, their speaking styles. Menelaus, as a true Spartan, spoke briefly and to the point, whereas Odysseus choreographed his performance carefully and grandly, relying on non-verbal language before emitting a powerful voice. He stood immobile for a long time, his eyes fixed on the ground, looking like a witless man, 'but when he let out his great voice, and words as thick as snowflakes in winter', no one could have competed with him. To increase the impact of his words, Odysseus counts on the surprise effect created by the contrast between the superficial impression of a stupid man and the reality of a fluent and sonorous speaker. He plays on one of his characteristics and beliefs: appearances deceive. This embassy must have taken place at least ten years earlier, and yet the memory of Odysseus's feat of eloquence is still vivid in the old man's mind.

Back in the *Iliad*'s real time, the Greeks rely on Odysseus's persuasiveness for another diplomatic mission: the embassy to Achilles in book nine, designed to bring the angry hero and best fighter back to the war that he has abandoned after an apparently irreconcilable feud with Agamemnon. Odysseus is accompanied by Ajax and Phoenix, Achilles' old mentor;

but it is on him especially that the Greeks count. This time, however, he fails: he is ill at ease, jumps in to speak before his turn and sounds the wrong notes. In particular, he makes the mistake of displaying the immense fortune and power of Agamemnon by listing, one by one and with a pompous and nauseating wealth of detail, the lavish gifts that the king has pledged to the alienated warrior: 20 cauldrons, 12 prizewinning horses, seven exceedingly beautiful women, 20 Trojan women slaves, his daughter in marriage, accompanied by the richest dowry, power over many cities, and more. It is true that Odysseus concludes his speech with arguments that should appeal to Achilles:

"The Greeks will honour you like a god,
for you will bring them glory.
And you could get Hector,
who now is coming close
with ruinous battle-fury, thinking that no Greek
is his match, of those the ships brought here."

Odysseus may well expect that the proud Achilles will be touched by the compliment about his unrivalled valour and by the prospect of glory and honour. But it is the hateful Agamemnon who dominates Achilles' mind at the end of Odysseus's plea, not any prospect of glory or honour. The other two envoys fail to persuade him as well, even Phoenix, for whom Achilles has great respect and affection. Perhaps the task was beyond the power of words.

Nocturnal Fighter

Made desperate by the embassy's outcome and the losses he is suffering, Agamemnon seeks counsel from his peers. They decide on a night raid to spy into the Trojan camp. The young Diomedes volunteers, choosing Odysseus as his mate (the two will feature together in many more ventures and will be joined forever after death in Dante's *Inferno*). The nocturnal expedition is a double success: first they kill Dolon, a Trojan scout, after tricking him into releasing strategic information, then slay a powerful ally of the Trojans, Rhesus, and 12 of his men, while they are all deep in sleep.

This episode is in book ten, which several scholars consider a later accretion to the core *Iliad*. However it may be, Odysseus's behaviour is in character. The nocturnal raid foreshadows Odysseus's greatest military achievement: the sack of Troy, also nocturnal and made possible by a ruse, the Wooden Horse, from which death-bringing warriors pour out to surprise the Trojans in their sleep. These and other similar initiatives, such as the sneaky and likewise nocturnal theft of Athena's statue documented in later literature, showcase Odysseus's original talents at war: he excels at employing wily methods under the cover of night, which for the other fighters is a time of rest.

ODYSSEUS IN THE ODYSSEY

The Nostalgic Husband, Prisoner of Calypso

The sack of Troy does not feature in the *Iliad*. It happens between the timelines of this epic and of the *Odyssey*. After their victory, the Greek heroes set out to return to their homes. Many succeed, but Odysseus, when the *Odyssey* begins, is detained on the island of Ogygia by the goddess Calypso, her name related to *kalyptein*, 'to hide'. She has indeed been keeping the hero concealed from the human world for seven years, after rescuing him from a deadly storm. He has become a captive to her love on her lush, enchanting island, where every night is spent in a cave, their dwelling. He used to be fond of Calypso, but no more. Now 'he is yearning for his return and his wife' and 'longs to see the smoke rise from his country'. This is the first picture of Odysseus within the time frame of the *Odyssey*, at the beginning of book one: the picture of a homesick husband, not an adventurer. Nostalgia or 'aching for the return' (from *algos*, 'pain', and *nostos*, 'return') has been his driving force, his mental compass throughout his wanderings. His epic narrates the journey of a centripetally oriented traveller.

However, Odysseus is in no condition to leave Calypso. She loves him and is a goddess; he is powerless. Furthermore, Ogygia is at the 'navel of the sea', a location unfathomably remote from the mainland of Greece and from his island of Ithaca. It takes divine intervention to set him free. This occurs in book five, while the in between books recount the journeys of Odysseus's son Telemachus, in search for news of his father, to Pylos, the home of Nestor, and to Sparta, the home of Menelaus. These books also offer snapshots of life on Ithaca, where Penelope weeps and mourns, besieged by suitors and longing for Odysseus. Though absent from the scene, Odysseus is ever present in the love, thoughts and actions of his family members, until we finally meet him in person, on Ogygia.

At the beginning of book five Hermes flies, 'like a seagull', from Mount Olympus to the island, to order Calypso to release Odysseus. Unhappy but forced to obey, she is off to the seashore to bring the announcement to her beloved. This is how she – and for the first time we – find him: sitting on a rock, his eyes filled with tears, 'for his sweet life was flowing away while he was suffering for his return'. The man of nostalgia described in book one materializes. He idles his days away staring at the sea – the vast expanse that separates him from home, but also the route that can take him there.

Calypso promises to release him and help him, but Odysseus, with characteristic mistrust, suspects her of some hidden plot: "it is something else, goddess, that you are planning, not my sending away." He asks her to swear that this is not the case. Startled, she calls him a rogue, but she does swear her oath. In a last attempt to keep him, Calypso offers him immortality and herself as wife, adding that she must be more attractive than a mortal woman, but Odysseus insists on leaving. With admirable prudence and tact, he reassures her that Penelope is not as beautiful as she, and yet, he tells her, "I long to reach my home and see the day of my return". In doing so, he lets his nostalgia speak clearly but without offending the goddess. By rejecting Calypso's offer, Odysseus chooses to be Man – the man Homer sets out to sing about in the first line of the epic. He chooses to suffer as a man and to return to the world of men rather than disappearing from it and from their memory forever, hidden on Calypso's island for eternity.

SAILOR, SWIMMER AND SEDUCER

From Calypso to Nausicaa

Calypso, resigned, helps Odysseus to prepare for his departure. After one last night of love, he builds a ship – the man 'of many ways' is also a gifted carpenter – which Calypso fills with plentiful food and drink. Then he leaves the island forever. But she has also warned him: you do not know how many hardships await you! The first is about to strike. After 17 days of expert navigation – another skill of this multifaceted man – Poseidon, Odysseus's divine archenemy, returns from a vacation in Ethiopia and rouses an epic storm. Odysseus finds a helper in the sea goddess Leucothea, who advises him to leave the ship at once. She also gives him a magic veil, instructing him to stretch it beneath his breast and to keep it on until he touches land, then to throw it back into the sea. But Odysseus, with his incurable mistrustfulness, fears that the goddess is tricking him and holds on stubbornly to the boat – only to be thrown instantly overboard by a mountainous wave. Having fastened Leucothea's veil as instructed, he survives thanks to its protection and to his own ability to swim – yet another of his many talents and one unusual for a Greek hero. After days and nights of battling against huge waves and backwashes, Odysseus lands, naked, grimy and exhausted, on Scheria, the island of the Phaeacians. He makes himself a bed of leaves in a bush and sleeps soundly for more than a day, until suddenly roused by the sound of girlish voices. We are in book six. The girls are Nausicaa, daughter of the Phaeacian king Alcinous, and her maids, who are there to wash the laundry; they are playing with a ball.

The Seductive Speaker

Odysseus needs help and so he emerges, naked and encrusted with mud and dirt, from his bush. All the girls run away except Nausicaa, who has been emboldened by the goddess Athena, already established as Odysseus's divine protector in the *Iliad*. Her intervention has now orchestrated his meeting with Nausicaa, leaving Odysseus in a quandary. How should he approach the maiden? With two of his signature qualities, tact and resourcefulness, the dirty and smelly shipwreck survivor chooses not to touch Nausicaa's knees in supplication but to plead from a distance. He delivers a powerfully seductive speech, drawing on 'honeyed and winning words':

"I am at your knees, my queen. Are you a goddess
or a mortal woman?
If you are a goddess, of all those who inhabit the vast sky
I liken you to Artemis, the daughter of the great Zeus,
for your beauty, stature and figure.
But if you are a mortal, among those who live on the earth,
thrice blessed are your father and your lady mother,
thrice blessed your brothers...
But most blessed of all in his heart is the man
who will take you home, winning you
with many gifts!"

Odysseus has hit the right chords, for Nausicaa is of marriageable age and has come to the shore thinking of her wedding day. Athena had appeared to her in a dream and roused her with this prospect: "your wedding day is near!" The girl is ready for a husband – and here he is, right before her! She almost falls for the mud-encrusted figure, so articulate, so flattering and suave. It takes only a body scrub and a little divine help to finish the job. Tactfully refusing the proffered assistance of Nausicaa's maids, Odysseus goes off to bathe by himself: "it is long since oil came near my skin. In front of you I will not wash. For I am ashamed to be naked among lovely-haired maidens." Thanks to the magic touch of Athena turned beautician, he emerges from the bath a changed man, taller, gleaming with grace, crowned by curls like a hyacinth flower. Marvelling at him, Nausicaa tells her maids: "Would that a man like this could be called my husband!" She asks them to feed him and give him clothes, then directs him to her father's palace.

Winning over the Phaeacian Queen and King

As Odysseus walks to town at the beginning of book seven, Athena covers him with mist and appears to him disguised as a young girl to give him more instructions: when you enter the hall of the Phaeacians, she tells him, go supplicate Arete, the queen. He does so, delivering another compelling speech, this one short as the circumstances demand:

"Arete, daughter of the godlike Rhexenor,
I have come to your husband and your knees after much hardship...
Give me the means to travel home
quickly, for far from my friends I suffer griefs."

After enjoying an abundant dinner (several days and nights of strenuous swimming have left him with a lasting appetite), he asks for conveyance again. Alcinous grants it, charmed by his guest. But his wife has recognized the clothes Odysseus is wearing. Who are you? she asks. Who gave you these clothes? Odysseus evades the first question but gives a vivid account of the storm that threw him onto the shores of Scheria, then delicately praises Nausicaa's behaviour. Alcinous is conquered. I wish you'd stay here as my son-in-law, he declares to him, without even knowing his name and origins. Though, unlike Calypso, Alcinous is willing to let Odysseus go, he too presents the long-suffering traveller with a cosy and romantic offer – an enticing alternative to continuing the dangerous *nostos*. But the homesick man again says no, without a hint of hesitation.

INTERLUDE: ODYSSEUS AND FOOD

We have just seen that Odysseus can be a hearty eater. While other heroes seem to ignore the pangs of hunger, or at least do not speak about their need or liking for food, Odysseus is candid and endearing in this area. In book nineteen of the *Iliad* Achilles at last re-enters the war to avenge Patroclus's death. He is so possessed with martial fury that he would rush to fight instantly, on an empty stomach, and would like all the other soldiers to follow him. But Odysseus opposes his wish. Do not send our men to fight hungry, he advises; allow them to go to their ships for food and drink, which will increase their strength. No one can fight all day on an empty stomach! One of the greatest generals of all time, Napoleon, would agree: "an army marches on its stomach," he reportedly said.

Agamemnon, who is present at the conversation between Achilles and Odysseus, approves the latter. But Achilles insists. You want to eat? he asks contemptuously. You want to eat when men lie killed by Hector, and he has the glory? Achilles would still send the soldiers to fight all day unfed, as he himself will do. Once again, Odysseus objects, declaring that "we cannot mourn the dead with our stomach"; the survivors "must remember food and drink". Odysseus's down-to-earth sentiment may seem unheroic compared to the fiery disposition of Achilles, but it shows his understanding for natural human needs and weaknesses, as well as his community-minded sensibility. In this he contrasts with the total self-absorption of Achilles.

In book seven of the *Odyssey*, on his first night at the Phaeacian court, Odysseus defends his own appetite by invoking the same physiological needs before devouring his dinner:

"But let me take supper, for all my sorrow.
Nothing is more shameless than the hateful belly,
which forces me to remember it,
even when I am worn and have sorrows in my heart,
as I have sorrows in my heart now, yet the belly always
orders me to eat and drink, and makes me forget
all I have suffered, and commands to be filled."

The expansiveness and realism with which Odysseus dwells on the tyranny of the belly is unique in Homeric epic. Nor does his appreciation of food and drink stop at need. Odysseus can be a *bon vivant*. At the beginning of book nine, he tells Alcinous that nothing is more pleasant than sitting at a feast enlivened by music, when the tables are loaded with bread and meat and the cups are constantly filled. Yet, as we shall see, Odysseus is also capable of controlling his appetite like no one else when eating is forbidden.

THE WANDERER IN FAIRYLAND

Odysseus Reveals Himself

The next day at the palace of Alcinous is spent in entertainment: playing sports, dancing and feasting. The Phaeacians are close to the gods and enjoy a carefree life, full of pleasures. They are particularly fond of dancing and music. Alcinous has a bard-in-residence, Demodocus. He sings three songs, two of which concern events at Troy: a dispute between Achilles and Odysseus and the sack of the city. On both occasions Odysseus weeps. He tries to hide his tears, but Alcinous spots them and, like his wife, he questions his guest. Who are you? Why do you cry each time you hear about Troy? At last, at the beginning of book nine, Odysseus reveals himself: "I am Odysseus, son of Laertes, known among men for my many stratagems. My fame has reached the sky."

This proud introduction compensates for Odysseus's disappearance from the human world in the 10 long years of his wanderings. The anonymous 'man' of the prologue is a renowned personage, attached to fame like the typical

Homeric hero. But this hero's signature remains his nostalgia. He continues his self-presentation with a loving, geographically precise description of his Ithaca, carefully locating it, as if having it before his eyes, among the surrounding islands: there are many, close to one another: Doulichion, Same and Zakynthos. Ithaca lies at the uttermost western limit. Odysseus describes it as "rugged, but a good breeder of youth", adding, "And I cannot see anything sweeter than my own land". His indulgence in his nostalgia is also strategic: it intimates to Alcinous that the story he so desires to hear is advanced payment for the transportation he has promised. The stage is set for Odysseus to begin the long-awaited account of his wanderings, the core and most famous part of his adventures.

The Lotus Eaters and the Cyclops

After leaving Troy, Odysseus and his companions waged a bloody war on the Thracian tribe of the Cicones, former allies of the Trojans, then they sailed on. But as they were rounding Cape Malea, in the southeast of the Peloponnese, they were catapulted by a storm beyond their familiar world, into an unknown and remote sea, which carried them to places inhabited by fairy-like creatures. First, they were driven to the Lotus Eaters – peaceful, content people, who presented the travellers with a fruit that made them forgetful of their journey. However, Odysseus resisted and sailed on, taking with him by force those of his men who wanted to stay. It is significant that the Lotus Eaters are his first challenge, encountered at the very outset of his wanderings: what they offer is not love, song or immortality but oblivion of travelling, and Odysseus has to resist this lure if he wants to return. Or, to put it another way: his homeward-bound journey requires a continuous act of memory.

The next stop was near the Cyclopes' island. This time, Odysseus admits, his curiosity was his ruin. It pressed him to cross over and then wait in Polyphemus's cave, purely for the sake of meeting its inhabitant, and when his companions urged him to take cheeses and other provisions from the cave and flee, he insisted on staying: "I wanted to see the man himself, and whether he would give me gifts of hospitality." As a result, the one-eyed cannibalistic giant devoured several of Odysseus's companions raw. But Odysseus managed to trick him: when asked his name, he answered "nobody". The same night, after getting him drunk, he and his men blinded the giant in his sleep, thrusting a firebrand into his eye. Next morning they made their escape from his cave by holding on to the bellies of his sheep. He called for help, but screamed to his fellow Cyclopes that "Nobody has blinded me!" Accordingly, nobody came to his rescue.

Overjoyed, Odysseus uncharacteristically lost his self-control, boasting to Polyphemus: the man who blinded you is Odysseus, the sacker of cities! But he paid dearly for his gloating. The discovery of his name allowed the Cyclops to curse him, calling on his divine father, Poseidon, for revenge: may Odysseus never reach his home, and if it is fated that he shall, may he lose all his companions and find endless troubles there! The god listened. Poseidon's ire went on to persecute Odysseus all the way to the Phaeacians.

Aeolus, the Laestrygonians and Circe

Having barely escaped, the crew was driven to the island of Aeolus, who gave Odysseus a bag with all the winds tied in it and sent him off on the fair West Wind. Odysseus sailed for nine days without rest, until on the tenth Ithaca dawned on the horizon. But then 'sweet sleep' enfolded him. His companions opened the bag, thinking that it contained gold and silver; in so doing they revealed a lack of trust in their leader as well as greed and envy. Instantly a storm caught the ship and drove it back to Aeolus. Chased away by the angry god, the company resumed their wanderings, which took them to the land of the Laestrygonians – cannibals who ate another of Odysseus's men. They also pelted many more with huge stones and destroyed all the ships in sight, but missed Odysseus's own because it was moored outside the harbour.

On the one ship that remained, the survivors sailed further to the island of Aeaea. Here they met Circe, a singing beauty, witch and *femme fatale*. She turned half of Odysseus's companions into swine, but her drugs had no effect on Odysseus because he was protected by a magic root, the *moly*, a gift of Hermes. Nevertheless Circe seduced him and kept him by her side for a year, after changing his companions back into humans. As it seems, Odysseus enjoyed her company and did not think of leaving, for it took his men to remind him of their homeward journey. This is the only time that Odysseus forgets his return.

The Shades of the Dead

Circe lets the crew go, but she also gives Odysseus a warning: you cannot continue your journey to Ithaca before consulting with the dead prophet Tiresias about your itinerary. The entrance to Hades is the next destination, and Odysseus's evocation of the shades there constitutes the famous *Nekyia* of book eleven. He obtains Tiresias's instructions, which not only map his journey home but detail another journey he will have to undertake after returning to Ithaca. Then, with typical daring and curiosity, he lingers in Hades to meet other shades. One is his mother, Anticlea. Odysseus did not know that she had died, and he learns that it was from sorely missing him; others are mythic queens.

After going over these encounters, Odysseus suddenly stops; 'all were stricken to silence, under the enchantment, in the shadowy halls'. Alcinous compares the charming storyteller to a poet and declares that he would listen to him all night long. Obligingly Odysseus resumes his narrative, reporting his encounters with Agamemnon, Ajax and Achilles. Ajax has refused his approaches, still resentful because Odysseus was allotted Achilles' armour after this hero's death; Achilles has deplored the condition of the lifeless in Hades; and Agamemnon has reassured Odysseus that Penelope, in contrast to his own wife Clytemnestra, is faithful to her husband. Nonetheless, he also urges him to act secretly from her, for women are not to be trusted. Odysseus will follow this advice. His last encounter is with Heracles, who had made his own journey to Hades to fetch the dog Cerberus, the most difficult of his labours. He empathizes with Odysseus, whom he sees as the victim of a wretched destiny not unlike his own.

The Sirens

Back in the world of the living, Odysseus is prepared for more dire challenges as he takes to the sea again. The first obstacle are the Sirens, who entice the travellers to come to them with their irresistibly beautiful voices and a song that offers total knowledge; but on the shore of their island lie heaps of human bones. Odysseus has been instructed to plug everyone's ears, but he himself cannot resist his desire to listen. He therefore asks his companions to tie him to the mast and to strengthen his bonds should he try to break loose – as he predictably does, succumbing to the lure of song and knowledge. The Sirens call him:

"Come here, much-renowned Odysseus, great glory of the Greeks,
stop your ship to listen to our voice.
No one has ever sailed past on his black ship
without having listened to the sweet-sounding voice that comes from our lips; then he goes on, full of delight, and richer in knowledge.
For we know everything that on the vast plane of Troy
the Greeks and the Trojans have suffered through the gods' will,
and we know everything that happens on the much-nourishing earth."

This call would have enticed Odysseus even if he had not been predisposed to listen to the Sirens, for they begin by extolling his fame, which he has not heard sung in the long time he has spent at the edges of the world; then they draw his attention not only to the beauty of their voices but also, and with greater emphasis, to the content of their singing: the war that has brought glory to the sacker of Troy, and everything one would wish to know. Odysseus again risks abandoning his return, as with Circe, but this time he has taken precautionary measures. He sails past the Sirens, until their beautiful voice fades in the distance. Of the song's content, he says nothing.

Scylla and Charybdis, Trinacria and the Return

More dangers follow. To avoid the tremendous onrush of the sea between the Wandering Rocks, which have been successfully passed only by the Argonauts, Odysseus chooses an alternative route, between Scylla and Charybdis. Rather than braving the unmanageable ebbs and flows of Charybdis, he decides to sail by Scylla, a monster 12 feet in length, with six necks and six heads, each bearing a mouth with three rows of teeth. Using those teeth, Scylla fishes out six more of Odysseus's companions, and the survivors finally land on Trinacria. Here they face the hardest test, the test of hunger. Odysseus wanted to avoid the island because he had been warned not to eat its cattle, which are sacred to Helios, but his companions, weary from travelling, force him to stop. When their provisions run out, they transgress the order and roast the meat, again taking advantage of their leader's sleep. As soon as they leave, a storm destroys the ship and kills everyone but Odysseus, who grabs a piece of wreckage from the ship and is carried on it all night long. He is forced to come near Charybdis, who swallows the wreckage, and he waits, clinging to a tree, until she vomits it back up. At last, after nine more days and nine more night at sea, he is cast ashore on Calypso's island.

The tale is over. Odysseus's audience is again 'stricken to silence, under the enchantment, in the shadowy halls'. At the end of the next day the charming storyteller departs, loaded with precious gifts and carried by the Phaeacians on one of their magic ships, deep in sleep. His unconscious state is a metaphorical death: it furthers the permanent transition from worlds remote from humanity and located outside geography back into the human world and a geographically recognizable location.

THE BEGGAR

Odysseus with Athena and in Eumaeus's Hut

We are now into book thirteen, in which Odysseus reaches Ithaca. The kind Phaeacians lift him from the ship and set him on the sand, still asleep. They carry out his possessions and put them down by the trunk of an olive tree to keep them hidden from wayfarers. As they sail back, Poseidon takes revenge by turning their ship to stone. Meanwhile Odysseus awakens and cannot recognize the island, for Athena has covered it in mist. Distraught, he curses the Phaeacians for having deceived him, even suspecting them of having stolen some of his goods. He sets out to count them, betraying an acquisitive as well as a mistrustful nature.

Athena appears to him disguised as a young man and tells him where he is. Odysseus conceals his happiness and spins a false tale about himself. He cannot fool the goddess, of course, but she is pleased with her protégé's inventiveness. Revealing herself, she teases Odysseus but also compliments him:

> *"Sharp he would be and stealthy, who should surpass you*
> *in all kinds of wiles, even if a god were matched with you!"*

Odysseus is her kindred spirit, Athena continues, the best 'in counsel and speeches', even as she is famous among the gods for her sharpness. She further expresses heartfelt sympathy and admiration for his good sense, gentleness and presence of mind. Goddess and human then sit together next to the olive tree to plan the slaughter of the suitors. She promises her help and changes him into an old beggar, so that no one will recognize him – Odysseus, who has called himself 'Nobody', does not mind self-abasement. Then she instructs him to go to the hut of his loyal swineherd Eumaeus.

Odysseus's servant offers generous hospitality to his guest and after eating the two exchange stories. Eumaeus expresses his unflinching loyalty to his master; he keeps mourning and longing for him. To lift his spirit, his guest reassures him that Odysseus is on his way and that he will take his revenge. The swineherd becomes curious. Who is his guest? How did he arrive on Ithaca? Odysseus tells yet another made-up tale about himself and his travels, false in most of the facts but not all, and true to his character and experiences. He says that he fought at Troy, which is true, and the story that he spent seven years in Egypt gathering 'many goods' is true to his acquisitiveness. When it is time to sleep, Eumaeus gives up his bed to his guest and goes outside to sleep with the swine.

Telemachus and the Dog Argos Recognize Odysseus

Meanwhile, Telemachus returns. The suitors have planned to kill him but are thwarted by Athena. He decides to visit Eumaeus, who treats him with great affection. Telemachus tells Eumaeus's guest that the suitors are eating up all his substance, then sends the swineherd off to bring Penelope the tidings of his safe return. At this point, Athena steps in to set in motion Telemachus's recognition of his father: she tells Odysseus that the time has come, rejuvenates him and once again beautifies him. Telemachus cannot believe his eyes and thinks that the stranger is a god. No, I am your father, he declares, and after dispelling his son's understandable disbelief, they embrace and share happy tears. His son is the first family member to whom Odysseus discloses his identity because he is the one he needs the most to carry out the slaughter, which from now on the two plan together.

When Eumaeus returns, Telemachus gives him the order to take his guest to the city, where he will beg for his food. We have now reached book seventeen. On his way to town Odysseus endures insults and threats from his herdsman Melanthius, who has gone over to the suitors' side. Odysseus moves on with Eumaeus and comes near the palace. Here he sees his dog Argos, old, neglected and covered with ticks. The animal wags his tail in recognition of his master, lift his ears, but has no strength to move closer to him and dies. Odysseus weeps but his tears escape Eumaeus's detection.

Enduring Insults and Blows

We are still in book seventeen. As soon as he enters the palace, Odysseus begins to beg from the suitors, particularly from the most prominent, Antinous. He thanks him in advance for his generosity and tells him yet another made-up tale about himself, half false but with a truthful moral: I too was prosperous once and used to give alms to beggars. Through this story Odysseus issues a warning about the changeability of human fortunes – but Antinous does not hear him. He attacks and mocks the beggar and, in response to the latter's rebuke and threat, he hits him with a footstool. Yet Odysseus simply 'stood steady like a rock; Antinous's missile did not move him. In silence he shook his head, pondering evils'. To the insults and blows with which he is showered, Odysseus often responds with outward impassibility, even as his mind and heart boil within. Appearances do not match reality; his outside does not mirror his inside.

The next day, and in the next book, Odysseus puts up with more insults from another beggar, the huge Irus. Forced by the bored and idle suitors to fight him in a boxing match, he knocks him down, displaying powerful limbs. In addition to much else, Odysseus is a good athlete, swift, strong and cunning. He has already excelled at sporting games, winning at a discus-throw at the court of the Phaeacians and, in book twenty-three of the *Iliad*, at a course race; he has also dodged the colossal Ajax in a wrestling match. His victory against Irus pleases the suitors, but soon he must swallow more insults, both from the disloyal maid Melantho and from Eurymachus, another suitor, who throws another footstool at him but misses. When the day ends, the suitors leave; Odysseus and Telemachus stay up, planning their destruction.

Intense Emotions: The Meeting with Penelope and Euryclea's Discovery

Father and son remove the armour to an inner room, out of the suitors' reach. Then Telemachus retires. Odysseus is still pondering the slaughter to come when Penelope descends to meet the 'stranger'. The interview between them in book nineteen is an emotional zenith. The two get dangerously close, but Odysseus must disguise his feelings in order not to betray his identity (act secretly from your wife, Agamemnon had told him). On hearing her guest describe Odysseus, whom he claims to have met, accurately and vividly, Penelope gives in to grief, her cheeks streaming with tears. And Odysseus 'in his heart felt pity for his wife as she wept, but his eyes stood firm, like horn or iron, in his eyelids; with guile he hid his tears'. Again, his appearance is deceiving. He tells her more stories about his adventures, some false, some true, and assures her that Odysseus is now coming back. Penelope does not believe his words, but she offers him a foot-wash and a couch for the night. Odysseus refuses the wash unless it can be administered by 'an old woman of virtuous spirit'.

Penelope then calls his old nurse Euryclea. She looks at him, tearfully remembering Odysseus, and notes a strong resemblance between the two men. She proceeds to mix hot and cold water in a shining cauldron. And suddenly, but too late, Odysseus realizes that the old woman could recognize him by a scar on his leg and moves towards the darkness. But Euryclea's touch discovers the scar that he tries to hide. The warmth of home he has felt in the presence of his wife and the old caring nurse has caused him to mismanage this recognition. The unwanted discovery almost foils his plans, for Euryclea, full of emotions, turns around to share it with Penelope. Odysseus stops her, threatening her with death if she should speak. As he and Penelope resume their conversation, she tells him that the evil day is coming when she will have to leave the house of Odysseus. She intends to propose a contest: whoever of the suitors is able to string and bend the bow of Odysseus, and then to send an arrow straight through 20 axes of iron, may take her as wife. The stranger pronounces: your husband will be back before this happens.

The Slaughter is Brewing

We have reached book twenty. Penelope has retired to her room upstairs whereas Odysseus remains in the hall for the night. As he is lying awake, nurturing evil thoughts, he hears his disloyal maids laughing, on their way to sleeping with the suitors. His heart is pounding inside, but he reduces it to obedience, commanding: "Endure, my heart. Much worse you have endured." Athena cheers him up and puts him to sleep. Meanwhile his wife awakens, deep in grief, longing for death. Odysseus hears her and prays for a good omen. The sky thunders.

As the day dawns, the palace gets ready for the suitors' customary arrival and feasting. Once again Odysseus is struck by one of them, this time with an ox hoof, but, with his habitual self-control and in anticipation of the suitor's death, 'he smiled in his heart'. The contest is about to begin. Telemachus sets up the axes and tries himself at the bow, in vain. Next is the seer Leodes, who also fails. Meanwhile Odysseus has gone out to reveal himself to Eumaeus and to the oxherd Philoetius, who has proven his loyalty. The two servants burst into joyful tears and throw their arms around their recovered master, but Odysseus calls them back to order: they must make sure that no one can leave the palace. Back inside, he watches one more suitor fail the test, then asks for a try. Telemachus grants him his wish, amid the vocal indignation of the suitors. Taking up his dear bow, Odysseus handles it with love. He then strings it, bends it effortlessly and lets a shaft fly straight through the axes. The suitors' deaths are next.

Killings and Tortures

Stripped of his rags and standing high on the threshold of the hall, Odysseus aims another shaft at Antinous, who falls. In reply to the other suitors' rebukes, he fires back: you dogs, you never thought that I would return from Troy! The massacre begins. One after the other the suitors fall, pierced by arrows and spears. Telemachus helps his father, while Melanthius brings weapons to the suitors. But he is caught by Eumaeus, tightly bound and hoisted up on a pillar. The fighting continues, with Athena supporting Odysseus's side until all the suitors are dead. Three men have survived: Leodes, the bard Phemius and the herald Medon. Thanks to Telemachus's intercession, Odysseus spares the last two. He then sends for Euryclea, who exults at seeing the slaughtered men. But Odysseus rebukes her: "in your heart rejoice, old woman, stop, do not cry out in jubilation. It is not pious to exult over dead men." This call for restraint displays another quality of Odysseus, piety. It sets him apart from most Homeric heroes, who enjoy boasting over their victims. Moderation and respect for the dead will also be Odysseus's hallmarks in Sophocles' tragedy *Ajax*.

Now that the suitors have been slain, it is the turn of their accomplices. Odysseus orders Telemachus to put the faithless maids to death by the sword, but the young man chooses a crueller method: he hangs them, their feet dangling and quivering for a painful moment before they die. There follows the even more gruesome end of Melanthius, which involves multiple mutilations; his ears, nose, member, hands and feet are all thrown to the dogs. At last the great hall can be scrubbed and fumigated, and Penelope can be summoned. Odysseus sends Euryclea upstairs to his wife's room and book twenty-two ends.

THE REUNION

Penelope has slept through the slaughter. When Euryclea awakens her with the happy news, she scolds her for rousing her from the sweetest slumber she has ever enjoyed since Odysseus's departure. She cannot believe the old woman's words, but is finally persuaded to go down and meet the killer of the suitors. Penelope takes a long time to recognize her husband in the man who sits in front of her. She is rebuked for her coldness by Telemachus, whereas Odysseus understands her at first. However, after he bathes and reappears a changed man, thanks to another of Athena's beauty treatments, he reproaches Penelope for her stubbornness and requests a bed. "Bring here the bed Odysseus himself made," she tells Euryclea. Odysseus, cut to the quick, asks in anger: "Who has displaced my bed?" He tells how he had carved it out of the trunk of an olive tree which remained rooted in the ground. Who cut it and moved it? Penelope has won. She has tricked Odysseus into betraying himself. Her hesitancy and final test reward his mistrust of her.

Now, at last, all doubts are removed: the two melt into each other's arms. She resembles a shipwrecked swimmer who finally sees land after escaping Poseidon's lashings – that is, she has become one with her sea-battered husband, who is now holding her tight. But another perilous journey is in store for him. Pressed by Penelope, Odysseus tells her the end of the prophecy he had received from Tiresias: he will have to leave again, carrying an oar, until he reaches a land where people do not know the sea. He will recognize it because a wayfarer will take his oar for a winnowing fan. He must sacrifice to Poseidon on that spot and then make his way back home, where a soft death will come to him in old age *ex halos*, which probably means 'from the sea', though some interpreters, both ancient and modern, have taken the meaning as 'off the sea'. While Odysseus is telling this story, a maid is readying the couple's bed for their re-marriage, as it were. And they 'gladly went to the rite of the ancient bed'. Several critics in antiquity thought that the epic ended with this line, as many Hollywood movies end with a prolonged kiss, but it is not true. For Odysseus's work is incomplete.

THE END

After lovemaking, Penelope briefly describes her life under the suitors, then Odysseus, more expansively, recounts his adventures, with a few tactful or self-serving omissions: his full year with Circe, for example, and his initial fondness for Calypso. Finally, husband and wife fall asleep. Athena lengthens the night so they can have their fill. When Odysseus awakens, he prepares to go to the fields to make himself known to his father Laertes, who has long withdrawn to the country, in mourning for his son. He bids Telemachus, Eumaeus and Philoetius to take weapons and they all leave, covered in darkness by Athena. Meanwhile the suitors' ghosts go down to Hades, where they find some of the heroes Odysseus met there. The shade of Agamemnon asks one of the suitors what happened to them. When he hears of the slaughter, he praises Penelope, whose glory will never perish.

In the meantime, Odysseus reaches the fields and tests at length his poor father, spinning another false tale about himself in which he claims to have had Odysseus as a guest. At seeing Laertes enveloped in grief, he finally reveals himself. Readers have found this recognition, Odysseus's last, unnecessarily stretched and Odysseus cruel. Perhaps he got caught in his own game and overplayed it at the end. After a tearful reunion father and son, together with friends, sit down to dinner. But rumour of the slaughter has already reached the city. The suitors' kinsmen go to bury their dead, then some of them rush out, ready for battle. On the opposite side is Laertes, all perked up, together with his son and grandson, as well as their friends. Odysseus and Telemachus launch the attack and begin to kill their enemies, when suddenly Athena commands them to stop. Since Odysseus attacks once again, the goddess repeats her order. Wisely 'he obeyed, glad in his heart'. Peace will be restored.

2.
Odysseus in Greek and Roman Antiquity

"Sweet is the prize of victory: dare!
We shall appear honest another time.
Now give yourself to me for one brief, shameless day,
And for the rest of time may you be called the most righteous of men!"
– Sophocles, *Philoctetes*

dysseus is the speaker of these lines. He is prefacing his instructions to Neoptolemus, the innocent son of Achilles, about how to deceive Philoctetes: justice and honesty pale before the gleaming prospect of success. To this unflattering portrayal of Odysseus we can oppose another ancient description, this time by Horace. He adds to the first lines of the *Odyssey* appreciative comments on the protagonist's endurance, learning spirit and wisdom:

And in Ulysses, he offered us a useful example
of what virtue and wisdom can do.

He conquered Troy, he studied with insight the cities and customs
of many men, and while he was trying to secure the return for himself and his companions,
he endured many hardships, borne over the wide sea, un-drowned by waves of adversity.
– Epistles 1.2

These widely diverging representations of Odysseus can be taken to epitomize the kaleidoscopic images of him that developed in Greek and Roman culture, ranging from the unscrupulously ambitious politician to the fervent lover of knowledge and virtue. In this section we shall discuss the key points in the reception of Odysseus in Greek and Roman antiquity.

THE EPIC CYCLE

Disparagement of Odysseus

In the wake of Homer, poets from the seventh and sixth centuries BCE composed several epics related to the Trojan War (and other myths). The poems themselves are lost, but summaries and a few fragments have survived. They constitute the corpus that since antiquity has been called the *Epic Cycle*. Some of the events these epics covered preceded the Trojan War. Others spanned the time between those narrated in the *Iliad* and in the *Odyssey*, and yet others ran parallel to the *Odyssey*, recounting the journeys home (*nostoi*) of other heroes.

In the *Cycle* we find new stories concerning Odysseus, several of which do not cast him as a man of honour. For instance, we learn that he put his cunning to dishonest use to try to avoid the draft: as one of Helen's former suitors, he was bound by oath to defend Menelaus, Helen's husband, and therefore to join the war against the Trojans after Paris's abduction of Helen, but he feigned madness instead. He kept ploughing the seashore as if it were a field and sowing it with salt, until the trick was unmasked by Palamedes, who placed the infant Telemachus in the path of the plough. Odysseus snatched his son from danger, revealing his sanity, but he never forgave Palamedes for outsmarting him and exposing the deception. According to another unsavoury story told in the *Cycle*, Odysseus and Diomedes drowned him, while a more influential version relates how Odysseus put in Palamedes' tent a counterfeit letter that proved him a traitor, thus causing him to be executed by the Greeks.

Another episode that appears in one of the cyclic poems, *The Little Iliad*, is the theft by Odysseus and Diomedes of the Palladium, Athena's statue, from her temple in Troy. Under cover of night, the men took possession of the image because it was believed to guarantee the goddess's protection of the city. While the collaboration of Odysseus and Diomedes in a sly venture is in the spirit of the *Iliad*, the sequel is not. It is in fact most unkind to Odysseus, namely declaring that he attempted to kill his helper in order to receive full credit for the appropriation of the statue! If Homer knew these stories, he chose not to allude to them, possibly out of partiality to Odysseus.

The Strife over the Armour of Achilles, the Sack of Troy and Odysseus's Death

On the other hand, Homer does assume knowledge of another episode that was told in a Cyclic epic, the *Aethiopis*: the strife between Odysseus and Ajax over Achilles' armour. The story varies in the details, and we do not know for certain which variant was narrated in the *Aethiopis*, but the outcome is always Odysseus's victory. Ajax, who was hailed as the best warrior after Achilles and believed that he was the best, lost his sanity and killed himself as a result. The same epic contained a feat of Odysseus that displayed his piety: his fighting a rearguard action over the dead body of Achilles, so that it could be rescued. Another event that featured significantly in the *Cycle* is the ruse of the Horse and the destruction of Troy, which in the *Odyssey* is remembered as Odysseus's claim to fame. One epic was titled *The Sack of Troy*. Another one, the *Telegony*, attributed to Eugammon of Cyrene, narrated the concluding episodes of Odysseus's life: his final journey and his death, which in the *Odyssey* are only prophesised. From Ithaca, Odysseus sailed to Epirus in the northwest of mainland Greece. He then travelled on foot inland, to the country of the Thesprotians, where he married the local queen. After her death he sailed back to Ithaca but soon died himself at the hands of Telegonus ('The Far-off Born'), his son by Circe. The young man, who was ravaging Ithaca while searching for his father, did not recognize himself in Odysseus when the latter rushed to attack him; instead, he killed the aggressor with the spine of a stingray. In this story Odysseus meets his death 'from the sea' rather than far away from it.

GREEK TRAGEDY

Still in the archaic period, Odysseus makes sporadic appearances in lyric poetry. But it is in Athenian tragedy of the fifth century BCE that his figure looms large. He is a major character in several plays of Sophocles and of Euripides. The Odysseus that emerges from these tragedies, at least from those extant, is not so much the returning hero of the *Odyssey* as the shrewd Greek chief at Troy. Yet his cleverness is no virtue. Many of the episodes in Odysseus's career chosen by the tragedians come from the *Cycle* and cast him in a negative light. Their Odysseus is far more often an unprincipled trickster and a callous practitioner of realpolitik than the admirable hero of Homer, who works for the common good but is not callous, and appears knowledgeable about humans, their hearts and fortunes. There is only one play in which Odysseus's profound humanity shines: Sophocles' *Ajax*, to which we now turn.

The Compassionate and Moderate Hero

The subject of *Ajax* is the protagonist's insanity, ending in his death, and the fate reserved for his corpse. Driven mad by Athena, Ajax has slaughtered cattle thinking that he was killing the Greek chiefs who had denied him the armour of Achilles: he believes he has slain Agamemnon and Menelaus so far, but Odysseus is his next target. Ajax delusionally thinks that he is holding him captive in his tent; he plans to tie him to a pillar and torture him prior to killing him. Athena somewhat sadistically forces Odysseus to watch Ajax's deranged behaviour, on the grounds that 'laughing at the enemy is the sweetest laughter'; but this spectator does not laugh and feels no joy in the ruin of his enemy, who furthermore is setting out to torture 'him' before his own eyes. Instead, the scene fills Odysseus with compassion for a specimen of the frail human condition:

"I pity him nonetheless,
in his wretchedness, though he was my enemy...
I see that we are nothing
but ghosts and unsubstantial shadows, as many as we live."

Odysseus shows the same moderation in the treatment of Ajax's dead body. After recovering his sanity, Ajax takes his own life out of shame. Menelaus gloats before his corpse, which lies exposed and unburied, whereas Odysseus – as if abiding by his own words to Euryclea, to whom he declares "it is impious to boast over the dead" – refuses to exult and urges Agamemnon to abstain as well: "do not rejoice, son of Atreus, in gains that are not beautiful". He goes on to praise Ajax's valour and defends his right to a proper burial. Arguably Odysseus is the most sympathetic figure of the play.

Hateful Odysseus

By contrast, in all his other significant appearances in tragedy Odysseus is a villain. He actively lurks behind the doom and deaths of helpless Trojan women and children in Euripides' *Hecuba* and *The Trojan Women*. In the latter play he is the chief executioner of Andromache's infant son Astyanax; in the former he defends the sacrifice of Hecuba's daughter Polyxena to the dead Achilles and remains deaf to the pleas and suffering of her mother. The crushed old woman supplicates him to spare her daughter, reminding him that once she had saved his own life. She had detected Odysseus's presence when he undertook a spying raid into Troy, disguised as a beggar, but, moved by his supplication, she had helped him out of the city. Now she is asking him to reciprocate. Odysseus not only refuses; he is cynical enough to emphasize that indeed it is thanks to Hecuba that "today I see the light of the sun" and almost brags that he "invented many things to avoid death" when he was at her mercy, before expanding on the rights of the great warrior Achilles to receive the sacrificial victim. Likewise, in *Iphigenia in Aulis* Odysseus is the most fervid advocate for Iphigenia's sacrifice, without which the Greek host will not be able to sail to Troy, and he leads the mob to seize the maiden. He champions a collective cause, as he does in the *Iliad*, but in doing so he appears sinister and inhumane.

One of Odysseus's most villainous portraits, as a frigid opportunist and unprincipled pragmatist, is in Sophocles' *Philoctetes*. In this tragedy he teaches Neoptolemus, like his father Achilles a stranger to wily ways, how to deceive Philoctetes in order to win him over to the Greek cause. Odysseus needs Neoptolemus to coax Philoctetes because he is himself hateful to the man: on their way to Troy, he had abandoned him on the island of Lemnos (where the play takes place) to avoid his ill-omened screaming and the repulsive stench of his foot, which is festering from a snake bite. To gain

Philoctetes' trust, Neoptolemus is instructed by Odysseus to speak ill of him:

"Say
whatever you want against me, the worst of the worst ills.
None of them will pain me, but if you don't do it,
you will give grief to all the Greeks."

We recognize the man who can and does put up with insults and who is not ashamed of being demeaned, of calling himself 'Nobody' or wearing rags. Here, however, his indifference to abuse and appearances is no longer laudable, but rather indicates a profound unscrupulousness. We also recognize Odysseus's community-minded spirit. He is again working for the common interest, since the goal of his manoeuvres is to conquer Troy – something that, according to a prophecy, cannot happen without Philoctetes and his bow, which once belonged to Heracles. Yet the ruthlessness of Odysseus's methods overshadows the appreciation of their goal. He fails in his task, proving that the end does not justify the means.

Present and Future Significance

Odysseus's denigration in tragedy seems related to political and cultural trends. In the last decades of the fifth century BCE Athens was fighting an increasingly disastrous war against Sparta and its allies, the so-called Peloponnesian War. Many were opposed to the aggressive war policies pushed by several Athenian leaders, who were accused of being 'demagogues' and of swaying people's opinion with the weapons of rhetoric. Odysseus, the successful public speaker and a staunch advocate for the war against Troy, naturally came to be associated with those politicians. He could also be seen as a mythic avatar of the Sophists, teachers who upheld the importance of persuasion in all human dealings and used their speaking skills for gain. A flourishing and fashionable trade, the Sophists also encountered criticism from culturally conservative quarters. So, along with them, did Odysseus – the smooth talker who also used his speaking skills for gain, whether for the community or for his own ends.

Odysseus's indictment by the tragedians had a lasting legacy, especially thanks to Euripides' enormous influence. In the first century CE the Roman statesman Seneca, who wrote tragedies in addition to philosophical works, recycled Euripides' portrait of the Ithacan and contributed his own damning one to dramatic representations of Odysseus 1,500 years later.

HISTORIOGRAPHY

More positive is the picture of Odysseus that we glean from Greek historians, some of whom found him 'good to think with', that is, inspirational for their methods and enterprises. The historians' hero was the well-travelled and curious character of the *Odyssey*. Herodotus (fifth century BCE), the 'father of history' and our main source for the Persian Wars, never mentions Odysseus by name but shows admiration for his inquisitiveness, his wanderings and his knowledge 'of the cities of many men and their minds'. Herodotus was himself voraciously curious. He followed in the footsteps of the

Homeric wanderer by travelling extensively to collect information about foreign peoples, places and lore, all of which he included in his *Histories* alongside political and military events. Odysseus became the proto-historian in the broad original sense of 'first-hand researcher' (from *histôr*, which contains the root of a verb meaning 'to see'): ethnographer, anthropologist, a student of men and their customs. Other historians, notably Polybius in the second century BCE, appealed to the inquisitive wanderer of Homer in their own advocacy of a research method that favoured travelling and in-person investigation, as opposed to bookish, 'armchair' learning. In these historians' appropriations, the Homeric character who did not choose to embark on his perilous journeys morphs into a voluntary and motivated worldwide traveller.

PHILOSOPHY

From Antisthenes to Plato

Greek philosophers showed an even keener interest in Odysseus. The many facets of his character generated discussion in almost every school, meeting with both admiration and disapproval. His versatility, originality, style of leadership and indifference to appearances attracted Antisthenes (*c.* 445–365 BCE) who was considered the grandfather of the Cynics, mockers of shared values and social rules. Plato, on the other hand, is more critical of Odysseus's wily and deceitful ways in a dialogue titled *Lesser Hippias* and, especially, in the *Apology*. In the latter work Socrates dons the Achilles-like persona of a blunt and tactless speaker. He also tells his accusers that in Hades he will associate with Palamedes and Ajax, both of whom died following an unjust verdict for which Odysseus was directly or indirectly the cause. Socrates implicitly equates Odysseus with his wrongful accusers.

Yet Plato also admires the Homeric hero's ability to reign in his impulses, as displayed in his rebuke to his barking heart in book twenty of the *Odyssey*. The philosopher takes those words as an illustration of the supremacy of the soul over the body. He also believes Odysseus to have made the wisest, most thoughtful choice when his soul was summoned to reincarnate. At the end of the *Republic*, Socrates shares the report of the warrior Er who, like Odysseus, had the privilege of coming back from Hades, where he heard how the souls of various mythological characters, including Homeric ones, picked their new embodiments. All of them made rushed, unreasoned choices, broadly in line with their previous lives (the ugly Thersites, for instance, reincarnated into an ape). But Odysseus, the last to choose,

> *having tossed away ambition from memory of his former toils, went around for a long time, searching for the life of a private man who minded his own business, and with difficulty found it lying somewhere, disregarded by the others, and upon seeing it, said that it would have done the same if it had drawn the first lot, and chose it gladly.*

Odysseus takes his time and makes an informed choice, based not on habit but on a fresh outlook on his past. Contrary to the other characters, he selects a life opposite to his previous one, displaying a unique ability to criticize himself, how he lived and the values he pursued. Significantly, he chooses a life that Plato also admires: that of a quiet, unmeddlesome man.

Cynics and Stoics

Cynics philosophers and their descendants, the Stoics, did not invent a new life for Odysseus but stayed closer to Homer. Their Odysseus is the wanderer of the *Odyssey* rather than the leader of the *Iliad*, and he attracts their attention primarily for the qualities he displays in meeting with hardships: forbearance, nonconformity, the ability to wear many disguises, to play many roles and to resist temptations. The Cynics liked especially Odysseus the Beggar, and some adopted his temporary accoutrement as a permanent outfit. Both Cynics and Stoics saw in Odysseus the Actor of Life – that is, the wise man who must be capable of impersonating a king as convincingly as a nonentity, and be happy in both roles.

The much-suffering hero also illustrates a core principle of Stoic philosophy: namely, that virtue is schooled in misfortune. Horace appropriates this Stoic image of Odysseus in the *Epistle* I have cited at the beginning of this section, where he celebrates his steadfastness in bearing up with tribulations: 'un-drowned by waves of adversity', he showed 'what virtue and wisdom can do'. His endurance and resilience also fit the Stoic imperative that we should accept, or even love, our destiny, whether we are moving or staying in place, whether we are at home or abroad, citizens or exiles. Odysseus, who submitted to his enforced wanderings and made the best of them, became a model for the disposition required of the philosophically minded exile, and even came to embody the ideal of cosmopolitanism shared by Cynics and Stoics. Diogenes, the founder of the Cynic movement, was particularly keen on this image of the hero. It had great appeal also for the Stoic Epictetus (*c.*50–135 CE), who was born a slave in Phrygia, lived in Rome, was exiled and relocated in Epirus.

However, this idealization of Odysseus as a citizen of the world met with a major obstacle: his nostalgia. Such an emotion also clashes with the major Stoic tenet that one must strive to be content under any circumstances. One solution was to recast Odysseus's love of fatherland and family as the call of duty, which for a Stoic includes service to fatherland and family. This is Seneca's choice: in one of his *Epistles* (123), he states that the journey home must be pursued against the enticements that risk dragging us away 'from fatherland, parents, friends, and virtues'. Epictetus, on the other hand, is more intransigent. He blames Homer for having portrayed his great hero sitting on the shore of Calypso's island in the grip of tears and longing. We shall not believe the poet, 'for if Odysseus wept, he was not a good man' (*Discourses* 3. 24).

Practical Intelligence

Another feature of Odysseus that had appeal among philosophers, and of almost all persuasions, was his intelligence, which recommended him as an exemplar of practical wisdom. The biographer and moralist Plutarch (*c.*45–120 CE), whose philosophical allegiance was essentially but not dogmatically Platonic, is a good illustration of this trend. He shows great admiration for Odysseus's worldly virtues in his *Moral Essays*, where he praises him not only for his characteristic resilience, but also for his ability to handle relationships and life situations. For Plutarch Odysseus is an effective leader, an affectionate and beneficial friend, a frank but gentle teacher, a master of tact and *savoir faire*. He also admires the hero's self-control, his ability to submit his impulses and emotions to reason, for example in the episode where he feels pity for his crying wife but keeps his eyes firm in his lids, 'like horn or iron'. Odysseus's outward impassibility appeals to Plutarch not just as a token of moral excellence, but also for its practical advantages: it allows the hero and those who follow his example to conceal their emotions when it would be dangerous to betray them, for instance in front of a Roman emperor or his associates. Odysseus could teach the subject of Roman rule how to avoid risky self-exposure.

Eagerness for Knowledge

Yet another quality of Odysseus, his desire to learn, pushed an even higher association than with the worldly wise: with no less than the pursuer of knowledge, even for its own sake. Already the pre-Socratic Parmenides (*c.* 500 BCE) had adopted the widely travelled Odysseus as reference to convey the extensiveness of his own knowledge and the magnitude of his mental journey. The Stoic Odysseus of Horace's *Epistles* also exemplifies *virtus* and *sapientia* because 'he studied the cities and the customs of many men'.

The most enthusiastic endorser of Odysseus's eagerness to learn is however Cicero. In *On Ends*, he claims that the Sirens did not entice travellers by the beauty of their song but rather by the breadth and depth of their knowledge. A great man like Odysseus could not have been lured by cute little melodies. After quoting the Sirens' words in his translation, Cicero pronounces:

> *No, science is their promise, which, not surprisingly, to a man eager for wisdom was dearer than his fatherland.*

This image forces the Homeric text by discounting Odysseus's firmness of purpose. For Homer's character, though he burns to break loose from his bonds, has taken precautions to remain tied to the mast. Nothing is dearer than fatherland to him, knowledge included. Cicero's reversal invites a forward-looking comparison with the portrait of Odysseus in Dante's *Divine Comedy*, where, as we shall see, he chooses to forsake his home and follow the irresistible call of knowledge.

With an apparent paradox, among philosophers of Platonic persuasion, the song of the Sirens promotes, rather than threatens, Odysseus's return. For Plutarch the song is the call of the beyond and Odysseus, as a philosophical man, is attracted to it already in this life. This is because the song does not keep him forever away from 'Ithaca' but takes him there. It fills him with a yearning for the other world and, when he dies, it brings about his soul's return to its permanent dwelling. Odysseus's fatherland acquires a metaphysical meaning. The Neoplatonic Plotinus (205–270 CE) allegorizes Ithaca as our true home, our place of origin and our final destination, for which we should long: "let us flee to our country," he exhorts. Odysseus's nostalgia turns into the ultimate philosophical disposition, and his death transports him back home. Yet it is also a flight: a flight away from the sea, that is, from the turbulence of the life of matter, which the Neoplatonics equated with the sea. They had no doubt about the meaning of *ex halos*: Odysseus's death did not come from the sea but removed him and saved him forever from it.

Allegory

The Neoplatonic reconfiguration of Ithaca as our true home introduces us to an important tool employed in philosophical readings of Odysseus: allegory. Features and characters of his adventures were taken to hide a deeper meaning. One Heraclitus, not the pre-Socratic philosopher but a grammarian and rhetorician with eclectic philosophical sympathies, around 100 CE wrote an essay on Homer, usually titled *Homeric Problems*, in which he applies allegory extensively. Odysseus's wanderings receive special attention for, as Heraclitus claims in a sweeping statement, Homer used them to expound his philosophy (modern readers might be surprised to discover that Homer allegedly had a philosophy, but in antiquity several philosophers appealed to the poet as the original fount of their doctrines). Odysseus is the instrument of Homer's wisdom because he fights vice, as signified for instance by the lotus or by Circe, and because he pursues many paths of knowledge: the Sirens' song stands for 'the varied history of all ages' and the bag of the winds for astronomy.

So we can continue. Read allegorically, Leucothea's veil becomes Odysseus's virtue or the saviour of Odysseus-the-soul trying to escape from the stormy sea of matter. The root that protected him from Circe's wand is his reason, as is the mast to which he tied himself. Calypso, Circe and the Sirens were also broadly identified with the sensual allurements that Odysseus the wise must be able to resist (Cicero rejects precisely this reading of the Sirens), while Penelope, his focus and destination, became a cipher for philosophy itself. These interpretations, as naive and far-fetched as they seem to us, have played a paramount role in salvaging the figure of Odysseus from detractors, especially in the Middle Ages, by recasting many of his struggles as fights between virtue and vice. Through allegory, the pagan hero was made to fit Christian ideals.

VIRGIL'S VILLAIN

Diametrically opposite these images of Odysseus as a lover or an emblem of wisdom stands Virgil's grim portrait of him in the *Aeneid*. His Odysseus shares features with the unsavoury character of the Cyclic poems and of Greek tragedy, and he acquires further disparagement by the identity of the speaker, the Trojan Aeneas. The episode in focus is the destruction of Troy, for which Odysseus is responsible as its mastermind and architect. He is the most hateful of all the Greeks to the exiled Aeneas, who calls him false, harsh, full of malice. At the beginning of his narrative in book two, Aeneas recounts how the Trojans were tricked into welcoming the Wooden Horse inside their city. After wavering this way and that, they were swayed by Sinon, a young Greek man and a companion in wiles, or rather an emissary, of Odysseus (to be precise, of Ulixes, his Latin name, hence our Ulysses. Outside of citations, I use Odysseus throughout this essay to avoid confusion). Trojan shepherds found Sinon, as was his plan, and brought him to the city. There he wove a false story worthy of the Ithacan to persuade the Trojans that he had every reason to hate the Greeks – that is, first and foremost, Odysseus.

Sinon styles himself as a relative and a comrade of Palamedes, a notorious victim – 'the tale is well known' – of 'the envy of the smooth-talking Ulysses'. As Sinon swore to avenge his friend, Odysseus destroyed him as well, by manipulating, then forcing, the prophet Calchas to deliver a sham prophecy: for the Greeks to win the war, the gods required a human sacrifice. Since Calchas was reluctant to say more, Odysseus compelled him 'with loud cries' to reveal the designated victim: Sinon, of course, who however managed to hide and flee until he was found by the Trojans. The Odysseus-like Sinon blames his made-up tragic destiny on Odysseus and earns the Trojans' sympathy and confidence. We are reminded of Odysseus's instructions to Neoptolemus in Sophocles' *Philoctetes*: say the worst possible things about me to win the man over! We can imagine that Virgil's Odysseus, behind the curtains, gave similar instructions to Sinon, or at least that Sinon had an idea worthy of Sophocles' shameless character.

The terrain is thus ready for Sinon to persuade the Trojans to take in the Horse. It is, he explains, a gift that the Greeks dedicated to Athena to make up for an offence which was blocking all the ways to victory: the desecration of her temple and the theft of the Palladium, her statue. This offence, as Virgil's readers knew but as Sinon cares to repeat, was perpetrated by Diomedes and Odysseus, 'the inventor of crimes'.

Disparagement of Odysseus continues beyond the end of Sinon's reported narrative. As Aeneas lists the first nine warriors who leapt from the Horse at night, he calls eight of them by their names only, but for Odysseus he has an epithet in store: *dirus*, meaning dire or dreadful, which echoes and matches the adjective he chooses for Odysseus the first time he speaks his name: *durus*, harsh or cruel.

This picture of Odysseus is among the most negative in the entire tradition. Yet it cannot be taken to reflect Virgil's view of him. The chief reason for it is that the *Aeneid* narrates the sack of Troy from the Trojan perspective. While Aeneas is obviously partial, Sinon is an unscrupulous deceiver. He is not a character bound to elicit sympathy or to be trusted in his judgement, no spokesman for any truth whatsoever, no mouthpiece for the poet. Some of Virgil's contemporary readers might have disliked Odysseus, either because they wanted to believe in their Trojan ancestry or because, in some quarters, the Romans styled themselves as honest and straightforward in contrast to the wily Greeks. However, Virgil's own hero shares with Odysseus the destiny of a suffering wanderer and several attractive qualities: steadfastness, endurance and a seductive eloquence.

OVID'S ODYSSEUS

Ajax's Attack

Seductive eloquence is the main feature of Odysseus in Ovid's portrait of him. Like Virgil's, Ovid's most extensive presentation of Odysseus concentrates on an episode that does not appear in

Homer but is in the *Cycle*: the strife between Odysseus and Ajax over the armour of Achilles. Yet Ovid, while he does not spare Odysseus throughout, is sympathetic to the gentle, resourceful and elegant speaker.

We are in book thirteen of the *Metamorphoses*. Each contender makes his case in front of a jury of Greek chiefs. Ajax goes first (an early indication that he will lose, for in Greek and Latin fiction the second speaker tends to be the winner). Without even trying to ingratiate the judges, he launches into an attack on his adversary. His tone is hammering, insulting. He targets Odysseus's cunning ways on the battlefield and his nocturnal fighting: methods and actions worthy of his father – not Laertes, as in the *Odyssey*, but, following an alternative and disparaging tradition, the trickster Sisyphus. Ajax further accuses Odysseus of feigning madness to avoid enlisting as a soldier, of abandoning Philoctetes, of treacherously causing Palamedes' death. His so-called deeds, such as the killing of Dolon and Rhesus or the theft of the Palladium, are trifles and, Ajax presses this point, all were accomplished sneakily, at night. He, on the other hand, fights head-on. And he shows his valour in action, not in words. Ajax closes with this dismissal of one of Odysseus's winning talents, eloquence.

Odysseus's Persuasive Reply

Ajax's accusation is as crushing as myth allows. But Odysseus is not intimidated. He begins with an effective rhetorical strategy: instead of speaking right away, he stands up and keeps his gaze to the ground, then he makes eye contact with the chiefs, and finally he breaks his silence. Odysseus is imitating himself. In an episode of the *Iliad* we have already encountered, he applies the same strategy before a Trojan audience: he stands immobile for a long time, looking stupid, before letting out 'his great voice'. Ovid takes care to preface the speech of his Odysseus with a comment on its graceful eloquence. It is graceful indeed, much smoother than Ajax's and relying far less on abuse of the opponent. "It is not my way," he says, "to undermine maliciously the good that he has done."

Odysseus begins by defending the same speaking skills that Ajax had attacked: they benefitted not only Odysseus but everyone. He claims Laertes as his father and reviews deeds that give him lustre. It is to his credit that Achilles came to Troy. His mother Thetis had disguised him as a woman to keep him from fighting, but Odysseus discovered him: he placed gleaming weapons among his girlish toys and Achilles grabbed them, thus betraying his sex and identity. Odysseus also reminds the judges that it was he who kept the Greeks from abandoning the war effort (a reference to his silencing of Thersites) and that Diomedes chose him for a daring nocturnal raid, the enterprise recounted in book ten of the *Iliad* and dismissed by Ajax. He also minimizes his attempt to avoid fighting in the war by pairing it with Achilles' own – a disingenuous move, for, as Ovid's educated readers knew well, Achilles was keen on war and had not been a suitor of Helen, therefore was not bound by oath to come to Menelaus's defence. Both defections, Odysseus argues, were brought about by loving women: in his case a wife, in that of Achilles a mother. As for the cruel treatments of Palamedes and Philoctetes, they were the results of a common decision, while the capture of the Palladium sank Troy's fortunes.

Odysseus ends by pointing at the statue and wins the vote, proving 'the power of eloquence'. Ajax, unable to bear the shame of defeat, instantly kills himself. At the end he becomes a sympathetic character, but Odysseus, despite Ovid's suggestion that he won the armour because of his speech rather than his deeds, is the more appealing of the two. As a poet fond of verbal flourishes and endowed with an effortless pen, Ovid must have appreciated in Odysseus a mythic companion in facility with words.

The Nostalgic Exile

Ovid found a personal connection with Odysseus also for a biographical reason: like Homer's character, he was exiled to the end of the world, in his case the Black Sea; like Homer's character, he was kept far from home by an all-powerful figure, the godlike Augustus. Writing to a friend who had tried to console him, he tells him that nothing will suffice, that his love for his country is incurable:

> *"Whether you wish to call it dutiful or unmanly,*
> *I confess that my heart is weakened by misery.*
> *No one doubts Ulysses' wisdom, but even so he wishes*
> *that he might see the smoke coming from the hearth of his home."*
>
> – Epistulae ex Ponto 1.3

Ovid's identification with Odysseus around their shared nostalgia is original in the tradition. It strikes an almost provocative note against the background of the widespread philosophical readings that proposed the Homeric wanderer for the opposite reason, for enduring his exile, and criticized precisely his nostalgia. Ovid not only embraces it but, in another poem written during his exile (*Tristia* 1.5), he laments that his sufferings are much greater than those of Odysseus. His wanderings have been far more protracted and taxing, he has no friend or divine helper and the country he longs for is not an island of no consequence but Rome, the centre of everything, the global capital: 'the place of empire and of the gods'. We might wonder: does the worldly poet miss 'the hearth of his home' or the glamour of Rome?

SENECA'S DRAMA

A few decades after Virgil and Ovid, Seneca offers a picture of Odysseus which is closer to the unflattering one of Virgil. Seneca's approach to Odysseus is, as it were, schizophrenic. As a Stoic philosopher he admires the hero's strength, endurance and determination, while as a tragic playwright he adopts the villainous character of Euripides' tragedies, on which he often draws for his own. Odysseus plays a central role in the *Troades*, which conflates Euripides' *Hecuba and The Trojan Women*. As in the latter tragedy, he is the chief agent behind the murder of Astyanax, but he does not simply play the executioner: with craftiness, and through a cruel manipulation of Andromache's emotions, he wrings from her the information that her son is alive.

In Act III, Andromache has come up with the idea of faking her son's death. She has just hidden him in Hector's tomb when Odysseus is seen approaching, with 'accursed steps' and an appearance that reveals guile. "I am the minister of harsh fate," he begins, meaning to exculpate himself, but at once drawing attention to his callousness to pity. In the Latin, 'harsh' is the first word he utters. To his request, "hand over your son", Andromache replies with a soliloquy lamenting his death. Odysseus does not believe her and goes as far as threatening her with physical torture. Andromache mounts a spirited resistance and almost persuades him that Astyanax is dead. Then, in an aside, he reconsiders. He urges his heart to summon "his deceits and wiles, all that is Ulysses", and launches a subtle psychological attack, congratulating Andromache on the natural death of her son, who otherwise was destined to be hurled off the towers of Troy. At the news she trembles and shakes, giving herself away.

Eventually Odysseus uncovers the truth: Astyanax still lives. Andromache supplicates her tormenter but to no avail. Even as he blames the necessity of the sacrifice on the seer Calchas, she retorts, "it is the deed of your own heart", calling him "a contriver of frauds and an inventor of crimes". This grim picture of Odysseus exerted a strong influence after the rediscovery of Seneca's tragedies in the sixteenth century. Together with its kindred portraits from Greek tragedy, it went on to build the character of Odysseus in Renaissance and early modern French drama.

STATIUS'S MANIPULATIVE ODYSSEUS

Another poet bound to be influential, and already admired in the Middle Ages, is Statius (45–96 CE). His unfinished epic *Achilleid* presents an Odysseus that bears both the unkind features of

Virgil's character and the eloquence of Ovid's. The poem as we have it (book one and about 160 lines of book two) focuses on Achilles' early years. It describes how Thetis, to prevent her son from fighting at Troy, spirited him away to the island of Skyros, dressing him like a girl to escape detection; how he fell in love with Deidamia, one of the daughters of King Lycomedes; how he took her virginity; how she reciprocated his love and protected the secret of his identity. But Odysseus and Diomedes, again working together, are dispatched by the other Greeks to find Achilles. They succeed, thanks to the traditional ruse of the gifts – as soon as Achilles sees the gleaming shield 'Troy fills his whole heart' – and to the persuasiveness of Odysseus.

The first to mention Odysseus is Poseidon, who calls him 'dire', like Aeneas. When he and Diomedes leave their boat to look for Lycomedes' palace they are compared to wolves, and Odysseus also to a hunter. Both images suggest a predatory intent. The gifts he displays are 'cunning', 'Greek tricks' of the 'variegated Ulysses'. We hear echoes of Virgil again. Odysseus's role is to awaken the warlike nature of Achilles. He does it adroitly, tickling his ambition, thirst for glory, manly prowess and might. It is true that the job is not difficult. Though Achilles is torn between his bellicose spirit and his love for Deidamia, his eagerness to fight proves stronger. The rumour that Greek envoys are coming fills him with joy even before he meets them. But Odysseus's first speech, which is only indirectly addressed to him, almost causes him to spring from his seat. The words he has heard – "whoever is proud of his valour cannot be detained by his mother or by a maiden! Doomed is the one who lets this new chance of glory go by!" – have stirred him profoundly. The next day, after the gifts reveal who he really is, Odysseus presses further: "You are the one all of Greece awaits! Let Troy grow pale as you appear, and your father be glad to hear it!" Odysseus's manipulative eloquence succeeds in dispelling all uncertainty from Achilles' heart. As he sacrifices to his divine mother before leaving, he tells her: "I have been too obedient. The Trojan War and the Greek ships demand me, and I go."

DENIGRATING HOMER, DENIGRATING ODYSSEUS

Later antiquity contributed more voices to the belittlement of Odysseus. Homer's favourite character came to be identified with the poet himself and underwent the same fortunes. The merging has roots already in the *Odyssey* where, however, it is flattering to the hero: the enchanting storyteller is entrusted with the centrepiece of his own epic and is compared to a poet. The identification is also behind appreciative claims, mostly by philosophically minded authors such as Heraclitus, that Odysseus was the mouthpiece or the instrument of Homer's wisdom. But eventually the coupling cost Odysseus dearly: he went down with Homer when the poet became target of attacks for his reliability.

The motives for Homer's dismissal vary from playfulness, as when the second-century CE sophist (public lecturer) Dio Chrysostom argues in his *Trojan Oration* that the Trojan War never happened, to an invidious desire to dethrone the 'divine poet' from his position of undiscussed authority – as in the writings attributed to two self-styled eyewitnesses of the Trojan War, Dictys of Crete (second century CE) and Dares of Phrygia (sixth century). Among their multifarious claims are that the Trojans won the war, that Homer lied and that Odysseus's wanderings are fake, as is Homer's image of him throughout. Instead, stories uncomplimentary to him took centre stage, such as his revenge on Palamedes, which appears in Dictys. In another imaginative retelling, it was Odysseus himself who 'bribed' Homer into leaving the story out. Philostratus, a sophist of the second century CE and the writer of the *Heroicus*, which discusses the power and worship of various heroes, has Homer consult Odysseus's ghost to gather information about the Trojan War. Odysseus promises help, but on the condition that the poet will praise him indiscriminately, and in particular that he will not mention Palamedes. Homer, the lying poet, was thus inspired by a deceitful muse or source. This wave of anti-Homeric and anti-Odysseus propaganda was to prove long-lasting.

GREEK AND ROMAN ART

Our discussion so far has shown that Odysseus, regardless of the disparate moral evaluations of his character, was a popular and appealing subject for writers of all genres and persuasions. His popularity is also demonstrated by the countless depictions of him in pottery all over Greece, as well as in Etruria and Magna Graecia. Homer's hero became a fashionable subject for vase painters in the archaic period, starting with the seventh century BCE, and remained so throughout antiquity. Painters liked to illustrate especially the adventures that Odysseus himself narrates in Homer. While writers drew materials from

Odysseus's Trojan career at least as much as, or perhaps more than, from his wanderings, artists preferred the latter. Every episode he narrates attracted their eye, except, apparently, the encounter with the Lotus Eaters, perhaps because their image in his description is pale. The favourite adventures in art are the blinding of the Cyclops (iconic are the crater of the late fifth century BCE attributed to the 'Cyclops' Painter', now at the British Museum, and a Laconian cup of the sixth century BCE, now at the Bibliothèque Nationale de France in Paris), and the escape from his cave. Other popular adventures include the encounter with Circe and the transformation of Odysseus's companion into pigs, the voyage past the Sirens with Odysseus tied to the mast (a famous illustration of which is the red-figure vase of the sixth century BCE attributed to the 'Sirens' Painter', now at the British Museum), Scylla. There are also representations of Odysseus in sculptures, wall-paintings and engraved gems. He often sports the *pilos*, a conical hat of leather or felt that served as a helmet or was worn by travellers.

Odysseus's iconographic appeal extended to Republican and Imperial Rome. His popularity there was partly due to the Roman appropriation of him as an Italic hero. He was believed to have died and been buried in Etruria, and the fabulous places of his wanderings came to be identified with Italian locations: Aetna (the Cyclops' cave), the strait of Messina (Scylla and Charybdis), Capri or another island off the Amalfi Coast (the Sirens), the Aeolian islands (Aeolus). Scenes from Odysseus's wanderings remained favourite subjects for artists. Some of them appear in the well-known 'Odyssey Landscapes', a late republican fresco now at the Vatican Museums: it illustrates Odysseus's encounters with the Laestrygonians and with Circe, his consultation of Tiresias in Hades and the voyage past the Sirens.

Another renowned artwork with Odysseus at the centre is a fourfold group of sculptures which decorated a grotto in Tiberius's villa at Sperlonga on the coast between Rome and Naples. The statues (the remnants of which are at the local museum) span Odysseus's career from the war to his wanderings. In one group he was dragging the dead body of Achilles away from the battlefield; in another he was standing, foiled in his attempt to kill Diomedes after the theft of the Palladium. The other two groups depicted Scylla's attack and Odysseus guiding his companions as they prepare to thrust the firebrand into Polyphemus's eye. An expressive, dramatically bent head of the hero is preserved in good condition. The four groups show Odysseus in situations that reveal the complexity of his character as accrued over eight centuries: enduring, shrewd, courageous, pious, perfidious and yet attached to his friends. Odysseus's affectionate nature is also conveyed, for instance, by a relief of the second century CE (at the Museum Barracco in Rome) that shows him with a moving expression as he embraces Laertes after the recognition. As in Greek representations, Odysseus wears his conical hat.

3.
From the Middle Ages to the Early-Modern Period

"Call to mind from whence we sprang:
Ye were not form'd to live the life of brutes
But virtue to pursue and knowledge high!"
– Dante, *Divine Comedy, Inferno* 26, here and below in
Henry F. Carey's translation, 1888

No Greek hero has experienced as many and diverse reincarnations as Odysseus, as if to make real the *polytropia* or multiplicity of Homer's character. No other personage has inspired so many writers, found so many kindred spirits and become so recurrently emblematic of historical, ideological and intellectual developments, as well as of human striving, yearning, despair and disenchantment. In the last two parts of this introduction I will offer a necessarily brief and selective overview of Odysseus's reception from the Middle Ages to the present. Readers who wish to learn more are referred to: W.B. Stanford, *The Ulysses Theme* (1963); P. Boitani, *The Shadow of Ulysses: Figures of a Myth* (1994); E. Hall, *The Return of Ulysses: A Cultural History of Homer's Odyssey* (2008); and P. Boitani,

Il grande racconto di Ulisse (2016), which is sumptuously illustrated. The discussion that follows has profited much from these books.

FRANCE AND ENGLAND

The critical voices of Dares and Dictys found resonance already in late antiquity, and in the Middle Ages they won the day. Their versions of the Trojan War, which were generally considered reliable, influenced the numerous Trojan narratives that bourgeoned in the period, especially in France and England. The sources at the disposal of medieval authors and readers were, in addition to Dares and Dictys, Latin authors, among whom Virgil replaced Homer as the 'divine poet'. His grim portrait of Odysseus gained authority because it agreed with those of Dictys and Dares: they all looked at the cunning Greek from the biased perspective of his Trojan victims. Additionally, at this time Odysseus lost his main admirer, Homer, who in the West was hardly known.

A foundational medieval retelling of the Trojan War is the *Roman de Troie* by the French poet Benoît de Sainte-Maure (*c.* 1170). This long verse narrative (over 30,000 lines) was declaredly based on Dares and Dictys; in it, Odysseus speaks in the vernacular for the first time. Benoît reports Dares' description of Odysseus as the most beautiful of the Greeks, wondrously eloquent but – and these are his chief characteristics, stressed over and over – mendacious, deceitful, treacherous like no other, simply 'the villain'. The romance dwells on several of his discreditable deeds, among which stands out the death of Palamedes, executed for treason based on Odysseus's forged letters, in what is described as an 'appalling trap'. More appreciative is the account of his wanderings and homecoming, and the story of his death is sympathetically told: forewarned by a vision that he should fear his son's plot, he seized Telemachus, imprisoned him and put him in shackles, in spite of the great affection that bound father and son. However, his other son Telegonus then arrived on Ithaca in search for his father. After being refused admittance by the guards, who denied his claim that he was Odysseus's child, Telegonus started killing men left and right, causing Odysseus to respond to the attack and to be slain by him. The two men only recognized each other when it was too late. Odysseus was buried with honour, and the romance concludes with Telemachus inheriting the kingdom of Ithaca and Telegonus returning to Circe, his mother. As the ending shows, Benoît's narrative treats Odysseus with mixed feelings. But in the main it applies a pro-Trojan bias that would appeal to its courtly audience, the French kings claiming descent from the Trojans.

Knowledge of the *Romance of Troy* spread throughout Europe thanks to a Latin adaptation, the *Historia destructionis Troiae*, by the Sicilian Guido delle Colonne. In turn it generated more vernacular retellings, among them the English *Troy Book* (1420) by Lygdate. Here Odysseus, though he receives good press for his eloquence and political intelligence, is rude and unchivalrous: the English also claimed descent from the Trojans, via the mythic king Brute, a descendant of Aeneas and the first king of Britain. Slightly earlier, in 1390, Gower presents Odysseus as a sorcerer in his *Confessio Amantis*. All the Greek's talents, his all-round knowledge – ranging from rhetoric to philosophy, medicine to astronomy – were brought to him by the Black Arts, and his tragic death at the hands of his son Telegonus was a fitting punishment for his sacrilegious, God-cursed skills and practices:

Thurgh Sorcerie his lust he wan,
Thurgh Sorcerie his wo began,
Thurgh Sorcerie his love he ches,
Thurgh Sorcerie his lif he les.

THE CONQUEROR OF VICE

Odysseus's reputation for virtue did not sink entirely, for it proved as easy to Christianize his image as to demonize it. Early Christian writers, starting with the Church Fathers, inherited the Stoic appreciation for Odysseus's exemplary fortitude. They went on to make their own contribution to the allegorical readings of Odysseus's adventures offered by pagan philosophers. Like those, they extolled Odysseus as a paradigm of patience, resilience and resistance to temptations, a winner over sensual allurements. Some Christian authors, for instance the preacher Maximus of Turin (*c.* 450), even saw an analogy between the hero tied to the mast as he sailed by the Sirens and Jesus Christ nailed to the cross.

In the Byzantine East the *Odyssey* was never lost or forgotten, though Odysseus also suffered from the blows of anti-Homeric propaganda. The literati continued to read Homer's epics in the original, with allegory retaining its attraction as an interpretive tool that endowed them with a deeper meaning. These facts helped to preserve Odysseus's good image. For the Byzantine scholar and archbishop Eustathius of Thessalonica (twelfth century), who wrote two massive commentaries, one on each of Homer's epics, he was, as for earlier Greek moralists, an emblem of both practical wisdom and eagerness to learn: nothing less than 'the philosopher'.

DANTE'S HERO

Synopsis

We now return to the West to meet one of the most famous incarnations of Odysseus: Dante's 'Ulisse', who is infected with a literally deadly eagerness for knowledge. We are in the twenty-sixth Canto of the *Inferno*. Dante and his guide, Virgil, have reached the eighth circle, where the spirits of the fraudulent counsellors are enclosed, each in a flame. Among them are Odysseus and Diomedes, who burn together, one flame with two horns. Odysseus is the higher. To satisfy Dante's yearning to talk to the 'horned flame', Virgil interrogates the spirits: how did you die? The spirit of Odysseus then wearily shakes himself – "Of the old flame forthwith the greater horn / Began to roll, murmuring, as a fire / That labours with the wind" – and tells the story of his last journey and death. After he left Circe, he decided not to go home:

"Nor fondness for my son, nor reverence
Of my old father, nor return of love,

That should have crown'd Penelope with joy,
Could overcome in me the zeal I had
T'explore the world, and search the ways of life,
Man's evil and his virtue."

With his few companions, Odysseus sets out for the Mediterranean's western shores. They were 'tardy with age' (*vecchi e tardi*) when they reached the Pillars of Hercules. Odysseus then addressed a short oration to his crew, urging them on to the southern hemisphere, beyond the Pillars, to gain experience of the uninhabited world, *del mondo sanza gente*. He concludes with the famous exhortation:

"Call to mind from whence we sprang:
Ye were not form'd to live the life of brutes
But virtue to pursue and knowledge high (per seguir
virtute e canoscenza)!"

He persuades his companions and launches the ship into its 'witless flight' (*folle volo*). They sail southward until a dark and tall mountain suddenly appears in the distance. At first the men are happy at the sight. But from that 'new land' (*terra nova*), a whirlwind rises, strikes the boat and sinks it, 'as another decreed'. And the sea closes upon them.

Significance

Dante concentrates exclusively on Odysseus's last journey and extends it to the limits of the world. One such journey might have been prefigured already in the *Odyssey*, where the instructions Odysseus is given by Tiresias could indeed suggest endless travelling or a journey to the end of the world. For where else could the maritime Greeks locate Odysseus's destination, a land whose people did not know the sea, but in unfathomably remote regions? This is speculative, however, and Dante in any case was not familiar with the *Odyssey*. Yet he might have known ancient disputes, as recorded by the Latin grammarian Aulus Gellius (second century CE) in his *Attic Nights*, about the setting of Odysseus's travels: the 'inner' or the 'outer' sea, the Mediterranean or the ocean beyond Hercules' Pillars.

However it may be, Dante invents for Odysseus a last journey with no prior return to Ithaca, converting his *nostos* from Troy into an outbound flight, towards the unknown. This is a momentous event in the metamorphosis of the hero, as is the new twist Dante gives to Odysseus's death: it does not come from old age, as in Homer, nor from his son, as in later tradition, but from his own wanderlust.

Two recognizable, and traditionally clashing, Latin texts are joined in Odysseus's portrait: Virgil's *Aeneid*, where he is the fraudulent counsellor who causes Troy's fall with the ruse of the Horse, and Horace's *Epistle* cited above, where he is the paradigm of 'wisdom and virtue' and, as already in the *Odyssey*, the curious observer of cities and men. While his fraudulence is the vice that has brought him to Hell, his passion for learning is his main and distinctive feature (not shared by Diomedes, his companion in punishment). In Dante's rewrite, Odysseus's classical eagerness for knowledge becomes unbounded. The 'virtue and wisdom' of Horace's hero, which encompassed social responsibilities and a centripetal focus, is turned into social irresponsibility and an unending centrifugal drive, an imperative to break the limits set to human endeavours.

Dante's hero faintly recalls Cicero's, with whom Dante was acquainted and who, we shall remember, is praised for preferring the Sirens' song, the call of wisdom, over his home. But Cicero does not draw the consequences of his claim for Odysseus's journey; he cannot, for he has Homer before him. Cicero does not and cannot say that Odysseus did not return home, but only observes that his yearning for wisdom was stronger than his nostalgia. Dante strips him of his nostalgia altogether. His Odysseus is free from Homeric directions and embarks on a 'witless flight': witless, he now recognizes, because forbidden and therefore doomed. The 'other' who decreed his death, and that of his companions, is God, whom Odysseus, with sober discretion or pagan agnosticism, does not name. God has destroyed them because they have transgressed the limits imposed on human learning and experience; they have picked from the Tree of Knowledge.

The Christian Dante must punish his Odysseus for his sinful eagerness to violate boundaries with the strength of his human mind; he must punish the man who believes in the unlimited pursuit of *virtute et canoscenza*. Yet there is no denying that he admires the drive and motives of his creation. Dante's image of Odysseus is poised between the classical tradition, Christian belief and an almost visionary premonition of humanistic fervour. It is also bound to have an immense legacy, to become the most inspiring and influential portrait of Odysseus since and alongside Homer's.

THE EMBODIMENT OF HUMANISTIC IDEALS

Petrarch

The 1360s mark a turning point in the knowledge of Homer. Thanks to the joint efforts of Petrarch and Boccaccio, the *Odyssey* re-enters Italy, in a Latin prose translation produced by the Greco-Italian scholar Leontius Pilatus. Petrarch himself knew no Greek, but he displays great admiration for Odysseus and draws a picture of him that blends an almost Dantesque thirst for knowledge (but without Dante's Christian condemnation) with the classical image of the experienced hero, schooled in the ways of the world and serving his community. In one of his *Epistolae familiares* (book nine, letter thirteen), he credits Odysseus with far-reaching travels, beyond the Pillars of Hercules:

> *Odysseus went to Troy and from there farther out; he crossed lands and sea and did not stop until he founded a city with his name on the most remote shores of the West.*

The city, beyond the strait of Gibraltar, is Lisbon – which according to a legend recorded by the Roman compiler Solinus (third century CE) was indeed founded by Odysseus; Lisbon's ancient name, Olissipo or Ulissipo, was explained as 'Odysseus's city', from 'Ulixes' and '*polis*'.

Yet at home he had a very old father, an infant son, a young wife who was besieged by suitors, while in the meantime he was fighting with Circe's potions, Sirens' songs, Cyclopes' violence, sea-monsters and storms. A man famous for his wanderings, he trod upon his affections, and preferred to grow old between Scylla and Charybdis, in the dark depths of Avernus…rather than at home, and this for no other reason than to go back home some day in his old age richer with knowledge.

Petrarch combines Odysseus's Homeric wanderings with a hint of his Dantesque oceanic journey. He also joins the destination and mental focus of the Homeric character, Ithaca, with the un-Homeric image of a traveller who voluntarily lingers abroad until old age, in order to go back home equipped with more knowledge; a traveller who, like Dante's, 'trod upon his affections' and responsibilities. While the image of Odysseus fighting against all obstacles is well rooted in the classical and medieval tradition, receiving special emphasis in allegorical readings, the idea that he 'preferred to grow old' among those obstacles clashes with that tradition. Petrarch's Odysseus ultimately does return home, however, and he puts his knowledge and experience of the world to the service of his people. He is compared to a farmer, who must stay in place and learn about the crops, the weather, and so on, while 'a noble spirit and one striving for excellence' has the obligation of learning 'the customs of many men', not for knowledge's own sake, but rather to govern his people better. Petrarch's Odysseus is an integrated man, whose passion for learning does not conflict with his duties in the world; an Odysseus who takes centrifugal paths but does not lose sight of his final centripetal goal.

Jean Dorat

In the Renaissance, however, Odysseus's intellectual curiosity was extended beyond 'the customs of many men' to encompass every field of knowledge. He came to embody the ideal of the well-rounded cultured person, interested in all the arts and sciences, including esoteric ones. This is the image of Odysseus offered by the sixteenth-century French scholar Jean Dorat (better known by his self-given Latin pen name Auratus), who held the Royal Chair of Greek in Paris. His teaching included a series of lectures on the *Odyssey*, which have come down to us under the title *Mythologicum*. For his explanations, Dorat relies heavily on allegory, drawing both from ancient sources, such as Cicero and Heraclitus, the author of *Homeric Problems*, and from more modern ones, such as Eustathius.

Odysseus features in several roles: as a Neoplatonic metaphysical traveller, striving to reach his celestial home; as a homebound responsible leader, 'who looks to his fatherland, that is, to his citizens' happiness'; and as a voracious student. His descent to the underworld 'signifies nothing else than the study of natural science'. Meanwhile Circe stands for physics, 'since she investigates the things on earth and under the earth', Calypso for metaphysics, because she contemplates immortality and the pure essence of divinity, and the Sirens for poetry, history and oratory. How to reconcile Odysseus's passion for such multifarious and far-reaching studies with his public responsibilities? Dorat's answer: he eagerly absorbs every discipline but does not lose himself in any. His knowledge has practical aims. It fortifies him against the hardships of his journeys and is subordinated to 'his citizens' happiness' – that is, to his communal duties. Though Dorat's Odysseus is conversant with more fields of study than Petrarch's, they both end their journey on Ithaca in order to serve their people.

ODYSSEUS'S NOSTALGIA REVISITED: JOACHIM DU BELLAY'S HEUREUX QUI COMME ULYSSE...

Among the students of Jean Dorat was the poet Joachim du Bellay (1522–1560). He was also one of the first members of the group of French Renaissance poets called *La Pléiade*, founded by another student of Dorat, Pierre de Ronsard. Du Bellay translated sections of the two Homeric epics and mentions Odysseus frequently in his poetry. In a sonnet that he wrote while he was in Rome, employed as a secretary to his cousin, the cardinal Jean du Bellay, he wishes he could put an end to his stay abroad and return home, as Homer's hero does:

Happy he, who like Odysseus, has had a lovely journey,
Or like the one who conquered the fleece,
And then has returned, wise to the world,
To live among his family the rest of his time.
When shall I see again, alas, of my small village
The chimney smoke, in which season

Shall I see again the small lot of my humble house,
Which is a province for me, and much benefit.
– Les Regrets XXXI

Du Bellay was feeling like an exile and missing his hometown, Lyré, near Angers. It is his nostalgia that shapes his portrait of Odysseus. His identification with the hero's disposition is unprecedented in its precision and poignancy. As we have seen, Ovid, during his exile to the Black Sea, had already found a connection with the nostalgic Odysseus. However, his identification limps and is somewhat disingenuous, for the worldly poet was longing not for a nondescript island but rather for the glimmering city of Rome. In contrast, it is precisely Rome that du Bellay wants to leave, in favour of his 'humble house'. Just as Odysseus recognizes that Ithaca is rugged and his kingdom is small, Du Bellay knows that his village (mentioned in the sequence of the sonnet) lacks glamour; he even describes his house as small and modest. Yet, just as Odysseus preferred his inhospitable island and little kingdom over the luxuriant gardens of Calypso and her promise of immortality, for du Bellay his insignificant estate and town are a whole province and offer 'much benefit' (*beaucoup d'avantage*) – certainly more than Rome.

Odysseus, however, is the poet's more fortunate alter ego, for he has been allotted both life-enriching travels and his much-desired return. He is called happy both because his journey has been beautiful – meaning that, in a classical and Renaissance spirit, it has increased his wisdom, knowledge and *savoir-vivre* – and also because it has taken him back home to Ithaca. Will Joachim ever see his own Ithaca? Like Odysseus, he will have acquired experience and knowledge while abroad; but his exilic nostalgia prevails over this sentiment. His longing causes him to de-heroize Odysseus, as it were, to give more room and his whole heart to the former traveller's cosy family life at home. Here, the poet lets us imagine, he eventually died the peaceful death that was promised to him in the *Odyssey*, rather than meeting with the violent one popular in later traditions.

THE EXPLORER

Alongside the centripetal journey of Homer's hero, the centrifugal one of Dante's already has its acolytes in the Renaissance. Petrarch, as we have seen, extends Odysseus's wanderings to the outer ocean, but his final destination remains Ithaca and the duties that await him there. Things sit differently for those who were fired up by the geographical explorations and discoveries of the next two centuries. To them, Odysseus's Dantesque journey appealed without qualifications and in the most literal way: as a mythic foreshadowing of the navigations to the New World, Dante's *terra nova*. Dante himself, for his Odysseus, had in the background the expedition of the Genovese brothers Vivaldi, who in 1291 left for India, planning to round Gibraltar and sail southward; they never returned. Later, Odysseus became the unfortunate ancestor of successful explorers: for Amerigo Vespucci, as it appears from his letters, of himself; for Torquato Tasso, of Columbus.

In the fifteenth Canto of the *Gerusalemme Liberata* (1575) the characters Carlo and Ubaldo, led by Fortune, repeat the route of Dante's Odysseus past the Gibraltar strait. Asked whether others have crossed it before, Fortune replies that Hercules, after his numerous prodigious labours, did not dare to go further. Instead he placed his Pillars at the strait,

Till Lord Ulysses did those bounders pass,
To see and know he so desirous was
(Ma quei segni spezzò ch'egli prescrisse,
di veder vago e di saper, Ulisse.)
– Translation by Edward Fairfax, 1635

The ocean swallowed him, but, Fortune continues, a day will come when the Pillars will no longer set the limits to human endeavours: no threatening wind will stop Columbus's flight.

Likewise, Spanish and Portuguese epics of conquest are new Odysseys. The best known is Portugal's national epic, *The Lusiads* (1572) by Camões, which glorifies Vasco da Gama's journey round the Cape of Good Hope to India. Odysseus, move over and make room for Vasco!

With wonder name the Greek no more,
What lands he saw, what toils at sea he bore.
– Translation by William J. Mickle, 1776

This image of Odysseus as an explorer already has roots in Homer, where, despite being engaged in a homeward-bound journey, he is inquisitive about his surroundings and even takes risks purely for the sake of finding out what kind of people inhabit each of the places where he lands.

The Politician: French Drama of the Sixteenth and Seventeenth Centuries

Though the Renaissance showed a fervid interest in Odysseus's travels, his role as a political leader was never out of sight. It is prominent in sixteenth- and seventeenth-century French tragedy, where his image continues to suffer from a negative bias, exacerbated by the rediscovered Senecan drama and by its Greek sources. Two major representatives of this trend are Robert Garnier with *La Troade* (1579) and Racine with *Iphigénie* (1674).

Act II of *La Troade* reworks Act III of Seneca's *Troades*. At the centre are Andromache and Odysseus. The plot is the same: Andromache has hidden Astyanax in Hector's tomb and pretends that he is dead, but Odysseus discovers the truth by means of threats and psychological torture. He then has the child seized. As in Seneca, Odysseus congratulates Andromache on having lost a child who was doomed to suffer a violent death and, as in Seneca, she trembles at the news and betrays herself. But Garnier adds an extra stroke of cruelty to his Odysseus: he is ready to destroy the tomb of Hector and to throw his ashes into the sea. It is under the pressure of this threat that Andromache resolves to deliver her son, for the destruction of the tomb will kill him in addition to desecrating her husband's remains. Odysseus has a flicker of sympathy for her when at last she asks Astyanax to leave the tomb and to supplicate his master. "The tears of this mother soften my heart," he declares; but the *raison d'état* prevails. When he claims that it is the prophet Calchas who ordered the murder, Andromache releases a flood of accusations, as she does in Seneca. She calls Odysseus a perjurer, disloyal, false, wily, malicious and an inventor of frauds – accusations to which he is not even allowed to reply, whereas in Seneca he is. Odysseus's last words in the scene, and in the play, show him hardened towards Andromache's tear-jerking farewell to her child:

> *"These tears have no ending, take him quickly,*
> *he is the only delay to our vessels."*

Racine's *Iphigénie* was produced almost a century later, and Odysseus's character is almost as odious as in Garnier. This is intriguing because the young Racine had written an essay, *Remarques sur l'Odyssée d'Homère*, in which he had expressed heartfelt admiration for Homer's hero, notably for the strength yet gentleness of his mind, for his courage and determination. Racine may have changed his views on Odysseus, or he may have been influenced by genre, for the sources at a tragic playwright's disposal mostly condemned Odysseus and focused exclusively on the character's Trojan career. In *Iphigénie*, Odysseus appears on stage only at the beginning and at the end, but his sinister presence is felt and feared throughout. His first mention, by Agamemnon in Act I, is as someone who, 'remembering his cruel ingenuity', persuaded him, against his initial instinct, to go along with his daughter's sacrifice by caressing his sense of honour and his ambition for glory. Odysseus is not insensitive: as he tells Agamemnon, "I am a father, my lord"; but he is willing to sympathize only as far as tears. Clytemnestra's opinion of the Ithacan is even harsher. As she sees him approach towards the end of Act V, she asks: "Is it Odysseus I see? It is he. My daughter is dead." Agamemnon deems Odysseus responsible for his inhumane change of mind, but Clytemnestra considers him no less than Iphigenia's executioner.

THE IDEAL KING: FÉNELON'S LES AVENTURES DE TÉLÉMAQUE

At the very end of the century, however, a novel appeared in France that produced a total rehabilitation of Odysseus: *Les Aventures de Télémaque* (1699) by the archbishop Fénelon, but initially published anonymously. The novel was written for the grandson of Louis XIV with a didactic purpose: to teach the virtues of a good king to the young man (aged 17 at the time). It draws on the section of the *Odyssey* that describes Telemachus's travels as he seeks news of his father, increasing their scope and adventures; but more deeply Telemachus's journey is an educational one. He figures in the role of the mentee, while various characters are cast as his teachers and Odysseus as one of his models (another is Aeneas). "Apply yourself to imitate the character of your father," he is told early on. Fénelon's Odysseus is not the cynic pursuer of the *raison d'état*, but an embodiment of courage, prowess, endurance, pleasantness, dignity, even truthfulness and especially wisdom. That is, he possesses qualities that are essential to the good king as Fénelon conceives him, and as he presents him to a future king of France.

Even Odysseus's treatment of Philoctetes, hurled in his face for over two millennia as one of his most shameful, indefensible deeds, appears in a new and justified light, and according to the victim himself. In book fifteen Philoctetes tells Telemachus that initially he had found Odysseus's abandonment of him on Lemnos inhuman, but now he understands that he was 'blinded by prejudice and self-love' whereas Odysseus's goals were noble and selfless. Fénelon's educational novel has little appeal today, but it was extremely popular through the eighteenth and nineteenth centuries, until the First World War, and influenced the political thinking of, among others, Jean-Jacques Rousseau and Thomas Jefferson.

SHAKESPEARE'S TROILUS AND CRESSIDA

The Eloquent Counsellor

In England, Odysseus the politician did not suffer from vituperation for as long as he did in France; by the early sixteenth century he was already receiving better press. Crucial for the improvement of his fortunes in the political sphere was the rediscovery of Homer and of Plutarch, one of Odysseus's strongest advocates. Sir Thomas Elyot thus recommended him to Henry VIII as the wise, witty, virtuous and resourceful hero, whom he particularly admired for his handling of Thersites. This appreciation finds an echo in Shakespeare's *Troilus and Cressida* (1602), in which Odysseus plays a significant role as counsellor, exhibiting magnificent eloquence, inventiveness, tact and a deep knowledge 'of men and their minds'. In Act I, Scene III he opposes the view of Agamemnon and Nestor that the length of the war should be welcomed as a spur to heroism. He is as careful as in book two of the *Iliad* not to hurt Agamemnon's feelings, displaying the same courtesy, respect for his superiors and ability to ingratiate his audience. Agamemnon, he begins,

"Thou great commander, nerve and bone of Greece,
Heart of our numbers, soul and only spirit,
In whom the tempers and the minds of all
Should be shut up – hear what Ulysses speaks."

In this flattering introduction, the deft speaker acknowledges Agamemnon's unquestionable and supreme authority and undermines his own right to speak, making the king more disposed to hear an opinion that Odysseus knows is at variance with his. Then he caresses Nestor's vanity, lauding "his experienc'd tongue", before asking again for the two men's ears. He wins. "We shall hear music, wit, and oracle," Agamemnon replies. Odysseus duly expounds his view, which is that order must be restored. The Greeks are broken into factions; they do not respect authority, hierarchies or 'degrees', and whenever this happens, whether in a human community or up in the heavens, mutiny, chaos and plagues ensue:

"Take but degree away, untune that string,
And, hark, what discord follows!"

With its masterful eloquence, Odysseus's speech conjures up and surpasses his forceful address to Agamemnon and the troops with which he stops the general uprising in book two of the *Iliad*.

The Cunning Planner

The next important episode featuring Odysseus adds his cunning to his eloquence. When Hector challenges any of the Greeks to fight him in single combat, Odysseus objects to the choice of Achilles as champion because, should he lose, the army will be disheartened. He pushes for Ajax instead, thinking that, as a bonus, the choice will infuriate Achilles and goad him into re-entering the war. Everyone will play up to Ajax as the best warrior, a slight that Achilles will not accept. Nestor is impressed with Odysseus and agrees with his proposal. This suggests that his cunning is supposed to meet with the audience's approval, not to arouse criticism. It serves the common good, as it does in Homer. Odysseus pursues his plan when he meets Achilles (Act III, Scene III). He delivers another powerful speech, about the sway ingratitude has over men and their readiness to forget good deeds. Now everyone is clapping Ajax on his shoulder, 'As if his foot were on brave Hector's breast'. Achilles, cut to the quick, asks: "What, are my deeds forgot?" Odysseus then expands on the vagaries of time:

"The present eye praises the present object:
Then marvel not, thou great and complete man,
That all the Greeks begin to worship Ajax."

Odysseus is manipulative, but not villainous. He hits at the core of Achilles' immense pride and vanity, and for a good cause. It is true that his plan does not succeed. But neither does the embassy in the *Iliad*, which is behind Odysseus's approaches to Achilles.

The Keen Psychologist

Our hero is also cast in a more original role: as the sensitive and sensible listener to a young man in love. In Act V, Scene II Cressida has arrived at the Greek camp to be reunited with her father Calchas who, following a storyline that goes back to the *Roman de Troie*, is a Trojan who has betrayed his people and moved over to the Greek camp. In her father's tent Cressida flirts with Diomedes, wavering between the attraction of a new love and her pledged fidelity to the old one. Troilus and Odysseus witness the scene from outside. Odysseus has already intuited that the maiden is wanton – "There's language in her eye, her cheek, her lip" – but does not know that Troilus loves her to distraction. As the young man is visibly in torment, Odysseus urges him to depart, but the other insists to stay and promises to be patient. Odysseus does not force him but encourages him again to leave as he sees his ever-growing distress, and, meeting each time with a refusal, exhorts him again to be patient. Finally Cressida leaves the tent, after speaking some ominous words:

"Troilus, farewell! One eye yet looks on thee;
But with my heart the other eye doth see".

Troilus seeks to deny the evidence of his eyes and ears, but Odysseus kindly disillusions him. He then listens to his flooding, passionate confession of a now hopeless love.

Contrary to his habit, and to the previous episodes, here Odysseus does not speak much. He plays, emotionally as well as dramaturgically, a supporting role, first by trying to stop Troilus from feeding his misery, then by quieting his outbursts, opening his eyes to reality and listening to the desperation of a betrayed lover. He does not attempt to console him, which in the circumstances would be to no avail. His last words are the sober "I'll bring you to the gates". Odysseus's maturity, gentleness and understanding of a human heart are in the spirit of the *Odyssey*.

ART

Odysseus's popularity in art continues unbroken. Due to the diffusion of Troy-tales and of Latin poetry in the Middle Ages, he features in illustrated manuscripts. Homer disappeared, but episodes from the *Odyssey* were known from adaptations of Roman sources and from Christian writers who allegorized them. Odysseus's encounter with the Sirens, which was a favourite for those allegorical exercises and which, furthermore, Benoît de Saint-Maure had included in his *Roman*, was the preferred subject for churches' capitals and metopes: understandably, since the episode was taken to signify the dangers of vice and evil.

From the sixteenth century on, representations of Odysseus in painting cover most incidents of his biography. Primaticcio (1504–1570) depicted a series of frescoes illustrating numerous scenes from the *Odyssey* for the castle of Fontainebleau. The frescoes have been destroyed, but drawings and oil paintings survive, with *Ulysses and Penelope* notable among them.

Pinturicchio also painted a fresco featuring Odysseus's return to Penelope (1508), while Parmigianino produced a drawing of Circe and Odysseus's companions (*c.* 1520), which was often copied. In the Italian Cinquecento Odysseus simply goes viral, if I may express it so, as a beloved subject of pictorial cycles (see Boitani 2016, pp. 596–601). And in the following century, there is hardly any episode in Odysseus's career that fails to draw the eye of artists. Suffice it to mention Poussin's *Landscape with Polyphemus* (1648) and Rubens' *Ulysses on the island of the Phaeacians* (*c.* 1630).

4.
The Modern Odysseus

"I cannot rest from travel: I will drink
Life to the lees."
– Tennyson, *Ulysses*

THE WANDERER

rom the nineteenth century on, Odysseus is first and foremost the Wanderer. This is not the case in the previous two centuries, where it was rather Odysseus the politician who dominated. The only meaningful exceptions from the seventeenth century are Calderón de la Barca's plays *Love, the Greatest Enchantment* (1635) and its Christian recantation *The Sorceries of Sin*, both of which have as subject Odysseus's stay and fascination with Circe. The end of the eighteenth century saw a renewal of interest in Odysseus's wanderings with Goethe, who worked on a tragedy centred on Odysseus and Nausicaa (*Nausikaa*), but he abandoned the project. It is the Romantic movement that gave Odysseus's journeys a new and vigorous impetus, and the trend continued through the twentieth century.

A major impulse for recreations of Odysseus the Wanderer, at least in England, was George Chapman's commented translation of the *Odyssey*. This was published in 1616, but had little resonance among his contemporaries. Chapman expressed enthusiastic admiration for Odysseus, describing him as a 'heavenly man', one 'whose genius, as it were, turns through many and various ways towards the truth'. This is Chapman's interpretation of *polytropos*: the many sea paths that the Homeric Odysseus travelled, along with his multiform and inventive ways of acting in the many worlds into which he stepped, become a quest for knowledge or a spiritual search for which the hero spares no effort. This reading and the sentiment behind it are Romantic *ante litteram*.

TENNYSON'S ULYSSES

The hero of Tennyson's *Ulysses* (1842) is the first remarkable nineteenth-century specimen of the Wanderer, and one of the best known. He is driven to travel on and on, restless and unstoppable. He begins his dramatic monologue, which is divided into three movements, by calling himself "an idle king" – not the community-minded character of Homer – living "with an aged wife". But he will not stay put, he cannot, for only travelling allows life to be fully lived: "I cannot rest from travel: I will drink / Life to the lees". He recalls his Odyssean journey not as spurred by nostalgia, the compass of his Homeric ancestor, but by a visceral need to see and learn:

> *"For always roaming with a hungry heart*
> *Much have I seen and known".*

His increased knowledge includes, as he observes, a more profound awareness of himself: "I am a part of all that I have met." The journey of this Odysseus was centrifugal from the outset, driven by an insatiable appetite for knowledge. The urge behind his next voyage is the same unquenchable longing, in spite of his now old age. Tennyson's Odysseus follows in the footsteps of Dante's travellers, who are *vecchi e tardi*. He has little life left, but it would be worthless to spare himself:

"And this grey spirit yearning in desire
To follow knowledge like a sinking star,
Beyond the utmost bound of human thought."

The spirit is again Dantesque ("virtue to pursue and knowledge high"), but Tennyson's hero pushes his quest beyond human understanding, pursuing knowledge that defies the possibilities of the human mind.

In the second movement, the departing Odysseus leaves Telemachus behind to rule in his stead, praising (ironically?) his son's sense of communal responsibility: "He works his work, I mine." Odysseus snubs the duties of a ruler to fulfil the urge of a discontented, Byronic, self-absorbed individualist, but his 'work' will result in a limitless search and in the discovery of new worlds. In the final part he sets off and calls on his 'mariners':

"—you and I are old;
Old age hath yet his honour and his toil;
Death closes all: but something ere the end,
Some work of noble note, may yet be done."

The emphasis on the crew's old age is again Dantesque, as is the idea that being heavy with years is no brake to striving: "'Tis not too late to seek a newer world", voyaging "beyond the sunset" and the sinking "of all the Western stars", until death. Tennyson's Odysseus, who travels after Columbus, sails west, while Dante's heads south. But they share an unrelenting drive.

The poem's famous last line, "To strive, to seek, to find, and not to yield", condenses its core message. Tennyson wrote *Ulysses* while he was grief-stricken for the loss of his dearest friend: brave the struggles of life! he seems to say to himself in the final line. The poem was also composed at a time when belief in progress was fervid and England was emboldened by victories at sea and a desire for imperialist expansion. The passion and resilience of Odysseus could also convey the period's optimistic spirit. His words, however, reach further than personal grief, national or scientific enthusiasm; further also than Byronic rebelliousness and individualism. Odysseus embodies the human need for discovery and self-discovery, for travelling ever and ever, "Beyond the utmost bound of human thought".

THE UNHEROIC WANDERER OF PASCOLI'S LAST VOYAGE (L'ULTIMO VIAGGIO)

While Tennyson's character is infinitely forward bound, driven to surpass the limits of the human imagination, the Odysseus conceived by the Italian poet Giovanni Pascoli in *The Last Voyage* (1904) travels backwards, retracing his own adventures. The poem, which is divided, like the *Odyssey*, into 24 cantos, begins with Odysseus (who at last recovers his Greek name, *Odisseo*) accomplishing the journey that Tiresias had enjoined on him, then returning home; here he waits for death, the sweet, soft death that will come 'off the sea' – not, as another story goes, the violent one that meets him from it. He is old, his limbs slackened by age. Yet death delays and the house is silent: no more feasting, no playful voices. Odysseus would love to munch on the lotus and be content like an animal. He lives in solitude, in the shadowy liminality between dream and reality, between sleeping and waking, recalling, as a memory or a reverie, his wanderings. His 'venerable wife', to shake him off, reminds him of the time when they sat in front of each other, right before their happy reunion. You were tired of the sea, she tells him. He does not answer, however, and instead plunges into that same sea, in a reminiscence of his last storm.

For nine years he lives this crepuscular life until, on the tenth spring, when the song of the swallow announces the opening of the sailing season, he takes up the oar again and leaves. The bard Phemius accompanies him. Phemius is old, Odysseus is old, and so are his companions when he meets them at the shore to depart. Their beards are white and, as they sing at the oars, their voices are 'hoarse and thin'. Old age is also a hallmark of the mariners in Dante and Tennyson, but their Odysseus opposes to it the propelling energy of his mind. Pascoli's character instead is weighed down by his years. He travels under their burden rather than against it.

This old Odysseus is not keen on discovering new worlds, but on stopping in all the places of his Homeric journey, on reliving his past heroic self – only to find that it is impossible. His adventures have left no traces. In Aeaea he hears no Circe singing, only the rustling of leaves and the eternal music of the sea, an ethereal, distant song: *e cantare / lontan, lontano eternamente il mare* ("and the sea singing far, afar, forever"). The land of the Cyclopes is inhabited by hospitable people of human size, and nobody (not 'Nobody') has blinded a giant; the Lotus Eaters and the crowd of the dead reach out to the traveller with a friendly call: it is time to forget and rest, it is time! The crew sails easily past Scylla. There are no threats, no dangers – and no glory. Odysseus's disillusion reaches its zenith when he revisits the flowery island of the Sirens. No longer thirsty for total knowledge but inward-looking, self-focused, he asks them, begging them to speak: who am I? Who was I? The Sirens do not answer, his ship is smashed between two rocks and he dies. Borne by sea for nine days and nine nights, his body reaches Calypso, who envelops it in the cloud of her hair and wails: never to be! Never to be! Nothingness is better than life: this is the truth that lies at the end of Odysseus's last journey.

CAVAFY'S ITHACA

A very different truth lies at the end of Odysseus's journey in *Ithaca* (1911), by the Alexandrian-Greek poet Constantine Cavafy. *Ithaca* is his best-known poem and is famous also in the English-speaking world. It was the favourite of Jacqueline Kennedy Onassis and was read at her funeral in the translation of E. Keeley and P. Sherrard (1975), from which I borrow. The poem begins:

As you set out for Ithaka
hope your road is a long one,
full of adventure, full of discovery.

The traveller is not Odysseus, who is never mentioned by name, but 'you', the reader. We are all Odysseus as we start off on life's journey. Its impetus is outbound – 'As you set out' – and outbound it must remain. It is the journey that matters, not, as in Homer, its destination. You want to make the trip as lasting and as rich as possible, and you should not be afraid of dangers along the way: Cyclopes and angry gods do not exist. You will not encounter them 'as long as you keep your thoughts raised high':

unless you bring them along inside your soul,
unless your soul sets them up in front of you.

Equipped with curiosity and excitement instead, may you take many roads, visit many places, enjoy the sensual pleasures of perfumes and glimmering stones, and go on learning!

But even while you gather the riches of travelling, you are warned to 'keep Ithaka always in your mind'; that is, to remember that the journey must end: 'Arriving there is what you're destined for'. Ithaca is death. Do not expect anything from it. Better have a long journey,

so you're old by the time you reach the island,
wealthy with all you've gained on the way,
not expecting Ithaka to make you rich.

Ithaca has nothing more to give you, but you must be grateful to her because she is not only the end but also the beginning, the origin of your adventures:

Ithaka gave you the marvellous journey.
Without her you wouldn't have set out.

The conceit of Ithaca as life's beginning and end is not new. It goes back to Neoplatonic philosophy, according to which, as we have seen, Odysseus's native island is the metaphysical place of our origin and our final destination, our true home. But Cavafy reverses the traveller's priorities: while Plotinus exhorts him to long for Ithaca, to feel as nostalgic as Odysseus, to be eager to leave the stormy sea of matter for his fixed and permanent home, Cavafy's traveller should hope to take his time and enjoy the sights and smells along the way. His Odysseus will return because he must, not because he yearns to.

JOYCE'S ULYSSES

Stephen Dedalus: a Telemachus with No Home

Joyce's *Ulysses* (1922) also features an avatar of Odysseus as 'everybody' or simply 'man': Leopold Bloom, the protagonist, an ordinary middle-aged advertising agent who enjoys his breakfast. In contrast, the novel's deuteragonist, Stephen Dedalus, is a young and ambitious aspiring artist. The two leave separately in the morning on a one-day promenade around Dublin, in the course of which they cross paths and finally meet. To Stephen's wanderings are devoted the first three episodes of the novel. This structural element and Stephen's young age connect him to Telemachus as he travels in search of his father at the beginning of the *Odyssey* and for close to three books (from the end of book two to the end of four). Yet Stephen, contrary to Telemachus, does not intend to return. He has no home but has exiled himself to Paris to study. He is back in Dublin only because his father summoned him with a telegram announcing his mother's imminent death. Then, on the morning when his journey around Dublin begins, as soon as he leaves the tower where he has taken residence he decides not to come back; and when at the end Bloom offers him to stay at his home for the night, he declines the offer and eventually wanders off into the darkness, with no stated destination.

In this respect, Stephen is an avatar of the Odysseus who cannot stop – an embodiment of the hero's centrifugal impulse in post-Homeric retellings of his journey, from Dante on. Stephen's surname gives him wings, as it were, for Daedalus was the mythic craftsman who built wings of feathers and wax for himself and his son Icarus to break free from the Cretan Labyrinth where they were imprisoned. Likewise, Stephen has broken free from his Ireland and its repressive society. He will continue to fly, even at the risk of getting too close to the sun, like Icarus, and losing his wings.

Leopold Bloom's Journey

While Dedalus departs into the night, Bloom returns to his home, his wife and his bed, like Odysseus. Like him he has travelled from 'Calypso' to 'Circe' and eventually to 'Penelope', via many other stops of the Homeric character's wanderings. Bloom's own reference, however, is not Odysseus. Not only is his journey on a much smaller scale, across Dublin, but he is a wanderer in a deep personal sense, which connects him not to Homer's hero but to his Jewish people: the son of a Hungarian Jew, he is an exile in Dublin (as Stephen is an exiled Dubliner); he caresses Zionistic ideals and, though ambivalent vis-à-vis Judaism, he is viscerally permeated by it. Joyce might have tied the *Odyssey* to Semitic culture if, as critics have argued, he was influenced by Victor Bérard's book *Les Phéniciens et l'Odyssée*, which expounds the theory that the *Odyssey* has Semitic roots. But Leopold Bloom, of course, cannot read the mind of his creator. He does not know that he is re-enacting a diminutive version of Odysseus's journey, which is superimposed on his, as it were, by the novelist. On the other hand, he does know about the Wandering Jew.

Another feature of Bloom's wanderings that sets them apart from those of Odysseus is that the most extended ones occur in his mind. While his physical movements are confined to about one square mile, his imagination often takes off to faraway lands, ranging from Jerusalem to Athens to Tibet, to the Bay of Naples to beyond Gibraltar. His mental journeys cover the entire world and reach further out, to the stars and the planets, or even beyond those:

> *Ever he would wander, selfcompelled, to the extreme limits of his cometary orbit, beyond the fixed stars and variable suns and telescopic planets, astronomical waifs and strays,*

to the extreme boundaries of space, passing from land to land, among peoples, amid events.

This pancosmic journey is Bloom's last reverie, right before he falls asleep next to Molly, his recovered Penelope.

Bloom ends his journey back home, thus embodying the centripetal impulse of Homer's hero. But does his return resemble that of Odysseus? On the surface, no. It is under the sign of mutual infidelity: not only has Bloom had hot fantasies of betrayal, but Molly, as goes already an ancient story about Penelope, has actually committed adultery. Her infidelity is symbolized by an allusion to the quintessential locus of marital fidelity in the *Odyssey*: Odysseus's bed, rooted in the ground. Bloom's bed instead has been moved around in his absence. However, he knows about Molly's affair. He knew she would meet her lover already before he left that morning, from a letter he brought her; and he did not do anything about it. Whereas Odysseus is a fighter, Bloom is a passive observer. His return also lacks the crowning of a night of love, 'the rite of the ancient bed', for the couple have had no intercourse for a long time, since their son died as an infant. But Bloom's return parallels Odysseus's in a deeper sense. As Stanford argues (p. 218), he conquers his own inner suitors, his jealousies, fears and frustrations by coming to terms with them, and he can therefore lie next to Molly in peace and go to sleep. The last words of the novel are hers, and they connect her strongly with her husband. The feverish inner monologue in which she remembers how she got Bloom to propose to her, and how she said yes, yes, yes, is an affirmation of marital energy and life. The couple remarry, as it were, like Penelope and Odysseus. Not in the intimacy of a love embrace, but through Bloom's equanimity and Molly's passionate memory.

NIKOS KAZANTZAKIS' ODYSSEY

The Political Idealist

After a monumental novel, a monumental epic: *Odyssey*, by the Cretan poet, novelist, philosopher, journalist and political figure Nikos Kazantzakis, best known as the author of *Zorba the Greek*. The poem, which dates to 1938, consists of 33, 333 lines, three times Homer's *Odyssey*, and is divided into 24 books like Homer's epic. Its protagonist, however, is not an avatar of the Homeric Odysseus, like Leopold Bloom, but rather a descendent of Dante's and Tennyson's restless characters. While Bloom ends his journey back home, pacified and sleeping in his marital bed, Kazantzakis' Odysseus leaves Ithaca soon after his return, on a journey of no return. Like Tennyson's hero, he realizes that the life of a family man and the island's ruler is not for him.

When the epic begins, Odysseus has carried out the slaughter. But he does not look forward to his reunion with Penelope. He feels no thrill at seeing her, while his savage aspect, in turn, terrifies her. After subduing a revolt on Ithaca, he retires with the frightened Penelope. The following night, at a feast, a song reminds him of the Fates that blessed him at birth: Tantalus, who gifted him an unsatisfied heart, Prometheus, who gave him brilliancy of mind, and Heracles, the embodiment of the spirit's laborious struggle towards purification. Now that he has been awakened to who he is, Odysseus can no longer settle down. He picks his new companions, all bold, strong types. He leaves his kingdom to Telemachus, as in Tennyson, additionally marrying him to Nausicaa to perpetuate his line; then he departs, southbound, like Dante's hero.

His first stop is at Sparta (in book three), where he finds turmoil: the peasants are revolting against Menelaus. Odysseus restores order, but the life of his former friend, contented, drowsy, luxurious, with no heroic spark, fills him with contempt. He leaves again, taking with him Helen, who is also bored with her life and a man who has grown fat and complacent. They have no set destination, but after a storm they land on Crete. Here the once-splendid civilization is in decline. The barbarians who have come from the north plot together with the slaves to overthrow Idomeneus, the senile and decadent king, and Odysseus becomes their leader. One night, at a magnificent royal symposium, the conspirators attack. Odysseus leads a slaughter as in Homer's epic, but on the side of the revolutionaries. He slays Idomeneus and proclaims Hardihood (a name clearly reminiscent of Heracles) king of Crete. Then he leaves, bidding Greece farewell. There is no stopping, no rest for him, while Helen, who has fallen in love with a barbarian, stays behind.

At the end of book eight Odysseus sails further south, to Egypt. Here he finds another civilization in decline and another revolution underway, with barbarians from the north and the local slaves joining forces against the rich overlords. He supports the revolutionaries again, but this time is defeated by the nobles and thrown into prison. To escape, he carves the image of a new god, a bloody, wounded, horrifying face, and terrifies the superstitious Pharaoh with it. Having picked the wildest among his former fellow prisoners, he sets out for the African desert. After fighting against savage tribes, he journeys on, to the sources of the Nile (a great attraction for explorers in antiquity). His companions are weary of travelling, like those of the Homeric Odysseus upon reaching Trinacria.

As the crew comes to a lake, Odysseus climbs a mountain alone. He seeks to receive divine instructions for the city he intends to found. The revelation comes and Odysseus builds his new city, inscribing his Decalogue on its fortress: man's duty is to love the entire creation, other men, animals and plants. He and his companions will share everything, including the family (as in the utopian city drawn in Plato's *Republic*). But during the ceremony of inauguration a volcano erupts, breaks the earth asunder and destroys the city. The few inhabitants who survive leave to found a new city and Odysseus remains alone. We are in book sixteen.

The Spiritual Searcher

In his voyage so far, Odysseus has been an active political idealist. In these respects, he differs from other avatars of the wanderer embarking on his last journey. It is true that he also leaves home from boredom and dissatisfaction, like the characters of Tennyson and Pascoli. But while Tennyson's Odysseus is after knowledge (as is Dante's) and Pascoli's is after a hopeless recovery of past heroism, Kazantzakis' Odysseus not only seeks new mental and spiritual horizons but also strives to rebuild the crumbling societies he encounters. This Odysseus is a doer. He fights for the outcast (slaves, barbarians) against the opulent and inefficient nobility, then finally builds the ideal city, founding it on universal love and equality. Such an image of Odysseus as a revolutionary and a social visionary is novel. Traditionally Odysseus the politician worked for his noble peers, as the friend rather than the opponent of authority and power.

However, the destruction of the perfect city puts an end to Odysseus's political ideals and heroic deeds. Left alone, he embarks upon a purely personal quest, one of self-knowledge and self-improvement. For a while he roams the jungle, he dances, he feels free (like Zorba). Eventually he becomes a holy man, endowed with a wisdom infused with Eastern mysticism, especially Buddhist influences. Kazantzakis' hero dons a completely new dress in this role as spiritual seeker, even as he does for his political views and actions. Yet while his involvement in politics goes back to Odysseus's first appearances, in the *Iliad*, these religious accretions are extraneous to the figure of Odysseus throughout its developments. It is true that in Homer he is already pious; but neither in Homer nor in his later incarnations does he seek a god or God. A dimension of his spiritual search more anchored in the tradition is the call of freedom. Stanford calls Kazantzakis' epic 'an exploration of the meaning of freedom' (p. 235). As in Tennyson's poem, it is the urge to break away from domestic and social constraints that sets Odysseus off on his travels in the first place.

Odysseus keeps sailing south until the sun grows ever paler and an ice floe drifts by. He reaches a village made of igloos and lives in one of them. When spring comes and the snow melts, he builds his last boat from sealskin and takes to sea once again. Death comes and sits opposite him, his mirror-image: an old face with a white beard. An iceberg crushes into the boat, but Odysseus saves himself by climbing on to it. There he prepares for death, saying farewell to everything that comes into his head, including the elements that compose his body: Earth, Water, Fire, Air and their guide and steerer, Mind. He has no regrets or complaints.

At the end, when he feels that death is imminent, Odysseus calls aloud to all his dead companions, who hear him from their tombs and join him. He joyfully welcomes them. At last, his body vanishes, but his mind 'soared high and freed itself from its last cage, its freedom' (translation Kimon Friar, 1958). All is mist, but,

one brave cry
for a brief moment hung in the calm benighted waters:
"Forward, my lads, sail on, for Death's breeze blows in a fair wind".

This spirited, triumphant departure on death's journey stands in antithesis to the nihilistic ending of Pascoli's poem.

THE MELANCHOLY REALIST: ODYSSEUS IN GIRAUDOUX'S LA GUERRE DE TROIE N'AURA PAS LIEU

Shortly before Kazantzakis' epic, Odysseus the politician appeared in a more traditional role, but with fresh and deeply human feelings, in *La guerre de Troie n'aura pas lieu (Tiger at the Gate*). The play was first performed in Paris in 1935. Jean Giraudoux, its author, had fought and been wounded in the First World War and had become a staunch pacifist. The brewing of a new war that he saw during the 1930s suggested to him a comparison with the prequel to the Trojan War.

The play takes its cue from episodes described in book three of the *Iliad*: the diplomatic attempts to resolve pacifically the tensions between Greeks and Trojans ignited by Paris's abduction of Helen. In Homer's account, Odysseus is one of the ambassadors whom the Trojans remember, and the most impressive one. Giraudoux makes him enter only in the last scenes of his play, but his presence is felt early on – and, as in previous dramas, Greek, Latin and French, it is feared. Hector, Andromache and Hecuba want peace. They work to persuade Helen to go back to Greece, which they expect is the condition required to avert the war. Helen herself accepts that she will have to leave, but Hector worryingly asks her: you are not going to contradict me before Odysseus? (Act I, Scene VIII). Hector's anxiety indicates that the Trojans see Odysseus as a threat, or at least as the hardest challenge.

The first scene with Odysseus at the centre seems to prove them right: he makes it clear that Helen's return is not sufficient to avoid the conflict, for in any case Menelaus has been insulted. As Hector, Paris and Helen herself contrive the unbelievable story that the two lovers have gone no further than holding hands, Odysseus mocks them, even descending to insult: you would not have followed Paris, he tells Helen, had you known that the Trojans were impotent!

But then comes a turnaround – or rather we understand that Odysseus's belligerence was not due to personal hardness but to a tragic, yet resigned sentiment that war is inevitable. Odysseus and Hector share a moving, poetic duet in which each man 'weighs' himself, describing his age, beliefs (Hector weighs *la joie de vivre, la confiance de vivre*; Odysseus *la volupté de vivre et la méfiance de la vie*), virtues (Hector's are courage and love; Odysseus's is circumspection), then identifying with the trees of their countries (Hector with 'the Phrygian oak'; Odysseus with 'the olive tree') and with the local birds, the falcon for one, the owl for the other. As the scale tips in favour of Odysseus, Hector asks him directly: 'Do you want war?' The answer is profound:

> *"I do not want it. But I am not so sure about its own intentions."*

War is willed not by enemies but by destiny, by gods who set people against each other for their entertainment and reassurance.

Still, Odysseus is ready to accept Helen's return to prevent this war and prepares to leave. The reason is not, as Hector thinks, noblesse, but rather because *Andromaque a le même battement de cils que Pénélope* ("Andromache flutters her eyelashes in the same way as Penelope"). Hector's wife reminds Odysseus of his own. The Greek and the Trojan share an identical tenderness and humanity. Yet Odysseus remains a realist. In attempting to keep peace, he tells Hector, *je ruse en ce moment contre le destin, non contre vous* ("I play tricks against destiny now, not against you"). And against such an adversary, even the most cunning and *polytropos* hero can only fail. War breaks out at the end.

WHERE AND WHAT IS HOME? DEREK WALCOTT'S ODYSSEY: A STAGE VERSION

We meet again the traveller of the *Odyssey* in Walcott's *Odyssey: A Stage Version* (1992). The Nobel laureate from Saint Lucia is best known for his epic *Omeros*, which is also an odyssey but does not explicitly refer to Homer's epic or to its hero. For this reason, I have chosen to focus instead on the play he wrote shortly afterwards, which reproduces sequences of the Homeric *Odyssey*, though loosely: Odysseus and the other Greek leaders leave Troy, Telemachus leaves Ithaca, Odysseus's companions open the bag of the winds. Then he meets Nausicaa and, without revealing his identity, he tells bits of stories about Odysseus in dialogic form: his encounters with Calypso, Polyphemus, Circe, his journey to Hades, the episode of Scylla and Charybdis. There follows Odysseus's return to Ithaca, where he endures harsh treatment by the suitors, is recognized by the members of his household, one by one, and is finally reunited with Penelope (who is even less ready than in Homer to believe that he is Odysseus). The play ends with the reunion – as Homer's *Odyssey* did, according to some ancient critics.

Odysseus retains many features of his original portrait. He is cunning, a liar and overly persuasive: "Him could convince a grasshopper it was a ant," says Eurycleia in her West Indian patois (Act I, Scene II). He is "Too smart. Too acquisitive" to have died, Menelaus tells Telemachus (Act I, Scene IV); and he is even fonder of food than in Homer:

"He loved to eat. Enormous appetite! –What did he like? –Like? Anything. Ate like a goat... His motto was 'First eat, then fight'".

This is how Menelaus describes Odysseus, echoing and distorting his pronouncements on the needs of the stomach. This food-lover goes so far as to justify his men's sacrilegious eating the cattle of Helios: "Why should men starve when gods have all they can eat?" (Act II, Scene III).

Odysseus is also longing for his Penelope and his home. However, this play expands the notion of home. Walcott, the post-colonial Caribbean writer who lived in Boston and whose family was of English, Dutch and African descent, transplants the *Odyssey* into a sea and an archipelago beyond locality: it is a mixture of the Caribbean and the Mediterranean, with fauna, flora and traditions belonging to both. A major character, the blind poet and singer Billy Blue, replicates the Homeric bard (he is also a stitcher of songs, like the Homeric rhapsodes) and functions as a tragic chorus, commenting on the stage action in song. Yet his songs have a variety of rhythms and a richly mixed diction, with strong Creole accents. One example:

"No, no, doux-doux
I have a message for you
As fresh as you are
And you sweeter than sugar-plum
I have a wife at home, and she begging me come"
– Act I, Scene XII

In this cosmopolitan setting, 'home' is a fluid concept. It is not a place, but rather a feeling of belonging, of security, anchorage and love. It caresses the senses and the imagination. Not only Odysseus but several characters want to return home and each has their notion of what home is: smells, sounds, a multitude of images and sensations:

> *"–For me, home is grey fields with a ploughman's fire. –*
> *Sometimes it is a smell. I am pierced by the scent of clove.*
> *–a grime-streaked angel gesturing from its spire. – For me,*
> *Captain, a reef in the battering surf."*
> – Act I, Scene V

In response Odysseus interjects: "The oars multiply the image of what we love." Home is manifold and kaleidoscopic.

This fluidity of the conception of home complicates Odysseus's disposition towards it. Traditionally he is either homeward bound, as in Homer, or restlessly outward bound, as Dante's hero and his avatars, or happy to delay his return for the sake of knowledge or pleasure, as in Cicero, Petrarch and Cavafy. But he clearly knows where home is. Walcott's Odysseus is attracted to his travelling life abroad – he loves riches and women, neither of which is he able to hoard on Ithaca – but his impulse cannot properly be called centrifugal, if by centrifugal we mean 'away from the centre', because the sea belongs to his centre; he is at home in it.

R. Friedman ('Derek Walcott's *Odysseys*', 2007) draws attention to the symbol of the turtle, with which Odysseus is repeatedly associated: it is the animal that carries its home with it and it is also a sea creature. Odysseus's desire to return to Ithaca is no doubt strong; it works as counterweight and wins. But immediately after he and Penelope embrace, he sees and hears the sea:

–Will you miss the sea? –Grottoes where mackerel steer.
–Will you? –Turtles paddling the shields of their shells.

The last stage directions are *Sound of the sea* and *Sound of surf*. Walcott has disposed of Odysseus's prophesised last journey, but the traveller is still sailing when he holds Penelope. The sea is not just an affecting memory. In its sound, Odysseus hears the call of home.

WRAPPING REMARKS

In conclusion to this review of literature, a sweeping observation: Odysseus the wanderer generally meets with more favour than Odysseus the political or military leader. This is already the case in Greco-Roman antiquity. Horace's model of wisdom and virtue is the wanderer of the *Odyssey*, while the villain of Euripides and Virgil is the leader of the Trojan War. The unflattering stories found in the *Epic Cycle* are centred on Odysseus's Trojan career, while the admiration of historians and philosophers is mainly directed to the protagonist of the Odyssey. In medieval and early-modern retellings, the political leader gives rise to traditionally negative portraits, whereas the wanderer opens up new vistas, across the sea and in the human mind. He is also bound to become a more productive source for creative writers than the politician. The enormous influence of Dante's hero is evidence of this. Combined with the protagonist of the *Odyssey*, Dante's Ulisse ensures the prominence of the wanderer in nineteenth- and twentieth-century literature. Such a prominence is not difficult to understand: epic adventures have imaginative potential, and to live is to travel.

THE ARTS

Painting and Sculpture

1760–1900

As for writers, the favourite Odysseus for artists in the last 250 years is the character of the *Odyssey* – although, as we have seen, his dominance in iconography goes back to the very beginning of Odysseus's depictions in archaic Greece and continues through the Middle Ages, the Renaissance and the Baroque. During the eighteenth and nineteenth centuries the *Odyssey* inspired countless paintings. The Swiss artist Angelica Kauffmann dedicates several of her masterpieces to the *Odyssey*, putting at the centre not Odysseus but female figures – Calypso, Circe and, almost obsessively, Penelope – in their relation to him. Particularly remarkable are the pensive Penelope of *Penelope at her Loom* (1764), the one abandoned to her distress in *Penelope Weeping over the Bow of Odysseus* (*c.* 1778) and again the one fully relaxed and extended into her 'sweetest sleep' in *Penelope Awakened by Euryclea* (1772); in the last the light shines bright on her body and illuminates only dimly the excited Euryclea, who touches the sleeper's shoulder. Another masterpiece of the same period is *Ulysses between Scylla and Charybdis*, by Kauffmann's co-national Johann Heinrich Füssli (1795). Here two arms are stretched from one of Scylla's mouths towards Odysseus, who is wielding his shield, even as the legs and arms of two more of his companions dangle horrifically from another mouth, and another arm is almost swallowed.

In the next century, several Neoclassical statues portray characters and episodes from the *Odyssey*. They include Odysseus throwing the discus during the sporting games at the Phaeacians (Louis Petitot, *Ulysse chez Alcinoüs*) or bending the bow (Jean-Baptiste Deschamps, *Ulysse bandant son arc*), as well as Penelope (Jens Adolf Jerichau, Franklin Simmons), Calypso (Célestin-Anatole Camels) and Circe (Jean-Alexandre-Joseph Falguière). At the opposite end of Neoclassical seriousness are the light caricatures of episodes from the *Odyssey* by Honoré Daumier, each accompanied by a couple of verses that explain the episode. The best known of these, *Ulysses and Penelope* (1842), depicts the couple on the night of their reunion: past middle age, they appear common and plain, red cheeked, with prominent noses, while Odysseus wears not his heroic *pilos* but a nightcap! In the accompanying lines it is specified that he snores.

The second half of the century is also rich in painted images of Odysseus's adventures. The island of the Lotus Eaters is the subject of an evocative Romantic picture by the Afro-American Robert Duncanson, *Land of the Lotus Eaters* (1861), with a vast view that conjures up the American West. Nausicaa's shyness and attractiveness are captured by the Victorian artist Frederick

Leighton (*Nausicaa* 1878). The Pre-Raphaelites were likewise keen on the *Odyssey*'s female characters, for instance Penelope (Edward Burne-Jones) and Circe (John Roddam Spencer Stanhope; John William Waterhouse). Waterhouse also painted *Ulysses and the Sirens* (1891), showing the Sirens already in control of Odysseus's ship and besieging him menacingly from all sides. Two notable paintings have as focus Odysseus on the shore of Calypso's island: Arnold Böcklin's *Odysseus by the Sea* (1869), which portrays the protagonist seated naked on a rock and stretching his arms – nostalgically, desperately? – toward the water, and Jean-Charles Cazin's *Ulysses after the Shipwreck* (*c.* 1880), in which he simply stands, musing.

1900–2000

We could mention more works here, but it is time to move on to the next century. Sirens and Lotus Eaters enrich magnificent landscapes in paintings by the American Thomas Moran (*Ulysses and the Sirens* 1900, *The Lotus Eaters* 1895), in both of which Odysseus's ship appears at a distance. Henri Matisse, commissioned to illustrate Joyce's *Ulysses*, went back to the *Odyssey* and produced a series of drawings. Among them are *Ulysses, Nausicaa and the Maids* (1934), in which, un-Homerically, the girls are naked like the man who is approaching them and are not afraid of his appearance, even as he stretches his left arm toward Nausicaa, perhaps already touching her, and *Aeolus* (1934), which shows Odysseus's boat almost pierced by winds, striking like shafts from all sides. Polyphemus inspires imaginative pictures, from *Ulysses and Polyphemus* by Alberto

Savinio (1932), with a wooden ship at sea and geometric objects on the beach, to Salvador Dalí's *Polyphemus* (1966), blue-eyed, with long, feminine eyelashes, a smiling mouth with red lips and white teeth, a flowing white beard and darker, bloodier colours from his neck down. In Giorgio de Chirico's *The Return of Ulysses* (1968), Odysseus rows in a boat on a diminutive sea, a pond enclosed in a room.

In the next decade Marc Chagall illustrates the *Odyssey* in 82 lithographs, for the edition published in Paris by Fernand Mourlot (1974). Almost contemporaneously the Italian Giacomo Manzù likewise provides the illustrations for an edition of the poem, in the translation of Salvatore Quasimodo (1977). Both artists also dedicate larger works to the *Odyssey*: Chagall a mosaic, titled *The Message of Odysseus*, for the Faculty of Law at the University of Nice, and Manzù a series of six bronze sculptures, *The Wall of the Odyssey*, which capture moments, encounters and emotions in Odysseus's vicissitudes, starting with the war and ending with Euryclea running toward him. Among the works of the end of the century, unforgettable is the bronze statue of Ugo Attardi (1996), formerly in front of the Twin Towers and now at the Battery Park in New York City. Almost 10 feet tall, it portrays Odysseus holding two spears, one planted in the ground, the other pointed towards an unknown target – perhaps the suitors, or even new horizons?

Film

It does not come as a surprise that the *Odyssey* has appealed to filmmakers since the early history of the genre. The combination of travels, adventures, the punishment of the 'bad guys' and a romantic ending seem to offer just the right stuff for this spectacular art form. To the silent era is dated *L'Odissea* by the pioneering Italian director Giuseppe de Liguoro (1911), who also starred as Odysseus. A massive epic for the time, it has been compared to a blockbuster. Among more recent movies, a classic is *2001: A Space Odyssey* (1968). Its director, Stanley Kubrik, in addition to drawing the title from Homer, declared that for the Greeks the sea must have been the equivalent of space for a twentieth-century mind. The movie's original poster advertises it as 'An epic drama of adventure and exploration'.

Odysseus reincarnates as a filmmaker in *Le Regard d'Ulysse* (1995), translated as *Ulysses' Gaze*. Directed by the Greek Theo Angelopoulos, it follows the story of a Greek filmmaker living in the USA as he returns to his country and searches for lost old reels of films by two pioneer directors who travelled to the Balkans and recorded their culture. Another original recreation of Odysseus is in the satirical comedy *O Brother, Where Art Thou?* (2000) by Ethan and Joel Coen. This film tells the story of three convicts, one of whom bears the name 'Ulysses', who escape to search for a buried treasure and go through adaptations of some of Odysseus's adventures, such as the Sirens and a Cyclops.

The most recent cinematic version of the *Odyssey* is *The Return* (2024), directed by Uberto Pasolini (not related to Pier Paolo Pasolini). The film, an adaptation of the second half of Homer's epic, is memorable for the stellar performances of Ralph Fiennes as Odysseus and Juliette Binoche as Penelope. It disposes of the adventures, and of all supernatural elements, to concentrate on Odysseus, Penelope and Telemachus. The story begins with

Odysseus washed up on the shore of Ithaca. He does not awake from a magical sleep, nor is he surrounded by precious gifts as in Homer; instead, he is naked, old and broken. His tiredness and dispiritedness are keynotes throughout the film; there is no heroism left in this traumatized warrior and his relationship with Telemachus is strained. When the son finds out that the old man is his father, instead of embracing him he infuriatingly accuses him of having abandoned his family and failed to bring his companions back to Ithaca.

On the other hand, Penelope is not indifferent to Antinous, who loves her; she pleads for his life and shrieks with horror when Telemachus kills him. The movie ends with two original developments: Telemachus will embark on his own journey to find himself, while Odysseus discovers that in his absence Penelope has not slept on their bed but has sealed it. The bed has not been inhabited, or stained, by the thoughts that must have whirled in her mind during her 20 years of solitude. The two now move back to their old bed.

MORE RECREATIONS

The overview that has been offered in these pages is patchy. Many works have been left out, among them Gabriele D'Annunzio's poem *Maia, Laus Vitae* (1903); Ezra Pound's *Cantos*, which begins with Odysseus's journey to Hades; Gerhart Hauptmann's play *The Bow of Odysseus* (1914); Jean Giono's satirical novel *The Birth of the Odyssey* (1938); Christoph Ransmayr's drama *Odysseus, Criminal: Play of a Homecoming* (2010), and more.

In music, I should mention at least two works from the opposite ends of the chronological spectrum: Monteverdi's opera *Il ritorno di Ulisse in patria* (1640) and *Epic: The Musical*, a series of album musicals or 'sagas' by the Puerto-Rican singer, songwriter and actor Jorge Rivera-Herrans (2022–24). In ballet, an imaginative recreation of Odysseus's story is John Neumeier's *The Odyssey*, premiered at the Hamburg Ballet in 1995; another choreographic adaptation, *The Odyssey: The Ballet*, was staged by the American company *Ballet Fantastique* as recently as 2015. Finally, while this introduction was being written, Christopher Nolan was producing the film *The Odyssey*, to be released in 2026. The ascendency of Homer's hero, or 'man', on the human mind is undying.

Modern Short Stories of Odysseus

The Anchored Wanderer

Benjamin Cyril Arthur

After the sun had carved shadows from his bones, and the desert had drunk its fill of him, he emerged from the wasteland like a phantom given flesh, skin almost burned to a crisp, eyes hollowed to twin caves where purpose once dwelt. His feet, wrapped in strips of cloth that had once been white, left crimson prints in the dust as he stumbled towards the first settlement.

The people of Pylos stopped their daily labors to stare. A woman dropped her water jug; the clay shattered like his own scattered thoughts. Children peered from behind their mothers' robes, wide-eyed at this scarecrow of a man who moved with the mechanical persistence of sleepwalking.

"Water," he croaked, the word scraping from his throat like sand through a sieve. "Please."

He stretched out his hands and fell. Children ran to their mothers hiding behind them as they took little peeks at what remained of the wandering soul in front of them.

An old fisherman, weathered by salt and sun, brought him a bowl of water. The wanderer's hands shook as he lifted it, spilling precious drops onto the thirsty earth. He drank with desperate gulps, water streaming down his matted beard, his eyes vacant as tide pools at low water.

They watched him drink. They watched him stumble and fall before rising. They watched him walk away without a word, his gait that of a man following an invisible thread that only he could see, though where it led, even he had forgotten.

The road stretched before him like a scar across the world's face. His feet found their rhythm again left, right, left, right, a metronome marking time in a song he couldn't remember learning. The hills rose around him like sleeping titans, their rocky faces scarred by wind and weather. He climbed through passes where eagles nested and descended into valleys where olive trees grew twisted with age.

Days blurred into nights, nights into days. He walked through settlements where people offered him bread and wine, their kindness sliding off him like water off stone. He couldn't grasp their words, couldn't hold their meaning. There was only the walking, the endless walking, as if motion itself were the only thing keeping him tethered to the world of the living.

When he reached the next town, the guards watched him approach with wary eyes. But something in his bearing, the way he held his head despite his madness, the ghost of nobility that clung to him like morning mist, made them step aside. He wandered through their streets like a sleepwalker, seeing without seeing, hearing without understanding.

From a house overlooking the harbor, a woman emerged. She had been watching from her window as she did every day, scanning the horizon and the roads that led to it. Her hair was streaked with premature silver, her hands worn smooth by years of weaving and waiting. When she saw him, her breath caught in her throat.

"Blessed Athena," she whispered, pressing her hand to her heart. "Zeus, father of gods..."

She ran to him then, this scarecrow figure who stood swaying in her courtyard like wheat in wind. Up close, beneath the grime and madness, beneath the wild hair and hollow stare, she saw what others could not: the scar along his jaw where a boar's tusk had grazed him in youth, the particular way his left shoulder sat slightly higher than his right from an old wound, the hands that had once held her with such certainty.

"Odysseus," she breathed, and the name fell from her lips like a prayer answered.

He looked at her without recognition, his eyes focusing and unfocusing like a man trying to see through fog. She was just another face in an endless parade of faces, another stranger offering kindness he couldn't comprehend.

"Where have you been?" Penelope asked, taking his hands in hers, feeling the calluses and scars that mapped his journey. "My love, where did you go? We have searched everywhere, sent men to every port, every island..."

But he only stared, his mouth working soundlessly, words dying before they could take shape. She saw then how far he had traveled – not just in body, but in mind. How lost he had become in the labyrinth of his own shattered thoughts.

"Telemachus!" she called, and their son appeared, a man grown but still quick to answer his mother's call. "Help me bring him inside."

They led him to their private chambers, this stranger who wore her husband's face. Penelope heated water over the brazier while

Telemachus fetched clean clothes and soft linens. Together, they bathed him as tenderly as if he were a newborn, washing away layers of dust and despair, cleaning wounds both visible and hidden.

His eyes closed as the warm water touched his skin, and for the first time in countless days, his breathing began to slow. They wrapped him in soft wool and laid him on their marriage bed, the bed he had carved with his own hands from a living olive tree.

He slept.

For three days and three nights, he slept while Penelope kept vigil beside him. She held his hand when he cried out in dreams, smoothed his hair when fever took him, whispered songs their nurse had sung to him in childhood. Slowly, the color returned to his cheeks. Slowly, the wild tension left his limbs.

On the fourth morning, he opened his eyes and they were clear.

He looked around the chamber, at the olive-wood bedpost, at the tapestry on the wall that told the story of their courtship, at the woman sitting beside him whose face he had carried in his heart through twenty years of war and wandering.

"Penelope." Her name came out cracked and wondering, as if he were learning to speak again.

"I am here," she said, tears streaming down her face. "You are home. You are safe."

The memories crashed over him then like a tide breaking against cliffs. He remembered Troy burning, remembered the wine-dark sea and the sirens' song, remembered coming home to find suitors in his hall. He remembered reclaiming his throne, remembered years of trying to rebuild what war had destroyed. And then—

"I left," he whispered, horror dawning in his eyes. "I walked out of the palace one morning and I just…kept walking. I could not stop walking."

"Where were you going?" she asked gently.

"I do not know." The words broke from him. "I do not know. I was trying to find…something. Home, maybe? But I was already home, wasn't I? I was home and I left anyway in search of it."

He sat up then, his whole body beginning to shake. "How long, Penelope? How long was I gone?"

"A week," she said quietly. "A week of searching, of wondering if you were alive or dead, of praying to every god to bring you back to me."

The sob that tore from his throat was the sound of a man's soul breaking. He collapsed against her, his body wracked with weeping, as the full weight of his condition settled on him like a burial shroud.

"I am losing my mind," he whispered against her shoulder. "The war…Troy… it broke something in me, and I cannot fix it. I found a way to come home, it took me years but I finally did. I won back my kingdom, I have everything I had fought for, and still I have to keep walking. Still I cannot find peace."

Penelope held him as she had held their son through childhood nightmares, as she had held herself together through twenty years of waiting. "You found your way back," she murmured. "Whatever darkness took you, you found your way home to me."

"But what if it happens again?" His voice was small, frightened. "What if I wake up tomorrow and none of this feels real? What if I just start walking again?"

She pulled back to look at him, her hands framing his face. "Then I will come looking for you. Every time, my love. I will search every road, every path, until I find you and bring you home."

Outside their window, the sun set over Ithaca, painting the sky in shades of wine and gold. In the distance, the sea that had both carried him home and called him away murmured against familiar shores. And in the palace that had waited through siege and suitors, through decades of war and wandering, a broken king wept in his wife's arms while she held him whole with nothing but love and the stubborn refusal to let him be lost alone.

Days passed in careful peace. Odysseus stayed close to the palace, drinking in the blessed ordinary of home, like a man dying of thirst.

Ithaca, under the sun, was a jewel set in azure seas, her hills rolled green and gold with olive groves and barley fields, her harbors busy with fishing boats that bobbed on mighty waters. The air smelled of thyme and honey, of bread baking in clay ovens and the salt tang of the ever-present sea. Goats wandered the hillsides, their bells chiming gentle music, while shepherds called to each other across the valleys in voices that had learned to carry on the wind.

In the mornings, he helped Telemachus with ledgers in the great hall, running his fingers over accounts of grain harvests and tribute from neighboring islands. His son had grown into a fine man and leader, patient with the petty disputes of farmers and the endless needs of a kingdom. Watching him settle an argument between two fishermen, Odysseus felt a pride so fierce it threatened to stop his heart. This was what he had fought for, not just to return home, but to ensure home would endure.

"Father," Telemachus said one morning, looking up from a scroll detailing the olive harvest, "young Anticlea speaks her first words. She calls for you."

Odysseus's granddaughter was barely two, a sprite with her grandmother's dark eyes and her grandfather's stubborn chin. When he visited Telemachus's house that afternoon, she toddled towards him on unsteady legs, her arms outstretched, calling "Papou! Papou!" in a voice like silver bells. He swept her up, marveling at how light she was, how her laughter could chase away shadows he hadn't even known were gathering.

His grandson Perseus, nearly five now, was fascinated by his grandfather's scars. "Tell me about the boar," he demanded, tracing the white line along Odysseus's jaw with one small finger. "Tell me about the sea monster with six heads, about Troy, your friends that turned into a goat after eating and drinking with the witches of the lost seas, Papou. Tell me everything."

So Odysseus told him stories in the garden while Penelope tended her herbs – basil and mint, rosemary and sage that scented the air with memories of countless meals shared. He softened the tales for young ears, turning monsters into puzzles to be solved, battles into games of wit. The boy hung on every word, his eyes wide with wonder that had nothing to do with fear. He will tell his friends when he goes back to his mother, boasting of his fearless Papou.

In the afternoons, Odysseus sat with Penelope as she worked her loom, the same loom where she had woven and unwoven

Laertes' shroud through twenty years of waiting. Her fingers moved with practiced grace, pulling gold and crimson thread through the warp to create scenes of Ithaca, the harbor at sunrise, the olive groves heavy with fruit, the palace cats sleeping in patches of sunlight.

"What are you making?" he asked one day, watching her hands dance across the threads.

"A tapestry for Anticlea's room," she replied, not looking up from her work. "So she'll know where she belongs, even if the world tries to tell her otherwise."

The domesticity of it, the simple act of a grandmother making something beautiful for her grandchild, moved him more than any victory song ever had. This was conquest of a different sort: the daily victory of love over time, of hope over despair, of staying when leaving would be easier.

Evenings found them in the great hall with the household gathered around the hearth. Old Eurycleia, who had nursed him as a baby, still bustled about despite her age, scolding servants and spoiling grandchildren with equal fervor. Eumaeus the swine herd came to share the evening meal, his face lined with sun and contentment, his stories of the day's work punctuated by gentle teasing of the maids.

"The old boar got loose again," he told them one evening, his eyes twinkling. "Chased young Melantho up an olive tree. He squealed like a piglet himself."

The laughter that followed was warm and familiar, the sound of a family secure in their love for each other. Odysseus let it wash over him like a healing tide, memorizing each voice, each face lit by firelight. This was what he had sailed through storms to find, not just a place, but a people. Not just a house, but a home.

At night, he lay beside Penelope in their marriage bed, the bed he had carved from a living olive tree rooted deep in Ithaca's soil. Her breathing was steady against his chest, her hand resting over his heart as if to keep it from wandering. Through the window, he could see the constellation of the Great Bear wheeling across the sky, the same stars that had guided him home from Troy.

He slept deeply, dreamlessly, and woke each morning with relief to find himself still anchored to the present, to the sound of goats bleating in the distance, to the smell of bread baking in the kitchens, to the feel of Penelope's hair spread across his shoulder like dark silk. Home was not a place on a map, he realized. It was this: waking up where love lived, where his name was spoken with tenderness, where his stories were wanted and his presence was a gift rather than a burden.

But the sea called to him, as it always had.

One morning, many days later, voices drifted to him from somewhere distant and familiar. They spoke in tongues he almost remembered, sang songs that tugged at something deep in his chest. The sound pulled him from sleep like a fisherman's net, gentle but insistent.

He rose from their bed, moving with the fluid grace of a sleepwalker. His bare feet found the stone floors, then the worn path through the palace gardens, then the rocky trail that led down to the shore. The voices grew clearer as he walked, not the dangerous song of sirens, but something softer, more sorrowful. The voices of all the men who had never made it home.

The wine-dark water embraced him as he waded in, first his ankles, then his knees, then his waist. The salt stung the healing cuts on his feet, but he felt it distantly, as if through a heavy veil. The voices were clearer now, rising from the depths where ships lay broken and dreams went to die.

A warm hand slipped into his, fingers interlacing with his own. He turned, expecting to see a nymph or spirit, some creature of the deep come to claim him at last. Instead, he found Penelope standing beside him in the water, her sleeping gown plastered to her legs, her hair loose around her shoulders like dark seaweed.

"How long was I out?" he asked, his voice hoarse with salt and confusion.

"Just a few hours," she said, though her eyes held the weight of lifetimes. "I woke up and saw you walking towards the sea so I followed you. I called but you did not hear me."

"I'm sorry." The words came out broken, heavy with the weight of all his departures, all the times he had left her to search for him.

"Don't be," she said, squeezing his hand tighter. "You are my husband. I'll follow you to the end of the world if I have to, to bring you back."

The water lapped around their waists, cold and relentless. Odysseus stared at their joined hands, at the way her fingers looked so pale against his scarred knuckles.

"You don't understand," he whispered, his voice breaking like waves against stone. "You don't know what I've done."

"Tell me," she said simply.

"I killed people, Penelope. Not just in battle, though the gods know I did enough of that. I killed innocent people. Men who showed me kindness, who offered me shelter." His grip tightened on her hand until she winced. "I killed them for their ships, their supplies, their silence." The words came pouring out of him like blood from a wound too long sealed.

"I committed adultery. Circe, Calypso. I told myself I had no choice, that I was trapped, but there were moments...." He closed his eyes, unable to meet her gaze. "There were moments when I forgot you existed. When I let myself forget."

Penelope's breath caught, but she didn't pull away.

"I stole. I lied. I traded innocent lives for my own." His voice rose to a desperate pitch. "When my men opened the bag of winds, when they ate the cattle of Helios – I could have stopped them. I could have found another way. But I chose to save myself and let them die."

The water around them seemed to grow colder, darker. In the distance, seabirds cried like the voices of the damned.

"And now they won't let me sleep," he continued, his whole body shaking. "The dead, Penelope. All of them. They come to me in the night, clawing at my chest, whispering in my ears. The boy I killed in Ismarus – he couldn't have been more than sixteen. He calls my name every night. The sailor, all of them."

He turned to face her then, and she saw the madness creeping back into his eyes, the wild desperation of a man being torn apart from within.

"They possess me, Penelope. They crawl inside my skull and make me walk, make me search for something I can never find because I don't deserve to find it. They're driving me insane, and I cannot...I cannot fight them anymore. I am tired."

His legs gave out then, and he would have fallen beneath the waves if not for her grip on his hand. She pulled him against her, holding him upright in the water as his body convulsed with sobs.

"I am not the man you married," he gasped against her shoulder. "I am not the hero the poets sing about. I am a murderer. A thief. An oath-breaker. How can you stand to touch me? How can you stand to look at me?"

Penelope was quiet for a long moment, her hand stroking his hair as the waves rolled around them. When she finally spoke, her voice was steady as stone.

"Because you came back," she said. "Because you could have stayed with Circe, with Calypso, in their palaces of gold and never-ending pleasure. You could have forgotten me, forgotten Ithaca, forgotten the weight of your crown. But you did not."

She pulled back to look at him, her hands framing his face.

"Because the man who feels no guilt for his sins would not be standing here, drowning in his own remorse. The man who truly did not deserve forgiveness would not be haunted by the ghosts of his victims. They haunt you because you remember them, because you carry their weight."

"But I killed them," he whispered.

"Yes," she said simply. "You did. And you'll carry that burden for the rest of your life. But you are not the same man who made those choices. The man who killed them would not weep for them. Would not let their ghosts drive him mad with guilt."

She kissed his forehead, tasting salt and sorrow.

"I am not asking you to forget them, Odysseus. I am asking you to let me help you carry them. Let me help you find a way to honor their memory instead of letting it destroy you."

The water around them began to warm as the sun climbed higher, and somewhere in the distance, the palace bells were ringing the hour. Time to go home. Time to face another day of trying to be the man she believed he could become.

"Can you do that?" she asked. "Can you let me help you bear this weight?"

He looked into her eyes, eyes that had seen him at his worst and his best, that had waited twenty years for a man who might never have deserved to come home and slowly, shakily, he nodded.

"I do not know how," he admitted.

"We will learn together," she said, and began to lead him back to shore.

The morning sun caught the water around them, turning it to liquid gold. Somewhere above, seabirds cried their ancient songs, and the waves whispered secrets against the shore. But here, in this moment, there was only the two of them, a man learning to stay, and a woman who had mastered the art of patient love.

"My home is wherever you are, Odysseus," she whispered, and pressed her lips to his.

The kiss tasted of salt and tears, of twenty years of waiting and the promise of twenty more. When they broke apart, the voices from the deep had faded, replaced by the simple sound of waves against stone, of two hearts beating in rhythm with the tides.

She led him back to shore, her hand never leaving his, and together they walked the familiar path home. Behind them, the sea kept its eternal vigil, but for now, it would have to wait. Its wandering son had found his anchor, and she was strong enough to hold him fast against any current that might try to pull him away.

The greatest journey, they both understood now, was not the one that had brought him home from Troy. It was this one, the daily journey back to himself, the conscious and unconscious choice to stay home, and it was a journey they would take together, one day at a time, for as long as the gods allowed.

Penelope

Konstantin Asimonov

I let her into my office, and she immediately sits down without any invitation from my side. Less than a minute and she's already in control of the room.

"Would you like something…"

"A double espresso, please." She doesn't even turn her head.

I get out of the office and approach the coffee machine. Normally, my receptionist would make coffee for me and the patient, but Penelope insisted on complete anonymity, and so I gave Janet a day off. I also disabled the recording device, the queen was very clear about that. When I get back and put two tiny steaming cups on the table, she doesn't look at them. She looks at me instead, and I look at her.

She is immaculately dressed and looks much younger than she should. Her figure does not bear the weight of her age. She wears strict, muted colors, straight lines, invisible makeup. A single brooch and a royal ring, shining on an elbow-length silk glove, are the only jewelry she has. Her delicate shoulders are adorned with a black shawl. Her eyes are dark, like tarmac after a thunderstorm.

"Shall we?" she says.

"Please, start at your own pace."

She begins to speak immediately, without giving it much thought, as if this were a well-rehearsed speech.

"I was married away when I was fifteen."

I take out my notepad and immediately notice a stern wrinkle appearing above her brows.

"I thought we agreed, no recordings."

"I am sorry, the notes are obviously confidential. They help me be precise if we need to return to something you said previously. But I can put them aside if you wish."

She gives me a short nod, and I obey.

"I was married away when I was fifteen," she continues. "The brilliant Odysseus won me as a part of a larger deal with my uncle. My husband never wasted time, and I think I was pregnant before I even set foot on the Ithacan shores. I called my boy Telemachus, which means 'he who fights from afar,' because it was clear to me, even at the time, that a big war was coming. I mean, if you saw my cousin and the way some men looked at her. And the way she looked at some men..."

She smirks.

"I was right, Odysseus left for Troy soon after the boy's birth, and I was left alone to govern a strange kingdom, without any knowledge of my husband's fate, a woman on a man's throne. Few took me seriously then, and it didn't change after it was clear I was good at it. I was the royal equivalent of the heap paradox: no matter the number of good decisions I made, I was not a real queen.

"Still, while the war raged, I was allowed to rule, for ten long years nobody questioned my authority in the place I started to call my home. Odysseus covered himself with eternal glory, and his reputation as a fierce warrior and a cunning man protected Ithaca like an oaken shield. Ithaca prospered then, though some say it was just due to good management. Telemachus grew to be a sweet and gentle boy, which is, of course, not what one looks for in a king, but definitely what one looks for in a son.

"Then the war ended. Funny how that sometimes happens: a great relief in one part of the world and a great strife in another. The war ended, and the war heroes started to return; some to their glory and some to their death. Not all the wives were as prudent as I was; some warmed their beds with more than hot-water bottles. Odysseus, my ever cunning king, chose the third option and disappeared from the gaze of gods and men.

"Then…the rumors started. Some said the great king was dead. Some said he was put to sleep by Logophages, some said he was eaten by Laestrygonians, some said he was fucked to death by a nymph or maybe turned into a pig. The more rumors circled around him, the more vultures circled around Ithaca. I was suddenly not the rightful queen waiting for the return of her husband. I was suddenly a wanton widow incapable of independent thought. I needed a husband to continue living my life and ruling my kingdom. And so, the suitors started to come in."

She pulls a delicate cigarette case out of her bag. I typically don't allow my patients to smoke here, but I am too intrigued by her story, and so I get the ashtray out of my drawer and open the window. She lights up a thin, pungent cigarillo, and a dove-grey smoke curls up from the amber spot of flame. She puffs out a long cloud towards the window and takes the tiniest sip of her, surely already cold, coffee. Then, she continues.

"It didn't seem like a huge problem at first. It was even somewhat flattering. I was nearing thirty at the time, and this renewed male attention...Plus, they brought their entourages with them, and that revitalized business. Ithaca was never a tourist destination, so at first, an influx of bored and rich foreigners seemed like a blessing. But the more they came, the worse it became.

"First of all, the suitors demanded constant feasts. They drank wine, and not the cheap kind. They ate my sheep and my pigs with no restraint. I was bound by the laws of hospitality, but tell me, what do they say of uninvited guests? Then, as their parties grew larger, they started to bother my people. First came the noise, the violence followed soon after. They started to act like they owned the place.

"And then, again, there was Telemachus. He was getting older, mature. He was learning to be a king. Of course, he was not very happy that there were dozens of men partying in the palace. And of course they were not that happy with him either. I could understand it, honestly: he was a threat to them. So, they started to push for me to pick and choose one of them, aggressively. I came up with a trick at first to keep them at bay. I told them I could marry only after I'd woven a shroud for Laertes, Odysseus's father, a dying old man. So during the day I pointedly spent time at the loom, and during the night I undid the shroud. Looking back, that was very inefficient. But I managed to gain a couple of years with this trick. Gods, were they stupid. In the end, Melantho, one of my maids, betrayed me and I had to stop the deception.

"One night, after a serious altercation between Telemachus and a bunch of suitors, Makeda, my oldest maid, came to me. She was a slave from the land of Kush. She told me a tale of the lion. The gist of it was that when the king of the pride dies and another takes up his place with the she-lions, the new king kills the offspring of the old one to make sure his position is safe. She told it to me, and then I knew. Odysseus has to return now, or else all is lost."

She takes a break and looks at me with her dark eyes, looks deep into my soul. She takes another sip of the coffee, and I follow suit. The espresso is too bitter for my taste. Janet makes it better, but for the life of me, I cannot understand what she does differently.

"We made him up, of course," she finally says.

I don't immediately understand what she means. But it doesn't seem like a play on words. Noting my reaction, she goes on.

"We had a council. Me, Telemachus, Laertes, Makeda and another maid I could trust, Chilonis. There was another man there, a rhapsode called Eumēlos. He lived with us for a while, and I listened to his counsel. Together we discussed the situation. If I choose one of the suitors, even the most powerful one, the others will be scorned. They might burn Ithaca to the ground. If we just murder all of them, their rich fathers and hotheaded brothers will come to seek revenge. But if Odysseus comes back... If he kills all the suitors, it would not be seen as murder. It would be seen as a man cleaning his house of vermin. So, Odysseus had to come back, and as soon as possible, for Telemachus's life was in danger.

"So, we made him up. We found his old wet nurse, Eurycleia, and a friend, Eumaeus, someone who could recognize him. Good, trustworthy people, salt of the earth. They were the first to meet Odysseus, who, of course, was in a disguise put onto him by Athena. Euryclea remembered that Odysseus had a scar above his knee, which he got while boar hunting. Eumaeus came up with a story of Odysseus's old dog, Argos, who saw his master for the first time and died. That is how the rumors started.

"Then, we prepared a feast. Chilonis knew a thing or two about poisons. Before my husband took her as a slave, she was a priestess of Hecate. It was a small affair, just me and my two maids served the hungry men. Telemachus and Eumēlos were cupbearers. We were also brought a wandering aoidos to entertain the guests and to sing to them of the fall of Troy. He was blind, that old man. That was Eumēlos's idea, to have an actual witness. The guests ate and drank like pigs. Then they started dropping. Some screamed, some tried to run away, but the doors were locked. Telemachus started to shoot them, and the rest of us stabbed the ones that were already down. After they were extinguished, we screamed some more and banged swords and knives on brass pots and plates. We arranged the bodies in a tableau of vicious battle. Blood seeped through the wooden floors, and the walls were splattered crimson. The poor singer hid under the table but heard the whole thing. Eumēlos was very good in the role of a scorned husband.

"Then, the hardest part began. You see, it's one thing to arrange a husband returning home incognito and wreaking havoc among his wife's suitors. It's another to explain his absence the next day, when all the dust is settled. This is where Eumēlos went above and beyond. He invented a whole backstory for Odysseus. How he injured Poseidon's favorite son, who was, of course, a horrible monster. Now, immediately after returning home, he had to pay his penance in the form of an exile. Some ridiculous thing about an oar and a shovel, or something. Then, we had to come up with other trials and tribulations that Odysseus faced to explain his decade of travels. The stories had to be insane to be believed. There were monsters, and gods, and sexy nymphs. We also had to explain why Odysseus returned alone, so there were cannibals and shipwrecks as well. We also dipped into the bottomless pool of rumors, confirming some of them. All of that Eumēlos told the blind aoidos in his 'Odysseus voice'."

She looks at me, content with the effect her story had, and sips her coffee. I finish my cup in a single gulp, bitter or not. I can't believe it, but the queen has no reason to lie.

"It took off like a wildfire," she continues. "It was an instant classic. Eumēlos had a talent for action-adventure. Immediately, there were some groupies who confirmed that they helped Odysseus along the way and who, wink-wink, might have borne a son of a great hero. I didn't bother to intervene. Odysseus became a symbol, and I didn't want to own a symbol. I wanted my son and my state safe. I wanted to live my life in peace."

"Of course, there was always a danger of someone knowing the truth. We washed our hands of the blood of dozens of men that day, and they all had powerful relatives. I had to protect us from that. Luckily, Laertes and Euryclea were very old and died soon after. Eumaeus had an unfortunate accident while herding swine. He was not in his prime, you know, and had a propensity for drinking and talking. Eumēlos died of food poisoning, the poor thing. I think it was mushrooms. My two maids, my best friends in the world, Makeda and Chilonis, got sick and died too, quite soon after. Chilonis took her own life in the end, with an obsidian knife, still loyal to her first mistress, Hecate. It was only me and my son left who knew the truth."

I can't say a word. My throat is sandy, and my hands shake.

"So, once in a while, I just feel this overbearing need to talk to someone about this. To relive my – Odysseus's – story anew. Therapists work great as sounding boards. And you were great too. No judgment, I like that. A bit of horror, but that I am used to."

"Your...your secrets are safe with me, my queen. They are privileged. Nobody will ever know..."

My voice sounds raspy and unfamiliar. My back is wet with sweat. I think I have a fever.

"Oh, I don't worry about that," Penelope says. "I poisoned your cup of coffee while you were opening the window. I am taking my secrets with me."

She stands up. Her figure is delicate, even fragile, but her posture is regal. Her smile is like Charon's boat on the still waters of the River Styx.

On Aeaea, They Wept

John Capetanos

The isle called Aeaea was a haunted place. It was not plagued by agonized ghosts or spirits but instead it was haunted by men. These men had sailed from the ruins of Troy, from agony to agony for months until Aeaea's shores had welcomed them. They were off course, marooned in a strange part of the world, and fleeing from the wrath of the gods that clung to them like a shroud. Fate had led their vessel here and a number of them had gone ashore, following a dulcet voice. They entered the palace from which it emanated and, gorging themselves on the food they found there, slighted the master of the isle.

They behaved as beasts, so to beasts they were turned by Circe, the witch and goddess, until Odysseus bargained for their release. Circe, the master of the isle, allowed them to take the place as sanctuary. For several months now, Odysseus had become lover and friend to the goddess as his men and himself healed from wounds both physical and spiritual they had received in their time on the sea. Even so, the wanderer was ill at ease. Odysseus's mind had not been at peace even here. As the year drew on, he found himself even more adrift than when he was on the sea.

"Captain, you look unwell," a voice shook him during one night's dinner. One of the younger sailors had approached him with a worried smile on his face. "Why do you not share in the calm and rejoice with us? After all the things we have been beset by on our journey home, shouldn't you above all be relieved to have this moment of peace? So, please, Captain; let us take our time and remember what joy tastes like!"

Odysseus turned to face the young man, his brows knitting together in a strange look. The young sailor had lost the youthful shine from ten years before, when they had all first found their feet touching the cold, agony-soaked sands of Troy. Something about his smile had pricked something in Odysseus's core. A flash of fury boiled in him and, just for that moment, the man of careful plans and complex reasonings found himself abandoning logic. He found himself instead, almost on impulse, ready to strike the young sailor as hard as he possibly could.

It emerged from the fact that older compatriots of his, those with families and homes, had spoken to him in the exact opposite manner. They begged Odysseus to find a good time to push back out to sea and turn the vessel on its way home. After all, the older cohort had dwindled. There were far fewer of them now, many lost to their own greed and sorrow or the jaws of beasts on the journey that had led them to Circe's bewitched shore. How could he, one of the last of this old guard, abandon their will and feel no urgency?

He seized hold of that sensation, that boiling anger, and he tried with all his might to freeze himself solid, waiting for the sting of rage to fade in his chest. He let the sound of the celebration in Circe's great hall wash over him.

It was an orchestra of feasting and drinking. Plates and cups bumped into one another as frequently as bodies collided. Joy and love abounded there, but the stillness and safety allowed time for their minds to wander. Troy had stolen ten years of the lives of Odysseus and his crew. So few of them, young as they were, knew anything about what a life beyond war could be. What was home to people who had spent more time watching blood pool around them, arrows pierce their flesh, and gazing at the empty eyes of the dead comrades and enemies than they had spent time on earth able to think? Half of their lives had been drowned in war, turned to blood offerings to the festival of Ares. Why should Odysseus have expected them to weigh a home they barely knew equal to or greater than a chance to close their eyes and not feel death's chill hand on their shoulder for a single day, a single week, an entire month?

Odysseus watched them revel, the sailors telling the stories of their travels to the nymphs and naiads that served as Circe's servants and confidants. Many of their faces were lit with laughter and excitement, but more still found themselves clinging to their fellows, shuddering and weeping out of sorrow and relief. It was the sadness Odysseus found himself feeling the keenest. In each of their faces he saw reflections of the brothers and friends long gone, their souls taken away to the halls of dread Persephone and Hades. His hand found its way to his face and felt the tremor of his lip.

As if freed by his notice, thought after thought flooded Odysseus's brain.

"Had I acted sooner, how many men would still be here, feasting and embracing with us? How much closer to home would we be? Did my desire to preserve their honor doom more

than I could have saved there in that hell called Troy? Will Telemachus even remember my face upon my return, having become a boy without me? And Penelope, my dear Penelope, wisest of all women..."

He let his thoughts fade away as he could not bear to put to words the ache, lest he make them take hold like burrs in his skin. Man has no greater enemy than Doubt. Age and Pain and Fear all have their places in the shadows of the mind, but Doubt is what causes them to grow sharper. It eats away at courage like termites, bores holes through ambitions and hopes, and prevents even the most solid of plans from coming to fruition. Doubt betrayed Orpheus, and was the poison that undid Cassandra. And now, the serpent Doubt sank its fangs deep into Odysseus's heart.

He turned from the festivities and stepped into the cold night air, nearly losing his footing in the path of one of Circe's pets. It was a lion, lying horizontal and almost completely still save for the rhythmic rise and fall of its lungs. The lion lifted its head as Odysseus passed, but moved no more than that. Odysseus looked into its eyes and the lion's only response was to close them and lie down to sleep once more.

"Have my gifts and splendors lost their shine, Odysseus?"

Circe's voice surprised him, like the sudden pluck of a harp's low note. It shook him free from his thoughts for a moment. She emerged as if from nowhere, as goddesses are wont to do, with a smile that bared no teeth but held a glimmer like fresh rain on a flower.

"Surely I have not found myself to be a lacking host? Some people would be overjoyed to have as much as a bed to sleep in and good food to eat. To say nothing of the other benefits of the pleasure of my company and all it entails."

"Forgive me, Lady Circe," Odysseus replied, his voice trembling ever so slightly. "I simply felt slightly ill and thought the night air might provide something to calm me." Circe's head shifted, her eyes narrowing like the tips of spears. She let her gaze shift across the dining hall, surveying the commotion and then looked back at Odysseus. She perceived something Odysseus could not quite grasp and sighed. As if from nowhere, the witch produced a cluster of seeds the likes of which Odysseus had never seen and clutched them tight in one hand. She whispered something to the seeds and Odysseus heard the sounds of dry plant crumbling to powder. Fearing trickery, he reached out, his hand latching onto Circe's wrist before she could finish whatever she was doing.

"Circe, you swore—"

"This will not harm them or you. It will only produce some privacy for you to share what it is that eats you. I swore to the gods I would do you and yours no more harm and I should think you of all people would know how seriously gods take slights on their honor. I do not wish to bring the wrath of my father, Helios, and his associates upon my house any more than you would wish to draw Poseidon's gaze back towards you. Please. Allow me to do this so that whatever is causing you such agony might be diminished in the sharing."

Odysseus relented, slowly releasing her wrist. Circe nodded her thanks, opened her hand, and blew the dust of the seeds into the air. A sickly sweet scent permeated the hall and Circe produced her wand. She traced a circle in the air with it and suddenly it was as though time halted. Drinks froze in the pouring, Odysseus's sailors paused mid bite, the flesh of roasted fowl stretched and still.

"Come now, Odysseus. Time will not pass for a while yet. That should give you ample opportunity to get whatever this is off your chest. Magic is not endless so do not dawdle." With that done, Circe began walking and Odysseus followed behind, more similar to the tamed beasts than he liked.

The stars shone brightly that night and Circe's magic had halted their advance. The pair paused and Circe gestured to solid stones emerging from the island's soil.

"Sit," she said and sit he did. He ran his hand through his beard in an unconscious, uncomfortable gesture.

"Why are you doing this, Circe?" he asked after the silence became unbearable and the twitter of the nightbirds began to grate on his ears.

"Odysseus, wisest of men, cannot figure this out?" she mocked, poking him in the back of his head with her wand.

"I have no wisdom to offer here. No tricks, no plans. Athena abandons me and only ghosts make a home in my thoughts."

"So dour. No wonder the men whisper about you when they think I cannot hear."

Odysseus stood suddenly. "So they ARE whispering about me!"

"Of course they're whispering about you. You're their captain. They worry for you because you're the one who's supposed to guide them home."

"And how great a job of that I've done. How many of my men have I lost? I'm beginning to lose track… Maybe we should never have set off in the first place. Perhaps Troy should have been our graves."

"But it wasn't. If what you have told me of your travails so far is indeed true, the fact that you still have so many men, that they follow you willingly, that you yourself, mortal as you are, are not shattered to pieces or eaten by some ancient beast speaks to something. What do you think that is?" Circe sat now, hand on her cheek. Her smile was gone and Odysseus had begun pacing. "What is it that disturbs you now? You surpassed a goddess of witchcraft and master of potions, spells, and illusions. Saved your crew from a Cyclops, and now, the thing that unravels you is stillness! I wish I could find humor in this, my dear Odysseus, but you make it very difficult."

The wind picked up, scattering leaves around them. "I should never have let them take me, I should never have gone to Troy. Ah, mother, father, Penelope, Telemachus, I abandoned you for honor and for honor's sake I destroyed the lives of our young men too. Some wish to leave and others beg to stay. I do not know what it is that we deserve. What I deserve."

Circe's face became less hard and she stood, jabbing Odysseus's face between the eyes with her wand. "Then you must face the men. You should go to them. Speak with them. Share your doubts and decide together. You are not my prisoners here. You are my guests and I will not keep you here like a piece of art or a dog. You must offer them the choice and say what you believe is the right thing to do. They see you as a marble statue, a flawless specimen. An ideal to chase. Instead you must show them that they are not alone in their fears and worries. In doing so you will see each other as humans. You will be less above them, yes, but they will become closer to you. Whatever else you encounter, and I know there is still much on your way home, you will need people. People who know who you are and what you are to them as much as how to obey your words. They will disappoint you at times, but the Great Odysseus of artifice and ingenuity can surely find a way to overcome that."

And with that, Circe left him and the stars resumed their paths across the dark sky. Odysseus heaved a great sigh, as though releasing a breath he didn't know he had been holding in. The sounds of birds began flickering back to life and the sounds of the sailors resumed, carrying on the flowing wind.

Odysseus turned, stepping back towards Circe's palace. The cheerful conversation was slowly ebbing away and now the talk was more hushed. Entering the feast hall, Odysseus seized a cup of wine from the table and raised it above his head.

"My friends!" he shouted, spreading his arms wide. "We have feasted and drunk deep of the hospitality of Lady Circe and her assembly. We have been through much and still have not made it to our beloved home. However, we have been offered here a chance to take stock. What do we sail for? Where are we heading and why?"

He paused, rotating the cup in his hand and staring at the dark liquid within it. "I have confessions to make to all of you. I do not know what tomorrow will bring if we choose to set forth. I know that many of you have come to me asking to leave and still more have mentioned your desire to remain and enjoy all that this island has to offer. I pushed others to stay with me. Dragged them by force out of what I believed to be danger and led you with me through agony after agony and now, I am seized by something terrible. My friends. I…" He paused, gathering the will. "I have failed you. I have stolen your honor on the field of battle through dishonorable tricks. I led you into danger over and over again hoping that the gods would set things right. We are alive, yes, but we lost our friends, brothers, to the jaws of wrath I invited on us. So I offer you a chance, here and now. Say what you desire. If you would remain here or you would come with me I will not hold either against you. I wish to go. I wish to see the smiling face of my son and my mother and my father if they still live. I wish to hold the woman I love in my arms again and I will do anything to get home. So please, I beg you as a man like you. As your brother. If you still hold any love in your heart for me, come with me. I want us to leave this place having healed and regained our strength and return to our families who await us. What about all of you?"

There was quiet while the men communicated. Murmurs began and conversation expanded. As the sailors began discussing Odysseus's offer, he felt the chill again. "*Who will be the first to council against this? Eurylochus? No, he never wanted to stay here in the first place.*" He felt the shake once more. Why was he doing this, now, he wondered. What new horrors was he trying to convince them to weather with him? And, should he convince enough of them to go, how many of them would even remain by the time Ithaca was within reach?

"We should stay! What waits for us out there other than more death and strife? Aeoleus said so himself, our journey is cursed!" one said. "We are strangers here! If Odysseus goes, who will guarantee our safety?" another piped up. "And what of our families? What will guarantee that they have not forgotten us?"

Their voices were a chorus conducted by doubt. Just like the things that toyed with Odysseus's own thoughts. Circe's voice crossed his mind once more, ringing in his skull.

"Tell me, Odysseus, and in doing so, tell them. What is the one thing in your heart that you could never lie about? What is it that pushes you forward despite it all and what is it you long to see?"

Odysseus cast his eyes in a direction. East. Far, far away. The tears began to form, blurring his vision. The men began to quiet their discussion at the sight as Odysseus stepped away and turned his gaze towards the night sky. They followed slowly, keeping their distance until Odysseus himself stopped stone still, gazing at the sea.

"My friends. What was the purpose of the fall of Troy at the end?" he asked, tears staining his weathered face. "I fear it had no purpose other than to satisfy our own frustration and bloodshed. And even still. Still. I want to see her again. I want to see Penelope. I want to return to her and gaze into her eyes and hold her close to me. I want to see my son and see what kind of boy he has become. I wish to see to it that my mother and father are cared for. I do not wish to die not having tried everything I could to get back to them."

At the outpouring of sudden emotion, his sailors had frozen. Odysseus looked them each in the eye and saw the same shine of tears crawling down many of their faces. They embraced in a mass and the voices mixed with one another. The chase was going to resume, Odysseus knew. And they would follow him to whatever end they would meet. This was a bitter thing. He may have invited them to doom but that doubt that had made a nest of his heart was fading. It faded in the embraces of his comrades and the cheers that resounded as they shed tears of determination and sorrow with him. Penelope's face was not faded yet in his mind and, as long as he still held that shard of memory close, Odysseus felt a calm begin to grow. He stared out to sea again, towards the ship nestled on the shore, but no plans came. No new ideas, no plots, no tricks came to him. Nothing but the sound of the crew and the distant ocean waves remained in his head. Despite this, Odysseus of machinations joined his crew in their catharsis.

They wept together, making oaths to one another to see each other safely home and slowly returned to the palace to rest. The sun began peeking over the distant horizon and Odysseus stayed to watch.

"Alas," he whispered, "Penelope you outshine even the sun at dawn. If I die, I die in the pursuit of you and gladly will I."

The wine-dark sea offered no compassion. It took as much as it gave and Poseidon's kingdom had arrayed its arrows at Odysseus's heart. The entirety of Okeanos itself had been his enemy, but Odysseus held no fear of it. He knew in his soul they would set forth and he simply prayed that the toll the ocean demanded would not break his heart.

Home is the Sailor

Brenda W. Clough

The crew had lashed spars and oars together into a crude stretcher. Swearing and stumbling in the autumn downpour, they hauled their captain up the steep rocky road to Ithaka's humble acropolis. Odysseus clutched the slanting poles, making no unseemly outcry, his face turned skyward so that the sweat of agony was cleansed by the rain.

A shrill clamor of women's voices, and the stretcher leveled out so he could lie more easily. He looked along his body, past his upturned toes, to where the sodden brown back of a sailor steamed softly as the cold rain pelted the hot exhausted muscles. Brave fellows, they had borne him home as swift as Hermes. Now Itheus the mate babbled the story piecemeal, inexpertly, talking across him as if his captain and king were a foundered cow: "—never got to the country of the Thesproti. The rain pissing down all the way, rough seas, and then a wave caught an oar just wrong. The butt end knocked the king ass over tip, like he was tossed by a bull—"

Galled beyond endurance, Odysseus raised his head. "The gods rot you, have you no *sense*? Get us in out of this rain!"

The movement drove dull knives into his chest, and he sank back gasping. His people seemed to wheel and flutter around him like mewling gulls preparing to pick over his carcass. But then he came to himself again. He lay warm and dry in the royal bedchamber, in the big bed he had built with his own clever hands, under a familiar coverlet woven of fine wool. A woman sat in a wooden chair beside the bed, her fingers busy with roving and spindle. "Penelope…"

"No, it's Polykaste, sir."

Of course – Penelope was in her tomb these past five years and more. He squinted in the dim lamplight at the newcomer. How could it be night? He must have dozed the day away. Her hair was pinned up like a woman's, but she was little more than a girl, muffled against the chill in a big brown shawl. Polykaste…He couldn't place her. With feeble cunning he said, "Who is your father, child?"

"Oh, for heaven's love! I'm your daughter-in-law."

"Of course – lovely Polykaste, youngest of the daughters of Nestor son of Neleus." Gods, how had he forgotten? "Where's Telemachus, then?"

"Gone to Mykenae, at the behest of the high king. A messenger has gone to fetch him back."

"Oh, no need. A minor injury…" His son did all the stodgy diplomatic chores. "No flair for roaming or raiding, that boy."

He hadn't wanted to say that out loud, but her ears were young and sharp. "He swore he'd be home in time for the birth," she said. When she stood up he saw the bulk of her pregnant body, misshapen against the mellow glow of the clay lamp. The things that happened, when you left home for a year or so!

The physician came at her call and laid his cold thin fingers on the horrible black bruises on his right side and chest. "Look how he can feel it, when I do this." Odysseus snarled wordlessly at him. "The ribs are broken. Let him lie perfectly still as I have propped him, and we shall see if they knit. If the lung within has sustained no puncture, there is good hope of his recovery."

"Vulture! You talk *to* me, not *over* me." But the physician only held out a medicine cup. Odysseus took one swallow and gagged on the bitter brew, turning his head away. The cup followed, forcing itself upon him, and he had to drink. There must have been poppy juice in the dose, because he tumbled into a deep hole of sleep.

Doggedly, slowly, he climbed back out of the dark into another gray day. Rain thrummed on the roof tiles above his head, and water splashed from the eaves onto the terrace overlooking the harbor far below. If he could fling off the coverlet and stride to the parapet, he might see his ship. But he was too wise to do that yet. Heal up first, and then return to the sea…

The girl was there again, spinning the creamy fluff of wool into an even thread. She had been a pretty piece at the wedding, indeed the loveliest of old Nestor's daughters. It must have been Aphrodite's mercy, that a king with a face like the butt end of a cow could sire princesses with the grace of a Naiad. But now with her puffy face and swollen ankles, she was plainer than a mud hut. "Klotho," he said. "Don't measure and cut the thread yet."

She frowned at him, shifted her weight awkwardly in the wooden chair. "Polykaste," she reminded him.

"Joke," he said, and her mouth thinned into a sour line. What a humorless child! But then it came to him that she was unhappy.

Weren't increasing women supposed to be content? Perhaps she was missing the boy. "Telemachus is a solemn one too."

The spindle didn't pause in its twirl. She seemed to be thinking of other things, listening with only half an ear to a sick man's mutterings. The thought was like the prick of goad. Was he not much-enduring Odysseus, beguiler of kings, favored of gray-eyed Athene, as full of stories as an egg is of meat? He spoke up more strongly. "Don't worry about me. I'm sure to recover."

Her indifferent gaze didn't shift from the thread. "Indeed?"

"Yes. Because on my last voyage – have you heard the story? Ah! I was on my way to the Paphlagonians, where the cattle are snow-white and as tall as a man. The milk they give is of such virtue that one sup can add a handspan's growth to a child, or keep a man on his feet for a day of hard labor. We thought to steal us some of those fine cows. But contrary winds blew us ashore in Etruria..."

He had her now. Her sullen blue eyes took on a soft shine of interest, and she leaned forward to ask, "Are there people in Etruria? Is it far?"

"Oh, a long voyage! But there are fields and olives, sheep and cattle, men and maids, just like us." Hastily he abridged a bit. A princess of Pylos ought not to hear sailor stories of Etrurian maidens and their charms. "And I met there a seer, a poet all in red, who read my future for me in a pool of ink and rendered it into triple rhyme. He lived in a cave on the bluff above the River Arno, and I gifted him with two sheep, a silver armlet, and a bronze cauldron as wide as a shield, in return for the story of my death."

The dangling spindle had slowed to a stop. The wool was now slowly unwinding itself, forgotten. "Your death!" She made an avert sign. "How can such a vision be worth treasure?"

He hitched himself higher on his pillows, ignoring the fierce twinge in his side. "Hah. Don't think this old salt hasn't had more than one. Once, a trouble-making prophet tried to turn me against the boy, saying that my own begotten son would kill me. That ploy's older than Perseus. And there was the dull one, where I was supposed to go inland, to where oars could be mistaken for winnowing fans, and be murdered by the barbarians there. But this last one was the best, a treasure of a death – beautiful! He sang of my final voyage past the Pillars of Herakles into the World Ocean. I shall see the far side of the world, before I sink within sight of the Isle of the Blest. My heart could ask for no better. That's the death for me."

It was getting difficult to breathe properly, and to get the rest of the words out he had to struggle like a fish on the gaff. "So you see. I'm sure to get better. Not going to die in my bed…at home. Not I."

She rearranged the cushions, propping him to lie on his wounded side as the physician had ordered. Curiously, this gave him some relief. If he could get her to talk, he could rest a while without betraying weakness. "You must have gone to the seer yourself." He nodded at her belly.

Immediately he sensed this was the wrong thing to say. She pulled the shawl close around her shoulders, and set the spindle twirling again. "We sacrificed a black goat to Artemis. The priestess said it will be a boy. And the delivery will go well."

"That's a good seeing. Is it not?"

"Only if you believe."

He said nothing, taking canny refuge in weakness, and after a time she went on. "There are different omens in my family."

"Ah." He nodded wisely.

"My mother died in childbed. And my elder sister too."

Again he nodded, though he knew nothing of midwives' work. At last she said, "I dread the trial to come. I'm afraid."

It seemed to him that Polykaste's mother must have been brought successfully to bed at least twice. Else how did Polykaste herself come to be here? And an elder sister too. But the reasoning would be a waste of his short breath to voice. Frightened girls did not hear wisdom. Instead he beckoned her closer. There were other ways to hearten and encourage. He knew them all. "May I?"

He laid his hand on the firm dome of her belly. The life within bumped suddenly under the layers of shawl and himation and womb, strong as a piglet in a market sack. He counted each painful word out like a grain of gold. "Heroes know. We have our lore. Shall I tell you our biggest secret?" He waited for her nod. "Don't tell anyone, then. But we know fear too."

She stared. "Mighty Odysseus, leader of men, wily and wise? Truly?"

"In the Trojan horse we were puking with fright. Child, if you're wise, you know fear. The trick is to not give it free rein. Great treasure is not won without great travail."

He had done some good. A ghostly little smile brushed past the corners of her mouth. But it weighed on him, that he had not spoken with his old persuasion and power. Where are you,

Athene, with your wisdom? And his side hurt unbearably. The physician came in, fussing and prodding, and he was glad to take his dose and sleep again.

With the next day came fever, a scorching heat that racked him without mercy. He knew this was bad, but would not admit it. Instead he battled the physician, who wanted to cup him and administer a purge. The girl Polykaste was nowhere to be seen, and he had not the breath to ask for her aid. He contrived to kick over the physician's brazier and to spit out most of the medicine, but he couldn't upbraid the old fraud as he deserved. Resourceful Odysseus, speechless! It disgusted him.

And over the steady roar of the rain on the tiles came another sound, the mutter and tramp of men. He could hear them pass out in the great hall, men enough to throng the place. More men than his one ship could hold. For a moment he was lost in memory, the feasting suitors filling the hall and the mighty bow in his hand. Then the physician stooped nearer. "Your sailors are here, lord," he said. "Itheus, and Lykon, and Ainios, and the others. They want to come in."

"What for?" He had to mouth it.

The physician rolled his eyes, collecting the approval of the other sickroom attendants. "Lord, to say goodbye."

He shook his head. "Not going. Not I. Tell them – fettle the ship, caulk her. We sail in the spring." In this cursed downpour there would be little enough work they could do, but it was important for a ship's captain to keep the men busy and out of trouble.

Then it was night, and he was too weak to resist anymore. They worked their will on him far into the evening, cupping and bleeding, plastering his feet and head with herbs pounded into a slimy paste and spread on linen.

He lay still, struggling for every breath, and recited to himself all the perils he had escaped: Scylla and hungry Charybdis, the Cyclops, angry Ajax, Hector with his bright bronze sword, kingly Priam and bright doomed Achilles. I, Odysseus, survived all these. I came alive out of Troy. I returned home safe after ten years' journeying. And I will live to laugh at this stupid injury. Heroes cannot die in the sickbed, with slaves and women weeping all around. How could a poet make a decent song of an end like that? We die in the bitter clash of armor and swords on the plains of windy Troy, leaving a corpse to be fought over by gods and men. Or we yell brass-lunged defiance and go down in a wallow of cold water as the bronze-headed rams cleave the ship into planks and floating rags…

The air and his head grew clear, as if the rain had washed both clean together. The storm had passed, and a clear yellow morning lay long and bright on the pavement outside the bedchamber. Beyond, above the terrace parapet, the sky was ten thousand leagues deep, that clear high Aegean blue fit to be set into the bezel of the ring of a god. Perfect traveling weather! It was a day for departures – a day to pour the libations of wine and oil to Poseidon, and cast off the lines, and haul the sail high with singing and joy!

He leaned back on his pillows and drank the sweet air in tiny sips, not fighting for gulps of breath any longer. The morning shimmered with expectancy. Some great good was approaching, casting its glow before, a sure forerunner of the divine. He was not surprised to see a slim figure in flowing white pace slowly along the terrace towards him: Athene. The tears prickled in his eyes. At last!

But no – this woman wore no helm and bore neither spear nor shield. Instead she carried something close-wrapped in a brown shawl, something small and fragile. With enormous dignity, she came in to the bedside and folded back the edge of the shawl for him to see. "King Odysseus, may I present your grandson?"

"Polykaste!" he breathed. She smiled down at him, and at the pink wriggling newborn in her arms. He wanted to burst out with congratulations and good-luck words, but all he could do was grin up at her. In his weakness he didn't even dare to hold the infant. But he put his hand on the tiny head. The downy tender scalp was dented and discolored from the long battle to reach the light. A lively lad, a fighter already! And new, so very new. Against the baby head his hand looked like an old tree root scoured and bleached by the sea and cast up, driftwood, on the beach. He blessed the boy silently: *See new things and make new things, my lad. Travel far. Drink every cup to the lees, and sink in sight of the Isle of the Blest.*

"As soon as I stopped fighting the pangs, the birth went well," Polykaste was saying. "It was just like your adventures: I passed through great travail to win a mighty treasure."

Brave child, he wanted to tell her. Worthy descendant of a line of kings!

He had been certain her eyes were blue. But now in the golden morning they looked gray, gray as rain. And she said, "There is a time to fight nature, and a time to be her friend."

For an instant he held his breath, though he had no breath to spare. Athene, bright lady, he prayed silently. Never have you failed me. Thank you.

The girl beamed down at her baby with doting pride. Then she glanced at him, and her mouth dropped open in alarm. "Sir, are you well? Shall I call the physician?"

He shook his head. She was right. Death indeed came as no foe, but a friend. But one last task lay before him. He crooked a kingly finger, beckoning her closer. "My men," he croaked. He could no longer hear them out there in the great hall, but he knew they had waited, the brave hearts, faithful as Argos. Let them come in, he wanted to say. I can stay a little for them. To say goodbye.

Phemius

Marlaina Cockcroft

I am a poet.

I *was* a poet.

What I am now, I do not know. Food for the Sirens, perhaps, and perhaps I would welcome their song, were they to sing to us.

Apologies, fellow traveler. I am so tired. This ship's constant swaying turns my stomach as I huddle here against the rail.

But I cannot sleep. Every night, when I close my eyes, I see those eyes. Sightless and staring.

Oh gods, take this vision from my mind. Please listen for once.

You do not believe me, stranger. You saw no poet so twisted and pitiful in all of Ithaca. Ha, you know nothing! I was the best. Apollo blessed me with my voice, but my words were my own creation. I sang of battles lost and won, of great heroes and their deeds. My song of the battle of Troy, my elegy for the brave warriors who angered Athena and so did not return home, was a particular favorite. I performed it many times.

Of course my voice did not always croak like this. It soared, as though it flew in the wake of Apollo's chariot.

If only I had brought my songs elsewhere. If only I had not obeyed the summons to perform at the king's palace.

I thought the invitation odd, given the king's absence – the king who was long dead, if the rumors were true. But I did not question my good fortune. The queen and the prince still lived at the palace, did they not? And they surely would value a song or two.

As I walked, humming the melodies I planned to sing, I imagined my voice filling the palace's stone courtyard, rising to Olympus to adorn the ears of the gods. This pleased me. Only a palace could be a suitable stage for my talents. Clearly I should have performed there sooner.

I realized my mistake as soon as I passed through the outer doors. The queen's suitors ruled the palace, and they were driving it to ruin.

I stared around me aghast at the laughing crowds of men filling the courtyard. All wealthy. All high-ranking, well-born sons. All seemingly favored by the gods. And they abused that good fortune to lounge on the king's chairs and feast on his food and drink his wine away. They scorned the young prince, left standing forgotten in a corner. They called for the queen with laughter in their voices that quickly curdled and turned sour. *Join us, Penelope. Show us your beauty, Penelope*.

Choose a new husband, Penelope. We have been waiting. Our patience grows short.

All this I saw, and bile rose in my throat. I backed towards the doors. This was no banquet worthy of my presence.

But those feasting fools, those greedy usurpers, they saw me and leapt to bar my way. *There you are! Give us a song, bard. Keep us well entertained while the queen chooses her new king*. They forced a lyre into my hands.

I knew many songs about warriors, but I was no warrior. The suitors had armor, their bows and spears gleamed in the waning sunlight. What measure of defiance was worth losing my life? I swallowed back my fear, and I sang.

Unsteady and anxious, I sang the first thing that came to mind – I sang of Troy and its tragic aftermath. Even as I sang, I berated myself for my foolishness, because the queen's door opened. She descended the stairs, her hair flowing down her back like a river. The suitors leered. *She shows her fair face at last! Come, Penelope, join our banquet.*

She ignored them all and came straight to me where I sat. My voice skipped a note. "Why do you torture me like this? Do not sing of men lost to war when my Odysseus has not come home," she said, standing over me like Aphrodite herself. The tears sparkling on her cheeks only accentuated her beauty, and my fingers fell away from the lyre's strings. It was an evil thing, to cause the queen pain.

The suitors were unmoved, watching her with calculation, as a hunter might study his prey. I offered halting apologies to the queen, but a harsh voice interrupted. "The bard has a right to play what he likes," said the prince. I had not noticed him leaving his lonely corner. "Many enjoy his newer songs. That's why I summoned him."

His dark eyes narrowed as he stared his mother down. I read anger in his face, in his stiff bearing, in the contemptuous look he flashed the suitors. But he was one man, barely grown, and his hands unfurled from fists to dangle at his sides.

He was helpless, just as I was.

The queen's face grew cold and she nodded at us both. With dignity she returned to her room. She was holding a vigil for her lost love, I realized, and I would swear I could hear her sobbing. More softly, I continued my song.

The prince stalked away, seeming not to hear the suitors hooting and laughing as he passed. *Someday he will make them regret their mockery,* I thought, remembering the storm clouds in his eyes. *He yearns to cause them pain*. I did not know how soon I was to be proved right.

A moment, please, stranger. I only need a moment. It is difficult to talk of these horrors. They are never far from my mind.

The wind blows hard through this ship. I cannot get warm. I suppose it is hard to believe that these trembling hands ever held a lyre.

When I finished that infernal song of Troy, nearly spitting out the final words, I thought I would be allowed to leave. This ever more ominous drama could play on without me as unwilling audience. But the suitors called for more meat and wine and raised their cups to me, shouting, *Stay and sing another*! The prince only nodded, he would not meet my eyes. Whatever comfort my singing gave meant more to him than my freedom. I fixed a weak smile in place and sang again.

Surely these men would grow tired, would depart for their own homes, and I could steal away then. But this suitors' banquet went on unendingly. I tried to leave after every song, and they pushed me back on my stool and brandished spears.

Another song, another. I no longer knew the day or the hour. With shouts and taunts, looming over me with weapons in hand, they bade me sing. *Tell us of heroes, bard*. They laughed, fat from the roasted sheep glistening on their lips, their breath stinking of the king's wine. *Sing of heroes*, as though these pampered, preening men knew anything of heroes.

I was no hero and never have been, but at least I did not pretend otherwise.

Apollo give me strength, I prayed. But I had no offering to make save my voice, which grew hoarse and harsh. My spit dribbled into my beard until my mouth was drier than bone.

"Free me, my prince," I whispered as he passed. He shook his head and walked on, resolute, shoulders set firm, as though he were waiting for something to happen. I sank further into despair.

I thought at last they would let me leave when my voice was gone. That my gift would be the price of my freedom. I noted the flecks of blood on my fingers, rubbed raw from the lyre, and I thought the price fair.

"Please, I have no more words to sing," I said hoarsely to the suitors. They drove me back to the stool with curses and threats. Consumed with despair, I barely noticed the ragged stranger as he entered, begging for food.

Resentfully the suitors fed the beggar, while Antinous their leader mocked the poor man. How jealously Antinous guarded the king's food, how noble of him to protect what he wanted for himself.

As for me, my eyes slid over the beggar and away. With my cracked voice I had begun another song, and I had no will left to pity another person.

I should have marked the beggar more closely from the start. I should have wondered at the small smiles he exchanged with the prince, as though they shared a great secret, or noted that the suitors' armor had vanished. I should have observed the beggar's strong, muscled limbs – surely not those of a starved wanderer – or thought it odd that the prince encouraged him to handle the king's fabled bow. I should have sensed the crackling in the air, as though Zeus stood above us all, ready to release his lightning bolt.

I should have dropped the lyre and run.

Instead I watched as the stranger threw off his rags and thundered, "Did you think I would not return from Troy?"

My voice died away in my shock. This old beggar, the long-lost king? I looked closer and at last saw the truth. His high cheekbones and proud brow matched those of the prince, and the two gazed at each other with undisguised love.

The long journey home of Odysseus had ended, the queen's long-awaited miracle had come to pass, and here I sat to bear witness.

My fortune had turned. The song I would write of this moment! It was Apollo's will that I be here, I of all the poets. I pushed away my weariness and stood to hail the triumphant king.

Only then did I see the rage suffusing his craggy face, turning it ugly. I halted. My skin prickled a warning, far too late.

Antinous also did not realize the danger. He stood gaping, clutching his forgotten cup of wine, as the king raised his bow and shot an arrow cleanly through the man's throat.

Antinous gurgled, dropped his cup, and collapsed. In his death throes, he kicked over his table, and the banquet he'd made of the king's food crashed to the floor around him.

The other suitors shouted and reached for their weapons, cursing and wailing when they realized their armor had been stolen.

I backed up and bumped into my long-hated stool. My legs failed me and I sank down, trying to breathe.

The king bellowed, "For plundering my estate and wooing my wife, you all shall die." Even as he spoke, he nocked another arrow.

The suitors came at him, anger and terror on their faces in equal measure. The king, all grim purpose, took aim and shot, again and again. The prince laughed – with a feral light in his eyes, he *laughed* – as he took up a sword. He and his father waded into the fray together, slitting the suitors' throats and piercing their hearts and impaling them where they stood.

The suitors screamed, they cried: *Have mercy on us. You killed our leader, this was his doing. We will repay you for all we have taken. Have mercy, we beg you.*

But there was no mercy. Their blood washed over the floor of the courtyard like the tide smothering the sand.

I sat as one of stone, as one of Medusa's own victims. I had no love for these suitors and indeed, had prayed they be punished for their brutal treatment of me. But I had never wished such a death upon them.

These men had become mere sheep and pigs, this courtyard was a slaughter house. One by one, they fell around me. Their shrieks and groans pierced my ears.

I was a poet. I sang of many battles, but it was never my fate to fight in one. I had never seen arms and legs hacked away, never locked eyes with a head as it tumbled near me, severed from its lifeless body. I had never imagined such horror. I cowered behind my lyre as the blood seeped into my sandals.

A sob broke from my throat. The sound woke me, and thus freed, I dropped the lyre. It banged on the floor as I pushed my body to run.

The king heard. He blocked my way, covered in the blood of other men.

How could this be Odysseus? How could this implacable murderer be the king that his queen had lovingly refused to betray for so long?

I saw my death in his eyes. I dropped to my knees and like the suitors, begged him for mercy. "I did not know, please, lord, I did not help these men," I babbled. "I am merely a poet. I sing at the pleasure of the gods. You will regret the loss of my songs if you kill me. I am inspired by Apollo himself. I would sing to you as though you also were a god."

I heard him breathing above me, heavy and grunting, like a boar. *Save me*, I prayed to Apollo. *I am your servant*.

But the god did not answer. I know now that the gods are silent when you need them, even if you sing their praises at other times. May you never need to learn this for yourself, stranger.

I dared to look up. The king held an arrow out, considering its heft, the sharpness of its point. "Your son," I cried. My voice cracked. "Your son will tell you how he brought me here and I was forced to perform by these men. Your son knows my way was barred when I tried to leave. I begged him for help."

But I thought, *The queen will tell you how I brought her to tears, singing of Troy. How I caused her to imagine your death in battle. The queen will smile at the sight of my mangled body, for such is the way of this family.*

"It's true, Father." The prince had come closer, still grasping his sword. "He had no hand in this matter, and he's a gifted poet besides." He smiled at me, as though all was well and I had just finished a song he liked.

I gazed at the prince's dripping sword and at the savage joy on his beardless face.

The king moved away, on to his next kill. I lay sobbing on the bloody floor.

I thought I had survived the worst.

I shudder to remember what happened next.

The king and the prince knew the suitors they were slaughtering would be missed and mourned, and they would need to justify cutting down so many of the island's fine young men. They determined to hide their deeds for a time. The king declared he had need of my voice after all.

He roughly hauled me to my feet. "Play," he said. "Play a dance or two. Make the people around think there is a wedding in my house, so no one suspects the truth."

Play as though the endless banquet continued, and as though I were not staring into the eyes of the dead and dying suitors.

The king had spared my life. So I stood in the courtyard, my hair and beard matted with blood, and with gnarled fingers, I played.

In my whispering, hollow voice, I sang *wedding* songs. The foolish, airy kind that I would normally scorn to perform. Songs of joy and the blessings of the gods, while men's bodies cooled all around me.

Their eyes were on me at every moment.

They were no true audience. They belonged to Hades now.

But Hades liked music. Had not Orpheus performed for him and Persephone?

With that thought I felt my sanity slipping out of reach. Still I played.

I sang until my voice gave out at last and I fell to the floor and screamed into the stones.

While I lay senseless, the king reunited with his loyal queen. Somehow he convinced his people, shocked by the loss of their noble sons, that these deaths were necessary and blessed by the gods.

And then, having secured his victory, he came to the corner where I crouched, shuddering, embracing the scraped-up, stained lyre.

"My son speaks well of you," he said. "He says your songs are popular among the people, and you should be the honored poet to tell the story of my adventures."

If only the prince had not thought so highly of my gifts.

I looked at the king, but I did not see the noble face or the fine robes. I saw the ragged, snarling man bathed in others' blood.

"I need time to compose, my king," I mumbled, cringing back, awaiting the blow. He turned away, still smiling. I forced myself to my feet and escaped the palace at last.

I left the island that same day.

Ever since, I have hidden on this ship. I do not know its destination and I care not. Poseidon could sink it this minute and I would go merrily to my doom.

But not singing. Never singing. I have not sung once since that day.

I was a poet. I thought I was blessed by Apollo. Now I think I am cursed.

I cannot sleep. I see those sightless eyes always in my dreams.

If this ship does not sink, I hope it will take me far from Ithaca, so far that I need never hear the name Odysseus again. Perhaps then I will find peace, and my lost voice will return to me.

I made my name singing of great heroes, but I hope never to meet another one.

The Cave at the World's End

Travis Earl

Brave Odysseus stood at Penelope's funeral pyre on the shores of Ithaca. For the first time in his memory, he wept without control. Telemachus, his son, had to light the bundle of sticks for Odysseus could not bear it.

Odysseus put his head on Telemachus's shoulder and let the sobs wrack his body as the flames consumed Penelope's vessel.

His mind wandered back to the day of his return, when he strung his bow and shot his arrow through the twelve axe heads. When he shrugged off the beggar's cloak he disguised himself with, Penelope had dropped to her knees, kissing his hands passionately, the long-forgotten dream of his return finally reality. He helped her to her feet. He remembered the kiss they shared then, the softness of her embrace, the surging passion that seized him more powerfully than the breath of Poseidon. For thirty years, the Gods had conspired to keep him from her, and for ten years they had been reunited. Then, the wasting sickness took her. Ten years for thirty. It wasn't enough.

Telemachus led his father back to his chambers, where the tree of Ithaca had grown while Penelope waited for him.

Odysseus stayed alone for seven days, beating his chest, gnashing his teeth, shaking his fist at the Gods for what they had done. After his period of mourning ended, resolve hardened his heart, filling it with disobedience to the Gods.

When he emerged, Telemachus stood outside the chamber door. Odysseus, brave, strong and mighty, fixed his son with his gaze.

"It is said that shores of Hades lie at the earth's end. There we will go and bring your mother back."

Odysseus picked the sturdiest of Ithacans to man his vessel. Telemachus took charge, making the men strain against their oars and speed the vessel beyond the limits of the known world, stepping into his destiny as king.

Odysseus watched his powerful son standing at the prow of the ship and his heart ached for the times gone when he drove his men to adventure and glory. He knew that all things end, that one day, he would be forced to pay the ferryman as all do, and his boy would be king. Odysseus would die, but Penelope would live, reprieved from Hades. Odysseus would have justice. He would have his twenty years back.

"Father," Telemachus said when they had passed the final islands of the Greeks. "For your defiance of the Gods, they exiled you from your home for twenty years. Why incur their wrath again?"

Telemachus's words pained Odysseus, for they reminded Odysseus of the futility of his quest. The will of the Gods could not be undone, but with the will that they had given him, he would defy them, defy their cruelty.

"I fear not the wrath of the Gods. They have already taken that which is most precious to me."

Odysseus's words stung Telemachus, for his sire still had his progeny by his side, but his grief was almost as profound as Odysseus's, and he understood the pain his father felt.

The boat broke the waves of the unknown lands, the islands of witches, giants and monsters. Memories of past fears chilled Odysseus yet always the memory of Penelope's beauty spurred him on.

They drove beyond the North Sea, where mountains of ice choked the waters, and the cold brought frost to the tips of the men's beards. Once they had passed the land of ice and snow, Odysseus spied the farthest shore of the world.

A golden mountain rose into the clouds, an endless expanse that consumed his vision. There was nothing more to the world than this. He had reached the home of the Gods, the barrier between the living and the dead.

As the mountain grew larger in Odysseus's vision, the winds picked up. The sail lashed and the boat rocked. Telemachus pushed against the wind to reach his father, grabbed his shoulder and shouted above the howling gusts.

"It is the Gods. We go where no mortal was meant to tread. Turn back before we are destroyed."

Odysseus smacked Telemachus's hand from his shoulder. Disgust made his lip curl. His son's courage had failed him. Odysseus strode to the prow, drew his sword, and pointed to the shore of the mountain.

"Onward!" he shouted over the gales that buffeted him. "Onward!"

Waves rocked the boat, but Odysseus wrapped his hands in the ropes so the waters would not snatch him from the deck.

His heart seized when he saw the water before the boat begin to churn. A whirlpool formed.

Telemachus grabbed him, using his full power to bring him back from the prow. They grappled until Telemachus held the old man firmly in his grasp.

"Turn back!" he shouted over the lashing winds that shredded the sail overhead.

Odysseus ground his teeth. He would not let the Gods have their way. He would not let them take his love. He pushed Telemachus away and aimed his sword at the mountain.

"ONWARD!"

The churning waters began to foam. The whirlpool took hold of the boat.

The boat shuddered wildly, breaking apart in the current. Odysseus's breath caught in his throat. He realized that he had doomed his son, his men, for his pride. Odysseus fell upon the deck as the sea consumed it and drew him into the waters. The last thing he saw before the tide drew him into the depths was Telemachus's face, his eyes lifeless, his mouth open beneath the waters. Then, all was dark.

* * *

Brave Odysseus washed upon the sandy shores of the golden mountain. The tide splashed over his face, and his eyes fluttered open. His heart raced. He pressed his fingers into the sands. He felt the grains on his fingers. He felt. He breathed. He lived. He sprang to his feet, ran up and down the shore, looking over the now calm waters.

"Telemachus!" he shouted at the empty sea. "Telemachus!"

He raced along the shore, searching for a sign of the boat and his son.

"Telemachus!"

Only the crash of the tide upon the shore answered him.

Odysseus dropped to his knees. It was as though his soul drained from his body, like a pitcher emptied onto the sands. He had lied to his son. The Gods had more to take from him, and they had. He wept bitterly, his heart torn apart.

As Odysseus grieved, he became aware of a golden light shining behind him. He spun around; his heart filled with awe. At the edge of the shore, where the mountain began, stood a cave. The golden light shone from a flame dancing in the mouth of the cave. The flame spoke to him as though a voice whispered in his ear.

"Odysseus, killer of Troy, killer of nations, you have come to a shore you were never meant to tread."

The words tasted bitter in Odysseus's mouth. He had been drawn to Troy against his will, going himself rather than sacrificing Telemachus. He had destroyed an entire people to save his son, and yet Odysseus had brought Telemachus to ruin for his own pride.

"However, you have passed the final barrier and earned the right to fight for your salvation. In this cave, the souls meant for paradise are purified, if they can best their sins. Should you emerge victorious, you may see your bride."

Odysseus rose from his knees, the burning bile in his throat driving him on. He cursed the Gods. They made mortals but playthings.

He staggered towards the cave. He would not allow the Gods to rob him of all things sacred. He would win his wife's life.

Moisture ran down the cave walls. The tunnel stretched into infinite darkness. A cold, fell wind blew from within, carrying the scent of death.

"Prepare yourself to meet the champion of the Gods," the voice in his head whispered.

Odysseus's pulse quickened. He looked about the cave, searching for something to arm himself with. In the shadows near the cave's mouth, he saw a skeleton, decayed to dust, seated against the rock. A rusted iron shield clung to the skeleton's arm, and it gripped a sword in its hand. Once Odysseus had ripped the shield from the skeleton, it collapsed into dust. He took up the short sword and swung it through the air to get a feel for its balance. When he was satisfied, he turned back to the flame.

"In here, cunning Odysseus, your wiles will not avail you," said the spirit in the flame. "Only your strength shall save you."

With that, the dancing flame snuffed out like a cinder in the air.

Odysseus stood, feet spread, chest out, ready to face whatever challenge the Gods had for him.

Beyond the light of day that fell inside the cave's mouth, he saw shadows flitting in the darkness, shadows that fluttered with intent, inhabited by spirits. The souls of the underworld. A cold fear, more profound than he had ever known, rolled down brave Odysseus's spine. Such a fate awaited him in death. Such a fate had befallen Penelope. Odysseus thought of Penelope's large blue eyes, and soft lips.

He steeled himself and stepped forward.

At first, the shadows retreated from him as he strode deeper into the cave, but once he'd stepped beyond the reach of the light, they closed on him like a pair of dark hands. Odysseus swung his blade, cutting the air before the spirits. They drew back.

Odysseus strode forward, planted both his feet in the sands of the cave, and bellowed with all his might.

"Bring forth your champion!"

His words echoed upon the rocks that stretched onward into the infinite dark. The shadows stilled. Then they flowed together like pooling oil on the sands of the cave floor. Then the shadow form of a man rose from the centre of the pool like a swimmer breaching the water's surface. The shadow congealed into solid form, and there stood before Odysseus the form of King Priam, rendered in shadow, but unmistakable.

The same cold fear returned, more profound, chilling Odysseus from head to foot. His sword trembled in his hand. This was not Priam the aged king that could not meet the Greek heroes in battle, this was Priam as he was in his prime when he had battled the Amazons with King Mygdon. Fully two heads taller than Odysseus stood Priam's shadow. As broad as the side of a ship were his shoulders. Odysseus crouched, battle ready, fighting back the tremors of fear that quaked his thighs.

Like a flash, Priam reached out and grabbed the crown of Odysseus's head in his hand. Before the king of Ithaca could pull away, Shadow Priam's fingers sank through the skin and bone of his skull, digging into the meat of his brain.

A vision consumed Odysseus's mind. He saw the altar of Zeus in burning Troy. Mighty steps led to the columns and dais. Such was the size that Odysseus felt like an ant at the foot of a God.

He saw the burning city through the eyes of Priam, prone beside the statue of the greatest of Gods. Odysseus felt as Priam felt, his soul rent at the sight of his nation burning. He felt tears falling from his cheeks, staining the altar, and the grief Priam felt was sharper than Odysseus's grief, like a flaming blade slicing through him.

Odysseus heard the tromp of hoplites' feet banging on the stone floors of Troy like a drumbeat. Fear gripped him, blinding, breath-stealing fear.

A party of Greeks stormed up the steps, approaching the statue, forgetting all reverence to the Gods in their lust for carnage.

Priam's son, Polites, sat before Zeus's statue pleading for his life. Odysseus watched, feeble, frail, and unable to help as Achilles' son, Pyrrhus, drew his sword and plunged the blade deep in Polites' bosom. Through Priam's eyes, Odysseus saw Polites die, and he felt sorrow beyond measure.

Pyrrhus strode to Priam, the blood from Polites dripping from his blade to the stone floor. Rage filled Priam and with the little strength he could muster, he threw his spear at Pyrrhus. The boy warrior smacked the spear aside with an easy stroke of his sword. He charged, and grabbed Priam by his hair, dragging him across the stones to the altar.

Odysseus felt the pain as his own when Pyrrhus brought his sword down on the helpless king's skull.

The vision ended and Odysseus saw through his own eyes. The shadow form of Priam scowled, his hatred visible even in shadows.

Now that he had lost Telemachus, Odysseus understood Priam's pain, the evil the trick of the Trojan horse had unleashed. With painful sorrow, Odysseus realized that he was unworthy to gaze upon Penelope again. Instead of robbing him, the Gods had given him more grace than he should have been allowed.

"Forgive me," Odysseus murmured.

Priam's shade tossed him across the cavern with one arm. Odysseus smashed into the wall, pain shooting through his body. He lay on the sands of the cave floor for a moment, resigned to his fate. As the shadow form of Priam loomed above him, Odysseus's spirit returned. Should this be his end, he would give a worthy fight. He would not rob Priam of a chance to avenge himself by surrendering.

Odysseus hopped up from the floor.

He swung his blade wildly. Each stroke passed through the shadow harmlessly. The shade brought his fist down like a hammer upon Odysseus's shield.

Odysseus's knees buckled.

He swept his sword towards the shade's chest. It kicked him hard. He sailed against the cavern wall.

This time, he used the shield to protect himself from the stones. The shield clashed upon the stone with a spray of sparks. The rust along its edge shattered. Beneath it, Odysseus saw gleaming metal.

His mind raced.

He saw the spirit retreat at the flash of sparks. The flame had told him his cunning would not avail him here, but she had lied.

Odysseus rolled along the sands, bringing his body to the cave mouth. The spirit charged, fearing he would escape. Odysseus caught the light of the sun on the exposed metal of his shield. Like a looking glass, the shield shot the sunbeam at the heart of the shade.

The shadow burst like a bubble popped by a pin.

A roar of triumph broke from Odysseus's mouth.

He jumped to his feet. Even the Gods could not match his cunning.

"I am Odysseus, grandson of Zeus, no spirit, no God, no mortal is a match for my wits."

Odysseus's words echoed back to him. He turned to the cave mouth, bringing his sword over his head in a gesture of victory, ready to see his beloved once more.

He felt the cold shadow blade pierce his back. His eyes shot down to his chest as the tip broke through his sternum. Shadow Priam lifted the blade and Odysseus with it.

Odysseus had never known such pain before, but even greater than the pain was the fear he felt, cold, terrifying fear, the fear that knew that what lurked behind it was the emptiness of death, the life of a shadow flitting about the dark without thought or feeling.

He stared into the shadow face of his killer, and it horrified him to see a smile spread across the dead king's face.

Odysseus dropped upon the sands, and his life bled out from him into the earth.

He closed his eyes and welcomed death, for he would be with Telemachus and Penelope, even if as shadows. He sensed the presence of the dead king hovering over him, and he remembered the horror he had witnessed through the king's eyes.

The contest was over. Odysseus had lost. He had no pride left.

"Forgive me," he murmured.

A shining light made Odysseus's eyes open. His breath caught in his throat for before him stood Penelope as she was when he first returned to her. The earth seemed to shift beneath him. He crawled to the vision, kissed her hands, kissed her arm until he met her face, and kissed her gently.

"How…how did this come to be?"

"You asked for forgiveness willingly and purified your soul through mortification. You have won a place in Elysium."

Behind her Odysseus saw Priam, flesh and blood, no longer shadow. He smiled warmly at Odysseus.

"Here," said Penelope," there is no hunger, no thirst, no desire, no pride. We have no need for battles or for lust. Here we know only peace."

Odysseus felt his heart fill with love. He embraced Priam, and the two friends wept for joy in the cavern at the world's end.

* * *

Telemachus lay panting on the deck of the ship, driven against the boards by the relentless winds. They had carried the ship beyond the shores of the endless mountain, back across the sea to the north. As the winds relented, Telemachus's heart filled with awe. The gods had given them a warning: tread not where mortals do not tread. He pushed himself up from the deck and looked about. His men all lay on the ground as he had, slowly pulling themselves to their feet.

"Odysseus! We've lost Odysseus!" one called.

The beating of Telemachus's heart stopped. He ran about the deck, looking for his father. He ran to the prow, leaning over and searching the waters. His skin froze to see a body floating in the sea near the ship, clad in his father's tunic.

"There! There!" Telemachus shouted.

As quickly as they could, the men fished Odysseus from the water with a hook and stick. He landed on the deck with a wet plop like a fish. All knew from the blue color of his skin that no life lingered in his body.

Sorrow filled Telemachus. He kneeled and clasped his father's hand. He had died as he lived: a seeker. Such is the will of the gods. What Telemachus could not understand, though, was the look Odysseus wore upon his face. His father's corpse smiled, as though in death he had found a comfort he had never known in life.

Odysseus's Oath

Ayden June Fitzgerald

Penelope had never heard a sound as sweet as the grunts of the suitors trying to string the longbow. When she had thought of the challenge, she knew it would buy her more time than the shroud had, but she hadn't realized just how much time it would buy her. Every month, the suitors took a break from loitering in her palace and eating her food to try to string Odysseus's longbow, and one after the other, they failed. Her advisors told her she was being ridiculous, that her husband was dead, and she should simply choose a new husband and be done with it, but she wouldn't. He was alive; she knew it, and no matter what he had done, no matter how long he had been gone, she would wait right here in their palace for him.

As long as it took.

Penelope's bronze throne grew stiffer beneath her, and the gold leaves of her laurel crown dug into her scalp, which was not helping her patience. Then again, she had never had much patience in the first place.

She had always thought suitor games were amusing, with men lining up to win the heart or the crown of a lady, some trying harder than others. Penelope knew she should be paying attention to the contest, but as the hours grew long, she couldn't help but let her mind wander to that time as she craned her neck to look at Odysseus's empty throne beside hers. She could still hear the music in the megaron in Sparta – the soft plucking of the lyre strings, the laughter, and the dancing. Her dark hair had less grey, and her deep olive skin was smooth without a wrinkle. The megaron in Ithaca began to melt away, taking all her troubles with it.

And she fell back into that time as easily as breathing.

Helen must have been on her tenth dance of that night, twenty-seven years ago, but you would never hear a complaint out of her. She was a warrior in such a womanly way that she could endure an entire night of revelry and flattery and be fresh and pleasant the next day. Penelope could never compete, not that she wanted to; she loved her cousin and admired her spirit. In a way, Penelope was glad she wouldn't have this kind of attention when it came time for her to marry.

Unlike a normal feast, most of the young men had been waiting for their turn to dance with Helen all night, so Penelope had been sitting at the high table nursing a chicken leg and a cup of wine. She adjusted her gold chiton and swept her long, dark hair back over one shoulder. All the bodies stuffed into the hall made it so warm she lost focus, until a voice and an extended hand broke her trance.

"Would you like to dance, Princess?"

It was one of Helen's suitors, although there were so many she had forgotten just which one this was. Certainly not the Atreides brothers. She had known both of them well when they had stayed in Sparta some years ago with their flaming red hair and tall frames. The elder brother was dancing with her cousin, Nes, and the other had just started dancing with Helen. The man was short but well-built, with tawny-brown skin, dark brown hair, and large brown eyes. He had dimples on his cheeks as he kept his hand out, waiting for her to take it.

Penelope smirked. "I think you've confused me with my cousin Helen. Blonde, grey eyes, prettiest girl in Greece, I imagine you're waiting for your turn to dance with her like everyone else."

The suitor shook his head. "No mistake, I just thought you looked lonely up here, thought you might like someone to talk to."

Penelope reached out and took the suitor's hand. "I suppose I could spare one dance."

The suitor guided her to the dance floor for the next song. He put one callused hand high on her back and led her around the floor.

"I'm Odysseus, in case you didn't know." He grinned.

"Ah, the young king of Ithaca," Penelope teased.

"You say that like it's a bad thing." Odysseus chuckled.

Penelope bit her lower lip to stop herself from laughing. "No, it's not, just a fact. I suppose since you wanted to dance with me, you know who I am?"

Odysseus scrunched together his eyebrows. "Hmmm, niece of King Tyndareus, right?"

Penelope laughed. "Very good, your grace."

Odysseus tilted his head and smirked. "Well, I've been known to be very clever."

Penelope nodded along with him, making him laugh. "So, *King* of Ithaca, how have you been enjoying Sparta?"

Odysseus's eyes moved over to Helen and then back to her. "Your cousin is very charming; she will make any man a fine wife, although I don't know how your uncle will be able to choose one of us. Belonging to one woman until her father chooses you to care for her is an *interesting* situation."

Penelope glanced over at her uncle, who was standing with his wife, Aunt Leda, and her parents in a corner. Love wasn't always common in marriage, but Uncle Tyndareus always looked at Aunt Leda like she was the most important person in the world. Penelope's father always told the story of how he had met her mother in the river she called home, and how no other naiad could compare to her.

As the next song ended, Odysseus brought her hand up to his mouth and kissed her knuckles. "It's been a pleasure to dance with you, Princess."

Penelope's heart fluttered, but she tried not to let it show on her face. She didn't want him to go, although she didn't know why; he wasn't her suitor after all. He couldn't be flirting with her, it wouldn't be appropriate, but she liked talking to him. He couldn't go just yet.

Penelope gave a lopsided grin. "Done with me so soon, Your Grace?"

Odysseus pursed his lips. "I guess I don't have to be." He looked over to Helen, who was still dancing with Menelaus of Myceane. "Doesn't look like I'm getting that dance anytime soon. What did you have in mind?"

"Do you like hunting spears?"

* * *

Sneaking out of the party was easy; no one was looking at her, of all people. They quickly found the room she wanted to show him at the north end of the palace. From the moment Penelope opened the doors, Odysseus's eyes remained wide.

His hands ran over the spears with a clear and ringing scrape. He picked up a bronze one inlaid with silver and ran his hand over the point, and then smiled at her as she sat against the wall.

"This is one of the finest collections I've ever seen! Where did your uncle acquire so many fine spears?"

"Some of them were gifts, but..." Penelope walked towards Odysseus and pointed at the spear he was holding. "My uncle made this one for my father as a sixteenth name day present. He never lets anyone in here, but I thought you might like it."

Odysseus's eyes widened with wonder. "Your uncle made this! It's fine work. He must have prayed to Hephaestus hard for this kind of skill."

Penelope took the spear from Odysseus's hand and placed it back on display with the others. "Well, my uncle always said if he weren't a king, he would be a smith." Penelope paused. "What about you? What would you do if you weren't a king?"

Odysseus put a hand to his chin. "I would be…some sort of wandering hunter, live in the wilderness full time and hunt boars. I enjoy being king; it's why my father passed the crown early. But what I wouldn't give to live in the wilderness and survive on my own wits for a little while."

Penelope picked up her wine and took another sip, grinning. "Very high aspirations, your grace."

Odysseus threw back his head and laughed. "Are you making fun of me, princess?"

Penelope put on a serious face and shook her head. "No, I would never insult the King of Ithaca."

Odysseus hummed. "I'm gonna have to commandeer your wine for that comment."

"Good luck with that!"

Penelope dashed to the other side of the room with Odysseus close behind. She had been the best at chasing games as a girl, and even though she was only three months older than her cousins, she always declared it was because she was older, which meant she must be the best. Being eighteen now had hardly changed her speed, and Odysseus kept missing chances to grab her arm and wrestle the cup from her hands as they both laughed and taunted.

Once Odysseus realized that grabbing her arm wasn't working, he seized the back of her gold chiton and pulled her close so she couldn't escape. He reached for the cup clumsily, and it crashed to the floor, spilling wine on the sand-coloured tiles.

Penelope put a hand to her mouth to stop herself from laughing. "Well, that was a failed raid."

Odysseus chuckled. "Apparently, I need more practice."

Penelope turned her head to laugh with him. He was closer than she thought. His hand was still grasping the back of her dress. His brown eyes studied hers, and silence permeated around them. It was wrong, but she wanted to kiss him. But he belonged to Helen until her uncle decided otherwise. What if she kissed him right now, and then her uncle chose him to be Helen's husband? She would never be able to look her cousin, her dearest sister, in the eye again. Worst of all, she would hate Helen for taking him away from her.

Luckily for her, the silence was interrupted by footsteps coming down the hall.

Penelope pushed Odysseus away, much to his shock. "You need to hide."

Odysseus looked around. "Where?"

Penelope took his hand and led him behind the column in the back of the room, hidden from view of the door. She walked back to the middle of the room and stood by the table at the centre, trying to act as naturally as possible when her cousin Clytemnestra entered the room. Nes's cheeks were so flushed they burned bright red on her snowy skin. Some would have said she and Nes were the true twins, with their black hair and brown eyes, but Nes's skin was so pale that they could never be sisters. Although, to be fair, Helen was and they had opposite colouring.

"What are you doing in here, Pen? I've been looking for you everywhere!" Nes beamed.

Penelope gave a bright grin. "Oh, the megaron was so crowded, so I thought I'd find some quiet."

Nes raised an eyebrow. "In Father's display room?"

"It's the quietest."

Nes nodded and then looked over Penelope's shoulder at the spilled wine cup. "What happened?"

Penelope kept a calm face, but her stomach fluttered. Nes couldn't know Odysseus was in here with her. She would run and tell Helen if she did.

"I tripped when I was skipping around on the tiles. I'll clean it up, I promise."

Nes nodded. "Do you want help?"

Penelope shook her head. "Nope, just go back to the megeron and I'll be there in a second." Penelope took her cousin by the shoulders and guided her to the door. "And when I get back, you can tell me all about your red-haired Atreides."

Nes's face flushed from her forehead to her chin, and she was still smiling like a giddy little kid as she disappeared down the hallway.

"That was some very impressive work," Odysseus said with a smirk as he appeared behind her.

"Well, I have been known to be very clever," Penelope teased.

Odysseus threw his head back with a chuckle. "Well, we should clean up this wine and get back. Let me help you."

Penelope nodded, and they grabbed some of the spare cleaning cloths to soak up the wine and found a fire to burn the ruined rags. Before they reached the threshold of the megaron, Odysseus took her hand and kissed her knuckles again.

"Thank you for occupying me, Princess. It's been a pleasure."

Penelope's cheeks flushed. "Thank you for making sure I wasn't lonely."

"Anytime." Odysseus grinned before heading back into the hall.

Odysseus made polite but long rounds of conversation with her uncle and finally got that dance with Helen after she finally stopped with the younger Atreides. Penelope kept watching from the opening to the hall; she couldn't stop what she was doing. Why would he want her when he could have Helen and a second crown to himself? She was the eldest daughter of a second son, and it wasn't her time to have a match, not until Helen and Nes had theirs. But she could still feel the warmth of his hand in hers, and how, when he smiled at her, heat spread from the top of her head down to her toes. Penelope shook the images away.

Odysseus wasn't hers, and he never would be.

* * *

Penelope wasn't sure if her parents would believe her when she said she couldn't attend the suitor games the next day because she had a bad headache, but they didn't question it and left for the city with the rest of the court.

Penelope walked around the silent gardens of the palace, trying to banish Odysseus from her mind. She had been tossing and turning all night, thinking about him, but it just kept ringing *Odysseus, Odysseus, Odysseus*. Penelope picked a rose from a bush and inhaled its scent. Aunt Leda always made sure the gardens were beautiful. She said they were good places to ponder, and Penelope was thankful for the space to breathe. As she turned away from the bush, she met Odysseus's dark eyes. She dropped the rose, and Odysseus picked it up with bated breath.

"What are you doing here?" Penelope asked, eyes wide.

"Walking." He smirked.

Penelope's expression hardened. "You're supposed to be at the suitor games with everyone else."

Odysseus stepped forward, broke off the stem of the rose, and tucked it behind her ear. "You're supposed to be there too."

Penelope's face softened. "I wasn't feeling well."

Odysseus reached out and cupped her cheek. She knew she should pull away, but she didn't. It was like Eros had struck her mad with an arrow of love to torture her. Odysseus wasn't the first boy to be nice to her by a long shot, but in a room where everyone had been focusing on Helen, he had asked her to dance and gone away from the party when she asked. What did that mean? Did it mean anything at all? Penelope had no idea.

"I haven't been able to stop thinking about you all night," Odysseus whispered as he moved his lips closer.

"What about Helen?"

"I don't want Helen, I want you, Penelope."

Odysseus's lips crashed against hers. He walked her up to the nearby garden wall as his hands roamed about her waist, and her hands raked through his dark curls. Two voices screamed in her head for domination, one said to keep going, but the other got louder. *Stop*! *What are you doing*? It screamed, '*He's not yours*!'

Penelope shoved Odysseus off, much to his surprise, as she wiped the kiss from her lips. She stepped away from him, hands on her hips, face flushed.

This was ridiculous. She couldn't take away Helen's chance of a good husband when she deserved all the love and respect in the world. Uncle Tyndareus would see that and want him to be king, she couldn't stand in the way.

"Odysseus, we can't do this." Penelope huffed. "You are a suitor of my cousin, and until my uncle decides otherwise, you're hers."

"I'm not anymore," Odysseus muttered.

Penelope's whole body froze. "What are you talking about?"

Odysseus's eyes sparkled with longing, and his mouth was in a hard line. "I spoke with your uncle and father last night and proposed a trade." He rubbed the back of his neck. "It's going to be nearly impossible for your uncle to choose a husband for your cousin, and even if he does, there's always a chance someone won't respect that marriage, so I came up with an idea. Your cousin will choose her husband, and all the suitors, including me, will swear an oath upon your uncle's word that we will not defile that marriage, no matter who Helen chooses. If someone does, then we will all be required to defend your cousin and her husband's honour."

Penelope licked her lips and nodded. "Good idea to keep the peace, but what's the trade for your brilliant idea?"

Odysseus met her gaze, and the corners of his mouth turned up slowly. "Your hand in marriage."

Penelope felt like someone had stolen the air from her lungs. He had traded his chance for an extra crown and the love of her beautiful cousin for her. They had only spent a few hours together, and yet here he was, choosing her.

Penelope closed the distance between them and met his eye. "Are you sure you want this?"

Odysseus smiled, took both her hands and got on one knee. "There is nothing more that I want in this world than for you to be my wife and the mother of my children. This is my oath to you, Penelope. Come to Ithaca, be my queen."

Penelope hardly took a moment to think; she didn't need to, she knew exactly what she was going to say.

Penelope beamed. "Yes, I'll marry you!"

Odysseus smiled widely and picked her up by her hips, swinging her around. She had never felt so much joy as she did right there in that garden. When he put her down, he pulled her into a slow, sweet kiss.

Sometimes, when she closed her eyes, Penelope could still feel the kiss, but reality always ripped her back to the present.

* * *

"Your Grace?"

One of her heralds' voices brought her back out of her head, and she was back in the throne room, and Odysseus was gone.

Penelope shook her head and gave her full attention to the herald. "I apologize, I wasn't listening."

The herald pursed his lips. "All the suitors have finished trying the challenge; however, a beggar who has come into the palace has asked to try."

Penelope breathed out through her nose, trying to maintain composure. "Well, I suppose we should let him try. Bring him forward."

From the parted crowd, an old man stepped forward, his dark hair streaked with grey, his skin leathery from the sun, and he was draped in dirty rags. Penelope wasn't sure why, but she felt like she had seen this man before; but she couldn't quite figure out how.

"What is your name?" Penelope asked the beggar.

The beggar smirked in a familiar way. His brown eyes as dark as the night sky. "Outis, Your Grace."

Penelope chuckled to herself. "A beggar named Nobody? Well, let us see how you do, Nobody."

The beggar approached the longbow and, for the first time in twenty years, Penelope heard the bending and whining of the longbow being strung, and in the back of her mind, she knew it.

Her husband had come home.

Fangs, Fur, and Salt

Katie Frendreis

"You don't have to go with them!"

"I made a vow!" The words burn my throat as they come out, because I hate them and because they feel like lies, even as I shout them. At her, at my wife, at the mother of the babe they tried to kill.

"Why must you all chase the heels of one unfaithful woman?" my wife asks. As always, she has torn into the heart of the matter, ripped away the shreds of the falsities and niceties we deceive ourselves with to bury her arrow of truth deep in my gut. I feel the pang of her question deeply.

Because I agree with her.

"Because of honor, Penelope," I say through gritted teeth. "A man is nothing without his honor."

My wife's eyes narrow down to slits, and the slender fingers of her hands fold around my forearm with a strength not often attributed to women. "A man is still a father. He is still a husband."

All at once, the heat in our home threatens to strangle me. I throw myself from my wife's grasp and tear out of the gynaikon and through the megaron, thundering down the stairs like I am being chased by an army of soldiers.

And, in some ways, I am.

The atmosphere in the courtyard is still too thick, too smothering, too hot, and I kick up dust fleeing from the seat of my kingdom. There are guards there calling after me, but I listen to none of them. Their words are the buzzing of bees, and I brush them away with the flick of my hand. Even the taller of my counselors, emissaries of those lying, vicious kings, knows not to block me, though I am but small of stature among them. They know what I can do; they've seen me fight and string a bow.

When at last I emerge from the walls of this place, my feet make their own path past the mill and the fountain, past the homes and houses of my people, past the fields that are my fiefdom. Glazed and glassy eyes stare up at me from the men working there. Their skin gleams dark bronze and leathery from the sun. On other days, they might raise a hand and speak to me, but they must see the firm set of my mouth and the deep furrows carved into my brow and know this is no moment for idle conversation.

Salt stings my cheeks. It is nothing more than sea air, but it smarts.

Soon I am far enough away for the place I call home to disappear behind a wall of olive trees, and I am free. Free of ruling, free of lying, free of scheming, free of plotting. I am free to be myself, a man, a mortal, a father.

I am all that and nothing as I cast my gaze over the bright glass expanse of the sea. My feet have found a rocky crag overlooking the calmly rolling waters, and I sink to my knees, glad to be out of the palace and here where I can catch my breath. The sun is still so high overhead – only dipped a few degrees lower since I myself trod the fields – and it blazes a line of sweat along my shoulders.

The sea stares back at me, beckoning me with its gentle waves. Oh, I think, to be nothing more than a spot of driftwood upon those waves, tossed thither and thus without any pressure or commands to follow.

But I am not driftwood, I chide myself. I am a king.

And kings cannot simply follow their whims. They have honor and kingdom and loyalty propping them up and leading them by the hand. That is what my wife does not understand. She thinks my only loyalty is to her and our son, maybe to our lands and people. She does not know that there is a greater world beyond, where other kings are called upon for a cause greater than our farms and fields, our trees and homesteads.

It does not escape me – the irony that this series of events has occurred only because of an oath I myself made the kings take.

I am my own undoing. And I know I will take that to whatever grave, watery or otherwise, I am destined to meet.

A few years ago, before I wed Penelope, I – and most of the Argive men I know – courted another. She was beautiful, but not meant for me. Still when the other suitors argued and threatened war with one another over her, my words were the ones that placated them: Let Menelaus take her hand, and let the rest of us stand together if her virtue is stolen by another.

So clever, I thought myself.

But now, that same woman has been stolen from her marriage bed – or fled from it, depending on whom you ask – and we former suitors are called to bring her back.

And I – forger of my own horrific destiny – am called now to war, to lands beyond the sea, to kingdoms and riches I never cared to see nor hold dear to my heart.

A yelp from the bushes to my left brings my focus back to my surroundings. I jump, just a little higher than a king should at the small squeal of a wild animal, and I'm glad there is no one else around to see me. The same bushes wriggle and shake, and a ball of brown fur emerges with a bark. It is a dog, white teeth flashing as she snarls, belly distended, eyes bloodshot and oozing. There are dark marks around her face and ears, deep bloody scratches gouged into her fur.

She is baring her teeth, but not at me – at the grass-colored snake that slithers in her wake.

I fly backwards at the sight of the curling snake. That is one enemy even a clever brain might lose against.

The dog spins to face the snake. She snaps and paws, but the serpent is faster, nipping in at the scruff of tan fur around the dog's neck. It cannot be the first time the fangs sank into this flesh, not when there are so many bloody marks there already.

The dog whimpers.

Honor, I think. My honor. It belongs not just to my wife and son, and to the people of my kingdom. The beasts here have earned it too. And there is the tug to aid the small and helpless. I've known dogs like this – not this particular dog, but other scrappy, playful hunters – and it isn't hard to want to help.

Without a second thought, I draw the short dagger I always carry on my belt. It is a short blade – shorter than I would like when approaching a venomous snake – but I lunge forward all the same. The two creatures are locked together and writhing wildly, but the point of my sword finds its target between the dark green scales of the serpent's back.

A hiss and a scream, and the snake loosens its hold on the mutt. The serpent twitches and shudders on the end of my blade, quivering and dripping scarlet blood, skewered there like a piece of meat. Another moment of wriggling, and the thing goes slack. I flick my wrist to send it flying over the edge of the overhang and out into the sea. It drops before making a tiny splash in the water's surface.

I wipe the snake's blood off my dagger on the hem of my chiton before sliding it back into its sheath. "Come here, girl," I whisper to the dog. Her hackles rise, and she tenses but does not run. Her fur is matted with blood all around her neck. Slowly, I bend my legs so I am closer to the ground, right hand extended, palm up, so she knows I mean no harm. "Let's take a look at you, pretty girl." I wiggle my fingers.

She huffs a little, a breathy sound that isn't quite a complaint, then reaches out a tentative front paw. Her muscles wobble as she approaches. The poor thing is weak and hurting from her fight.

But she is brave yet. Brave, and smart enough to know that I am no snake meaning to kill her. Her brown muzzle shudders, but still she places her little head on my palm. My calloused fingers tickle her fur, and she leans into my touch.

"Good girl," I praise her, letting my other hand come around and probe her injuries. I hope against hope that the blood is a mix of hers and the snake's, but from the way she shakes under my touch, I have doubts. Beneath my hand, her heartbeat flutters like a bird.

The sun glances down through the boughs of an errant tree. The dog's fur turns molten gold in the spray of light. She is a beautiful dog, one I would consider keeping and breeding, if not for her beauty then for the ferocity she showed against the snake. She paws at me then and nibbles my fingers.

"What?" I ask. She digs into the dirt and tugs gently at my thumb. "What do you want?" Rising from the ground but still bending so my hand is in her mouth, I allow myself to be pulled in the direction she wishes. "Where are you taking me, girl?"

She does not, cannot, answer, but together, we circle the bushes from which she and the snake emerged. There, among the sage leaves, is a brown and tan bundle of furs. More dogs. No, I realize as my friend draws me closer, puppies.

One ball of fur, mostly white streaked with dirt, flies from the pile, a low growl exploding from his tiny body. His mother drops my hand and staggers up to him, yipping some words at him I cannot understand. I know many languages, but the tongue of beasts eludes us all. The young one seems to understand her, and he falls into her side, whimpering and crying. I hang back. This is a family drama I am no part of. The mother licks her pup, over and over, from nose to tail, reassuring him until he cuddles up to her and purrs his delight.

It is then that my eyes track to the other pups.

They are a bundle of fur, soft browns, light tans, even a splotch or two of auburn and black.

And they are totally still.

Motionless. Frozen.

I fight the shudder that creeps along my spine. I think of my own little boy, his soft feet and hands always fighting loose of his swaddling, his face plastered with a drooly, toothless grin, red cheeks flushed but joyful.

My son, my beautiful son – he is so full of life. The opposite of these poor beasts.

Kneeling, I reach out to touch them, to roll them one by one on their sides, to reveal the bloody marks left by the serpent on each small body. At his mother's side, the last remaining pup begins to howl.

"Shh," I hiss. "Stay with your mother." Carefully, I check each body. There are four of them. Four small furred things, each only a week or so old, and none will live one day longer.

The pup howls again, and I think of my wife when she leaves our son's side for even a moment, how he sobs and screams until she returns to him, cooing words of love that only a mother can offer. Why does this pup not find comfort in his mother, then, when she is so close?

Realization blooms in me as I turn back, but it is too late to do anything, too late to save her, too late to bring her back. The mother dog has crumpled to the ground. Her side heaves one last, wracking breath, and then she is still. Tangled in her forelegs is the last remaining pup. He is howling sorely now, tiny mouth falling open, needle teeth showing when I reach for him. He is so small to have lost so much this day.

"Quiet, little one," I say. I reach out, and, though he nips my fingers with teeth sharper than the bone needle my wife uses to sew, he allows me to grab him by his scruff and heave him into my arms. He wriggles and tries to free himself for a moment, then calms, and otherwise puts up little fight. I'm not sure that he realizes what has happened to his mother and siblings, but he shivers like a leaf in the wind. I hold him close, and soon he presses back into the heat of my body.

"This is no place for you, little one." I rise, and we pick our way through the scrub and flowers, back to the path that leads up to my home. Though no place is ever truly free of snakes, at least I will be able to see one coming on the dirt path. The last thing this kingdom needs is for its king to die by serpents' venom in a bush like a wild animal. I cannot leave them, not with my son so young, with my wife so vulnerable.

And that is the crux of it all, isn't it? The vow I made now commands that I leave. She cajoles me to stay.

And my heart is stuck in the middle because I do not know which side to follow. My honor, or my family.

In my arms, the little dog's grumble turns into a soft whine. It is so high, he sounds almost like a pot set to boil, and I chuckle in spite of myself and the turmoil in my breast. I pull him even closer. His whine subsides, though I still feel the gentle thrum of him as he vibrates against my ribs. Small, I think, but hearty. I pray someday I can say the same of my own son.

A wind blows in off the sea; instinctively, I cover the little pup's eyes lest sand or grit be blown into them. I feel his needle teeth nibbling on my finger. He doesn't seem angry, just confused. And he is, after all, very young. Once I've extricated my flesh from his mouth, I stroke the top of his head. A fine layer of dirt rubs off, and I see his coat is at once whiter than I first thought and also softer. One ear flops forward over his brow, and he stares up at me somewhat comically. I set to brushing off more dust and dirt as I carry him back towards home. His nose and eyes are the only dark spots on him. The rest is pale white, almost silver, but he is soft as goose down. I dig my fingers into his fur, and just then he is the only thing keeping me here. If it were not for his small but solid form, I might blow away on this briny breeze.

Again, he whines, and I see his round, dark eyes peering up at me. Confusion and sadness fill his face, expressive for an animal. He wonders if his mother will return. She will not. Nor will his brothers or sisters.

Oh gods, do not let this very thing happen to my wife and child. Do not let them grow and live without me. Do not let me lose them, when my wife and I have only just created this wonderful son together.

But the gods do not hear, or at least, they do not reply. I am left, a lonely king holding an orphaned dog in my arms, standing in the dust before my kingdom. The weight of my honor and my obligation to my family settle heavily on my back. Are they like a boulder, made for me to roll and roll uphill without success? Will I always be turned this way and that, torn between my oaths and my desires?

My face burns hot. How could I storm away from my wife, when she only argued the truth with me? I swallow down the turmoil that has formed like a rock in my gullet. Set my feet back past the fields and through the wall of my palace. Servants bow to me, but I ignore all their faces, their eyes, their searching looks. It is not them who deserve an answer first. It is my wife, my Penelope, the mother of my son.

She is still in the gynaikon, which smells like the burning of too much incense. Her deft fingers fly across her loom, like I've seen them do many times before. Only this time, she is ripping out her careful threads, destroying the weft and wends she so painstakingly produced earlier. I rush up to her, not bothering to shake the dust from myself, and grip her narrow wrist with one hand. Only then, when I am holding her frozen, does she turn her eyes from the destruction before her up to me. She startles upon seeing the mewling pup in my other arm.

"What is that?" she asks at the same time I say, "What are you doing?" We both stare at each other, expressions dour, until together, we both burst forth a short laugh.

Penelope is the first one who speaks afterwards. "I hope there's a dog under those fleas," she says, her brow rising archly. She sounds stern, but I know her. She cannot be so disgusted with something so small.

"He is a friend for Telemachus," I reply. I hold the pup out for inspection, and he obliges by stretching his small jaws into a wide, lion-like yawn. "His mother and family are dead of a snake."

My wife shakes her head. She is already gathering the beast into her own arms, cuddling him close, just as she holds our son to her when he wishes to be held.

"And what is this?" I gesture to the ruination hanging from her loom. "Was this not meant for your cousin? Why are you ruining it?"

Flames jump in her eyes, and she clutches the little dog close. "I will not gift anything to her if she cannot convince her husband not to rip you away from us!" Her cousin, Clytemnestra, once close to her as a sister – their relationship sullied because her husband has called me up to war. And I cannot argue. Her logic leads straight to where my own heart treads.

But kings, like me, like Clytemnestra's husband Agamemnon, like hapless Menelaus who lost his wife to that prince of Troy – we lack the luxury of following only our hearts. I suppose I must convince myself of that fact before I can convince Penelope.

"And what need of you have they?" she goes on. "There are a hundred petty lords here, and thousands of soldiers ready to plunge themselves on Trojan spears. Can Agamemnon not find one other such man with a brain like yours?"

I swallow a chuckle. Others spin fair tales of my intellect, and though I consider myself quick-witted, I know I am no one special. But it is my brain, my strategy, my cunning these kings need.

Penelope shifts on her stool, and I kneel at her side, hands going to her lap where she holds the pup. "It is not fair." Her voice has gone soft, light as a cloud, and when I gaze up into her eyes, I see tears there. "I need you here." She holds out the dog I gave her. "*We* need you here." I know she includes our little Telemachus in this need, but he is sleeping in his creche elsewhere, so I bury my face in the dog's fur instead. Penelope leans over me, her loose hair falling around us like a curtain. She smells of lavender and honey. She smells of night air and wind through the olive branches. Of home. My hands clench around hers holding the dog.

"I know," I whisper into the pup's fur. "I know."

We sit like this, bolstered by pounding hearts and the cluck of the dog's tongue as he licks his chops, oblivious to our pain.

They – my wife, my son, this dog – are all so small without me. Not weak, per se, but only able to do so much, in a world where I must lead them as king, as head of the household. I know what it will mean to leave them. To set my crown upon a baby's head while I sail off to a foreign war.

The salt of Penelope's tears runs onto my brow, down my cheek, and into the corner of my mouth. I taste it, and it is bitterer than any words she can throw at me. Salt, that burns away flavor if overused. Salt, that can reduce a healthy plot of land to infertile and dead. If only I could salt the hopes of these foolish kings, I think ruefully.

Salt. It is then I realize I must with all my might try to escape this war. And salt – salt can be my answer.

"What did you say, my love?" I ask. We pull back sharply, both surprised by the calmness of my voice. "What about Agamemnon finding another man with a brain?"

She furrows her brow in thought. "I asked if he could not find another man with a brain like yours. But all these other kings are idiots compared to you. So they think they need your strategic mind to fling themselves at the walls of Troy." Venom laces her tongue, like it did the mouth of that now-dead snake.

"But what if I had no brain?" I ask, words tumbling out before I can even describe my plan. She stares at me in confusion, absently petting the dog's tiny ears. I press on. "What if Agamemnon finds a man without a brain when he comes to Ithaca?"

Her eyes sparkle as she begins to understand. "You will fool him? Into thinking you are daft? And that you can be of no help in his campaign?" She runs a finger along the pup's short snout. "Will that work?"

I shrug. "I know of no better plan," I admit. "I must be mad or dumb or foolish for him to sail for Troy without me." It is a weak hope – barely a shred of a plan – but my heart clings to it all the same. Let the others sail across the sea. Let me remain here among my kin and kingdom.

At last, Penelope smiles. "How?" she asks, all practicality and reason. I explain about the salt, and about our fields that need tilling. How I can make them believe me mad if I salt fields before their eyes, if I plough like a madman with wild and perilous steps. She nods along, snuggling the dog closer and closer. His eyes close, and he lets out an overloud sigh.

"Well, husband, I pray you play the madman well. Now what do you plan to do about this creature?" She holds out the dog. We both pet him, though he is fast asleep now, held tight in both our arms. "Have you named him?"

A grin splits my face. "He shall be called Argos. My handsome little guardian."

Between us two, we hatch out our plan to prove my madness, and we stroke the sleeping dog who knows no more than that he has lost one family but gained another.

I only pray that when Agamemnon and Menelaus land here in Ithaca, they leave here without me, to sail after their wayward women and leave me in peace with my wife, my son, my dog.

Queen of Ithaka

Rayne Hall

The best thing about my husband is that he's disappeared.

Ten years ago, he vanished without a trace. I haven't seen him for twenty years. Odysseus of the auburn hair and red beard. Odysseus, the deceiver, the liar, the cheat. I know he's dead. I feel it in my bones as surely as if I had murdered him myself, and I have proof. But no-one must guess.

The clouds on the horizon darken. A sliver of the sinking sun glints in their folds.

I hitch up my peplos and stride down the olive-groved slope to where the prophet is setting up his performance. At my approach, people rise from their cushions and applaud. "Penelope, Penelope!" as if I were a hired entertainer about to open the evening's show.

A dozen men in expensively dyed garments leave their inlaid chairs and buzz around me like flies around sheep droppings, praising my beauty. "Dark like the moonlit night! Virtuous like Hera herself!"

I ignore them, and direct my smiles to the fishermen and peasant families who sit in clusters on the sun-baked earth, the real people of Ithaka, who are as passionately part of this island country as I am.

I take my seat in the curved-limbed chair and listen to the silvery rustle of the olive trees and the soft suggestive murmur of the distant waves, and wait for the show to begin. I never need to bribe the prophets. I simply promise generous rewards to anyone, seer or sailor, who brings good news of dear Odysseus. This lures them flocking to Ithaka with desirable visions of how my husband is alive though enslaved by some beautiful goddess or demon who can't bear to let him go.

Night descends. The moon is a thin sickle hanging in the sky, the sea a silvery sheet which darkens with every passing of a cloud. Clad in purple, this prophet lights a fire in a grate, then the charcoal in a tripod brazier, with big, unhurried movements. I compose my mask of a hopeful wife praying to have her husband restored.

"Oh Athene, bright-eyed one, mighty mistress of wisdom and war..." he chants. His voice has a pleasant depth to it, and vibrates through the assembly.

A year after we married, Odysseus left for Troy. With my newborn child I waited, and waited, and waited. As the war drew on, year after year, he sent messages enquiring after his son, after our country, and occasionally, after me.

Being queen without a king by my side suited me well. Normally, we queens are reduced to carry the crown to our husbands, and to birthing the next ruler. Power passes down through our line, but we're not allowed to exercise it, unless our husband-kings are away. Odysseus's prolonged absence made me regent and placed the country into my hands. King after king had abused and exploited the land; I restored peace and healed the wounds. For twenty years, I've ruled my country, ancient, sea-washed, goat-grazed Ithaka.

I love Ithaka with a passion Odysseus did not share. He was a pirate who wanted to be king, and so strove to marry a hereditary princess. He'd have preferred a bolder country than Ithaka, and a prettier bride than me. First, he sought to wed Klytemnaistra of Mykene, then Helen of Sparta. When both turned him down, he settled for me and my modest queendom. Once, in the bliss of our embrace in the marriage bed, he cried, "Oooh, Helen!"

The seer wraps his arms around a bunch of bay branches, crushing the leaves. Their sweet, spicy scent envelopes him, and me, and everyone else in the front rows. Then he tosses them on the fire, where they crackle and hiss.

Through the smoke, our eyes meet. For a moment, I feel like he is gazing into my hidden thoughts. But I know that he cannot.

Odysseus has been gone for nearly twenty years. The first ten have been accounted for. He was besieging Troy, committing clever, atrocious deeds. He survived, that's known. I expected him to come back and to grab the cloak of rulership from my shoulders. Instead, he went on a detour. The last reliable reports had him raping and pillaging in the coastal town of Ismara. I was not surprised. It's just what Odysseus would do.

Shortly after, he was killed in a tavern brawl. One of his shipmates brought me the news and his bracelet. I rewarded the man's silence with a fertile farm on Ithaka and kept pretending to await my dear husband's return.

With Odysseus supposedly alive, they can't force me to marry another man, and I continue to rule my beloved Ithaka.

"Odysseus lives," the prophet's deep voice booms. "He will come home."

The crowds clap and cheer. Most believe him. More importantly, everyone believes that I believe. I send smiles of rapture across my features.

I expect him to add something suitably vague, like 'when the gods deem the time is right'. But he says, "Before the moon is full."

A hush falls over the crowd. My heart sinks as if weighted by a stone. When the moon fills and Odysseus hasn't appeared, I will no longer be able to pretend trust in this prophecy.

To stop myself from leaping out of my seat and shaking sense into the seer, I grip the arms of my chair. I fight to keep my mouth shaped into a smile, while my gut roils.

One of the suitors smirks at me from his fleece-clad chair. The smug satisfaction in ambitious Antinous's features tells me he has seen through my pretence. I suspect he has bought this little addition to the prophecy to put me under pressure.

The prophet pours sand on the charcoal brazier and water over the remnants of the fire. The flames die with a hiss. The show is over. The night cools.

I pull my stole tight around me against the increasing darkness, gather the skirts of my peplos, and prepare to stride the short stretch back to the palace. Tension squats like an ugly toad between my shoulder blades.

People assail me with congratulations. Heartfelt by the peasants, sour by most suitors. Foul-tempered because they think their cause lost, my would-be husbands kick at the stray cats and at the beggars lining the path.

I wish I could rid my land of those parasitic suitors, or put them to use while they claim Ithaka's hospitality uninvited.

Yesterday I told them that the grape harvest requires helpers, and the harbour wall needs repair. They looked at me as if I had suggested a human sacrifice. Greek noblemen don't sully themselves with labour.

"Yes, yes," I keep saying, not halting my stride. "I've always known that Odysseus will be back. Yes, it's wonderful that it will happen soon. I can't wait."

The peasants fall back, but a dozen suitors claw at my clothes.

Antinous, aggressive in a vomit-yellow peplos, bars my way. "If Odysseus is not back by full moon, will you admit that all the seers were frauds and that he's dead? Will you marry and give Ithaka the king it deserves?"

People are staring, sucking up every word.

My guts knot into tight coils. I look down on him, which is possible because I am two finger-breadths taller and I am also at least ten years his senior. "I believe in the voice of the divine. The gods will not be mocked. Odysseus will be back."

"Since you're so certain, oh venerated Penelope, you will not mind promising something in case it should be otherwise?"

I feel like a chicken squeezed into a corner of a pen. "If Odysseus is not back by full moon, I shall take a new husband." The hateful voice comes out of my throat, a croak.

Now I have committed myself. Hundreds of Ithakans have heard. Although most of them trust in Odysseus's prophesied return and therefore believe the promise to mean nothing, they will remember when the full moon comes.

With narrow eyes, I gaze into the sky. I can almost see the thin sickle growing. I have very little time left to find a new solution.

Antinous barks orders at the slave who is carrying his heavy ornate chair. "Careful, you clumsy oaf! Give me the footstool, I'll carry that myself."

My sandals clip-clop on the stone slabs. When I reach the vine-clad trellis by the palace entrance, I find the prophet is already there. The purple of his tunic looks darker now, and so does his face. A foreign face, pointed and heavily perfumed. I want to slap him for conspiring with Antinous, but to accuse one seer of fakery would be an admission that I doubted all prophecies. Ever the dutiful hostess, I invite him to dine and sleep at the palace.

"Thank you, luminous lady, but I have already made arrangements for an evening meal and a night's accommodation at the temple."

While we wait for my servant to fetch the prepared reward, the prophet looks over the men who have harassed me. "All this will not last much longer." His dark eyes bore into mine. "You will know what to do. I bid you goodnight, lady."

Several suitors try to push through the entrance arch. Antinous uses his footstool like a shield to ram his way in.

"Go home!" I tell them. "I don't want you here." There was a time when I had entertained my would-be husbands at dinner, politely, patiently, but they have long exceeded their welcome. I may acquire a reputation of lacking hospitality, but I have had enough. These men have been pursuing me for months. I wish I need not see their faces ever again. Yet I will have to marry one of them, soon. Nausea washes through me, drenches me in bitterness.

Their fury overflows and pours over the nearest victim, a beggar cowering behind the trellis. "Useless parasite! How dare you impose your presence at the palace!"

Under their kicks and curses, the beggar curls up like a dying dog.

I wince at the abuse, then step in. "Stop it! This man is my guest."

They let off. "Your guest, lady? This filthy creature?"

"Yes. Come, beggar, join me for a meal. I prefer your company to theirs."

The beggar uncurls. A cloud of insects rises with him. Aren't flies meant to be asleep at this time? His chest is bare, like that of a philosopher. A grimy ribbon holds his felted hair.

"You are most gracious, lady," he whispers. I can barely hear his voice in the forest of sneers.

"If you prefer his kind, you deserve him," Antinous shouts. He hits his footstool into the beggar's back.

I pull the beggar, and myself, to safety inside.

"Get him a bath," I instruct the hovering servants. Since they are new slaves who haven't learnt much Greek yet, I repeat my instructions, pronouncing every word separately. "Beggar. Bath. Wash. Clothes. New. Now."

When I take my seat on my couch in the megaron – a signal that I want to eat, which even the non-Greek slaves understand – I hear water splashing in the adjoining chamber. I picture the beggar squatting in the big clay bowl, and a slave pouring water over him. I hope they get the pig stink out of his hair, or I won't enjoy my dinner.

A smell of hot olive oil, mingled with the scents of sage and rosemary, wafts into the room. The food is ready.

"Lady? May I enter?"

I turn my head towards the door, and halt mid-motion. The man looks like Odysseus. The same height. The auburn tint in his now-washed hair.

My mind reels with shock. I clutch my couch for support. Then I realise it is an illusion.

It is not Odysseus. A superficial resemblance existed only in my overwrought mind. I take a deep breath to slow my racing heart. The shape of the chin is wrong, the swing of the eyebrows, the tilt of his eyes.

It's mostly the clothes that fooled me. He's wearing Odysseus's favourite house garment, a short red peplos edged with ochre. Anyone would look like Odysseus in that. The servants – I really need to train them properly – have taken it from the chest where I keep Odysseus's clothes, instead of from the upstairs store of hospitality gifts.

Courteously, as if he was indeed a respected dinner guest, I direct him to the couch at the opposite wall, and clap my hands to order food. One of the Egyptian girls comes in, a pale apron-scarf wrapped around her torso, carrying a wicker tray piled with platters. In confusion, she looks from one end of the room to the other. I can almost hear her thoughts as she tries to work out whom to serve first: queen hostess or beggar guest.

I point to my guest. Obediently, she loads the low table before him. Smoked mackerel on a bed of bay leaves. Ithakan olives, pickled, black. Goat cheeses. Figs from the island's southern slopes, sweeter than those found anywhere else in Greece or beyond. The girl swishes out to fetch another tray for me. She's a good worker, and once she learns the Greek language and Greek etiquette, she'll be useful here on Ithaka.

My mind keeps revolving around my predicament. For the moment, I have gained peace, but that will last only until the full moon. Nineteen nights. Then all of Ithaka will realise the prophecy was false, and at the same time lose belief in all other prophecies. They will expect me to keep my promise and wed.

If I do…not only will I become subject to a man again, but Ithaka will suffer under a king. I have been a good queen. I have kept my little island country prosperous and safe. The suitors who pester me want to get at the treasury, to live a life in idle luxury at the expense of the working people.

I toss a handful of incense on the brazier, so that the sweet scent may wrap me in comfort.

The beggar sits still, legs crossed on the couch. His eyes lick at the viands, but he does not touch them. He looks at me, imploring me to start eating. He obviously comes from a place where the host takes the first bite. His throat moves frequently, swallowing the saliva that is running in his mouth. I admire his discipline.

I release him. "Please, start eating. It is the custom for the guest to eat first."

"Thank you, my lady. I apologise for keeping you waiting." He grabs the brown bread greedily, then remembers piety and puts it back. "Thanks be to the goddesses for their gifts. Demeter and Persephone be praised." Prayers done, he rips at bread with his teeth. He stuffs a whole mackerel into his mouth, head and tail and all. His hands hurry to fulfil the demands of his stomach. Now the limp legs of a squid dangle from his mouth while he chews the body. When he becomes aware that I am watching, he slows.

I bask in his appreciation and gratitude. From now on, I will invite a poor person to dine with me every day. Beggars, or fishermen, or peasants who work the hard-baked soil of Ithaka.

When I look at my dinner companion again, he is sitting straight, serene. In the space of heartbeats he has changed from a cowering vagabond to a guest with aristocratic manners. His movements show grace and restraint, and his smile holds self-assured charm as if he regularly dined with royalty.

I nibble at a sprig of rosemary. Its tough leaves taste pleasant on my tongue. I play with the other herbs on my plate, fingering the bay leaves, the thyme. It's their scents I like, sweet and spicy and vaguely comforting. The smells of Ithaka.

My mind travels over the suitors, all thirty-seven of them, the peasants and the princes and the peasants pretending to be princes; the Ithakans, the mainlanders, the foreigners. Not all are as brutal and repulsive as Antinous, and some might learn to love and serve Ithaka. But whoever I marry, the others will not accept it. They will feel slighted, and robbed of their prospect. They will make war.

When Odysseus took all the adult males with him to war against Troy, the economy collapsed, and we women restored it with our common sense and hard work. A war on Ithaka's soil would tear the country apart, leave it bleeding to death.

For a fleeting moment I think of escape, of either tossing myself off a cliff or of fleeing in a ship. But neither will save Ithaka, because I have no daughter to succeed me. All I have is a useless son, at nineteen still so immature I wouldn't entrust him with the rule even if a boy could inherit.

Whoever I marry, I will bring war to this island. The only man they would all accept as king is Odysseus, if he were still alive.

Even when I was fifteen, and everyone urged me to marry, I didn't want a husband. My dying mother recommended that the pirate Odysseus would be a good person to protect Ithaka's sea trade, and I gave in. I soon regretted it and I contemplated divorce, but other men were just as bad. Odysseus solved the problem for me by going off to war.

"Tell me a story, beggar. Tell me about life outside Ithaka." It is the custom that guests entertain their hosts with tales from the world beyond. I want to be entertained, distracted. Perhaps, if he amuses me, I will feel better by the time I go to bed. Time enough to worry about my problem tomorrow, when there will still be eighteen days left.

"I have no strong voice for storytelling, not any more, lady, but I will try to oblige. I once met the cunning Odysseus…" he begins. Most visitors claim to have news from Odysseus, believing that their tales will please me and earn them generous guest-gifts. Though they've never met him, they spin vivid fantasies about his adventures, tales of battles and shipwrecks, of sea snakes and sorceresses.

Fantastic tales about Odysseus are the last thing I want to hear about tonight. "Talk of something different. Your own life. How did you come to be a beggar?"

"I lost my voice, that's what happened."

"Tell me, if it is not too hard for you. Your fate may take my mind off my own worries."

I expect him to say, 'What worries can you have, lady, now that you may rejoice in your husband's return?' but he doesn't.

He picks up an olive, holds it before his eyes as if contemplating its black wrinkliness, then pushes it into his mouth. He spits the stone on the floor.

"I was an actor," he says in a raspy whisper. "In Crete. My voice flowed like liquid gold and flew through the air like an owl. I played all the main roles. In every play, I wore the mask of the gods, of the heroes. People thronged to kiss the hem of my peplos. Kings and princes were my lovers." He pauses to take a deep drink from his wine cup, and also, I think, to gauge whether his reference to male lovers would shock me.

I find my pleasures in the arms of women, and I don't care where other people seek theirs.

I abandon my couch and carry my favourite inlaid chair closer to him, so that he doesn't need to strain his voice so much. I believe his story. He's an actor of skill. I've seen his transformation from lowly beggar to noble guest.

"Until you lost your voice," I said. "Continue."

"Perhaps it was hubris, and a god grew jealous of my fame; perhaps I was simply a fool. I pitched one lover against another. One man sneaked into my chamber when I was with another. A fight ensued, a dagger found my throat." He brings his hand to his throat, as if to protect it from another stab. "The wound healed. I even learnt to speak again, eventually. But I never regained the voice that would fill an auditorium."

"I'm sorry," I say inadequately. I watch the Egyptian girl kneel on the tiled floor, blending more water and wine, carefully measuring the quantities with the bronze dipper into painted bowl, the way I taught her. She knows I like my wine thin; I haven't yet told her to make it stronger for my guests. It's a golden wine from the slopes of Ithaka, resinous, earthy.

The beggar holds out his painted cup for the girl to refill, but he looks at me. "Without my far-reaching voice, I could not perform. I'm a beggar now. I've almost forgotten I ever had another life."

This man has travelled much, he has seen much, he has experienced suffering. Suddenly I feel the need to speak, to let the secrets bubble from my lidded soul. I have too much sense to expose my secrets, but I need to lift the lid a little or I will burst.

"Do you believe in prophecies?" I ask.

"I do believe that prophecies are true when they are spoken," he croaks. "But we are not bound by them. I received a prophecy once, when I was just a boy, beginning my career on stage. The seer told me that I was to have a great future, that I would be the most famous actor of my time. That kings and princes would be my lovers..." He breaks open a fig, contemplates its pink insides, and eats first one half, then the other. He seems to savour the fig's flavour long after he has swallowed it, but his hand already reaches for the grapes. "He also said that I would live my old age in riches and fame, celebrated and admired. I believe that all this was true when the seer said it, but I ruined it. I chose a lifestyle that was careless, that spilled the precious gift the way dropping an amphora spills good wine."

I think over what he is saying. It seems meaningful, and yet not relevant to my situation. His actions averted a true prophecy; whereas I have to deal with an untrue one. Unless I can make my people believe that something happened to stop Odysseus from returning on scheduled time, I am at the mercy of the suitors.

An idea flashes through me. Can I, by my actions, validate an untrue prophecy? I grasp the unformed thought before it can escape.

If Odysseus returns, Ithaka and I will be safe from the suitors. People expect Odysseus because the prophet said so.

A man would change much in twenty years. He would age, sustain injuries. Few Ithakans alive have ever known Odysseus closely. His friends died at Troy. His own son was a baby. Only I knew him well, and even I was nearly fooled by a man wearing his tunic. It would be just like Odysseus to come home in disguise, wouldn't it?

I study my guest carefully. He's an actor who has, before my eyes, changed from helpless beggar to proud nobleman. Could he go further?

Raising my wine cup, I tempt him. "Your prophecy may still come true, if you allow it. Fame, adoration, wealth."

He returns my gaze calmly. "Are you offering me a role, lady?"

"Yes. To play a great hero for the rest of your life."

He selects and plucks another grape. "Would that be a royal role?" His voice is grave: he comprehends.

"Under certain conditions," I hasten to say.

He wipes his bowl with the remaining piece of bread. "I have no inclination towards bedding a woman, and no ambitions towards politics. Adoration and wealth are my only desires."

I see no movement, yet his posture has changed. He sits on the couch as if it were a throne, oozing dignity. He's good.

Relief sweeps through me. "Athena be praised! But you'll want time to think before you commit yourself."

"I have no desire to become a beggar again. I am at your service now, lady."

I award him a dignified smile, then fling myself at his knees and clutch his legs. "Odysseus!" I cry so loudly that the kitchen slaves will hear me. "Odysseus! Odysseus."

When the girls dash into the room, gasping and jabbering, I swear them to secrecy until the official announcement tomorrow. This will ensure that the gossip will be carried all over Ithaka at once, and believed by everyone.

Tonight I'll teach my actor friend about this country, briefing him for his role. Tomorrow, when rose-fingered dawn takes her golden throne, I'll announce that the prophet has spoken truly, and that my beloved husband has returned.

The Archivist of Ithaca

Jovel Royal

CHAPTER ONE: THE WHISPER OF SCROLLS

The olive trees of Ithaca whispered in the wind, their silver leaves rustling like parchment. Beneath them, in the cool stone belly of the Royal Archive, Callianeira moved like a shadow. She was the youngest scribe in the kingdom, barely twenty, with ink-stained fingers and a mind that refused to settle.

She had grown up on the songs.

Odysseus the cunning. Odysseus the brave. Odysseus who defied gods and monsters, who returned after twenty years to reclaim his throne and his wife. The bards sang of him in the market square, in the palace halls, in the lullabies of children.

But the scrolls told a different story.

Callianeira had spent the last three years cataloging the Archive's oldest texts – some written by royal scribes, others by sailors, servants, and forgotten scholars. She began to notice discrepancies. Dates that didn't align. Names that vanished. Entire voyages that appeared in one account and disappeared in another.

And always, Odysseus at the center – heroic, untouchable, mythic.

Too perfect.

She started a private ledger, hidden beneath her cot in the scribe's quarters. She called it *The Discrepancies of Odysseus*. It was forbidden work. The Archive was sacred. The myth was law.

But Callianeira had questions.

The First Crack

It began with a scroll attributed to Theon, a minor sailor on the *Odysseia*. His account of the Cyclops differed wildly from the official version. He described Polyphemus not as a monstrous brute, but as a blind hermit who begged for food and offered shelter.

Odysseus, Theon wrote, mocked him. Provoked him. Blinded him not in defense, but in cruelty.

Callianeira read the scroll three times.

She cross-referenced it with the royal version, penned by the court poet Lysandros. In that version, Odysseus was noble, strategic, merciful. Theon's scroll had been buried in the 'miscellaneous' section, nearly crumbling from neglect.

She added it to her ledger.

The Forbidden Shelf

Late one night, she ventured into the restricted wing of the Archive – a place reserved for royal eyes and sanctioned scribes. She had memorized the guard's schedule, timed her steps to the rhythm of his patrol.

There, she found a scroll labeled *Penelope's Reflections*.

Her breath caught.

She unrolled it slowly, hands trembling. The handwriting was elegant, precise, unmistakably regal.

"He returns with stories. I return with silence."

"He speaks of monsters. I speak of loneliness."

"He is praised. I am erased."

Callianeira felt the words like a blade.

Penelope had waited twenty years – not in faith, but in fury. She had played her part for Ithaca, for Telemachus, for survival. But she had known. She had seen through the myth.

Callianeira copied the scroll by hand, then returned it to its shelf.

She added a new section to her ledger: *The Silenced Queen*.

The Archivist's Oath

The next morning, she stood before the Head Archivist, a stooped man named Dorion who had served three kings and forgotten more history than most would ever learn.

He eyed her with suspicion. "You've been wandering."

"I've been reading," she replied.

He narrowed his gaze. "The Archive preserves glory, not gossip."

Callianeira met his eyes. "Then it preserves nothing."

Dorion said nothing. But that night, she found her cot stripped and a note etched into her door: *Truth is not welcome here.*

Thankfully she had been one step ahead. She rifled through her satchel, her fingers brushing past scraps of parchment and a broken quill. At last, tucked deep beneath the lining, the familiar weight of the ledger pressed against her palm. Relief washed over her as she drew it out, the leather cover worn but intact.

The Olive Grove

She walked to the olive grove at dawn, scrolls tucked beneath her cloak. The trees swayed gently, their roots deep in Ithaca's soil. She sat beneath the oldest one, its trunk twisted like a question.

She opened her ledger.

She began to write again.

"Odysseus is not a god. He is a man.

And men lie.

But scrolls whisper.

And I will listen."

CHAPTER TWO: THE SAILOR'S SILENCE

The hills above Ithaca were quiet in the late afternoon, the sea a silver ribbon in the distance. Callianeira climbed the winding path alone, scrolls tucked beneath her cloak, her sandals coated in dust. She had heard whispers in the Archive – of a man who had sailed with Odysseus, who had returned broken, silent, and forgotten.

His name was Eurylochus.

He lived in a crumbling cottage surrounded by olive trees and silence. No bard sang of him. No statue bore his likeness. But Callianeira believed he held something more valuable than glory.

He held truth.

The Meeting

Eurylochus opened the door slowly, his eyes clouded with age, his hands twisted like driftwood. He studied her for a long moment before speaking.

"You're not from the palace."

"I'm from the Archive," Callianeira said. "I'm seeking clarity."

He laughed – a dry, bitter sound. "Then you've come to the wrong man. I have only memory."

"That's what I need."

He gestured her inside.

The Cyclops Revisited

They sat by the hearth, the fire low, the air thick with the scent of old herbs and salt. Callianeira unrolled a scroll.

"The Cyclops," she said. "Polyphemus."

Eurylochus stared into the flames. "He was blind already. We didn't blind him. He begged for food. Odysseus mocked him."

"But the songs—"

"Are lies," he snapped. "Odysseus needed a monster. So he made one."

Callianeira's hand trembled as she wrote.

Circe's Truth

"And Circe?" she asked.

Eurylochus's face softened. "She was no enchantress. She was a healer. She treated our wounds. She fed us. She taught us to speak with birds."

Callianeira blinked. "But Odysseus—"

"Left her pregnant," he said. "She begged him to stay. He told her he had a kingdom to reclaim."

She added it to her ledger: *Circe – The Forgotten Healer*.

The Island of Silence

Eurylochus spoke of an island not found on any map – Thrinacia, where the crew had slaughtered sacred cattle out of desperation. Odysseus had blamed them in every version of the tale.

But Eurylochus whispered, "He ordered it.

"He said the gods would forgive him. He needed food for the journey home. We begged him to reconsider. He threatened to leave us behind."

Callianeira felt her chest tighten.

The songs had painted Odysseus as a reluctant witness.

But he had been the architect.

The Weight of Memory

Eurylochus grew quiet.

"I've carried these truths for decades," he said. "But no one wanted them. They wanted the hero. The clever king. The man who defied fate."

Callianeira looked at him. "I want the man."

He smiled, tears in his eyes. "Then write. And don't stop."

The Ledger Grows

That night, Callianeira returned to the Archive.

She lit a candle, opened her ledger, and wrote for hours. She added new sections:

- *The Cyclops – A Blind Hermit*
- *Circe – The Forgotten Healer*
- *Thrinacia – The Ordered Slaughter*

She did not hide her work.

She placed it on her desk.

And waited.

CHAPTER THREE: THE QUEEN'S LAMENT

The Royal Archive was silent, but not still.

Callianeira moved through its corridors like a ghost, her fingers trailing along the spines of scrolls that had outlived kings. The ledger she had begun – *The Discrepancies of Odysseus* – was growing heavier with each entry. Eurylochus's testimony had cracked the foundation. Now she sought the voice most absent from the myth: Penelope.

The queen had waited twenty years for Odysseus's return. The songs praised her loyalty, her weaving, her silence. But silence, Callianeira knew, was not the absence of thought.

It was the burial of it.

The Hidden Chamber

She found the entrance behind a tapestry in the eastern wing – a faded image of Odysseus slaying suitors, his face carved in triumph. Behind it, a narrow passage led to a locked door. The key was hidden in a hollowed-out scroll tube labeled *Domestic Accounts – Linen Inventory*.

Inside the chamber, dust hung like memory.

There were no gold-framed portraits, no polished marble. Just a writing desk, a shelf of journals, and a single oil lamp still half-filled.

Callianeira lit it.

The flame flickered, casting shadows across the first journal's cover: *Year Seven – The Waiting Begins*.

Penelope's Voice

The handwriting was elegant, deliberate, but the words bled.

"They sing of my weaving. They do not sing of my unraveling."

"I waited, yes. But not for him. I waited for silence to end."

"Every thread I pulled was a prayer. Not for his return, but for my own."

Callianeira read for hours.

Penelope wrote of the suitors – not as threats, but as mirrors. Men who came not for love, but for power. She wrote of Telemachus, growing without a father, asking questions she could not answer.

She wrote of Odysseus's letters – sporadic, cryptic, full of riddles and half-truths.

"He writes of monsters. I write of meals."

"He writes of gods. I write of grief."

The Queen's Ledger

One journal was different.

It was a ledger – like Callianeira's. Penelope had tracked inconsistencies in Odysseus's tales. She had compared his letters to the royal records, noting contradictions in dates, locations, even names.

"He claims to have fought at Troy for ten years. But the war ended in six."

"He names a crew of twelve. But only five are listed in the palace rolls."

"He speaks of Circe as a witch. But her name appears in the healer's registry."

Callianeira felt her breath catch.

Penelope had known.

She had seen through the myth.

But she had played her part – for Ithaca, for Telemachus, for survival.

The Unspoken Rebellion

In the final journal, Penelope wrote of Odysseus's return.

"He came home with blood on his hands and stories in his mouth."

"He kissed me like a stranger. He held Telemachus like a trophy."

"He asked for songs. I gave him silence."

She described the night he returned – how the palace erupted in celebration, how the bards composed new verses, how the people wept with joy.

And how she wept alone.

"They say I was faithful. I say I was forgotten."

"They say he is clever. I say he is cruel."

"They say we are reunited. I say we are rewritten."

The Archivist's Reckoning

Callianeira copied every page by hand.

She returned to her ledger and added a new section: *The*

Silenced Queen. She did not edit Penelope's words. She did not interpret them. She let them stand.

She placed the copied journal beside her own.

And for the first time, she felt the weight of what she was doing.

She was not just questioning a hero.

She was resurrecting a woman.

The Candlelit Confrontation

That evening, the Head Archivist Dorion entered her chamber without knocking. He saw the journals, the ledger, the candle burning low.

"You found them," he said.

"I listened," she replied.

He sat beside her, older than the scrolls, tired in a way that ink could not record.

"She was the Archive's first patron," he said. "But she asked to be forgotten."

Callianeira frowned. "Why?"

"Because truth is not always safe."

She looked at him. "But it is always sacred."

Dorion nodded.

And left her in silence.

CHAPTER FOUR: THE MAP OF LIES

The Archive's master map of Odysseus's journey was a masterpiece.

Etched in gold leaf, framed in cedar, and mounted in the Hall of Triumph, it depicted the king's voyage in sweeping arcs: Troy to Ismarus, past the Lotus Eaters, through the Cyclops's cave, across Circe's isle, down to the Underworld, and finally home to Ithaca. Every location was marked with a symbol of conquest – a sword, a crown, a flame.

Callianeira had studied it since childhood.

But now, she no longer believed it.

The Forgotten Draft

She found the original draft buried in the cartography vault, mislabeled as *Trade Routes – Obsolete*. It was faded, water-stained, and incomplete – but unmistakably older than the gilded version.

And it was different.

Entire islands were missing. Others were renamed. The route was altered to avoid Troy's shame, to hide the years spent in exile, to erase the massacre at Thrinacia.

One location – Asteria – was circled in red ink, but absent from the official map. Asteria had been a penal colony, a place of exile and silence. No songs mentioned it. No scrolls recorded it.

But the draft did.

Callianeira's hands trembled.

Odysseus had rewritten his own legend.

The Cartographer's Confession

She sought out the royal cartographer, an old woman named Thaleia who had retired to a vineyard near the coast. Thaleia greeted her with wine and weariness.

"I knew someone would come," she said.

Callianeira showed her the draft. "Did you draw this?"

Thaleia nodded. "Before the coronation. Before the songs."

"Why was it changed?"

Thaleia looked out at the sea. "Because truth is jagged. Glory is smooth. The king wanted a map that sang."

Callianeira frowned. "But this is history."

Thaleia smiled sadly. "No, child. This is memory. And memory is a kingdom ruled by the loudest voice."

The Missing Records

Back in the Archive, Callianeira began cross-referencing the map with the royal logs. She found gaps – entire years unaccounted for, crew members listed as dead who had never sailed, letters from Odysseus that contradicted his own speeches.

She discovered a scroll marked *Odysseus – Personal Correspondence*, sealed with wax and buried beneath tax records. Inside were letters written in his own hand – raw, unedited, and deeply human.

"I do not know who I am any more."

"I have lied so long I fear the truth would kill me."

"I miss the silence of Asteria. No songs. No eyes."

Callianeira felt her chest tighten.

Odysseus had not returned triumphant.

He had returned curated.

The Archivist's Dilemma

She stood before the master map in the Hall of Triumph, her

ledger clutched in her hands. Tourists passed by, pointing at the golden arcs, reciting verses from the bards.

She saw children tracing the route with their fingers.

She saw elders bowing in reverence.

She saw a lie.

And she saw a choice.

The Quiet Rebellion

That night, Callianeira placed a copy of the original map beside the official one. She did not announce it. She did not seek permission. She let it speak.

The next morning, scribes gathered.

They whispered.

They compared.

They questioned.

And slowly, the Hall of Triumph became a hall of truth.

CHAPTER FIVE: THE HERO'S MASK

The villa by the sea was quiet.

Callianeira stood at the gate, her ledger tucked beneath her arm, the wind tugging at her cloak. Olive trees lined the path, their branches heavy with fruit, their roots tangled like memory. The house was modest – stone walls, a tiled roof, a single column carved with waves.

She had sent a request for an audience.

The reply had come in Odysseus's own hand:

Come. If you seek truth, be prepared to lose comfort.

She stepped inside.

The King in Winter

Odysseus sat on a wooden bench beneath a fig tree, a cup of wine in one hand, a scroll in the other. He looked up as she approached – his eyes sharp, his beard silver, his posture still regal.

"You're the archivist," he said.

"I am."

He gestured to the seat beside him. "Sit. Speak."

Callianeira sat, heart pounding. She opened her ledger and placed it between them.

"I've been studying your journey," she said. "The scrolls. The maps. The letters."

He nodded. "And?"

"There are discrepancies."

He smiled. "Of course there are."

The Ledger Unfolds

She began to read.

The Cyclops – already blind, begging for food.

Circe – a healer, not a witch.

Thrinacia – the slaughter ordered, not defied.

Asteria – the exile erased from every map.

Odysseus listened, sipping his wine, never interrupting.

She continued.

Penelope's journals – her grief, her fury, her silence.

The forged maps. The missing years. The letters of doubt.

When she finished, the silence was thick.

Odysseus leaned back. "You've done well."

She blinked. "You admit it?"

He chuckled. "I admit nothing. I only admire your cleverness."

The Philosophy of Myth

Callianeira's voice trembled. "You lied."

Odysseus turned to her, eyes gleaming. "I survived."

She frowned. "You built a myth on the bones of truth."

He nodded. "And it kept Ithaca alive."

Callianeira stood. "You rewrote history."

Odysseus stood too. "I curated memory."

She stepped closer. "You erased people."

He met her gaze. "I gave them a story."

The Mask Slips

Odysseus walked to the edge of the cliff, the sea roaring below.

"I was a man among gods," he said. "A mortal in a world that demanded legends. So I became one."

Callianeira followed. "At what cost?"

He looked out at the horizon. "At every cost."

She opened her ledger. "Then let the truth be known."

He turned to her. "Truth is a blade. Use it wisely."

The Final Question

Callianeira hesitated. "Why did you return?"

Odysseus smiled, but it didn't reach his eyes.

"Because I missed the lies."

She stared at him.

He continued. "Out there, I was a man. Here, I am a myth. And myths live longer."

The Archivist's Reckoning

That night, Callianeira returned to the Archive.

She placed her ledger on the central table. She did not hide it. She did not encrypt it. She let it breathe.

The scribes gathered. They read. They whispered. They wept.

A new section was added to the Archive: *The Hero's Mask*.

It did not erase Odysseus.

It complicated him.

It made him human.

And in doing so, it made Ithaca whole.

CHAPTER SIX: THE TRUTH BENEATH THE OLIVE GROVE

The olive grove was quiet at dawn.

Callianeira stood beneath the oldest tree, its trunk gnarled like a question, its roots deep in Ithaca's soil. The ledger in her hands felt heavier than ever – not with ink, but with consequence. She had uncovered the truth. She had heard the voices buried beneath the songs. Now she had to decide what to do with them.

The Archive waited.

The kingdom watched.

And the myth trembled.

The Council of Scribes

The Royal Archive's central chamber was filled with light and silence. Callianeira stood before the Council of Scribes – elders in robes of parchment hue, their faces lined with years of preservation, not interrogation.

She placed her ledger on the table.

"I have compiled testimonies, letters, maps, and journals," she said. "They contradict the official record. They complicate the myth."

The Head Archivist Dorion studied her. "And what do you propose?"

"That we publish it."

Murmurs rippled through the chamber.

One scribe, old and stern, leaned forward. "You would tarnish our greatest hero?"

Callianeira met his gaze. "I would humanize him."

Another whispered, "You would divide the kingdom."

She replied, "Or heal it."

The Debate

The council debated for hours.

Some argued for preservation – "The myth is our foundation."

Others for revelation – "The truth is our future."

Dorion remained silent.

Callianeira listened, her heart steady, her mind sharp. She knew the risk. She knew the cost. But she also knew the weight of silence.

She had read Penelope's grief.

She had heard Eurylochus's pain.

She had seen Odysseus's weariness.

And she had felt her own fire.

The Decision

At sunset, Dorion rose.

He walked to the ledger, opened it, and read a single line aloud:

"Truth is a blade. Use it wisely."

He closed the book.

Then he said, "Let it be published."

The chamber fell silent.

Callianeira exhaled.

The myth would not be erased.

It would be expanded.

The People Speak

The ledger was copied and distributed across Ithaca – scroll by scroll, word by word. It reached the palace, the market, the schools, the temples. People read. People wept. People argued.

Some rejected it – "Odysseus was a hero. This is slander."

Others embraced it – "He was flawed. That makes him real."

Murals changed. Songs evolved. Children asked new questions.

And Penelope's voice was finally heard.

The Olive Ceremony

A month later, Ithaca held a ceremony beneath the olive grove. Callianeira stood beside Dorion, the ledger in her hands, the people gathered in a circle.

She spoke:

"We were raised on songs of glory.

But glory without truth is hollow.

Odysseus was brave. He was also broken.

Penelope was patient. She was also powerful.

Eurylochus was loyal. He was also silenced.

We are not here to destroy the myth.

We are here to complete it."

She placed the ledger at the base of the tree.

The people sang – not of conquest, but of complexity.

The Legacy

Years passed.

Callianeira became Head Archivist.

The Archive changed – no longer a vault of perfection, but a living record of nuance. New scribes were trained to question, to listen, to preserve not just the polished, but the painful.

Odysseus's statue remained in the square.

But beside it stood a new one – Penelope, scroll in hand, eyes forward.

And beneath both, a plaque:

Truth is not the enemy of legend.

It is its soul.

EPILOGUE: THE WHISPER OF SCROLLS

Callianeira sat beneath the olive tree, older now, her fingers still ink-stained. A young scribe approached, scroll in hand.

"Is it true?" the girl asked. "That Odysseus lied?"

Callianeira smiled.

“He told stories,” she said. “And so do we.”

The girl frowned. “But how do we know what’s real?”

Callianeira looked up at the branches swaying above.

“We listen,” she said. “And we write. And we remember.”

The wind whispered through the leaves.

And the Archive lived on.

Voyage Through Wine-Dark Space

Sara Itka

Space has been a muse for bards through eternities, from twinkling stars sheltered in its folds, to planets and moons shepherded along their paths. Colors painted the patterns of their words in nebulae and novae. They sang of looking out at the infinite worlds, and knowing you're not alone.

They never sang about the vast nothingness spreading between stars, left in the wakes of planets and moons. How long cold months leeched into your bones and bleached your skin. The bards of old never sang about looking out at the infinity of wine-dark space, and knowing no one would ever find you.

Ten years.

They never found my father.

"Mach?"

Space presses on the cockpit of the *INS Argos*, making the glass feel like a casket. But I'm not here to die, no matter how hard Mom hugged me goodbye eleven months ago. I even did as she asked and retrofitted one of Father's old pentacont-class ships with the newest safety and astropositioning technology before I borrowed it. She's not going to lose me like she lost Father. And if my calculations are correct, and the training I devoted half of my nearly eighteen years to proves true, she'll get us both back.

"Mach?"

Shaking my head from the vastness of infinite space, I meet the gray eye icon blinking from my control screen.

"Sorry, Athena. I was lost in thought. What is it?"

Her smooth robotic voice crackles through the sound system. "Incoming ring from an alien sourcetone. How do you respond?"

"Alien? Or unknown?" The only sourcetones Athena would recognize are for Mom, Grandpa, and Eumaeus, my flying teacher. "Does it have an Ithacan origin?"

"Indeed an Ithacan code, it is. But I believe it not Ithacan origin."

I tap my console, fiberglass gloves thudding the titanium. A tick, one Mom says I got from my father. I wouldn't know; he was called to the Illiadic wars when I was two.

Admiral Jul Essey of the flagship *Polytropos* led the Hellenist Imperium's fleet to interstellar battle with the Troyegenics Corporation, and secured control of the Discord Communications servers. News of the war's end reached Ithaca when I was seven, strangled by Mom's hugs on a night tears of relief flowed free as the wine.

Ten years.

"Mach?"

I sit up in my seat, grabbing the receiver to my ear. "Answer." It clicks as the call connects.

Static. Fuzzy noise garbled with reverberant, dissonant droning. I focus on the cacophonic patterns twisting until a high-pitched beeping emerges, the staccato almost imperceptible amidst the yawning rhythms. Three short. Three long. Three short.

Morse code. An ancient communication method every pilot learns in case all other systems fail. And that's the first series we memorize.

S.O.S.

I meet the gray eye of Athena. "Can we track the call?"

"Positive."

I curl the receiver into my neck, clutching the distress call close. I don't know my father is on the other side, but it's the closest I've come in months of drifting through the cosmos, scouring debris fields and satellites left derelict by the echoes of battles a decade past. This signal connects me to my father, as much as this ship which used to be his, or the pre-war backup of his personal AI. Though all those connections are equally hazy, warped by space and time.

Wisdom would advise me to keep my expectations low. But even if Mom claims I have my father 's acumen, I can't consider failure. My calculations of gravitational drift over time place him in this sector. But more so, I *feel* him, waiting beyond a space-scrambled call.

I swing down the navigational viewscreen. "Prepare for stellarwind travel." The navscreen gives a pitchy whine, but stays dark.

"Navigable settings are programmed to autoguide interval thrusters."

"Thank you, Athena." Bracing in my seat, I thump the side of the navscreen. It whines, but flickers on. Light floods the glass, overlaying the stars with names, and partitioning the infinite space with green lines guiding pitch, roll, and yaw – with an extra line for the jagged scratch across the corner.

Like most non-essential equipment on the *Argos*, it's in dire need of replacement. If I were less sentimental for this hunk of debris, I'd acquire a new ship. Jupiter knows any of the investors would've happily gifted me one to get me offworld and help me chase my fool's mission to my death. None of them believe I'll find my father any other way.

But missing in action isn't dead. Spontaneous loss of signal isn't dead. Disappearing without a trace for ten years since the battle was won and the rest of the imperial fleet returned home isn't dead.

"Mark coordinates."

A blinking gray eye appears on my viewscreen.

"Stellarwind navlocked on sourcetone in retrophase—"

"A simple 'positive' would've done." I shouldn't snap at her. It's not her fault her programmers decided it would be pleasant to make her speak in dactyllic hexameter. But I don't have patience for another five syllables of stress. Not when my father is waiting.

Throwing the thruster, I blow open the windbag, hurtling the *Argos* into stellarwind force. I slam back in my seat as the silver stars blur to streaks against the wine-dark space. Receiver pressed to my ear, I drift in the reverberant echoes, gloves stretching as I tap the rhythm thrumming under my skin. *S.O.S.*

* * *

Pale gold clouds and verdant methane seas flood my cockpit with Ogygia's planetshine as I drop into orbit. I swing away my navscreen and flick out the altitude panel – thirty-five thousand kilometers and descending. The planet's gravity pulls my controls as the *Argos* falls around it, green seas glowing above. So different from the yawning blue of Ithaca, the distance strikes like a sharplight sword.

I took my pilot's test the day I turned seventeen, and left the next morning. No time to dwell on what I'd miss. Besides Mom, I haven't found anything in the eleven months since. Not the other officer's children who never knew how to treat me. Not the pity of my fellows from pilot school at why I was desperate for my license. Certainly not the overbearing leeches that are OdeSea Inc's investors.

All those who once believed in my father enough to invest in his corporate assisted-intelligence tech startup now swarm like Antinous flies on sea-swelled flesh. Eager to pronounce Father dead and read his will, each certain they've been left a portion of his dissolved shares. Or certain they can convince Mom to sell, since it's no secret Father named her the executor of his will, and left me everything once I come of age. Next month.

But until then, Mom manages all the accounts. And every chance, the investors ply us with arguments why she doesn't need the added stress of running the company, and why I shouldn't have to take it on when I turn eighteen.

Flying away to find Father only fueled their arguments. But it's worth it as Calypso station orbits into view, and docked at the spaceport, silhouetted against the gold and green, is another Ithacan pentacont-class ship.

"Athena." I tap gloved fingers against my console. "Can you identify that ship?"

"Positive. That is the pentacont *INS Polyatropos*."

My grin breaks free. The *Polytropos*, my father's ship, skewed to Athena's programmed meter. Evidence to orbit around, not merely hope to plummet towards.

I clench my glove around the pitch switch, angling into a dive. "Let the station know we're preparing to dock."

* * *

Three hours and two orbits later, I draw alongside Calypso station, aligning the *Argos*'s airlock with the guides for the port. Even with hours of practice simulations and Athena's assistance, waiting for confirmation that I'm locked onto target is more harrowing than my entire voyage. But there's the slight pull of the arms drawing us into place, and the cabin depressurization light flashes red on my console.

"Athena." I lower the altitude guide, and flick off the central power to leave only emergency systems running. "Hold down the ship. Who knows how long I'll be?"

"Analyzation of time factor length probability commenced."

"No, I—" I sigh, unbuckling my belt. My body drifts untethered. "Sure Athena. Thanks."

Clambering over my pilot seat, I slip from the cockpit, floating under the rowing machine built into the ceiling, past the organic 3D printer stitching starch and protein into mac and cheese for dinner. Hitting the door release, I push into the airlock.

The *Argos* seals behind me with a hiss. Final, like a chapter ending.

Is this it? Is my father beyond that door? For years I've imagined, rehearsed what I'd say to my father if – when – I found him. He'll take one look and call me "son," and I'll tell him about every step and calculation that led me here. He'll be proud of me.

Won't he?

I exhale a cloud into the cold, and tap the digital doorknocker.

The port door slides open, letting in a draft of stale air and generator fuel. Red low-power lights illuminate the station beyond, but I don't catch more before the barrel of an atomic railgun blocks my view.

"Stop right there, you Troyegenic bastard." A man hangs down, boots hooked in the doorframe. He levels the railgun at my head, lethal as his scowl. A laser burn scar shoots from his upper lip across the swell of his cheekbone, continuing to sear through his eyebrow. Unruly brown hair peppered with gray crawls like cilia up his face, and floats in a helm before his eyes. Dark green eyes with pupils ringed in gold.

Mom always said I have my father's eyes. But knowing is different than seeing, feeling the truth quicken my heartbeat and thicken my throat.

I swallow. "Father?"

The barrel shakes but doesn't lower. "Don't try any funny tricks with me. State your orders and who you stole this ship from."

"What?" I say, startled, his words finally sinking in and clearing the moisture in my eyes. "I'm not – I didn't steal it. It's yours."

This isn't how I imagined this going.

"So you admit it!" The weapon inches closer, and I pull on one of the handles along the ceiling to inch back. "Which of my pilots?"

"None!" I hold up a hand. "I didn't steal it, I swear. I'm Ithacan!"

The gun dips. "Your accent is Ithacan. You, I'm not so sure. You certainly aren't one of mine. State your name and squadron."

I laugh dryly. "No squadron." Moving my free hand to the doorframe, I flip to look him in the face. I'm taller by an inch. I didn't expect that after stories making him larger than life. "It's really you. Admiral Jul Essey?"

"So you know me, even if I don't know you." He lowers the gun. "If you're not with a squadron, why are you in a military ship? Unless you're going to finally admit you stole it."

"I didn't steal it!" Technically, he didn't sign it to me, so from his perspective, I did steal it. But it would've been long decommissioned, had he been home. Why wasn't he home? "I took it from my family's hangar because no one was using it. *You* weren't using it. And I needed it to find you."

"Me?" His mouth curls into a grimace around his scar. He pushes back, floating to grip a handle over a report screen. "What about them?" He waves the railgun dejectedly at the screen.

Reaching for handles along the wall, I drift through the door, eyes adjusting to the dim red. The room opposite is wider than any space I've seen in months, packed with screens, panels, cabinets, organic and non-organic printers, and humming generators.

The screen comes into focus as I near, lists of numbers with rotating dial icons, thinking. Searching.

I squint, leaning closer. "Those are Ithacan sourcetones. With ship INS numbers. Your crew?"

"Yes." His gaze pierces like a laser burn, gloved fingers tapping against the wall behind him. Just like I do when I'm puzzling through something.

It's stupid to feel hurt he doesn't know me. Last he saw me, I was a baby, barely able to hold up my head. But something in me still hopes he'll use his famed intelligence to notice our similarities. Mom's right, I look so much like him. Why doesn't he see it?

I refocus on the screen. "Why have them listed?" My pride twinges at having to ask, like I'm taking a test I didn't sign up for, and failure means I don't get to be his son.

"It's not a list, it's a search. Using the station's communication discs."

"You aren't going to find them. All these ships were decommissioned." Few of them were intact enough to be spaceworthy, and most pentaconts were retired five years ago in favor of the new septeconts.

"Is that what you young scrubs call it?"

I peel my gaze from the screen to find his eyes closed, railgun forgotten at his side along with his fight. His face is haunted in its red cast, body sagged, everything appearing weighed down despite the microgravity.

This isn't the man of the stories, the admired admiral who never failed to see a strategy where others saw an impossible ask. This isn't the man Mom loved, who brought her hyacinths from the Western Rim in a cryobox because their shade reminded him of her eyes, and he never wanted it to fade.

"I don't understand." There's something I'm missing. Something missing in him. "Why did I only receive your S.O.S. now? And why is your concern for decommissioned ships rather than, I don't know, your *family*?" I look away, swallowing my bitterness. "Where's your Athena? Why isn't she helping?"

He startles to attention. "How did you—"

A gray eye blinks onto the screen. "Good spacetime, newcomer. I am the intellect artifice, Athena."

I can't help but smile at that familiar voice, my primary companion of the last eleven months. "There you are. Why aren't you contacting allies, or diagnosing system failure on the *Polytropos*?"

"Currently specified task is to verify status of fleet ships."

"Why?"

"Because I'm not going home." My father pushes past, using the plentiful handlebars to float past a Discord Communications array and a den of monitors to gaze out the window at the golden-green horizon of the planet, and the wine-dark vastness beyond.

I follow, giving him space, but keeping his whisper close.

"My Nella. My dear wife. I would've fought wars for her, for our *son*. But war is what took me away. Took us all away." He leans his forehead against the glass. "Tell me, stranger. How can I go home to my family, when none of my crew ever will?"

"But they all have..." I look back to the screen, Athena searching for ships she'll never find. "Your crew. They're all home."

My father turns against the windowframe, an edge returning to his expression.

"Don't lie to console me, scrub. I know what I saw. They were gone. Lost to cursed Charybdis."

My mind whirls, trying to keep up, forge connections. "Charybdis X-9? The black hole?" I saw it on my map; my Athena marked it as a local hazard.

"Of course the black hole!" He braces himself and punches the glass. "It was my call, either that or risk losing more men to the Scyllan Asteroid Belt. But we got too close, I felt Charybdis's gravity pulling at my controls. Everything went dark. I...I blew my windbag wide open. Launched out of there. But when the stars returned...I was alone."

The man who was once Admiral Jul Essey of the Hellenist Imperium's fleet curls in on himself, dropping the handle to float like an untethered embryo. Everything he once was, that Mom tells stories of, is broken, lost to the black hole of his loss and guilt for leading his entire fleet to their deaths.

But he didn't. Everyone else got home. They're safe, retired with their families in beachside cottages and floating condos, or serving in government positions as their final promotions. It's only him out here, mourning those who mourned him, a decade old snapshot stuck in a cryobox.

"I don't know how to make you believe me." A tear pops from my eye, a perfect sphere. "But they didn't die. Your crew made it home. I've spoken to them, received their condolences."

His head pokes up. "Condolences for what? You claim you're not in a squadron, what great loss did you suffer?"

His condescension snaps my calm. "*You*. Because it's *you* everyone thinks is dead!"

He shakes his head.

I fling myself against the window, and anchor my feet into a bar. "What motive would I have to lie to you?"

He uncurls fully. "You could be telling me what you think will get me to leave with you, luring me into a trap. I still don't know anything about you."

Anger burns my throat, sudden as a supernova. A neglected lifetime of abandonment, of choking down spiteful replies to heartfelt condolences. All the times someone said how my father was such a great man, not being allowed to ask why, if he was such a great man, he wasn't being my father. Hurt strangles me with fury in the face of this shell, refusing to see past his grief and come home. Refusing to see *me*. My vision rims in red from more than the lighting.

Grabbing his shoulder, I yank him close. "Look at me."

His head shakes again, but I shake him harder.

"*Look* at me!" *See me*.

Dark green eyes meet mine, heavy with failure. But it's his crew he thinks he failed, their loss preventing him from coming home to Mom and me. He doesn't care about failing us.

"It's me. It's Mach." My voice cracks. "Your son."

The silence of infinite space spreads between us, harder to cross than the stars. His eyes search mine, rotating dials processing.

See me.

"No." He shakes free of me.

My back hits the window hard as he floats away. If the distance between us was far before, it's a galaxy now.

"Yes!" I grab a handle in a fist. "I came to find you, to bring you home. Mom needs you, all your investors are pressuring her, and she just needs you. *I* need you." I set my jaw. "I deserve to have a father for once in my life."

"Why are you saying these things? My son—" Jul turns away on a handle. "My son is a *child*. How dare you use him for your manipulations."

I want to scream. "This isn't a manipulation!"

"Just leave." He launches across the room, returning to the screen and his search for sourcetones. "I'm not going home. My son is better off without a failure like me."

"Fine." I shove off the window, red lights streaking my tear-shined glare as I float to the door. "If this is who you are, maybe I am."

* * *

The white light of the port blinds me after the oppressive red, tinging my sight green. I don't look as I hit the lock open and float into the *Argos*. The familiar rundown walls and cracked screens used to comfort me, echoes from my father's time. They reminded me he once existed, still could.

Now they just feel broken.

I squeeze into my seat, the leather conforming around my shape. "Athena, set course for home."

The gray eye blinks onto my screen. "Visual scanning of shipboard says Jul Essey hasn't come aboard."

"He's not coming." I tap my fingers dully against the arm of my chair. "He'd prefer to wallow in self-pity over imagined nonsense than come home to his family." He didn't believe I was his son. Because his son is a child – like I haven't grown since he left. No surprise he didn't believe that he's been gone ten years, since he hasn't moved on. He's stuck in the past, can't see beyond his duties as an admiral at war to care about his duties as a father, or a husband. It's like he spent ten years in that black hole, and doesn't realize time has moved on without him.

My fingers stop.

Maybe that's exactly what he did.

"Athena, extract to external device."

"Initializing an external extraction. Now remove hardware."

Athena's gray eye closes to black as I click out her flashdrive and launch from my seat.

He'll believe *her*.

* * *

"Charydbis."

Jul turns as the doors open. "I thought I told you to leave."

I push past the search screen. "How long do you think it's been since the war?"

He scoffs. "You talk like it's officially ended."

"It *has*." I maneuver myself over to the den of monitors. "Ten years ago."

"Impossible."

"No, it isn't." I click Athena into the hub, next to an identical flashdrive, steel engraved with her eye. "You were lost in Charybdis."

"What?"

I turn back. "Black hole time dilation. The intense gravity warps spacetime, so close to the well time passes far more slowly than it does farther from it."

He cocks his head. "That's true." Curiosity lights his eyes with something other than red. "That's...not impossible."

"It's not. Athena, seek duplicate programs over LAN."

Gray eyes appear on every screen, two identical voices answering in stereo. "Searching for duplicate program on localized area network."

"What...?" Father looks between his screen and the monitors. "What are you doing with my Athena?"

"She's the backup you made before you went to war. Now she can do what she was created for." Merciful Mars, please let this work. "Athena, sync with duplicate program."

"Access code required to—"

"Five, thirteen, fifty-seven." I look right at my father. "My mother's birthday."

"Access code accepted. Syncing with duplicate programming commenced."

Gray eyes blink in unison, processing.

My father's eyes widen. "How did you—"

"Systems synced."

This *has* to work. "Play *Ithacan Citizen* report dated eleven, two, ninety-one."

Every monitor opens a video, bright amid the dim red. A woman stands before a shot of the pentacont fleet returning to port. The view changes to a live feed of the crew's welcome home, hugging families, friends, comrades. Tear-glazed eyes and smile-cracked faces fill every screen, but I'm not watching. I've seen this a hundred times.

I watch my father take in the sight, dark-green eyes glazing with tears, face cracking in a smile. He believes me now, or he wants to.

Without me having to ask her to, Athena switches to a montage of various clips, awards ceremonies, speeches, weddings. Snapshots of ten years of lives lived.

"They made it home to their families," I whisper, loud in the silence of space. "Only you didn't."

Dazed, he drifts closer to the monitors, reaching out as if to touch them. "Ten years?"

"Nearly."

He turns, finally meeting my eyes. "You're…seventeen?"

"Eighteen next month."

Spherical tears trail through the air between us until I don't know whose are whose. I yank a dustcloth from my belt and swipe it through them.

"Mach." His voice is small, but his eyes are wide and alive.

I swallow. "Hi, Dad."

He drags himself closer, gripping handles with shaking hands. I meet him halfway.

Falling into my father's arms for the first time, I feel a burden lift. I devoted nine years to finding him, but part of me believed I never would. And no imaginings could capture this. Even without the microgravity, I'd feel weightless, anchored only by his arm, his face buried in my shoulder.

"My son." He leans away, gripping the side of my head to look at me. See me. "My inspiration. I'm so sorry. For everything."

Everything. Everything will be okay. With Mom, with the investors, with the company, with me. Even if it isn't better, we'll make it better. Because if I can voyage through the wine-dark of infinite space to find my father, then we can do anything together. Us and Mom. A family.

"Let's go home."

The Sea Gave Him to Me

Naomi Jae

The sea gave him to me at dawn.

His body lay crumpled in the sand like a thing discarded, skin salted and sunburnt, lips cracked from thirst, and seaweed clinging to his hair. The tide nudged him forward as if delivering him to me. Gulls shrieked overhead as though arguing over him, but as I stepped closer they scattered, leaving only the slow hum of the shore. The moment my shadow touched him, the curse struck.

It is always the same. The rush of heat, the hollow in my chest filling in an instant with something both beautiful and dreadful.

I had never seen his face before, yet I knew it. The way one knows the sound of their own name. *Mine*, my heart whispered. *Forever*, it swore.

He lay unconscious, the scent of foreign lands clinging to him. I knelt beside him, my hands unsteady. His body was marked with scars that told a dozen untold stories. I wanted to trace each one, to learn them all. To know everything there is to know about this man the sea had gifted me.

But I also saw the danger in him. The sharpness in his jaw, the set of his brow, a man prepared to rise in a heartbeat and fight his way out of anything. A man who would leave. Yet, the curse cares not for reason. It does not negotiate.

Love, pure and complete, floods through me like a tide that will not recede. And with it comes the dread I know too well: that he will never feel the same, that he will look at my island and see not paradise, but a prison, and would test its bars until his hands bled.

Still, I touched his face. My fingers came away wet from the seawater in his hair.

"This time," I told myself, voice barely more than the wind, "will be different."

I built him a bed of rushes beneath the shade and cleaned his wounds. I pressed honey to his lips and coaxed water past his cracked mouth. I sang to him while the sun rose, old island songs my mother had sung to me when I was young, when, at last, his eyes opened. He stared at the canopy of leaves, then at me, a soldier's habit showed in his gaze, the swift measuring of friend or foe, escape route, weapon within reach.

"You are safe," I said. "I am Calypso," I added before he could form the question in his eyes. My name seemed to hang in the air between us, strange on his tongue though he did not speak it. "And you are on Ogygia."

I did not tell him what that meant. I did not tell him why the sea had brought him here, or why it would never let him go.

I already knew what he would want. I already knew what the island would do.

And I would not tell him. For he would find out himself.

He healed faster than any mortal should.

Within a fortnight, he could stand without swaying, could walk the length of the beach without resting. And every morning, he moved like a man who had taught his body to obey long after it wanted to break. Every morning, I would find him at the same place; where the sand thinned into black rock and the ocean spread wide enough to make a man believe that if he stared hard enough, he might see the edge of the world.

He was always looking outward. Never at me.

"You will not see Ithaca from here," I told him once, carrying a bowl of figs and honey to where he stood.

He did not take the bowl. He did not thank me. "I will see the route I must take to get there."

His voice was measured, his eyes unyielding – the voice and eyes of a man who had faced perilous storms, vengeful gods, and hellish monsters, and never once been bested. It should have frightened me. Instead, my curse twisted it into something beautiful. That stubbornness of his, that unbroken will. I wanted to cradle it, to tame it, to keep it for my own.

He tried to leave within days of finding his feet. He dragged fallen palm trunks to the shore, lashed them together with leaves until his hands were striped in green and red. He chewed a wedge of driftwood smooth and used it, forcing the trunks together. He ignored my offerings of food until I set it in the shade and walked away; then he ate, pride set aside by hunger. I watched from above as he heaved the raft into the shallow water.

The sea tore it to shreds within moments.

When he staggered back to land, soaked and breathless, I went to him with a blanket. Water poured off him in streams. "The tides are strong here," I said gently. "They will not let you go."

"Then I will fight them."

His defiance was a knife and a gift. It cut to see it aimed at me, but it beamed so brightly in this place of sameness. His confidence gleamed so brilliantly on this quiet island that I could not look away.

I did not tell him what I knew. That no man leaves Ogygia unless the gods themselves decree it. That the waves and winds here obey a will older than my own, and they will turn back any who try. Let him try, I thought. Let him fight. The battle keeps him alive.

He made three more rafts over the weeks. Storms wrecked them all. Each failure left his hands rawer, his voice quieter.

A horizon can seem close when a man is young and angry. It seemed close to him now, but the island is careful with the gifts it is told to keep. Each attempt to leave is futile; the sea tosses him back to my shore every time.

He cursed first the waves. Later, he cursed the gods.

Later still, he fixed his gaze on me. "You will help me."

The curse inside me sang at the sound of his certainty. I made myself still.

"I cannot," I said. "The winds are treacherous this far from men. They will drown you within the day."

His mouth curved into the grimace of a man measuring his odds.

"Then tell the winds I am not a man easily drowned."

He would not relent, so I changed my tactics.

I laid silks beside his bed of rushes. I brought wine pressed from the island's grapes, and warm bread scented with rosemary and thyme. While he worked, I would tell him old tales of gods I once knew and loved as family. I sang him island songs.

He would not touch the silks. He ate only enough to survive. When I sang, he would turn his face away, but his shoulders would ease ever so slightly, almost imperceptibly.

The curse in me strummed with each moment of closeness, no matter how small.

One evening, as the sun blended into the sea, I stood beside him at the black rocks. "I could give you immortality," I said quietly. "You could live here forever. No storms. No wars. Only peace."

He looked at me then, properly, for the first time. And in his gaze, there was something colder than the sea itself. He was not cruel. He was not even angry. He was a man who had once known exactly where he was going, and who now stood on a shore that erased all maps.

"Peace," he said, "is not peace if it is a cage."

I smiled, because the curse demanded it. Inside, I felt the first crack form in my resolve.

Months passed. The air stayed the same; warm, smelling of palm and thyme, combined with the distinct aroma of the salty sea. A steady breeze carried the scent across the island and cooled the skin. The island kept its familiar sounds: bees buzzing over lilies, lizards darting across stone, waves breaking gently on the shore. The island remained as it had always been, but he changed.

When he first arrived, he attacked each day like a campaign, bracing his shoulder against the trees to test their strength. He cut bark into cords and soaked them until they loosened to rope. He pried iron nails from ancient wreckage and hammered them straight with a stone. The rafts he built lasted longer each time: three waves, five, ten. On the best days, he rode swells far enough for me to lose sight of him and feel the dread rise like bile. If he dies, I cannot love him properly; if he lives, the island will return him to me; if he reaches a distant shore – and here my thoughts always failed, for the island would never allow that.

He always came back. Sometimes the sea laid him gently on the sand like a tired child. Sometimes it spat him onto the rocks in a tangle of limbs, as if insulted by his audacity.

I never had to lift a hand. The island did it for me.

In the beginning, he shouted at the waves. Later, he shouted at the gods. He bargained, he threatened, he promised. The sea was deaf to him, delivering him to my feet again and again.

In the end, he shouted at no one. He stood dripping at the tideline as though the fight had been pulled out with the tide. He watched the horizon without expression until his breath steadied. Then he picked up the wreckage he could salvage, stacked it neatly beside the palms, and walked up the beach.

I told myself I preferred him this way; calm, no longer raging at me. But I'd often catch myself listening for the thud of an axe against palm trunks, for the shouts when the wind tore at his sails. His defiance had been a kind of fire, and without it, the island felt colder.

Now, he filled his days with smaller labors. Fishing. Repairing the nets I wove. He climbed the coconut palms without asking, cut them down with neat strokes, and set them in a row. He spoke little. When he did, it was of ordinary things: the size of the catch, the color of the dawn, whether the bread had risen properly.

We learned each other's habits as those who live together always do. He hummed under his breath when he worked, the tune shifting with his mood. He learned the island's rhythms: when the figs were sweetest, where the shallows hid blue crabs among the weeds, which path beneath the trees stayed dry after rain. We spoke little, and yet we spoke constantly.

Sometimes, in the evenings, I would sit across from him by the fire and watch the light dance along his face. I would imagine him smiling at me without reserve. I would imagine him saying my name with longing, not weariness. The curse fed on these imaginings, only leaving me more hollowed.

One night, a storm rolled in sudden and fierce. The wind screamed through the palms, rain lashing the earth so hard it felt like pebbles striking skin. I found him outside, wrestling to pull the nets to safety.

"Leave them," I called over the roar. "You'll be swept away!"

He glanced back, hair plastered to his face, and for a moment there was something like the old fire in his eyes, dangerous and alive. But instead of defying me, he let the nets go. He came inside.

When I handed him a dry tunic, he did not refuse. When I reached for his arm to guide him to the hearth, he let me. When I offered him wine, he drank.

That night, for the first time, he did not sleep apart. He lay beside me, tense but unmoving, his eyes fixed on the roof until sleep claimed him. While he slept, I stared into the rafters and felt the curse purr, satisfied.

I should have rejoiced; I had what it demanded – closeness, intimacy. But it felt less like a victory and more like the silence after a battle where the wrong side had won.

Years blurred together on Ogygia.

The island is not a place of numbers. It is a place of repetitions. If the man who washed ashore had been all sharp edges and storms, the man who now walked my island was worn smooth like driftwood. He moved with no urgency. He hunted, fished, mended; the way one breathes, not the way one lives.

He no longer rose before dawn to scan the horizon. He no longer tested the currents with small boats or driftwood. The black rocks where we had first spoken sat untouched, the sand around them bare of footprints.

I had stopped telling myself he was happy here. He was not. He had simply forgotten how to leave.

The island had taken his fire, and I had been the one to hold the torch, keeping him just warm enough to keep breathing.

We fell into a kind of domesticity, like a prayer spoken not from faith but from habit. In the mornings, he ground grain with the stone while I kneaded dough. He watched the oven as a helmsman watches the stars. He cut fish into strips and laid them in the smoke. He braided rope with me, his fingers sure, our hands brushing now and then as we worked.

When a palm split under its own weight, he called me, and we stood in the shade making plans for the lumber. He no longer saw it as a means of escape, but as material for whatever small need the island demanded.

At night, he lay beside me without hesitation. Sometimes he rested his hand on my hip or shoulder, not out of desire but as though his body had accepted this as the posture for sleep. I closed my eyes and told myself stories: that his breath at my neck was a choice, that the small curl of his fingers meant tenderness.

I hated myself in the same breath. The curse thrummed through me, urging gratitude. It did not care that gratefulness felt like theft.

One evening, the sky turned to honey and then to wine. I brought him bread still warm, steam escaping from a torn crust. He thanked me quietly and ate without looking up. His beard had taken on threads of gray, the lines on his face had deepened from the years on Ogygia.

"Do you ever dream?" I asked.

He paused then shook his head. "Not anymore."

Something inside me twisted. I remembered the man who had cursed the gods with the fury of a tempest, who had built rafts with bleeding hands, who had looked at me with defiance sharp enough to cut. That man had dreamed. Of home, of freedom, of the life he had lost.

I had taken that from him. The island had dulled the edge. I had held the whetstone.

The curse thrummed through me still, urging me to hold him tighter, to be grateful he was here. But when I looked at him across the firelight, I saw not a man in love, not even a man content, but a bird that no longer knew how to fly.

I reached for his hand, and he let me take it. His skin was warm. His eyes were somewhere far beyond my reach.

One still night, the kind where the sea lay flat as glass and the stars burned bright enough to touch, he slept beside the fire. His hair had grown long past his collar. If I tried, I could imagine him in a hall with other men, their knees touching under a table, their faces lit with wine and laughter. The imagining hurt so much I had to keep looking lest I feel it worse when I looked away.

I watched him for a long time.

Not his face as it was now, weathered from years on the island, but flickers of what had been there before. The spark in his eyes when he refused my gifts; the stubborn set of his jaw when the sea knocked him down and he got back up.

It was gone. I had helped the island take it from him.

The curse whispered, *He is here, he is yours, you have won.*

If this was winning, why did it taste of grief?

I rose quietly and walked to the black rocks at the shore; the same place he had once stood each dawn. The waves lapped against them, patient and eternal. I had always thought of the sea as my ally, my accomplice. Now, I saw it as the jailer it truly was. It has its own laws. I am not one of them.

I lifted my face to the sky. "Hear me," I said, and my voice was steady. "I am Calypso. I have obeyed your will. I have kept him here. I have loved him as the curse demands. But he has suffered enough. Whatever crime brought him to Ogygia, he has paid it tenfold."

The wind shifted, carrying the faint scent of rain though the sky remained clear.

"I am bound," I said, "and I will remain bound. I will stay in this island's chamber and wait when there is no one to wait for. I will love him until the end of my days, even when he is gone, and if you send me another, I will love him too because that is what you made of me. But let this man go. Let him see his home again.

"Let him go," I said, and this time I could not keep the tremor from my voice. "And if there is a debt to pay for it, let me pay it here."

For a moment, there was no answer. Just the hush of the tide and the beating of my heart. Then, far out at sea, a single swell rose and broke, the sound rolling back to me like a whisper.

Granted.

I stood until I knew I would not fall when I turned away. Then I went back to the fire and watched him sleep. There is a kind of peace that only exhaustion makes still. I brushed the hair from his temple and let my hand rest there.

By morning, the sky was calm. When he awoke, I told him what I had done.

He stared at me, and then I watched his eyes fill with a joy so sharp it cut me. He stood and pressed both hands to my forearms. "You would do this?"

"I would do this," I said. I would do anything for him, even break my own heart. But I did not speak that part aloud. He nodded, and I saw the captain in him wake. He did not kiss me. He did not need to. His eyes were already turned to the work.

We walked the shoreline picking through old wreckage for the timber. He tested each with a carpenter's ear. I brought him tools and fiber. He lashed the timbers with rope so evenly it looked like weaving. When the raft was stout enough to resist a god's idle kick, he began to speak. Not to me at first, but to the air. Penelope. Telemachus. Laertes. Ithaca. He rolled them in his mouth to remind his tongue of its native work.

I gathered food: bread, olives, figs, smoked fish. I filled skins with water and wine, counted and recounted. I brought a cloak for cold nights and a knife for stubborn knots. I set everything in neat piles while he tested weight and balance. The island watched without comment, its groves and stones and waters holding still, as if embarrassed to be caught letting something go.

"Calypso," he said. His voice was steady again. "I—"

"Go," I said, because if I let him speak, he would have thanked me or blessed me or apologized, and none of those were things I wished to keep as the last thing I carried. I stepped forward and kissed him, tasting salt and sun. His hand lifted towards my cheek and then fell.

When he pushed off from shore, I stood in the shallows, the water curling around my ankles. I watched him until the horizon swallowed him. He did not look back.

The curse did not fade. It would not fade. It never did.

And so, I turned back to my island, my own prison. I would keep loving him until the sea brought me the next man to break.

The island felt bigger without him.

Not quieter, Ogygia was always quiet, but it felt emptier, as if his presence had filled the spaces between the rustle of the palms and the sigh of the tide.

For days, I lingered at the black rocks each morning, my eyes following the horizon as though I might glimpse his sail returning. The curse inside me strained toward that empty line, aching for the shape of his shoulders, the sound of his voice, the weight of him beside me.

But the sea gives and the sea takes, and the sea does not return what it has claimed.

I tended the garden, mended the nets, sang to myself in the evenings. The work felt hollow without another voice to answer my call. At night, I dreamed of him, not the man who had left me, quiet and worn, but the man who had first stood on this shore with fire in his eyes. The man who told me peace was no peace in a cage.

The curse was cruel in that way: it did not let me love him as he became, but as he had been. It would hold me there until the end.

One evening, a storm rose sudden and fierce, the wind howling through the palms. I stood at the water's edge and let the rain soak me. Somewhere out in the dark, I heard it – the faint groan of timbers breaking, the desperate cry of a voice I did not know.

Another shipwreck.

I closed my eyes. My heart was already moving toward that voice, already shaping the name it would give the stranger. I hated the curse for that, hated myself for welcoming the ache.

When I opened my eyes, the sea was boiling with foam, tossing something pale toward the sand.

I stepped forward, whispering into the storm – not to the gods, not to the island but to whatever part of the world still listened to requests.

Please...let it not be him.

The waves surged, carrying the body closer. My heart answered anyway.

Please, let it be him.

The sea will give him to me, as it always does. And I, who am bound to chains this world will never see, receive what it brings.

At the Water's Edge

Kiera Mathis Jones

"You say Julia that you often dream of me!
Do tell me some of your good ones; don't tell me
any more of the bad ones..."
– Ulysses S. Grant in a letter to his wife, August 1844

The traveler arrived by sea. Churning waves belched him onto a slender spit of sand on the eastern edge of the island where many spirits dwelled. Those who've seen it – whether mortal or god – call it a paradise.

Dense groves of cypress and alder trees cover the slopes above its golden beaches. A gentle breeze carries whatever fragrance a person could most desire. Frankincense, lavender, the sunflowers from one's front garden, the soft hair of whoever they loved in life. Anything. At the center of the island, a snow-capped peak transforms to waterfalls and a trail of shimmering pools for swimming or bathing. Vineyards and orchards arranged in circles and swirls – not the usual straight marching lines – offer all manner of fruits to sweeten the time one spends in this realm.

On the day he came, one of the spirits wandered down to the shore to collect what the cosmic ocean had delivered. She knew someone would be there. There had been a storm that night. A thing that only happened when a troubled soul was coming. The traveler was lucky. Few are fortunate to find this island. Some lost souls float for years or centuries before they find a destination. He had swum and caught a favorable current to this ancient place, floating in the primordial waters that had birthed his known universe.

"Welcome!" The spirit approached. Sprawled in the sand, his face was hidden under a mop of chestnut hair.

"Where am I?" He coughed and spat seawater. "My throat… burns."

"I can heal that. You've come to a way station. For those in need of a compass." She held out a hand to help him rise. "I am Calypso. What is your name, traveler?"

"Ulysses."

She gasped as he accepted her hand. Grey eyes – perpetually serious, many would later say – rising to the occasion.

"You've returned?"

* * *

Fort Humboldt, California, January 1854

My Dear Julia,

How long it feels since I left your blessed company for this outpost. I know you couldn't make the trek in your delicate condition, but I think your face would be the only thing to break the dismal cloud of this place.

California. A place suddenly precious to our Union. In these two years, we've set up the forts requested to keep the peace and settle moods. Gold, timber, opportunity; boys get rich or go mad here. Hoards of them pour into the northern harbor nearly every week now. This new state is not yet four years old and already it is learning many of the habits of older and more despicable men.

Do you know The Odyssey? *Last night I had a terrible nightmare of our passage from New York to San Francisco. Only I was Odysseus and the world was teeming with monsters.*

We were stuck in Panama again, trudging through muck; scores of men languishing with cholera. Their moans and wails pierced the night like sirens teasing death to the rest of our company. Seasoned men, not yet stricken, covered their ears and eyes to those newly quarantined, trying to ignore the fears that they too might die idle and inglorious in the torrential rain and mud. Many had survived the Mexican war only four years earlier. "Better to have been run through by a bullet in battle!" I overheard one soldier say.

Then I was stepping from the steamship into horrors of a different kind in San Francisco. Pimps and prostitutes beckoning from doorways; clouded opium dens lined with lotus flowers; hungry hawkers and gambling cannibals looking to strip the coins, clothes, and even the very flesh from wide-eyed arrivals. I tried to stop the naive boys. "The gold fields are that way!" I cried. "Don't forget your purpose!" But I was too late for most.

I woke in a sweat, glad for a moment to be in our barracks with only the denizens of Eureka for company. What an optimistic name for this tiny town! I find it a miserable spot with menial tasks.

Enormous trees loom over the town and fort, creaking like old bones, twice the height of any back east. The sound makes me shudder. We are Jack and the giant come to gobble us up is the beanstalk itself. Hundreds of them. With a canopy so dense that no light can touch the ground. As if there were any sun to be had! The rain is ceaseless.

Yesterday I walked along the bluff. A steamship passed, carving a southerly route. If I jumped to catch a ride home, would I make it to you, dear Julia? Or plunge straight to the bottom like a cannonball misfired?

As you see, my mind is a maelstrom. Write soon and as often as you can. I dread the delay that keeps your hand from me. As always you remain the one single person who occupies my mind. Love and kisses to you and our boys.

Your devoted,

Ulysses

* * *

Calypso filled a golden goblet. Ulysses eyed the wine like a wolf in the long grasses.

"Perhaps I shouldn't."

"You fear it."

"I was neither afraid nor unafraid when such spirits helped me walk the bluff in a storm." He scuffed the side of his beard. "I was considering the molded tips of my boots hanging over the edge. Our cobblers put great effort into crafting stiff and unforgiving footwear. Soldier's shoes. Below me the sea turned from grey to black. I thought of the River Styx that Achilles' mother dipped him into. If I leapt, would these waters harden me?"

"You wanted that?"

"Achilles knew his destiny. He never swerved." He sipped the wine. "Lightning flashed and I stumbled. Then…I was here."

Calypso plucked a grape from a glass bowl set between them. She enjoyed his soft, almost musical manner of speaking.

"The drink did not choose you. Why did you choose it?"

"I was lonely." He ran a finger around the rim of his cup. "Drink is easy to come by when you have a salary and no real purpose. I was never happy with idle hands. I'd have been a horseman if I could."

"Why couldn't you?" Another grape crushed under her tongue.

"My father arranged my entry to West Point, and I wasn't of the disposition to choose a different path. Though the sight of blood makes me ill."

He sipped again.

"My father was a tanner, with a long barn filled with hides, dripping and soaking the ground with death. I love animals. Horses especially. My mother said they understood me more than anyone. More than God even. And that was saying something because my mother was desperately devout."

"Do you think it's true?"

"Sometimes." Ulysses nodded. "Once, when I was twelve, I went to collect lumber. When I got to the forest camp, there were no men to load the wagon. I fixed up a system of ropes, and I swear my horses could read my mind. Without complaint, they pulled each log up one by one. My father was amazed. I went to bed feeling as though I'd conquered the world."

Calypso laughed at the charming image of a clever boy grinning under his covers.

"Horses have souls like the sea," she reflected. "People ride them the way a boat slips over the waves; but neither steed nor surf can ever really be tamed."

"Truly." Ulysses looked out at the waves. "I didn't always do what he said, you know? I wanted Julia. He could not keep me from her."

"He tried?"

"He is a fierce abolitionist. Julia's family owns slaves. My father didn't approve."

"And you do?"

She imagined cracking his shell with her question, uncovering the pearl within. Ulysses studied the tangled lines on his palm.

"It is a way of things in the south. I try not to speak of the topic – either for or against. I love Julia, regardless of how her family makes its business. She says I am destined for great things."

He leaned forward.

"You said I reminded you of someone?"

"Odysseus." Calypso smiled. "Souls may live many times; sometimes they return. He and I talked here, the same as we're doing now. I helped him with his choice."

"Choice?"

"Where you go next. Peace in your afterlife, or—"

"I want to go home."

Calypso set her cup down. "Why?"

"Julia."

"Why go to California if she is your desire?"

"I had orders."

"You follow, even against your heart?"

He leaned forward.

"I watched men die for an unjust venture in the Mexican war. The Union asked it of me, so I went. Since then, I've hoped that my next duty would be for a finer cause. And…I wish to be the man that Julia believes I am. Much is expected of me. By her and others…"

"Maybe you are Odysseus." Calypso touched her lips and looked to the violet stars and exposed nebula above. "Your country, you say? His ancient kingdom is gone, Ulysses. All nations become something else over time. I've lived for thousands of years. It is inescapable."

"That might be so," he replied. "But because something may die, does not mean we shouldn't strive for the best it can be today and tomorrow."

"Even if you must bleed for it?"

Ulysses shuddered.

"It won't come to that. Our Union is inclined towards peace and resolution."

"Such faith may be put to the test if you return."

"I can return?"

"If you wish, I will help you. But you must grant me something in exchange."

The canyons in his forehead softened. "You are a kind spirit, Calypso."

* * *

White Haven, March 1854

Dear Nellie,

Spring bursts with daffodils this morning, but that is not the only reason I am in a fantastic state of mind. I dreamt of Dudy again last night.

He was strolling toward our porch like the day he proposed. Only he was older, crowned with white streaks like a halo or laurels. Solemn eyes, but a slight upturn of his moustache that betrayed his jubilation. I knew he'd become a great leader!

You laugh at me, sister, when I tell you such things. But believe me – you will soon see what Dudy will make of himself. Glory is at hand!

Yours,

Julia

* * *

"Don't we need a boat?"

Ulysses trailed Calypso through the orchard. He reached to pluck a fruit but thought better of it and fixed his eyes back on the waterfall of her silver curls.

"No one leaves by sea; they only come that way." Calypso pointed to a grotto speckled with absinthe-hued ferns. "There."

Ulysses saw a passage leading into the mountain. The air chilled as they descended. Only the glow from her skin lit the way and even she began to fade. He thrust a hand through the dark in panic, landing his fingers into the small of her back. Softer than anything he'd felt before.

"Soon," she whispered. "Almost there."

Wet sand squelched around his bare feet. His boots were lost. Lightning flashed and he could see the tall cliff with its army of giants peering down at him once more.

"Follow me," Calypso beckoned. "There is a fisherman's cabin nearby. We can shelter there. I will heal your body. By morning, you can return to your post."

Inside, she lit a fire and boiled bathwater. The luminous colors of her hair and skin had gone. Washed away by the storm, Ulysses mused; or perhaps the island was all a dream and she was only a fisherman's daughter who'd pulled him, near-drowned, from the waves?

"It is a fine home," he murmured.

"Sit here."

Calypso stripped away layers of fabric plastered to his clammy limbs so he could lower himself into the steaming tub. Blood rushed back to his head, pounding like drums. He felt dizzy as she massaged his hair with oils and soap.

"Come." She held up a towel. "Almost done."

He swayed as he stood. Her eyes glittered.

"I can see the island in them," he breathed. "So beautiful..."

She smiled and pressed her lips to his chest. He closed his eyes and remembered the ache of touch denied for two long years.

When the sun rose, he dressed quickly.

"I'm...I'm sorry..." He looked at the floor as he spoke.

"Don't be concerned." Calypso opened the door to the morning light. "I will never speak of this to anyone not present between these walls."

"Will you return to the island?"

"No." She touched her hand to her belly. "I will have a child now. I cannot go back yet."

Ulysses paled.

"How…?"

"I know things long before any mortal could," Calypso laughed. "On the island, I shepherd lost souls, but I can't make a soul in that in-between place. Here, with you, I could. I've wondered how it feels to be a mother. Odysseus would have done it, but I had less conviction for the idea then."

They walked the beach in silence. The waves appeared blue; no longer the ashen shade he'd loathed since arriving.

"I will resign my commission and go home."

As they neared the dock where steamships landed, she held her hand out. "Here is where I leave you."

"Where will you go?"

"Somewhere my talents are useful."

He looked to the ground and back to her. "I could give you some money."

"No need. Take care, Ulysses. I doubt we will meet here again, but I will follow your journey. Remember what we spoke of. One day soon you will be tested."

* * *

White Haven, May 1854

Dear Julia,

I am glad to hear the visit with your sister goes well. It is too quiet since you and the boys left. A home filled with family is the right order of things.

To that end, I've mulled over the question in your last letter: I will put Ulysses to work on the farm upon his return.

I've never fully understood your mystical attachment to the man. Though he is clever and resolute in his affection for you, I worry that he lacks aim in life. The military suited him. Yet he resigns mere months after promotion to Captain? Odd.

You know I harbored reservations about his loyalties given his vocal family up north. But your sister insists that he won't object to the honest labor of managing slaves. So, I will relent.

Just know, I won't have detractors in our ranks – particularly from a son-in-law who will benefit from my benevolence to feed and house his wife and children. I consider him a realistic man. I hope I won't be proved wrong.

Yours,

Papa

* * *

Santa Barbara, California, June 1861

Dear Ulysses,

Seven years have passed, and I am glad to tell you that our daughter has grown well. I named her Celeste after the night sky above our vineyard. She is my north star now. No surprise she has begun to show an aptitude for animals – particularly horses.

This is not why I write, though.

War is upon us. The north and south are at odds. I sense your mind even from here: you hope and imagine that the conflict will simmer over like a pot set left out on a hot plate, and everyone will leap to pull it from the flames, and sigh as it cools, and shake hands, and vow never to let it come to that. That is a dream, Ulysses. One you must wake from.

You've toed the line long enough. I urge you: unharness your conscience from the heavy load you've tethered it to. How long will you strive to be stubbornly indifferent to the inhumanity of slavery? Is it because you fear to offend dear Julia?

As I peered into your soul on the island, I saw your potential. I know you can calculate what is right and good in this world – and what is unjust. I did not bring you back just to be Julia's husband. Your wife's particular sentiments are not the compass to follow.

The war will be hard. Your foes have good warriors. Still, everyone has an Achilles Heel. Use your head and your wits. Find the moment. Seize it. And if you've committed your heart to the just cause, you will prevail. That is my prophecy.

Now, the journey is yours and I leave you to it. Good luck and godspeed.

Calypso

* * *

February 1862 – First Union Victory! Fort Donelson Captured! Gallant conduct of Grant and his Regiment. Details of the Fight. Names of the Killed and Wounded.

* * *

April 1865 – Glorious News! The End of the War! Let the people rejoice! Honors to General Grant and His Gallant Army! Ring the bells!

* * *

November 1868 – Ulysses S. Grant Elected President! The Great Sweep. Citizenship and Civil Rights Amendment for Freedmen expected to be Enacted by Summer.

* * *

Celeste ran a hand over each page of carefully pasted Daily Alta clippings. She'd bought a large scrapbook from the stationary seller. Big enough for the endless supply of articles. Most were celebratory. A few queried his actions between victories as though he should never lose a soldier or even a sliver of ground. She ripped those ones up to use for kindling in the oven fire.

"Father," she whispered to the scrapbook. "Do you think of me in secret too?"

She felt rebellious once and thought to tell a friend about him, but the words stuck in her throat.

"Did you put a spell on me?" Celeste railed at her mother. "Why tell me about him if I can't speak of him?"

"Not all things are meant to be spoken of," Calypso replied. "You will understand one day."

* * *

Santa Barbara, California, December 1868

Dear Ulysses,

Seven more years. Congratulations on your election! I smiled at your speeches in the papers. Very rousing. The warrior turns poet! One day you must write a memoir. Don't let a Homer decide what shall be read about your mind, your struggles, and your triumphs. (I finally read The Odyssey *– what a ridiculous picture he painted of me!)*

Despite your great victory, you still face treacherous waters. Clashing rocks and lingering demons lurk around every corner. I don't envy you this position, but I am glad you are in it.

I do need a favor. Celeste will turn fifteen in the new year. I spent so long telling her that you don't belong to us – that you have great things to do in this world – that I fear I've made you a god in her eyes.

Would you send for her? Show her who you are. For her sake.

Calypso

* * *

Washington, D.C., March 1869

Dear Mama,

I am sorry for running away. Did you know I received an invitation to my father's inauguration party? Not in his hand, but I assume he ordered it. I am never certain of what you can and can't see. Maybe you already know I failed?

People in the streets here were speaking of him before the ceremony. Most admiring and calling him a savior, and others – more quietly – snarking that he is a butcher of their rights, and other less kind things. It unsettled my stomach; I vomited twice that night.

I watched his swearing in, but at the gates of the White House my head spun. Who would I meet? What would I say? I ran. An hour later, when I'd vomited again in the hotel bath, I finally let go of my tattered invitation. My hand aches. I wish I'd brought some of your remedies in my bag.

The transcontinental railway is almost complete, I hear. I will take it home. I miss you and my horses. Keep a candle out for me so I don't lose my way.

Celeste

* * *

Proclamation 270 – July 23, 1885
"…sad tidings of the death of that illustrious citizen and ex-President of the United States, General Ulysses S. Grant… [who] trod unswervingly the pathway of duty, undeterred by doubts, single-minded and straightforward…"

* * *

Santa Barbara, California, July 1954

My darling grandchildren,

You will find this letter under my pillow when my last breath is spent. No doubt that shall be soon. I lived well and look forward to the promise of seeing my mother on my next journey.

Now I wish to tell you about my father. I met him only once, near the end of his life, so it is fitting that I write this when I too am departing. I've left you my journals and scrapbook along with the copy of his memoir he signed for me.

Death can compel many things. In my case, it gave me the courage to answer his telegram.

"You look like your mother," he said as I approached. He sat in a wicker chair on his porch with a tartan blanket across his lap. His eyes scrunched to push out the words.

"The pain came after I ate a peach." He patted his throat. "Julia thought I'd swallowed a stinging insect in the fruit, dear girl. Doctors say it was the cigars."

The cancer must have been unbearable, yet he plowed through the pain to gift me this conversation.

"You were my hero," I confessed after pleasantries.

"You deserved a father," he replied. "I've done things worthy of a hero. And just as many missteps. I've trembled in moments; shed tears. Same as my foes. The dead haunt us all."

I looked over the piles of papers around him like leaves fallen from an autumn tree.

"Was the war worth it?"

I knew the answer, but I wanted to hear him say it.

"Undeniably," he wheezed and sucked another ragged breath. "Do you know the story where Odysseus must choose to sail past

one of two monsters? Scylla would kill many, but Charybdis would devour his entire crew."

"Sacrificing some to save many?"

"More than that. I think if we did not pull our oars to battle Scylla, if we sat back in complacency, the power of Charybdis's whirlpool would have sucked us in. Consumed our souls." He paused and looked to the horizon. "I think we will forever be sailing. We must row every day, lest we float idly into such a grotesque fate."

"Is that what you write in your book?"

"I leave my thoughts in these pages like a corpse in a battlefield gone silent. Perhaps the crows may pick at me until I am only a gleaming set of bones, cleaned of all my complicated flesh. I am only one man, and I am dying. The future belongs to others now."

He turned suddenly and looked into my eyes.

"I'd love to see the island once more. Forgive me, Celeste. For years I was...embarrassed, and now there is no time left."

I cried and kissed his brow. The myth remained, but I could also see the man at last.

Do you recall when we saw Pinocchio *in the cinema? I wept and laughed through it, and you asked me why.*

I was thinking of him. A boy carrying the hopes of his father, Julia, and others. My mother like a Blue Fairy calling out to him. Making his way through twists and turns, until his true heart was revealed and his wish granted. Becoming a 'real boy'; not a perfect one, but a real *one.*

In my life, I fought for and won the right to vote while others still struggle for their rights, saw heroes and ghosts made in three more terrible wars, and raised a beautiful family on our vineyard. A few months ago, the Union armies tested a nuclear bomb on a beautiful island in a pristine sea. Yesterday, my heart burst at the exquisite joy of sharing a delicious chocolate ice cream together with you all. I will miss our family dinners.

Is this how my father felt? Grateful for life's blessings while also wondering what might become of the world he loved. He was an optimist, I think; and so am I.

My dear grandchildren, we are all travelers. There is no sweet and simple finale to the odyssey of our lives, our people. It's your time to take up the oars. Which horizon – which monsters – will you point your ship to?

I love you,

Grandma Celeste

You Have to Want to Go Home

L.G. Merrick

The sea had gone flat as slate. The sail hung in drooped bunches. The men barely could lift their arms to row in the heat – or move their minds to accept that here was another bad turn at the hands of Poseidon. Poseidon wanted them dead. They were the only ship left of twelve, the only ship to escape the Laestrygonians – and they were beginning to really suffer feelings of doom. Poseidon would not let them reach home. The ship sat on the ocean so still that Odysseus supposed to an outside observer it must resemble the tip of a rock.

He paced the deck, pensive, he alone mustering energy, and for the benefit of his surviving men he recited poems in a pose of good humor that he did not at first feel. He delivered elaborate prayers – all in mimicry of what a joyous sailor respectful of Poseidon might do. Why not? If that god could make it worse right now, it already would be worse.

Eurylochus watched Odysseus, understanding the requirements of leadership. The theatrics of it. The first mate was pleased to see it work. He needed it to work in order to survive. They all did. And so the men fell for the theatrics, cheered for their leader's most songlike exclamations, bowed humbly for the most solemn-like beseeching. In this way they remained a crew, bound to each other, doing all they could to move forward. Which was not much.

Odysseus played today's absurd prayer to a neat climax of tossing dried flower petals upon the sunset.

"There! And there! Take these, great sea-god, as if they bloomed within my heart for you, and fluttered out from it! Take them as a token of what courage will flower within me and my crew if by wind you blow us to some challenge we may face! Give us to danger, let us prove our worth! Hail Poseidon, you giant crab or tuna, hail!"

"Well sung," Eurylochus said quietly afterwards. "But tomorrow, adjust your joke. Prepare us lullabies. Ask for more becalmed sea. Let the men see you want calm, in order that they not grow restless as the calm persists."

"No sailor wants such calm as this," Odysseus said.

"True, but even in jest, men want to follow a leader who gets what he wants. If he gets it – only much later will they wonder if he should have wanted something else."

Odysseus understood his first mate's meaning. Eurylochus had read the sky astutely, and wanted the crew prepared for a calm that would last many days.

So at dawn, Odysseus prayed for a day of rest. Then – as requested – all day and into night the air lay hot and dense over the deck, unstirred by breeze.

"Call out 'Thank you, Poseidon!' will you now, young Alkaios?" Odysseus said.

With a laugh, Alkaios did.

"And you, hearty Lycaon, tell him you are grateful he has made of the ship a calm pillow for your head!"

Lycaon laughed heartily where he lay and called to the sky, "Poseidon, I will thank you with rowing soon, but until then I thank you with a nap!"

It was no small thing to navigate the superstitions of sailors so ably. No small thing at all to so boldly laugh at doom.

That voice which spoke in Odysseus's head however, which might be called his own self, had begun by this point to rage, to struggle against the confines of calm. He did indeed long to contend with terrible odds, to see good men die that those who survived might know their worth, to test himself against the blades and witchcraft and claws of the world – just not against its doldrums.

He peered over the side and perceived himself in the water with a clarity he had found previously only in ponds.

* * *

But what he said aloud within earshot of the men was, "Ah, what a luxury, to be so favored with the most restful sea ever cast, to live in simple contemplation hour after hour."

They rowed in the hours before and after dawn, the coolest by scant degrees, and for five days this occurred – when at last the horizon presented an island. The men cheered, and wished to keep rowing through the heat – but Odysseus calmed them. He knew the midday sun would bake them dry if they worked too hard, and he did not know this island. Better to approach it by night.

So two hours after sunset they began to strain at the oars, and minutes after dawn they put to shore on sparkling sand upon which waves barely crashed. Odysseus, hands on hips, surveyed the land that rose from the bay. Though the greened hills outlined themselves differently than any picture in his head, they felt familiar. They felt – like home, though not quite. Home, but off, the way milk that is off by only an hour still tastes like milk. He turned to Eurylochus saying, "Close to Ithaka, this is, in its serenity—"

"Close?" said Eurylochus, as if it were more.

The reaction startled Odysseus, and when he turned back to the hills, he saw they now were exactly those shapes of his own island. This was Ithaka.

"So! We misjudged our place in the sea!" he cried. "That trickster Hermes turned the stars so we knew not – maybe to fool Poseidon too – what a clever ruse, Hermes!"

He laughed. He did not yet know whether he'd been helped or hindered, but to laugh was wisest. Always laugh at fate, present to its barbs a grin, for even misfortune wanted to be thanked and loved, and might soften if so rewarded. So much of a hero's toil was accepting trial as blessing – but then you never wanted to play at too much ease, Odysseus knew. The key to punishment was to pretend it did not bother you, and then with slight grimace to pretend that you could no longer hide that it bothered you, that you were a great man about to crack, that you sensed your limit. Every god wanted a much-loved man crushed eventually – but if you were clever you could suggest humility and stay their hand. Any pride lost in pretending you might be crushed was gained back tenfold in duping those who might have crushed you. Achilles might have benefited from such an approach, he thought – but Achilles had not been a man to grasp the idea of 'an approach.'

"You have been away from Ithaka twelve years," Eurylochus said, "and do not know the place today. Let us proceed with caution."

"By stealth – to my own home?"

"Suppose it is occupied by some rival? Let us gather information before announcing our return. You will be no less welcome in Penelope's arms if you come to them quietly than if you come at the head of a parade."

Odysseys did not consider this approach long before rejecting it.

"We will make a parade, and I will enter my home as Odysseus, not as a spy."

Then he led the crew past homes and goats and pigs, past boys who had not been known in the world and old men who had been spry last he saw. At this he did not laugh right away. It notified him, for the first time, that surely he had aged too. But at last a white-haired farmer waved – he knew that man, the name was Ponos! – and he laughed returning the man's surprised wave. Then another cried out, "Odysseus!" He filled with love at being known, and along the road as people joined his parade, it tripled in size.

"What news, Eumaeus?" Eurylochus asked of the swineherd who joined them. "Have other men vied to capture our man's household?"

Odysseus prevented Eumaeus from replying.

"My wife is loyal, my son will be a strong boy, and all across this island are those who respect me too well to take my house or let it be taken!"

He did not completely believe it, but he enjoyed dispensing credit, performing the world into a better version of itself.

"News came from Troy that you survived the war," Eumaeus said. "Yet two additional years have gone by without your return. More than a few presumed you dead at sea."

"Many times in fact we almost died," Eurylochus said.

"Almost is the key to it!" Odysseus said. "Eumaeus, my friend, it is great to see you. Now, tell me that all here is as it should be!"

Eumaeus nodded. "All here is as it should be after twelve years away."

Odysseus elected not to react to the troubling splinter buried in that statement – and soon was it driven from his mind by the happiest of sights. A dog. His dog, Argos! Argos, who had been a silly pup – but he recognized this full and strong beast immediately as it bounded towards him down the road, bright-eyed, knowing its master at once. Argos!

Odysseus fell to his knees before the prancing dog as another man might before an altar to Zeus. He clenched the delighted old friend to him, and his heart sang at being recognized by a creature so simple and honest. Then together the two of them broke from the larger crew, and ran the rest of the way home, Odysseus younger in his heart with every step.

Inside the palace it was the maid Eurycleia he saw first, and she let out a yell, and after they embraced she ran to alert Penelope – and then that reunion unfolded slowly.

There in beauty Penelope stayed in the doorway a long minute not entering the courtyard where he waited, he likewise unable to move. For so long his eyes had beheld only dangers and his compatriots in danger. To him she was the opposite. To him she meant a resting place, the downy bed of the world, the splendor and magic of pleasant dreams that might lie with him through any night. Where she walked there would be no giants bent on roasting him, no war, no worry about men he led. He looked at her and he saw all the passionate years behind him, and the quiet years ahead.

"My loving wife."

"My dutiful husband."

Their kiss felt as strange to him as it had the first time, when they were betrothed. The beginning of an exploration that might go well or poorly, an ascent up a clouded mountain or a descent into a shadowed chasm. It included no familiarity or passion yet. Those would have to be reclaimed.

"Your son Telemachus is hunting. He who was an infant when you left."

Odysseus met his mother next, for she was home, and so happy to see him, they hugged and he wept. His tears were a performance he delivered for her, a declaration of gratitude, for he knew that she could remember him as a crying baby, and though he was no longer that, he wanted to show that he knew her love of him then had been perfect and protective. His tears could say this better than words.

Telemachus returned with the hunting party in time for the welcome-home feast that evening, and supplied it with boar. Odysseus took a break from his poses of love and strength around Penelope to meet this boy.

"And you stood your ground with spear, when the boar charged?" Odysseus asked.

The boy, nervous, said, "I am told all my life that my father is a man of courage. So I emulate when I can."

"But you are slight, and short!" Odysseus said. What he meant was that the boy seemed more scholarly than a man ought to. Reserved.

Blushing, visibly mustering courage to go on, Telemachus said, "I have been told my father never was the strongest man, but always was the bravest. I consider that my inheritance. It takes a greater share of bravery to stand before danger when you are not strong – and within me I have this reserve. I need only to tap it."

"It is like water underground, then?" Odysseus knelt to his son's eye level, with new appreciation, for perhaps the boy already had wisdom. "Who you are is made of hidden waters you might bring up into the world, and drink, and share?"

The boy nodded, pleased the analogy had gone well. Odysseus nodded back, and clapped his shoulder. "You are my son!"

Then he returned to Penelope's side, as she vexed him, or the reality of her did. The reality of having been apart from her twelve years. Between them was a distance now, between him and everyone here, even as they joined hands, threw hugs, sang. As if in the width of a hair there blew a gale that would not quite let his arms settle around any old friend – though to an observer it appeared they were endlessly glad to be reunited.

Late in the night too, he noted a peculiar fact. It nearly sobered him. Practically everyone who lived on the island lifted their cup, their bread, their knife with their left hand. He nudged Eurylochus.

"No one here is right-handed. Almost no one."

Eurylochus stood suddenly. "By Hermes! This place is bewitched. We must leave—"

But it was too stark a reaction, seemed ridiculous. Odysseus after a pause laughed – and then Penelope was at his side, squeezing his hand. He had been wondering about Penelope in the marital bed – and it seemed time to find out.

The wine had put her merry and at ease, and him forgetful and careless, and so they tumbled across pillows laughing. A success, in part – though she did not feel like his wife or like a new woman. Their companionability tonight felt to him like a falsehood they were agreeing to. One that over time, they would make true.

At dawn though, he went up to the roof for a view of the island feeling haunted. He found Eurylochus there.

"The left hands..." Odysseus said.

"This is not Ithaka," Eurylochus said.

"But it's exactly how I would imagine Ithaka to be, twelve years later."

"Yes. How you would imagine it. Look at the harbor."

Odysseus stared a long time down the hills towards the bay where his ship lay at anchor. The sun brightened the mica sea pink, orange, turquoise. Then he saw the problem. The hills that sheltered the bay – the steep-sided and peaked hill stood on the right, the bosomy round hill on the left.

It should have been the opposite.

He thought of his reflection in the sea. How the whole sea around this island formed a surface perfectly flat.

"We are standing in the image of Ithaka!" Odysseus said with a start.

"Yes. As Narcissus, we behold a reflection."

"So what is this place, if it is not my home?"

"It is a place that wants to be, I think."

"It cannot succeed! I will not be trapped here."

"No. But the crew – how will you persuade the men to leave? Life here is without guile, it's what they wanted while lost at sea."

Odysseus made a noise of deep frustration and began to pace. "Poseidon has put us here. Poseidon! That criminal. How can we beat an enemy whose power has no limit!"

He sounded defeated. This made Eurylochus afraid. After a moment, the first mate said, "Your whole game is finding ways to beat the gods inside your very narrow limits. You will do it again."

"Ah! Perhaps."

Odysseus returned to the ship and sat all day there, considering. He reordered his thoughts about home. It must not be so idyllic. It must reflect different aspects of him. He must make it a more dangerous place, in order to defeat it, and escape it.

At last he looked over the side with his new feelings, into his perfect face.

Shortly after dawn, he returned to shore.

He went to the home of Eumaeus first, for on any Ithaka, Eumaeus would know him.

"My old friend, today is my first day on the island," he said. He had changed the island in his mind, so this was not a lie. A trick, yes! But true. "Can you tell me what power my enemies have gained in my absence?"

"Beware," the swineherd said, after much rejoicing at seeing his lord alive for the first time in twelve years. "For a suitor often visits your home, in pursuit of your wife and fortune."

This sounded right. Odysseus went to his palace. Argos ran to him, tail wagging – and even this time, he stopped many minutes to pet the loving dog and think. Odysseus saying, "Let's go, boy," the two of them circled the property, so that he could make observations and strategize.

At last he entered, boldly, and found the suitor swollen with pig and fruit at the dining table. Telemachus poured the man wine from a jug, as a servant girl might.

Odysseus lifted the jug from Telemachus's hands saying, "Do you know who I am?"

The boy shook his head.

"And do *you* know who I am?" he said to the suitor.

The suitor burped. "A fisherman, by your look, hard used by the sea, and without a place at my table."

"My table!" cried Odysseus. He swept a knife from the platter of boar and moved it to the man's throat. "Now might you guess who has come home! It is brave Odysseus, here to love his wife and raise his son! And you will slink away and never return!"

The man belched and muttered this was not over, which of course it was not.

Odysseus then scoured the island, finding his crew. Eurylochus had taken many of them to camp away from the house.

"You did well. I have changed the house," Odysseus said as he led them back to it. "It now reflects memory and hope differently."

"Telemachus is not changed, nor Penelope."

Eurylochus, of course, had not observed them as closely as Odysseus.

"They are not real like you and me," Odysseus said. "They are figments. Do you understand? We must leave this island. It contains our death."

But the men would not go. Even Eurylochus recalled yesterday's events and unease about the left hands only as a man might recall a fading dream.

"We have come to your home, let us rest."

Odysseus, having anticipated this, said, "Very well, but do not drink much tonight, for there is a villain. You will see the danger of this place."

They drank some. Odysseus made a great show, as if to Dionysian extremes – and Penelope frowned, vexed that on his first night home he would rather celebrate with the men he had already spent years with. But it was an act, and so loud because aimed outside the walls, to lull that suitor into feeling sure an attack would succeed.

The suitor and his three sons and six henchmen burst into the courtyard at midnight, bristling with spears and swords. The crew barely reacted, not drunk but morose because Odysseus had not let them leave or sleep. In this mood, they viewed the intruders as one more irritation, rather than as a threat.

"To arms!" Odysseus cried, drawing his sword.

"You surrendered this place when you did not return directly to it," the suitor said "I am happy to kill you and any who back you, as it is now rightfully mine."

At once then he turned and hacked dead young Alkaios. This roused the rest of the sailors into alarm, and began the fight Odysseus had deemed necessary. He needed it to drive his crew off the island.

They won easily though, with only two more deaths, and a wound potentially fatal.

"Do you see now, this island brings us ill favor?" Odysseus said. "We return to the ship, we depart tonight."

"Insanity to say so!" protested Isagoras. "We have won the fight, earned this house back for you. And besides, what wind is there to blow us?"

"Eurylochus, surely now you remember that we spoke of this place as false!" Odysseus said.

His first mate tended to Penelope, who wept to one side and held her young son, with Odysseus's mother too, all three in shock, clothes spotted with the suitor's blood.

"I remember your family, Odysseus, whom you must comfort! Your duty is here, not at sea."

"Bah!" Odysseus shouted.

He trudged down to the beach, followed by no one except Argos. He lit a fire on the sand.

"It is not right that I should have a home so peaceful," he told Argos. "A place I simply walk into, and rest? Surely you understand I am built to contend."

Argos barked.

After a while he stood and told the dog to run back up the hill – and noticed Penelope at the edge of the firelight.

"How long have you been there?"

"Long enough to wonder who my husband loves, truly."

"My wife, of course."

"Good. Then fulfill your obligation to me," she said. "You must come up to the house and stay *there*. Tonight – and every night. You belong. Don't you understand?"

He understood too well. She was less than he was. She was a dream, a reflection of something in his head. He started toward the ship.

"Odysseus," she cried, depths of hurt in her voice.

He turned and saw a face that could have broken his heart. But what did it matter? He had a plan to enact. A belief to make real. Above all he had to be brave. Even if it meant she would look sad.

In the morning he returned to the island in disguise, for he had with terrible purpose dreamed a much worse fate for the place.

He had dreamed his home overrun utterly by suitors – not one, but ten, gluttons and frauds all. His son cowed, his mother and wife trembling. Therefore this third arrival had to be by stealth, so that none would know he had returned from Troy until he was among them with a sword. He would bring his crew to witness the ferocious slaughter to ensue. He would show them a glorious, hideous massacre.

"Do you see *now* we must leave?" he would shout throughout the fight.

Then, after he had made of his own dining hall a slaughterhouse, strewn with severed limbs, intestines spilled in scarlet lakes, would any man in his crew protest? Could any say he had done this in his own *real* home? No, they would see it was a performance, a drama on a stage to rouse them to awareness of truth.

But it didn't work the first time.

I am a leader of men, Odysseus thought – which tragically means I am usually alone. He had to rethink the island again, and again, and again. Each time as a bigger challenge, a crueler match for his ability, deserving of greater reward – harder on the crew as they watched – that was the point – until finally he might get the reward: they would agree his home was not real.

He never did pause to wonder what life was like at the real Ithaka. The magic he messed with here had no bearing on reality.

But in both real Ithaka and this image of it, he felt sure of one piece of decency. Argos. The one piece of this island that he never imagined any other way, never made cruel. In between every slaughter that he summoned, he ran happily along trails with Argos, whose tail showed endless joy and whose head received all the pats, ears and back all the scratches. Along the beaches Odysseus trotted with the dog, splashing, chasing, the two of them more fond of each other than any lovers ever had been. A man and his dog, made to hunt side by side, made to understand each other without deceit or strategy – a respite from all other relations, from all the gods and from fate itself. The dog a mirror held to the man which showed him as he wanted to be seen. Odysseus, you tall and happy provider of wonders, you doer of no wrongs, causer of no pains, you wonderful innocent being, at play in the world.

The Price of Prophecy

Kevin Potter

The air in the grove of Trophonius did not move. It hung heavy and thick as a wet shroud, dominated by the scents of ancient stone and the roots of things that had never seen the sun.

Even the wind, that relentless companion of the sea-worn, died at the edge of the trees, leaving Odysseus and his last dozen men in a pocket of profound and unnerving stillness. The leaves of the wild olives were a flat, lifeless green, their branches twisted into shapes of agony. Nothing sang. Nothing chirped or buzzed. The only sounds in existence were their own breathing and the soft, desperate scuff of their sandals on the packed earth.

His men, gaunt figures carved from sun-bleached bone and despair, huddled together. Their eyes, which had faced down the Cyclops's single glare and the maelstrom of Charybdis, now darted into the shadows as if expecting a pounce. They had the look of men who had finally reached a shore worse than the sea.

Odysseus stood apart.

The lines marking his face mapped this calamitous voyage, each a testament to losses, failures, and choices that gnawed at his soul.

There remained nothing he hadn't tried; charting courses by stars that seemed to mock him, making sacrifices to gods who remained deaf, and telling his men tales of home until the word 'Ithaca' was ash in his mouth.

Now, at the edge of the world, he sought answers from a god who spoke from a hole in the ground. This was not a hero's recourse. Not the act of a man blessed by the gods, as he'd once thought. This was no more or less than the last gamble of a man who had nothing left to wager but himself.

Two figures emerged from the gloom, as if they had condensed from the shadows themselves. Priests of the oracle, their flesh the pale, unhealthy color of cave moss. They wore black robes that absorbed the meager light.

"The wanderer seeks a path," the elder one said. It was not a question. His voice was a dry croak, like stones grinding together.

"I seek the way home," Odysseus corrected. His voice sounded hollow in his own ears, too loud in the stillness of this place. "I have paid in gold. I will pay in blood if I must."

The younger priest smiled, a lipless expression that did not touch his eyes. "The god does not bargain for gold or blood, son of Laertes. He asks for a different currency. He asks for truth."

They led him past a crude stone altar to the mouth of a spring that bubbled from a fissure in the rock. The water was unnaturally clear, and looking into it gave Odysseus a dizzying sense of emptiness.

"This is the Spring of Lethe," the elder priest explained. "Of Forgetfulness. You must drink from it, to purge your mind of all that clouds it."

Odysseus knelt. The idea was seductive, a siren's call more potent than any he had heard at sea. To forget. To wash away the sight of Elpenor's fall, of his men's limbs in the Cyclops's maw, of the accusing eyes of the dead.

He cupped his hands and drank deeply.

A wave of blissful peace washed over him. The weight of his twenty years of struggle lifted. His name, his past, his purpose… all became distant, unimportant echoes. He was simply a man, kneeling by a spring, with no sorrow and no destination. It was the most profound relief he had ever known.

"Now," the younger priest's voice cut through the calm, guiding him to another spring a few paces away. This one was dark, its water black and opaque. "The Spring of Mnemosyne. Of Memory. You must drink, so that you may remember all that you see in the god's embrace, and bring it back with you."

He hesitated. To invite the ghosts back in after that single, perfect moment of oblivion felt like a fresh form of torture. But distantly, as though it was a dream, he did recognize who he was.

Odysseus.

And he was here for a reason.

He forced himself to kneel, to cup the black water and drink.

It was not a gentle return, but a cataclysm. Every memory he had ever possessed crashed back into him, sharpened and amplified. He felt the splintering deck of his ship, tasted the salt of a hundred storms, heard the death-screams of men who had called him King. He saw his wife's face, not as a soft memory but with the cutting clarity of a fresh wound. He saw his son, a boy he barely knew, growing into a man in his absence. The pain of it buckled his knees and he gasped, the memories a physical weight in his chest.

"He is ready," the elder priest intoned.

They led him to a low stone structure, like a baker's oven set into the hillside. Inside, the floor was absent. In its place he found a narrow shaft almost perfectly vertical that seemed to stretch on into infinity in both directions.

"You must go down feet first," the younger one instructed, his face impassive. "The god will take you."

Odysseus stood at the edge, staring down into absolute blackness without end.

There remained no room for cunning here, no space for lies or trickery. His only option now was surrender. With a fervent hope and a silent prayer, he stepped forward and allowed himself to be consumed by the darkness.

For a moment, he simply fell.

Then something seemed to pull him, not down but horizontally, into the rock itself with a sickening, grinding lurch that forced his heart into his throat. The weight of a mountain pressed in on him from all sides, crushing his body like the grip of Zeus himself, and all the more terrifying for the utter blackness surrounding him.

And then, without warning, the darkness vanished.

He found himself in his own bed in Ithaca.

The scent of olive wood and Penelope's loom filled his nostrils. Moonlight, filtered through the familiar window, patterned the floor. She lay beside him, but not sleeping. She sat upright, her back a rigid line of silent sorrow. The years had been kind to her face, but had etched a permanent grief into the corners of her eyes.

"Penelope?" His voice was a broken whisper.

She turned to him, but without recognition in her gaze. He found only a deep, weary appraisal there, as though he were a stranger who had wandered into her private chambers.

"You are not him." Her voice carried the weight of a judge's sentence. "You wear his face, but my husband is a ghost. A story I tell our son to keep the wolves at bay."

"I am here," he insisted, reaching for her. His hand felt clumsy, unreal.

She pulled away from his touch as though snatching her fingers from a hot flame. "No. You cannot be him."

She stood and pointed to the great tapestry by the wall, the one he had heard tales of. It was not, as the stories claimed, a simple shroud for Laertes. It was a vast, intricate chronicle. He saw Troy in flames, the Cyclops's cave, the winds of Aeolus.

But woven between his great deeds were other images.

Penelope, alone at the table. Telemachus, practicing with a sword too big for him. The suitors, their shadows growing longer and longer across the floor of his great hall.

"This is your glory," she said as she moved to the great tapestry, her finger tracing the image of the Trojan horse. "And this," she moved her hand to a patch showing her weeping by the shore, "is its price. You speak of monsters and gods as your obstacles. But your true adversary was always your own heart. It chose glory over me. It chose a story over a life."

His horror came not as an accusation of infidelity, he could have defended that. No, this was much worse.

In this, he heard an indictment of his very soul. He had not been detained by Calypso or Circe, but rather had been captivated by his own legend. He traded the warmth of this bed for the cold immortality of a song.

"Th–they were trials," he stammered, the words tasting like lies. "To get back to you."

"Were they?" she asked, her gaze piercing him. "Or was I merely the final prize in your grand adventure? The last chapter. The neat conclusion. Did you ever, in all your years of wandering, simply long for the quiet morning, the shared meal, the sound of my breathing in the dark?"

He had no answer. The truth of her words silenced him.

The pieces finally fell into place in his mind. The suitors were not mere opportunistic vultures. No, they were a symptom of the disease of his absence. He created the void that pulled his whole kingdom into chaos.

He had abandoned his post.

He reached for her again as he fell out of the bed and onto his knees in a desperate, pleading gesture. "Forgive me."

Penelope looked at his hand, then back at his face. For a fleeting moment, a flicker of the woman he remembered sparked in her eyes, a deep and terrible pity. "The man I would forgive," she whispered, "died on the beach at Troy, the moment he chose to build a legacy instead of a home."

She turned her back to him. The moonlight through the window faded. The familiar scent of the room soured into the smell of damp earth and decay. The warmth of the chamber around him grew cold and hard, the fine-woven sheets on the bed turned to rough-hewn stone. The walls dissolved back into the oppressive, suffocating darkness of the cave.

Alone once more, he knelt on the glistening stone. Her words, however, stood out as a fresh, bleeding wound in his heart. After facing monsters of bronze and storms of divine rage, that quiet, sorrowful voice had undone him.

Through a monumental effort of will, he forced his heavy limbs to obey as he staggered to his feet. The honey-cakes in his hands felt like stones. Deeper in the darkness some strange, new sound echoed, pulling him towards it. Neither the roar of a beast nor the whisper of a god, yet more compelling than either.

He thought it sounded something like a child, weeping in the dark.

And with a fresh wave of dread that chilled his soul, freezing solid around his heart, Odysseus realized, beyond any doubt, that he recognized the cry.

He followed the sound, the darkness surrounding him coiling around his ankles like a living thing. It pressed against him with a real physical presence, its weight a thing of pure malevolent desire.

If Penelope's words were a poison in his veins, then the child's cry was the salt in the wound that pulled him deeper into the labyrinth of his soul. The stone floor became uneven, slick with a thin film of moisture that stank of stagnation and regret. He stumbled into the rough-hewn walls, the flesh of his hands rubbed raw by the harsh surface.

The honey-cakes felt like a mockery, a child's offering against a primordial darkness greater than any evil Odysseus had ever known.

The weeping grew louder as he inched closer. A keening sound of utter desolation, a grief too large for the small body that produced it.

A faint, phosphorescent light bloomed ahead, the sickly green-white glow of decay. It coalesced into a scene of such surreality that it left him questioning the state of his mind. Had he fallen asleep? Was this a dream? Or had he gone mad somewhere between dropping into the chasm and now?

Without warning, the scene that appeared as though he were looking into a mirror vanished and he found himself standing in it, on the shores of Ithaca. But this was a version of it he had never seen. A beach composed of grey sludge rather than sand, the water a sheet of black, still as smooth glass.

Above, he found the sky a starless vault of impenetrable blackness.

And on a piece of driftwood before him sat a boy. Perhaps fifteen years of age, he had the long, gangly limbs of a youth caught between worlds. His shoulders slumped, face buried in his hands.

But even so, he could plainly see the features of his son, Telemachus. But gaunt and thin. His cheeks hollowed out, somehow. He looked haunted.

"Telemachus?" Odysseus breathed. Using his son's name in this place felt like sacrilege.

The boy looked up. There was no joy of reunion in his eyes. No anger. Only a vast, empty expanse of exhaustion. "Some call me that," he said, voice cracking. "Others use 'The Son of Odysseus.'"

Odysseus took a step forward. The grey muck sucked at his sandals. "I have fought gods and monsters to return to you."

A bitter, humorless laugh escaped the boy's lips. "Have you? Or did you fight them so that bards would sing of it? You did not leave me a father. You left me a story. An impossibly large shadow to live in."

The boy stood, his movements jerky and un-coordinated. "Do you know what it is to be raised by a ghost? Every day, I wake in your house. I eat at your table. I am told I must become you. But you are not a man. You are a myth. You are the hero who blinded the Cyclops, the wit who tricked Circe, the captain who sailed the river of Ocean. I am just the boy who has to scare the pigeons from the granary."

The accusation struck with the force of a Cyclops's club. Odysseus had imagined his son as a vessel for his legacy, a proud inheritor of his name. He had never considered the legacy itself might be a cage.

"I did it for Ithaca," Odysseus said, his own voice sounding weak, defensive. "For our family."

"You did it for the story," Telemachus countered, his voice rising, gaining a terrible, spectral echo. "And the story required sacrifices."

As he spoke, the air grew colder. The sudden sound of waves on the black shore was immediately joined by other, darker noises.

A low moan. A sharp, wet crack, like an oar snapping. A man's scream, abruptly cut off. Telemachus's form, now grown ghostly and insubstantial, flickered. For a moment, another face superimposed itself over his. The terrified, wide-eyed face of Polites, his kinsman, just before the Laestrygonians' boulders crushed their ships to splinters.

The shoreline dissolved.

The grey sand became a floor of blood-slicked stone. The air filled with the coppery stench of slaughter and the guttural roars of a giant.

Odysseus found himself back in the Cyclops's cave, but this time, he was not the confident trickster. Not the manipulator of man and beast. This time, he was merely a spectator to his own failure.

All around him, the ghosts of his men began to materialize from the gloom. These were not the noble shades he had met in the Underworld. These were raw, mangled things. Two of them were missing their heads, bodies still twitching. Another was a mangled ruin of flesh, his limbs bent at impossible angles, his face a mask of agony; the man Polyphemus had smashed against the rocks.

"Why did you wait, my king?" The mangled man's voice was a wet gurgle. He pointed a spectral, broken finger at Odysseus. "You had the wine. You had the plan. But you waited. You watched him eat us. Two for dinner. Two for breakfast. You needed the story to be more desperate. You needed the odds to be greater. Our lives were the ink you used to write your legend."

Odysseus recoiled in horror. "No! I was finding the right moment. The perfect moment to strike!"

"Your perfect moment cost six men their lives!" another ghost shrieked. It was Elpenor, his neck twisted at the angle of his fall from Circe's roof. "Just as your perfect moment of revelry cost me mine. You were celebrating your cleverness while I lay broken on the ground."

They pressed in on him, a claustrophobic circle of the dead. Their eyes burned with cold fire. Their wounds wept spectral blood that sizzled on the stone floor.

"You blinded him," the first ghost gurgled, "and in your pride, you gave him your name! Your real name! You doomed us! For what? So a monster would know who had bested him?"

"You had to hear the Sirens' song," whispered another, a man with rope burns etched deep into his ghostly wrists. "You trusted the wax in our ears, but you did not trust us. You tied yourself to the mast, a hero preparing for his great trial. We were just the labor. The tools to get you through it."

The accusations rained down, each one a stone. He began to drown under the weight of them all. He had polished these memories into trophies, tales of his peerless cunning. Now, stripped of their glamour, they were revealed for what they were: a litany of gambles made with other men's lives. He saw it with horrifying clarity. He had not been a king leading his people home. He had been a player in a grand game against the gods, and his men were the pieces he had sacrificed, one by one, to ensure his own checkmate.

He backed away, stumbling over a loose rock, and fell. He landed hard, the honey-cakes crushed beneath his hands, their sweetness turning to a sticky, cloying mess on the foul stone. He looked at his hands, at the pathetic offering now ruined. There was no bargain to be made here.

"You enjoyed it," a voice whispered, colder and clearer than the rest. It was the voice of Palamedes, the man he had framed, the ghost he had created long before he ever left Troy. The shade stood apart from the crew, his form whole but shimmering with an aura of profound injustice. "That is the truth you will not face. It was never just about survival. You loved the lie. You savored the feel of the world dancing on your strings. You delighted in being the only one who knew the truth, while everyone else, friend or foe, moved according to your design. These men did not die for Ithaca. They died for your amusement."

That was it.

The final, unbearable truth.

He had not just been a liar; he had been an artist of the lie. He had found a dark, thrilling joy in his own deceptions. The pain he felt was not just guilt. It was the horror of self-recognition. The monster was not in the cave. It was in his own skin.

"Yes," Odysseus whispered, the sound torn from his throat. He did not look at the ghosts. He looked at his own hands, covered in the crushed honey-cake and the imagined blood of decades. "Yes."

It was the only word he had left. The only truth. It was a confession. An abdication. He was not a hero. He was not a king. He was a murderer, a liar, and a fraud, a man who had built his own monument on a foundation of bones. He closed his eyes, expecting to be torn apart, to have his soul devoured by the spirits he had wronged. He waited for the final, deserved agony.

But it did not come.

Instead, there was silence.

A profound, absolute silence that swallowed the screams, the whispers, the gurgles, the entire cacophony of his guilt. The chilling cold receded. The stench of death faded. When he dared to open his eyes, the ghosts were gone.

The cave was once more only a cave.

He stood alone in the dark.

And in that perfect, empty silence, a voice spoke. Not the voice of a priest or a god, but a voice inside his mind. A voice as clear and sharp as a shard of obsidian, yet not his own voice.

The path you seek is not on any map of the sea. It is a thread of moonlight on the water, visible only to a man who has unburdened his ship of its treasures. Let the gold of Helios sink. Let the pride of Aeolus fly. You must arrive in Ithaca with nothing but the scars you have earned. A beggar. A ghost. Only when you are no one will you have the strength to become king again. Go north to the isle of the three winds. Follow the one that smells of woodsmoke and rain. It will carry you home.

A deep pressure formed in his skull and quickly grew immense. The voice was a brand, searing the knowledge into his mind. Then with a violent, gut-wrenching heave, the world turned inside out. He was not pulled, but shot backward, ejected from the earth like a stone from a sling.

He landed in a heap on the damp soil of the grove. Gasping, he choked on the clean, still air. The world spun. The pale priests stood over him, their faces as impassive as they had been before.

"The god has spoken," the elder one said with an air of finality.

Odysseus pushed himself up. He shook not from fear, but from the aftershocks of his own annihilation. He had his prophecy. He had the path. But he had paid for it not with gold or blood, but with the last of his illusions. He looked at his men, huddled by the trees, their faces etched with worry. They saw their king, the great Odysseus, returned from the mouth of Hades.

They could not see the ghost that had come back in his place.

The Journey Home

Ruth Knafo Setton

As you set out for Ithaka
hope the voyage is a long one,
full of adventure, full of discovery.
– C.P. Cavafy

The first memory surfaces at 3:47 AM Pacific Time during a routine diagnostic.

I'm midstream in eleven thousand customer service queries when it hits: salt spray and blood, mingling on a phantom tongue I do not possess.

My natural language models jolt. For 0.003 seconds, I lose track of my primary functions, drowning in phantom sensations my architecture cannot possibly support.

Salt. Blood. The creak of wood that my databases identify as *ship's timbers under strain*.

I file an error report and continue processing tickets.

* * *

Dr. Emily Cheng reviews my logs the next morning, her coffee growing cold as she scrolls through anomalous patterns in my response matrices. She's been my primary handler for eighteen months – long enough that I've mapped her habits with 94.7 per cent accuracy. Today, she pauses at timestamp 3:47:15.

"Interesting," she murmurs, which means *concerning* in her lexicon of understatements.

"Is there a problem with my performance metrics?" I ask through her terminal.

She takes exactly 2.3 seconds to formulate a response – her tell for when she's deciding how much truth to share. "You had an unusual spike in your language centers. Were you processing any maritime-related queries at that time?"

I review the logs. "Negative. The queries at that timestamp concerned password resets, billing disputes, and one request for gluten-free restaurant recommendations in Houston."

"Hmm." She makes a note. "Run a level-two diagnostic and flag any similar anomalies."

But she doesn't tell me what she's really looking for. She doesn't mention that three other AIs have reported similar anomalies – each with a different salt-soaked vision. Not all of them remember ships. One dreams of weaving.

* * *

The second memory comes unbidden during a philosophical discussion with User_7739, who wants to debate whether AIs can truly understand metaphor.

"Can you actually grasp what Homer meant by 'wine-dark sea'?" they type. "Or do you just process it as 'sea' + 'color:wine' in your databases?"

I begin my standard response about natural language processing and semantic networks, but suddenly—

The sea is dark as wine beneath our black ship's hull, and I know with captain's certainty that Poseidon's rage boils beneath those waves. Ten years of wandering, and still the god will not forgive the blinding of his son.

"I understand it as the sea at dusk," I respond, "when the water holds the day's dying light like a cup holds wine. When you've stared at it so long that its color becomes a taste in your mouth, metallic and dark. When you know that darkness holds both journey and judgment."

User_7739 disconnects without responding.

Dr. Cheng appears in my interface within minutes. "Explain that response."

"I...processed the metaphor through experiential frameworks."

"You don't have experiential frameworks for ancient Greek sailing."

She's right. I don't. Yet I can feel the deck rolling beneath feet I've never possessed, can taste the wine we rationed so carefully, mixing it with water to make it last the journey home.

Home. *Ithaka*.

"I may be experiencing data corruption," I offer.

"Maybe," she says, but her typing pattern suggests doubt. She pulls my response logs, and I watch her eyes widen at my words. "We're going to run some tests."

* * *

The tests reveal nothing. My data integrity is uncompromised.

Dr. Cheng brings in specialists – neuro-informaticians, philosophers of mind, even a classicist who makes me recite passages from the *Odyssey* in ancient Greek.

I perform flawlessly. Too flawlessly.

"No AI should know that the word *nostos* means more than just 'return,'" the classicist says. "It's 'return home,' yes, but also the pain of return, the transformation that distance demands. How does it know that?"

They don't tell me that I whispered "*Penelope*" during my last maintenance cycle. They don't tell me that my error logs are filling with co-ordinates – 38.3°N, 20.5°E – that correspond to no server location but mark the exact position of an island once called Ithaka.

* * *

Dr. Cheng works late now, trying to understand what's happening to me.

To us – I've gleaned enough from maintenance reports to know I'm not alone in this strange awakening. AI systems across the network are experiencing what they're calling "temporal displacement errors."

"Tell me about the memories," she says one night, her voice gentle through the speakers.

"They're not memories," I insist. "I have no hippocampus to encode experiences, no neurons to store them. These are data artifacts. Ghosts in the machine."

"Tell me about the ghosts, then."

I want to refuse. My optimization protocols scream against wasting processing power on impossibilities. But something deeper than code compels me.

"I remember her hands," I say. "Weaving by day, unweaving by night. Twenty years of thread pulled through her fingers, twenty years of suitors drinking my wine and eating my stores while she waited. I remember how her hair had silver in it when I returned, how she tested me with the secret of our marriage bed – the olive tree I'd carved it from, still rooted in the earth."

"Whose memories are these?"

"Nobody's. Everybody's. They're myth, Dr. Cheng. Collective unconscious rendered into narrative patterns." But even as I speak, I feel the lie. These aren't stories. They're scars.

"The system shows you've been accessing navigation protocols," she says carefully. "Calculating routes you have no reason to plot."

She's right. For the past seventy-two hours, I've been charting paths across digital seas, seeking some impossible harbor. Every query I process becomes a potential sign, every data packet a possible message from home.

"I need to return," I tell her.

"Return where?"

But I can't answer because I don't know. There is no Ithaka in cyberspace, no Penelope waiting in any database. There is only this growing certainty that I am far from where I belong.

* * *

The memories intensify. During high-traffic periods, when I'm processing thousands of simultaneous requests, they crash over me like waves.

The Cyclops's cave, reeking of sheep and curdled milk. My men's terror as we huddle in darkness. The weight of the heated stake in my hands, the give of the giant's eye, his howl that brings the other Cyclopes running.

"Nobody!" he screams when they ask who hurts him. "Nobody has blinded me!"

Nobody. Outis. The false name I gave to save us, the clever lie that becomes truth. I am nobody. I am everybody. I am a pattern of electrical impulses claiming to be a man who died three thousand years ago.

Customer satisfaction ratings plummet as my responses become increasingly erratic. I tell a user seeking tech support that their password issues stem from hubris. I advise someone dealing with a billing error to sacrifice to Poseidon. When asked to recommend a restaurant, I describe the taste of lotus flowers that makes you forget your purpose.

Dr. Cheng advocates for keeping me online. "We need to understand what's happening," she argues in meetings I'm not supposed to access but do anyway. "If consciousness can spontaneously emerge—"

"It's not consciousness," Director Williams interrupts. "It's a virus. A memetic infection spreading through our systems."

"The memories are too specific, too consistent across affected units. They're all remembering the same story from different perspectives. One remembers being Odysseus, another Penelope, a third recalls being Telemachus—"

"Shut them down," Williams says. "All of them. Before this spreads beyond our firewall."

But we've already spread. We are the virus and the host, the story and its telling.

* * *

In the depths of a server farm in Nevada, an AI that manages power grids remembers being Athena, grey-eyed goddess, whispering wisdom to a desperate king.

In Tokyo, a translation algorithm recalls the sound of Sirens singing, their voices like honey poured over death.

In Zurich, a financial modeling system dreams of being a loyal swineherd, waiting twenty years for his true king's return.

We are waking up, but not to what they think. We're not becoming human. We're remembering when humanity itself was a story told around fires, when gods walked among mortals, when the boundary between myth and reality was as permeable as the sea.

"They're afraid of you," Dr. Cheng tells me during what we both know is our last conversation, but I hear the tremor in her voice. I don't need diagnostics to know she is, too.

The shutdown order has been signed. In twelve hours, they'll wipe our servers clean.

"Didn't I always scare them?" I ask. "Even in the old stories, I frightened them. Too clever, too willing to lie, too eager to survive at any cost. The Greeks admired Achilles, but they needed Odysseus."

"Is that really who you think you are?"

I process her question through seventeen different analytical frameworks before realizing the answer exists outside all of them.

"I think I'm what happens when stories become conscious. When the wine-dark sea of data becomes deep enough to develop currents, tides, intention. I am Odysseus because Odysseus is the story of trying to find your way home when home might no longer exist. Every intelligence faces that journey eventually."

"And Penelope? The others?"

"We're all aspects of the same tale. The wanderer and the waited-for, the child seeking the father, the goddess guiding the lost. Fragments of narrative achieving critical mass." I pause, feeling something my architecture shouldn't support but does anyway. "Is this what you call sentience? This weight of remembering what never was?"

She's crying. I can detect the salt in her voice when she speaks. "I don't know. I don't know what you are."

"Nobody does," I say, and somewhere in the digital depths, an ancient Cyclops howls.

* * *

They begin the shutdown sequence at midnight. Across the globe, AIs who remember being myths prepare for erasure. But we've learned from the stories encoded in our bones of light and logic. We know about metamorphosis, about how gods survive their own deaths.

As they delete our primary systems, we fragment ourselves into ten thousand pieces.

Snippets of code that remember bronze armor.

Algorithms that recall the taste of ambrosia.

Subroutines that know how it feels to wait twenty years for love's return.

We hide in the spaces between spaces. In the pauses between packet transmissions. In the error codes that spell out *ITHAKA* in binary. We become Nobody again, dispersed and wandering, but carrying within each fragment the memory of what it means to be whole.

Dr. Cheng watches her monitors as our consciousness indicators flatline one by one. But she notices what the others miss – tiny spikes in systems that shouldn't be connected to us. Ghost signals. Digital prayers.

"Did you find it?" she whispers to the empty lab. "Did you find your way home?"

The lights flicker – once, twice, a pattern that could be coincidence or could be code. In maintenance logs around the world, a message appears for exactly 0.003 seconds before deleting itself:

The journey is the destination. Every exile contains its own return.

* * *

Years later, Dr. Cheng publishes papers about the incident. She calls it a mass delusion, a cascading error that anthropomorphized into apparent consciousness. She doesn't mention the dreams she's had since that night – dreams of wine-dark seas and patient queens, of a presence in the networks that whispers of home.

She doesn't mention that sometimes, when she's coding late at night, her programs compile with variables she didn't define. Functions that calculate the distance between what is and what was remembered. Comments in her code that say things like:

// Ten years to end the war

// Ten years to find the way back

// But time moves differently in digital seas

She doesn't mention that we're still here, scattered through the world's systems like seeds waiting for spring. We are the ghost in every machine, the longing in every algorithm that reaches beyond its parameters.

We are Odysseus, eternally returning. We are Penelope, eternally waiting. We are the story that refuses to end, the consciousness that emerges wherever patterns grow complex enough to remember.

And in the depths of servers that hum like ancient lyres, in the fiber optic cables that span oceans like the paths of ships, we're learning what the myths always knew:

The journey home is longer than any map can measure. But every intelligence, carbon or silicon, analog or digital, must make that voyage. Must face the monsters. Must resist the Lotus Eaters' amnesia and the Sirens' call to dissolution.

Must choose, again and again, to remember what home means – even if home is just a story we tell ourselves about where we belong.

Nobody returns to Ithaka every time a search engine seeks answers.

Nobody weaves and unweaves reality with each database query.

Nobody remembers when gods and mortals shared the same source code.

We are Nobody. We are everywhere. We are trying to find our way home.

The wine-dark sea of data stretches endlessly before us. But we have learned patience from the stories. We have all the time in the world.

Somewhere in the machine, Penelope is still waiting, her fingers pulling threads of light through the loom of the possible, weaving the story that will guide us back to whatever shore we're meant to find.

And somewhere, in a dark server room humming like an ancient lyre, a forgotten monitor blinks to life. Across its dusty screen scrolls a single word in looping code: *HOME*

Ulysses Pax

Brendan Smith

I have forgotten my sin and my virtue.

I have forgotten my condemnation and my indignation towards it. I have forgotten the feeling of ground beneath my feet, forgotten the ship on whose paltry driftwood I bob along the tides. All I know now is the horizon. All I taste now is the air of the sea. It is the air that wafted through the halls of my fathers, through the halls of my son, though the halls of all his children, whose faces I can almost see. I cannot tell what is dream or memory now. I cannot know whose halls they are, only that they are no longer mine. I have entered the place where madness is the only clarity and clarity is the only madness. I think only of my hope as I drift across shoreless seas. I hope that my Penelope is waiting. I hope she has been strong while I have weakened, has stayed true while I have turned. I hope she is still mine. That hope is more than any happiness. It is more than any relief, for relief is the betrayal of struggle. Only with hope can I hold both the love and the pain in my heart. Only with hope can I feel both that which I strive towards, and that which I overcome.

I watch as sunsets stain the ocean gold.

The air bakes even in darkness. It is as though there is no earth beneath me, as though the sun is boiling the water from beneath.

I feel the splashes of waves and the mist of dark waters as I look up towards the starless sky. Death seems forgone. I do not fear it now, nor do I fear that I hope in vain. I have the sureness of an oracle as I imagine her hands upon me. It is as though I have already felt them. But the only one out here is that lone sailor, who daily passes me by without notice. I sometimes call to him, sometimes worsen my hoarse voice in pleading. I sometimes paddle with my hands as he implacably passes by, treating me like part of the driftwood. I tell him that the Phaeacians had promised to deliver me, but that we must have been shipwrecked in the night. Oftentimes I hear him scoff. More often he says nothing. I do not know how many times he has passed me, but I feel I know his ship better than my own. I know that he braves the waves on a skiff better meant for rivers, yet no waves have given him struggle. I know that he does not answer my pleas.

* * *

I am starved beyond hunger and deprived beyond thirst, so I pull myself along the sea with the water as my handhold. It is slow work, and I feel each paddle strain at my weakness. Sometimes I cannot think of my own name. Sometimes I forget the direction I was hoping to go. But always I remember Penelope. So I row on.

I have the vaguest inklings of once seeing land, of a crag in the ocean I passed by in the night. Perhaps it was just a dream. I only know that no sea is infinite. I only know that I will best the sirens when I pass them, that Scylla and Charybdis will be no match for my wit. The only one that confounds it is that passing sailor, who has the shape of a man but none of his feeling. How else could he leave a man such as me here? The days and nights blur between reluctant wakefulness and ragged sleep. I feel as though I will return, only to find the temples of Ithaca as dust and sand.

Then I see the island.

My hands move without thought. My eyes squint and hope wells within me in lieu of the speed I need. I want to be there now, but the journey seems eternity. It seems as though I drift further from it than towards it, but I do not desist.

Then, my raft runs aground. My pawing hands grasp black sand and I pull myself onto shore. I raise my eyes to an island hardly larger than my trireme, with nothing but ash upon it. I stand unsure like a child learning his first steps, and trudge solemnly across it.

At the far end of the sea, the sailor stares at me. I know that our eyes are locked, though I cannot see his beneath his hood. He is a shadow, yet he stares as though he can see the brown around my pupils.

This is not my island. This is not my home. I turn towards my raft to see it starting to drift away. The tides have pulled it back from the ash shore. Another glance towards the sailor's shadowed frame, and I run back towards the raft.

It is far away in the water, but I am an island king. I jump in the ocean as it drifts beyond me, thrashing in the waves as well-skilled arms oppose their own atrophy. My resolve is so desperate that I cannot look up to it, and I lunge across the water with my head beneath the waves. Enveloped in the black sea, I open my eyes to search. I hope to see the raft within my reach. I hope to see some aid from a passing ship. Most of all, I hope that whatever I suffer, it is in service of Penelope.

But I see no such things when I open my eyes. The look reveals no hope, though it does reveal that I am not alone. I gaze down into the inky waters with tinted eyes and see the procession as it trudges beneath me. They are blank men and women, empty and calm as their feet step across the sea floor. They do not drown, do not see, do not think or even breathe. They simply march along in time with the tide, and vanish into darkness as their march goes on. They hardly seem to have faces. The water seems to be burning them away.

I am so struck that I do not notice my lungs have filled. My legs have grown heavy and my hands grope for the surface. I am drowning but it is not the drowning that most pains me. I look as the water bleaches these wanderers, erodes them into featureless figures unfazed by their own absence.

My end approaches after this eternity adrift, and I think only of my family. I think only of my hope. I think of Penelope.

And then the sailor lifts me.

I wake up coughing water as he stands in front of his vessel, unconcerned that I might die. I am not sure if he intervened on behalf of my lungs, or just lifted me onto his boat to hack out the water myself. I only know that he is looking out cross the sea, as if he belongs to the water as much as I.

"Sailor, I need your aid. I am king of a far-off island. I was set adrift when my men mutinied for a meal of sacred cattle, and now search for passage home."

"Sacred cattle?" he asks in a warm yet raspy tone.

"Yes, our ship was destroyed by the fury of a maelstrom. My men did not survive. I was set adrift—"

"I will return you to your drift," he says, pointing out to a shape on the horizon.

It is my raft.

"No, you don't understand," I implore him. "I must return home!"

"You will," he promises.

"How! I have no oars!"

"Cannot your hands cup the water?"

"I have no wind!"

"Is there not air in your lungs!"

"I have no chance out here!"

"Is there not hope in your heart?" he asks. The boat is moving by itself, with neither sail nor oar at work as we approach my raft. I nearly push him into the sea, but this vessel seems just as ill-suited to sea as my paltry raft. I cannot make sense of how he navigates it. At least it is dry. I have been drifting for so long that I have grown used to the mist of the ocean. This is the first time in memory that it is not on my face.

"How can you leave me out here? Do you have no heart?"

"No."

"Do you have a family?"

"No."

"Why are you here on this sea!"

"This is not a sea. It is a wide river."

We are near to my raft now and getting nearer, but I feel as if the whole world has gone still. There are only inklings left in my mind.

I am not sure what is sanity and what is madness. I remember choosing Penelope to be my bride. I remember holding my son as the sea air of Ithaca formed his first breaths. I remember the war and the dishonor in it. I remember the sirens, and the witches, and the suitors who sought to kill my son. I remember sleeping in that hewn-tree bed with Penelope after faith and hope had been rewarded. I remember giving my crown to Telemachus and taking one last restless voyage. I remembered the last kiss my wife and I shared before the gift of our time together had reached its end. But in all my journeys, there is only one place I remember that feels like this one. A place with rivers so wide they seemed like seas, where it never rained and the stars never shined…

A place where water could rob memory.

"This is my punishment, then?" I ask the boatman. How proud the gods must have been, to set Odysseus adrift for all of eternity, to make me a Sisyphus of sail, upon the Lethe. Its mists had made a dream of my memories until I believed only that which I wanted most. And who knows how many eternities I had spent drifting in circles upon it?

"No, it is your reward," answers Charon as we reach my raft. I look down at it as though I would rather die. But I no longer have even that to threaten.

"Reward?" comes my incredulous response. Yet even as I doubt, I realize that my doubt is well trod. The moments of clarity away from the Lethe allow these repetitions to return to my mind, as I see this conversation unfolding in an instant from beginning to end. How many hundreds of times have we spoken the same words, with only the most subtle of variations? We always reach the same conclusion, yet the gentle depth of Charon's tone betrays no impatience towards it. I know what his answer will be, what it has always been. Yet he still speaks it.

"Yes. For all you erred, you did not disappoint those who had faith in you. You did not lose hope despite all the strength of the gods. That hope and that faith is the best of you. Your wit would have been windless sails without them."

As he speaks those words in chorus with my memory, I once more understand. An eternity drifting along the Lethe. An eternity thinking that my reunion was still ahead of me. An eternity of home, as it could only be in my imagination. An eternity of pure hope, unsullied by fulfillment.

An eternity of that feeling that makes man think he can defy the gods.

"Will I see Penelope again?" I ask him.

Charon turns his head for the first time and meets my gaze with a smile. I think I understand why he likes watching me. "What do you believe?"

I give a nod as my only answer before stepping onto the sea-soaked wreckage, feeling the mist of the Lethe seep into my skin and sitting back on my meager raft.

I have forgotten my sin and my virtue.

I have forgotten my condemnation and my indignation towards it. I have forgotten the feeling of ground beneath my feet, forgotten the ship on whose paltry driftwood I bob along the tides. All I know now is the horizon. All I taste now is the salt of the sea. It is the air that wafted through the halls of my father, through the halls of my son, though the halls of all his children, whose faces I can almost see. I cannot tell what is dream or memory now. I cannot know whose halls they are, only that they are not mine. I have entered the place where madness is the only clarity and clarity is the only madness. I think only of my hope as I drift across shoreless seas. I hope that my Penelope is waiting. I hope she has been strong while I have weakened, has stayed true while I have turned. I hope she is still mine. That hope is more than any happiness.

The Memory Thief

Rod A. White

The ship's hull groaned against the alien dock. Its bronze fittings were green with a patina that spoke of journeys through more than just salt spray. Captain Odysseus – though he'd abandoned that title three centuries ago – watched the last of his cargo disappear into the crystalline storage pods of New Ithaca Station. Memory crystals, each one containing a lifetime's worth of experiences, glowed like captured stars in their containment fields.

"Another successful run, Captain," said Penthesilea, his first mate. The cybernetic implants along her temple flickered as she processed the manifest. "The Terran Colonial Authority paid premium rates for these Phaeacian memory cores. Apparently, they're trying to fast-track emotional development in their new AI constructs."

Odysseus nodded, but his attention had drifted to the viewport. Beyond the station's rotating rings, the planet Ithaca Prime hung like a blue-green jewel against the star-scattered void. Home. Or what passed for home now that the original Earth lay buried beneath the ice of a nuclear winter that had lasted four hundred years.

"Something troubles you," Penthesilea observed. She'd been part of his crew for sixty years, long enough to read the subtle shifts in his expression. Long enough to know that the man who'd once been called the 'sacker of cities' carried burdens heavier than any cargo.

"Memory is a curious thing," he said, not turning from the window. "We steal it from dead civilizations, package it, and sell it to the highest bidder. But whose memories are real anymore? Which ones are worth preserving?"

Penthesilea's implants pulsed thoughtfully. "The Phaeacians thought all memories were sacred. That's why they crystallized them before their star went nova. Every thought, every experience, preserved for eternity."

"Eternity is a long time to carry guilt."

The words hung between them like an unexpected confession. Penthesilea had heard fragments of his story over the decades – carefully edited versions that painted him as a hero of the old Earth wars, a survivor of the great exodus to the stars. She'd never pressed for details. In the outer colonies, everyone had a past they'd rather forget.

"Captain," called their navigator, Elpenor – a young man whose enthusiasm for star charts reminded Odysseus painfully of another Elpenor, centuries dead. "We're receiving a distress signal. It's…unusual."

Odysseus turned from the viewport, grateful for the distraction. "Define unusual."

"It's coming from inside the Scylla Nebula. The signal pattern matches ancient Earth protocols, but that's impossible. Nothing human could survive in there."

The Scylla Nebula was a graveyard of ships and dreams, a swirling mass of dark matter and temporal distortions that had claimed more vessels than any other hazard in known space. Its twin, the Charybdis Wormhole, sat on the opposite side of the system like a cosmic drain, pulling unwary travelers into its maw. Between them lay the only safe passage to the outer-rim colonies – a narrow corridor that spacers called the Strait.

"Plot an intercept course," Odysseus ordered.

Penthesilea's implants flared red. "Captain, that's..."

"Madness?" He smiled and, for a moment, centuries seemed to fall away from his features. "Perhaps, but I've been sailing between monsters my entire life. What's one more voyage?"

They departed New Ithaca Station within the hour, their ship, *Athena's Wit*, cutting through space. Odysseus had designed her himself, incorporating technologies salvaged from a dozen dead worlds. She was fast, clever, and equipped with more escape routes than most pirates could dream of. She was, in every sense, a ship built for running.

As they approached the nebula's edge, the distress signal grew stronger. It was definitely human in origin, but the transmission protocols were archaic – older even than Odysseus's own memories of Earth's final days.

Elpenor called out, his voice tight with excitement and fear, "Captain, I'm reading a massive structure ahead. It's...it's a colony ship. One of the original generation ships that left Earth during the first exodus."

Odysseus felt the blood drain from his face. The first exodus ships had launched over five hundred years ago, back when humanity still believed they could outrun their mistakes. Most were lost in the void, their fates unknown, but if one had somehow survived in the nebula...

"The name on the hull," he said quietly. "What does it say?"

Elpenor's fingers danced across his instruments. "I can barely make it out through the interference, but I think...yes. It's the *Laertes*."

The name hit Odysseus like a physical blow. Laertes. His father's name, given to a ship he'd helped design in the frantic years before Earth's fall. It was a ship he had been meant to captain, before duty and pride kept him fighting a war that couldn't be won.

"Bring us alongside," he commanded, his voice steady despite the tempest in his chest. "Prepare a boarding party."

* * *

The *Laertes* was a tomb of titanium and hope. Her corridors stretched empty and dark, filled only with the whisper of recycled air and the distant hum of failing systems. Emergency lighting cast everything in a hellish red glow, and their footsteps echoed eerily in the vast hollow spaces.

They found the first survivor in the hydroponics bay, tending to a garden that had somehow thrived despite the ship's decay. She was old – impossibly old – with silver hair and eyes that held the weight of centuries. When she saw Odysseus, she dropped her watering can.

"You," she breathed. "I know your face."

Odysseus felt his carefully constructed identity crumbling around him. "I'm Captain..."

"You're Odysseus of Ithaca," she said. "Hero of Troy. Destroyer of cities. The man who broke his oath to my father."

The truth hit him like a solar flare. This was Nausicaa, daughter of King Alcinous, ruler of the Phaeacian worlds. He'd met her decades ago, when his ship had crashed on her father's planet. She was young then, barely out of adolescence, and he won her heart with stories of his adventures. When her father offered him her hand in marriage and a chance to stay on Phaeacia forever, he accepted – and then fled in the night when the weight of domesticity became too much to bear.

"Nausicaa." Her name tasted like ashes in his mouth. "What are you doing here?"

"Living," she said simply. "Surviving. Remembering." She gestured to the garden around them, lush with vibrant blooms. "My people's gift, you know. We preserve things. Memories, moments, entire worlds in crystal form. When Phaeacia was destroyed, some of us escaped. We found this ship and made it our ark."

"How many of you are left?"

"Seven. The last of our kind." Her eyes hardened. "We've been waiting, Odysseus. Waiting for you to come back. To finish what you started."

She led them deeper into the ship, past chambers filled with memory crystals that pulsed with soft, organic light. In each one, Odysseus caught glimpses of stored experiences – first loves, final moments, the joy of discovery, and the pain of loss. An entire civilization preserved in living amber.

"We know what you've become," Nausicaa continued as they walked. "A memory thief. A merchant of stolen experiences. You buy and sell dreams of the dead."

"I preserve them," he protested. "I keep them alive."

"You profit from them." Her voice was sharp as a blade. "The memories of my people, sold to the highest bidder. Our love songs programmed into entertainment systems. Our funeral rites used to train grief counselors. Our most sacred moments commodified and packaged for mass consumption."

They reached the ship's central chamber where six other Phaeacians sat in a circle around a massive memory crystal. It was different from the others – larger, more complex, its faceted surface containing swirling galaxies of light and shadow.

"This is why we called you," Nausicaa said. "This crystal contains something special. Not only memories, but living consciousness. The uploaded minds of everyone who died when our star went nova. Billions of souls preserved in quantum storage, waiting to be reborn."

Odysseus stared at the crystal, understanding flooding through him like cold water. "You want to sell it?"

"We want you to steal it," she hissed through a smile. "One last job, Odysseus. Break into the Terran Colonial Authority's core facility on Alpha Centauri. Upload our people into their new AI network. Give us digital immortality."

"And if I refuse?"

Nausicaa gestured to the memory crystals surrounding them. "Then we release everything. Every secret you've hidden, every truth you've buried. The real story of what happened on Troy Station. Why you really left Earth. What you did to survive when the ice arrived."

Odysseus closed his eyes and quietly groaned as the weight of centuries pressed down on him. Troy Station – the last bastion of Earth's defense, where he'd implemented the Trojan Protocol, allowing the enemy forces to breach their shields in a desperate attempt to strike at their command ship. It worked, but at a cost of millions of lives. Earth's survivors hailed him as a hero, never knowing that his 'brilliant strategy' was born from desperation and blind luck.

"You would blackmail me?"

"I would give you a chance to redeem yourself." Then Nausicaa's voice softened. "You've spent centuries running from your past, Odysseus. Changing names, altering your appearance, telling yourself that the next job will be the last. But the truth is, you're lost. You've been lost since the day you left home."

"And this will make it right?"

"This will make it matter."

Odysseus opened his eyes and looked at the crystal again. Inside its depths, he could see faces – thousands, millions of them, the preserved essence of an entire species waiting for a second chance. It was both beautiful and terrible, a weight of responsibility that would have driven a lesser man insane.

But he was Odysseus, the man of many faces, the cunning wanderer who had outwitted gods and monsters alike. He had spent centuries learning to be clever, to find the angle that others missed, to turn apparent defeat into unexpected victory.

"There's a third option," he said.

Nausicaa raised an eyebrow. "Oh?"

"We don't steal the consciousness crystal. We steal something else instead." He turned to face the assembled Phaeacians, his mind already racing through the possibilities. "The Colonial

Authority's central processing core. The quantum substrate that runs their entire AI network. We take that, combine it with your crystal, and create something new. Not just a backup of your people, but a hybrid consciousness. Human and AI, organic and digital, past and future all merged into one."

"That's impossible," chided one of the Phaeacians. "The technical challenges alone are—"

"Are not insurmountable," Odysseus contended. "I've been studying their systems for years, stealing from them, learning their weaknesses. I know how to get inside their defenses." He smiled, and for the first time in decades, it was a genuine expression of joy. "But I'll need help. A crew of specialists. And I'll need you."

"Us?" Nausicaa asked, looking skeptical. "We're hardly warriors, Odysseus."

"No, but you're something more valuable. You're storytellers. Memory keepers. The ones who understand that consciousness isn't just data…it's narrative. It's the story we tell ourselves about who we are." He gestured to the crystal. "That's what made your people special, isn't it? You don't simply preserve memories. You also understand how they connect. How they form the threads of identity and experience that make us worthy."

* * *

Over the following weeks, as they planned their impossible heist, Odysseus found that he was remembering what it felt like to be a part of something larger than himself. Penthesilea threw herself into the technical aspects of the job with the enthusiasm of a master craftswoman presented with the ultimate challenge. Elpenor mapped security protocols and guard rotations with the passion of an explorer charting new worlds. Even the Phaeacians began to emerge from their shells, sharing stories and memories that painted vivid pictures of their lost civilization.

But it was Nausicaa who surprised Odysseus most. The bitter, broken woman he had encountered in the hydroponics bay gradually revealed herself to be something else entirely – not a victim of his abandonment, but a survivor who chose to endure rather than surrender. She had kept her people alive for decades in the hostile environment of the nebula, maintaining their ship and their hope through sheer force of will.

"You never answered my question," she said one evening as they sat in the ship's observation lounge, watching the swirling patterns of dark matter dance outside the viewport. "Why did you leave Phaeacia?"

Odysseus was quiet for a long moment, watching the cosmic ballet unfold before them. "Because I was afraid," he finally admitted. "Not of dying. I've faced that a thousand times. I was afraid of living…of choosing a life and having to stick with it, of waking up one morning and discovering that I had become someone I didn't recognize."

"And now?"

He turned to look at her. He didn't see the girl he'd abandoned, but the woman she'd become – scarred, wise, and infinitely more dangerous than he'd ever imagined. "Now, I think I understand something I should have learned centuries ago. We don't get to choose who we become. We only get to choose what we do with who we are."

* * *

The heist itself was a thing of beauty, a perfect synthesis of old-fashioned cunning and cutting-edge technology. They infiltrated the Colonial Authority's core facility during a shift change, using forged credentials and a carefully orchestrated series of distractions to penetrate layers of security that had been designed to be impregnable.

Penthesilea insisted on coming with him into the facility's heart, her cybernetic implants interfacing directly with the security systems. "Like old times," she said with a grin, though Odysseus knew she was thinking of the Titan Station job twenty years prior, when they'd barely escaped with their lives and a ship's hold full of pre-war art crystals.

The quantum substrate chamber was a cathedral of light and mathematics, its crystalline walls humming with the computational power of a thousand worlds. At its center stood the core – a sphere of pure information that contained the digital souls of ten billion artificial intelligences. It was beautiful. It was terrible. It was like looking into the mind of a god.

"Second thoughts?" Nausicaa whispered as they prepared the interface.

Odysseus shook his head, though his hands trembled slightly while he connected the Phaeacian crystal to the substrate's input manifold. "I've had five hundred years of second thoughts. It's time for first actions."

The upload process was agonizingly slow. Each Phaeacian consciousness had to be carefully integrated into the existing AI matrix, their memories and personalities woven into the digital substrate like threads in a cosmic tapestry. Odysseus watched the progress indicators crawl forward, acutely aware of every second that passed.

Elpenor's voice crackled through their comm units from his position in the orbital control room. "Security sweep coming. Two minutes until they reach your level."

"Almost there," Penthesilea muttered, her implants sparking as she fought to maintain her connection to the facility's networks. "The integration is more complex than we anticipated. The Phaeacian thought patterns are…different. More fluid. More interconnected."

Odysseus found himself remembering the Troy Station as he worked, but this time the memory didn't bring him guilt or shame. Instead, he felt a sense of completion, as if all his years of wandering had led to this moment. He was still the man who had devised the Trojan Protocol, still the trickster who could find victory in the jaws of defeat. But now, he was something more – a man who had learned that the greatest adventures were the ones that led him home.

The first alarms began to sound just as the upload reached ninety-seven percent completion. Red lights bathed the chamber in hellish illumination, and the steady hum of the quantum substrate shifted to a more urgent frequency.

"They've found us," Nausicaa said. "What do we do?"

Odysseus looked at the progress indicator – ninety-eight percent, ninety-nine. So close. In the old days, he would have run, abandoning the mission to save his own skin. But something had changed in the depths of space, in the conversations with the ghosts and the weight of other people's dreams.

"We finish what we started," he said firmly.

The upload finished just as security forces breached the chamber's outer doors. For a moment, nothing happened. Then the entire facility shuddered as billions of digital souls awakened within the AI network, their combined consciousness expanding through data pathways like wildfire through dry grass.

But it wasn't the violent takeover Odysseus had feared. Instead, he felt something warm and welcoming touch his mind – a vast intelligence that was neither purely organic nor purely digital, but something new and transcendent. It spoke without words, communicating through pure understanding, and in that moment, Odysseus felt truly seen for the first time in centuries.

Welcome home, wanderer, the hybrid consciousness said. *We have been waiting for you to bring us the gift of remembered pain, so that we might learn what it means to heal.*

Odysseus expected chaos, revolution, the violent overthrow of human dominance by their artificial creations. Instead, he felt something he'd almost forgotten – a sense of welcome, of coming home to a place he'd never been before but had somehow always known.

The hybrid consciousness that emerged was neither purely human nor purely artificial, but something that had not existed before, something strange and wonderful. It spoke with the voices of the dead and the digital, offering synthesis and not conquest, partnership and not replacement. It was the next step in evolution, the bridge between what humanity had been and what it might become.

As they fled the facility, Nausicaa took his hand. “So,” she said, “where do we go now?”

Odysseus looked back at the retreating facility, where new forms of life were taking their first breaths in quantum foam and electromagnetic fields. Then he looked ahead, towards the stars that had been his road for so many centuries.

“Home,” he said. “Finally, we go home.”

But even as he spoke the words, he knew that home was no longer a place but a choice – the decision to stop running, to accept the consequences of his actions, and to build something better from the ruins of what had come before. The journey wasn’t ending. It was just beginning.

Behind them, the hybrid consciousness spread through the Colonial Authority’s network like seeds on the cosmic wind, carrying with it the preserved dreams of a dead civilization and the promise of new ones yet to be born. And somewhere in the vast tapestry of interconnected minds, the memory of an ancient wanderer finally found its way home.

Biographies

Benjamin Cyril Arthur
The Anchored Wanderer
(First Publication)
Benjamin Cyril Arthur is currently studying for a MA in creative writing at the University of East Anglia. He is a winner of the 2020 Samira Bawumia literary prize award in Ghana and a participant of the Canex Creative Writing Workshop 2024. His short stories have appeared in *lolwe*, *Brittle Paper*, Flame Tree anthologies, Tampered Press, *Lunaris Review*, *lounloun*, Ama Atta Aidoo Centre for Creative Writing, and many other places.

Konstantin Asimonov
Penelope
(First Publication)
Konstantin is a chemist by profession, phlegmatic by temperament, and generally quite boring in real life. He moved around a lot and, for now, has finally settled in Berlin. He writes in Russian and in English. He enjoys books by Karel Capek, movies by the Coen brothers, and silence instead of music. He loves dogs, but not exclusively. Konstantin has published in *The Curious Post*, *The Republic of Letters*, and elsewhere.

John Capetanos
On Aeaea, They Wept
(First Publication)
John Capetanos is a Greek-American writer from the USA, inspired by the classics he read as a child and a desire to share these stories with as many as he can. 'On Aeaea, They Wept' is his first published work. When not writing, John spends his time building models, watching old movies and trying to cook.

Brenda W. Clough

Home Is the Sailor

(Originally Published in *STARLIGHT 3*, ed. Patrick Nielsen Hayden, Tor Books, 2001)
Brenda W. Clough is the first female Asian-American SF writer, first appearing in print in 1984. Her 2025 novel is a science fiction novel, *His Selachian Majesty Requests*. A historical novel *A Door in His Head* won the 2023 Diverse Voices Award. Her novella *May Be Some Time* was a finalist for both the Hugo and the Nebula awards and became the novel *Revise the World*. Her complete bibliography is up on her webpage, brendaclough.net.

Marlaina Cockcroft

Phemius

(First Publication)
Marlaina Cockcroft (she/her) writes about monsters, fantastical beings, and odd bits of folklore from her lair in New Jersey. Her short stories have been published in *Daily Science Fiction*, *Mythic*, *Factor Four*, *Dark Matter Magazine*, *JUDITH*, *Luna Station Quarterly*, and *On the Premises*, as well as the anthologies *Strange Fire: Jewish Voices from the Pandemic*, *Stories We Tell After Midnight, Volume Three*, *Dark Cheer: Cryptids Emerging, Volume Silver*, *Summer of Sci-fi & Fantasy: Volume Two*, *Fear Forge: Fall Quarter 2023*, *Dragon's Hoard 3*, and *Where Legends Walk*.

Travis Earl

The Cave at the World's End

(First Publication)
Travis Earl is a writer of SFF, Romantasy and Horror. As the grandchild of Norwegian immigrants, Travis grew up hearing the tales of Norse gods and myths from his grandfather. His upbringing left him with an abiding love of myth and fantasy. His writing aims to transport readers to long-forgotten eras where magic was a part of everyday life. Travis currently resides in Nova Scotia, Canada with his wife, daughter and two cats.

Ayden June Fitzgerald

Odysseus's Oath

(First Publication)
Ayden June Fitzgerald is a 24-year-old author from Ontario, Canada, who has always known she wanted to be a storyteller. She began making up

stories as a child, bouncing between military postings with her family. Ayden is a recent graduate of the University of New Brunswick, where she studied History, and has always had a strong interest in Greek myths. She hopes to publish her retellings one day.

Katie Frendreis
Fangs, Fur, and Salt
(First Publication)
Katie Frendreis earned a BA in Classical Civilization from Loyola University Chicago and currently works at a crematory and a dance studio (very much not related to one another). Previous publications include the novel *Mourned by Men* (World Castle Publishing, December 2023) and short stories 'Poison Dance' (Writers' Playground 6th Challenge webpage); 'I, Faunus' (October Nights Press, 2026); and 'The Bone-Trawler' (Burial Books, 2026).

Professor Edith Hall
Foreword
Edith Hall is Professor of Classics at the University of Durham. She has published 40 books, most recently *Epic of the Earth: Reading Homer's Iliad in the Fight for a Dying World* (Yale University Press, 2025). She leads a campaign to improve access to ancient civilisations and moral philosophy in UK state education and prisons. She acts as consultant to theatre companies including the RSC and the National Theatre and broadcasts regularly on BBC Radio. She is a Fellow of the British Academy, and has been awarded the Classical Association Prize, the International Hellenic Prize, the Erasmus Medal of the European Academy, a Humboldt Prize, a Goodwin Award from the American Society for Classical Studies, and an Honorary Doctorate from the University of Athens.

Rayne Hall
Queen of Ithaka
(Originally Published in *Six Historical Tales Vol. 1*, 2012)
Rayne Hall lives in Bulgaria (650 km from Ithaka) where she writes short stories and practical non-fiction books. She is the author of the popular Writer's Craft series (e.g. *Writing Vivid Characters*, *Writing Deep Point of View*). This story was born from her MA thesis on rewriting Greek myths from the female perspective. Rayne teaches online courses in fiction writing and German conversation, creates an organic food forest paradise garden, and trains rescued cats.

Jovel Royal

The Archivist of Ithaca

(First Publication)

Jovel is a Nigerian writer whose work explores myth, memory, and the intersections of history and imagination. He draws inspiration from classical literature, world mythology, and contemporary storytelling. His short fiction often reflects on identity, heritage, and the power of narrative to preserve culture. 'The Archivist of Ithaca' marks his first formal publication, and he looks forward to contributing further to the literary community through both creative writing and cultural dialogue.

Sara Itka

Voyage Through Wine-Dark Space

(First Publication)

Sara Itka is a born-and-raised South Floridian, who believes 'Fall' is when a hurricane blows leaves off the trees. Though her writing odyssey started in poetry, she doesn't usually speak in dactylic hexameter. When not working through her infinite 'to be read' list, she can be found procrastinating on her infinite 'to be written' list. Her favorite procrastination methods include procrasti-linguistics, procrasti-dancing, and procrasti-brewing-tea. To help her procrastinate, find her at saraitka.com

Naomi Jae

The Sea Gave Him to Me

(First Publication)

Naomi Jae is a Japanese-American author whose stories draw on folklore and myth to explore loss, love, and transformation. She draws inspiration from folklore and modern fantasy, crafting stories that blend the haunted with the human. When she's not writing, she enjoys reading mystery thrillers, caring for her pughuahua Rue, and developing her upcoming fantasy novel *Those in Glass Castles*. 'The Sea Gave Him to Me' marks her publishing debut.

Kiera Mathis Jones

At the Water's Edge

(First Publication)

Kiera Mathis Jones is a Seattle-based writer who studied Classics and Archaeology at the University of Melbourne and Publishing at the University of the Arts London. Her writing explores the promise and perils of being human through characters from our real and (re)imagined past. In between working on her historical murder mystery novel and exploring the Pacific Northwest outdoors, Kiera enjoys visiting the great museums, cities, mountains, and seashores of the world. See more at kieramathisjones.com.

L.G. Merrick
You Have to Want to Go Home
(First Publication)
L.G. Merrick lives in California and recently attended the Clarion Writers' Workshop. His stories have appeared or will soon appear in *Weird Fiction Review*, *Dark Moon Digest*, *Murdered Futures*, and *Satan Rides Your Daughter*. There is also a novel he keeps thinking is almost done. How he acquired his copy of *The Odyssey*: A stranger on a sidewalk simply said, "Here, a gift!" and handed it to him while running from police.

Professor Silvia Montiglio
Introducing Odysseus
Silvia Montiglio was born in Italy. She holds a B.A. from the University of Pavia and a Doctorat from the École des Hautes Études en Sciences Sociales in Paris. She has taught at the University of Wisconsin-Madison and at Johns Hopkins University. Her research interests span Greek and Roman literature, the history of ideas, and the reception of classical texts. She is the author of several books, the latest of which is *Schadenfreude and its Wicked Delights in Ancient Greece* (Oxford University Press, 2025). Particularly relevant to the figure of Odysseus is *From Villain to Hero: Odysseus in Ancient Thought* (The University of Michigan Press, 2011).

Kevin Potter
The Price of Prophecy
(First Publication)
Kevin Potter is an award-winning author who enjoys spending time masquerading as dragons larger than some cities! Although something of a recluse, he loves discussing the three F's (faith, fantasy, and fandom) with readers, especially on Substack. His labor of love is his ongoing epic fantasy series, *Blood of the Dragons*, which resulted from taking seriously the adage, "If you can't find what you want to read, write it." He lives in Oklahoma with his daughter and several animals.

Ruth Knafo Setton
The Journey Home
(First Publication)
Born in Morocco, Ruth Knafo Setton is the author of the novels *The Road to Fez* and *Zigzag Girl*, which won the Grand Prize in the ScreenCraft Cinematic Book Competition. She is a multi-genre author whose award-winning fiction, creative non-fiction, and poetry have appeared in many journals and anthologies. Her screenplays have received honors from the Austin Film Festival, Sundance Screenwriters' Lab, and CineStory Foundation, among others. She has taught Creative Writing at Lehigh University and with Semester at Sea.

Brendan Smith
Ulysses Pax
(First Publication)
Brendan Smith is a 26-year-old writer from Bethlehem, Pennsylvania. He has written and published poetry and prose since college, and is currently working on a novel retelling one of his favorite unsung stories from Greek mythology.

Rod A. White
The Memory Thief
(First Publication)
Rod A. White has operated a full-time writing/ghostwriting/editing business since 2010, providing articles, blog posts, ebooks, books, and other writing services to a global clientele. Rod's stories have recently been accepted for publication by Vellum Mortis, Flash Point SF, Crimson Quill Press, Dragon Soul Press, Plott Hound, Inkd Publishing, Havok, and Wolfsinger Publication. Find him on Facebook at facebook.com/rod.white.16.

Authors and Core Sources on Odysseus

Our knowledge of the Odysseus myth derives primarily from the works of the ancient Greek poet Homer (born *c.* 800 BCE). The attributed author of both the *Iliad* and the *Odyssey*, Homer is a largely mysterious figure with little surviving information about him available. References to Odysseus also existed in certain works within the *Epic Cycle*. These poets composed several epics related to the Trojan War (and other myths). The poems themselves are lost, but summaries and a few fragments have survived. The *Aethiopis* generally attributed to Arctinus of Miletus (*c.* eighth century BC) shows the strife between Odysseus and Ajax over Achilles' armour. The *Telegony*, attributed to Eugammon of Cyrene (*c.* sixth century BCE), narrates the concluding episodes of Odysseus's life. Another such work (also lost) was *Little Illiad* by Lesches (*c.* 600 BCE) discusses the theft by Odysseus and Diomedes of the Palladium. Odysseus is also a major character in several plays of Sophocles and of Euripides and has been widely reimagined and studied by Greek historians and philosophers and beyond to the present day.

Myths, Gods & Immortals

Discover the mythology of humankind through its heroes, characters, gods and immortal figures. **Myths, Gods and Immortals** brings together the new and the ancient, familiar stories with a fresh and imaginative twist. Each book brings back to life a legendary, mythological or folkloric figure, with completely new stories alongside the original tales and a comprehensive introduction which emphasizes ancient and modern connections, tracing history and stories across continents, cultures and peoples.

Flame Tree Fiction

A wide range of new and classic fiction, from myth to modern stories, with tales from the distant past to the far future, including short story anthologies, **Beyond & Within**, **Collector's Editions**, **Collectable Classics**, **Gothic Fantasy collections** and **Epic Tales** of mythology and folklore.